Outrageously IN Love

THE *Love in the City* SERIES
BOOK THREE

JEN MORRIS

Outrageously in Love Copyright © 2021 by Jen Morris

First edition September 2021

Kindle ISBN: 978-0-473-58646-1

Epub ISBN: 978-0-473-58645-4

Paperback ISBN: 978-0-473-58644-7

Cover illustration by Elle Maxwell

www.ellemaxwelldesign.com

For the sexiest geek I know.

Life begins at the end of your comfort zone.

— NEALE DONALD WALSCH

AUTHOR'S NOTE

Please note that this book contains sensitive topics such as high school bullying and self-harm. It also includes panic attacks and divorce. I hope I have treated these issues with the care they deserve.

1

"What's the most outrageous thing you've ever done?" My flatmate, Steph, leans across the sticky table in our local bar, one eyebrow arched as we consider her words.

The question is simple enough, and my first response is to grin wickedly, as if I have something juicy to share. But the longer I sit there, scanning the depths of my mind for crazy, wild stories, the more I realize I've done nothing outrageous in my life at all.

Nothing.

Not one, tiny, outrageous thing.

You'd think, in my twenty-eight years on this planet, I could have done *something* shocking. I've never even had a one night stand for Christ's sake.

I shrink into my chair and pretend to busy myself with the drink menu. These aren't even my friends, anyway. They won't expect me to answer.

"Ooh, I know!" Cassidy, a redhead with big teeth, exclaims. Everyone looks at her eagerly and she pauses for effect, drinking in the attention. "I once had sex with a guy in the middle of a rugby field."

Bloody hell.

"It was midnight and there was no one around," she clarifies. As if we'd all been picturing her straddling some guy during the second half of the World Cup Final while a ball whizzed past her head.

But still. It doesn't exactly sound fun.

"Okay, I've got one," Steph says, running a hand through her short, brunette bob.

I've always loved Steph. We met about ten years ago, at the cafe where I work in Baxterton, New Zealand. She worked there part-time while studying, and even though she left after graduation, we kept in touch and became flatmates a few years later. She puts up with me better than anyone and, God love her, she's always trying to push me out of my comfort zone. If it weren't for her I'd spend all my time at home surrounded by mountains of books. I'd be perfectly happy with that, but she insists I "need to get out sometimes." That's why I'm here with her workmates, drinking on a Tuesday night. She's trying to turn me to the dark side.

Steph giggles. "I gave a guy a handjob in the alley behind this bar."

I try not to groan. This is such a typical Steph story. She's a lot more, shall we say, sexually adventurous than me. Don't get me wrong, it's not like I haven't had the occasional fantasy of doing something like that. It's just that the opportunity has never presented itself, and I've yet to meet a guy so irresistible that I feel compelled to tear his clothes off on the spot.

"Alright, your turn," Cassidy says, gesturing beside me to

Heather. It seems we're going around the circle, and there's a pinch in my belly at the realization that I'm next.

I push my glasses up my nose and fix my gaze back on the drink menu, trying to extricate myself from this whole thing. I'm never coming out with Steph again.

Heather grins and flicks a wave of blond hair over her shoulder. "I once had sex with a married guy."

A married man? I bury my face in the menu to hide the frown tugging at my brow. I'm all for sexual freedom, or whatever, but something about sleeping with a married guy seems over the line.

What even was the question again? Why is everything sex-related? Is that the only thing that qualifies for outrageous? Has nobody, I don't know, gone skinny-dipping, or dyed their hair a wacky color, or sunk every cent of their savings into some crazy dream? Not that I've done any of those things, of course. I can't even send back food at a restaurant. Well, I hardly ever go to restaurants, so that example is more hypothetical than literal, but you get what I'm saying.

"Your turn, Harriet."

My pulse quickens and I pretend I haven't heard them, directing my attention towards selecting another drink. Mm, the cocktails sound nice, or maybe a bunch of tequila shots—

"Harriet?"

Heat creeps up my neck as I meet Cassidy's gaze. I glance at Steph with a silent plea for help, but she's engrossed in something on her phone. The other two watch expectantly and I swallow, my tongue feeling like sandpaper. I mentally search for something to get them off my back, but my mind is blank.

"C'mon," Heather presses. "What's the wildest thing you've ever done?"

Steph looks up from her phone and her face breaks into a grin. "You're asking the wrong person," she says, with a good-natured chuckle. My cheeks grow warm, despite the fact that she's speaking the absolute truth.

"What?" Cassidy laughs in my direction. "Surely you've done *something*?"

Steph shakes her head and speaks again before I can answer. "Harriet? Are you kidding? She spends all of her time with her nose in a book. Her hero is Hermione Granger."

She flicks me an affectionate smile and I roll my eyes. After I was taunted mercilessly in high school she's the only one I let tease me like this, because I know it comes from a place of love.

"Harriet prefers to read about adventures, not have them."

Her words sting. Is that really what she thinks? I might not have sex on a rugby field but I wouldn't say I don't do *anything* exciting.

"Her idea of doing something wild," Steph continues, as if I'm not here, "would be returning a library book after the due date." She nudges me and the other girls dissolve into giggles.

I shoot Steph a look of annoyance but she doesn't notice. I know she's being silly, but her words hurt a little. I mean, for one, I *never* return books late. And two, well, I'm not *that* boring.

Am I?

"Being outrageous requires spontaneity and that's not Harriet's strength," Steph adds.

What's so wrong with that?

Cassidy looks flabbergasted. "So you've never, like, jumped in the sack with a hot guy you just met?"

"Wait," Heather interjects, her kohl-rimmed eyes widening as she leans closer to me. "Are you a *virgin*, Harriet?"

My face burns. "No," I say, exasperated. Are there only two options? You leap into bed with random men you've just met or you're a virgin?

I've had sex with my fair share of men, don't you worry. I just don't go around broadcasting it, like this lot. You don't get to twenty-eight with Steph as your bestie without getting it on with a few guys. And I've had loads.

Okay, to be more specific, I've had sex with three men. I don't know what Steph is carrying on about, because each was more disappointing than the last. I didn't... reach completion, so to speak. Although I've never done that on my own, either, so perhaps that's not on them. It didn't help when my last boyfriend told me he'd been with much more attractive women. After that I didn't feel like having sex with him at all.

"Anyway," Steph says, slinging an arm around my shoulder, "Harri might play it safe, but she's always been there for me. She's the best friend anyone could ask for." She squeezes me. "Besides, I'm working on her."

"Thanks, Steph," I mumble, and down the rest of my drink. "But I'm quite happy with my life."

"I know. It wouldn't hurt you to get out there a bit more, though. Have a little fun, let your hair down."

"Literally!" Cassidy chimes in, then howls with laughter.

I raise a hand to my hair, pulled up into a tidy bun on the top of my head, the way I always wear it. What does my hair have to do with anything?

"Seriously, when did you last have sex? I had sex this morning." Cassidy beams with pride.

"Maybe you should talk to a guy now and get a number," Heather suggests, her gaze swiveling around the bar. "Ooh, what about him?" She jabs a manicured finger towards a guy with ruffled blond hair, wearing a leather jacket and ripped jeans. A motorcycle helmet sits on the bar in front of him. He's exactly the type of "bad boy" that women love, for whatever reason.

"Erm, no thanks." My phone buzzes on the table and I lunge to grab it, relieved for the distraction. I glance at the screen as I stand and slip outside. It's my sister, Alex, calling from New York. She moved there a year ago and met some guy called Michael and they've been inseparable ever since. They're getting married in a few weeks, which I've been trying to avoid thinking about. She asked me to fly across for the big day and be her maid of honor, but I came up with an excuse about having to work. The truth is, I can't imagine flying there. I've never been to a huge, foreign city like that. The crowds, the traffic, the possibility of being mugged... it scares the bejesus out of me.

"Hey, Harri," Alex says when I accept the call. "How are you?"

"Not bad." I push the conversation in the bar from my mind. "How are things?"

"Busy with writing and wedding stuff."

Sometimes I have trouble keeping up with everything Alex does. She writes for an online magazine called Bliss Edition, she works part-time at a bookstore, and when she's not doing those things, she writes romance novels. Now, of course, she's planning a wedding too.

"It's pretty full on," she adds.

"Mm," I say, distracted by a couple across the parking lot making out against the side of a Honda. Ugh.

She sighs at the other end of the phone.

"Everything okay?" I ask.

"It's Mum."

I nod, even though she can't see me. I know what she's going to say because I've heard Mum go on and on about this since Alex announced her engagement.

"She's beside herself that I'm marrying an American and not coming home. She keeps asking me if I'm sure I'm doing the right thing."

"Yeah," I murmur. "I know."

"I just got off the phone with her. This time it was, 'I'd hate to see you make a big mistake.'"

I grimace. "Shit. That sucks." Silence stretches between us and she sniffles. It's hard being a million miles away.

"Sorry. I just needed to talk to someone who understands what a nightmare Mum can be. Do you think you could have a word with her?"

"Absolutely," I say. It's the least I can do.

"Thanks." She sighs again. "I wish you were coming to the wedding. We'll miss you, but I know you're busy."

The guilt that's been gnawing at me for the past few months carves a hole through my chest. Alex has been so understanding since I gave my bullshit excuses about why I couldn't come, but after everything Steph and her friends just said, I'm suddenly questioning that knee-jerk reaction. I never for one second considered that I actually *could* go all the way to New York; I'd ruled it out as too far and too scary. Unlike Alex, who jumped on the first flight she could after breaking up with a guy. The thought of doing something like that makes me feel nauseous.

We've always been different. Alex is three years older

than me and we've never been especially close. She likes to go out, meet guys, go shopping—do all those "girly" things which I'm mostly indifferent to. The one thing we do have in common is our love of reading, but whereas I love fantasy and sci-fi, she loves romance. While I don't mind the odd romance novel—and I've read hers out of curiosity—I don't get what all the fuss is about. Not just the novels; the whole lot of it.

That's another difference between Alex and I: she's always dated, always been looking to meet "the one." I've seen her lose her head over a guy a hundred times and I've never once felt like that with a bloke. I've never been in love, never felt completely overcome by needing to have some-one, and—as sad as it might be to admit this—the men in real life have never quite measured up to the men in the books I love.

Maybe I'm missing the horny gene, or something. Alex certainly got it. Her romance novel is so steamy I can't bring myself to tell her I've read it.

"Anyway, I'll let you go," she says. "I didn't mean to inter-rupt your evening. What are you reading tonight?"

I blink, focusing back on her words. "What am I reading?"

"Yeah. You're usually halfway through some epic fantasy novel when I call at this time."

She prefers to read about adventures, not have them.

Steph's words run through my mind and my heart sinks. It's not just Steph and her friends who think I'm dull; even Alex believes I can't possibly be anywhere other than at home, doing something unremarkable. For the first time, when I think about heading home for the evening, I'm not comforted in the same way I usually am. I find myself wanting to prove them all wrong, wanting to show them that I *can* do something spontaneous.

"I'll come to the wedding." The words are out of my mouth before I can even stop to think.

"What? Are you serious?"

My pulse ticks up a notch. "I... yes."

"Oh my God!" Alex shrieks so loudly I have to pull the phone away from my ear. "Harriet! I'm so happy! I can't believe it!"

I force myself to take a deep breath and stop my clammy hands from trembling. A strange sense of nervous excitement ripples through me, and it takes me a second to realize that I kind of *want* to go; to throw caution to the wind for once and do something crazy.

Ha! I want to yell at everyone in the bar. *Look who's outrageous now!*

"When can you come?" Alex asks in a rush. "I'd love it if you could come soon, then we'd have a couple of weeks to go sightseeing and explore the city! I'll send you some ticket options."

The words *sightseeing* and *explore* make my stomach tilt. "Okay, but—"

"Will you be my maid of honor, then?"

In spite of my nerves, I smile, touched that she still wants me to do that after everything. "Of course."

"Harri, you have no idea how much this means to me." My heart squeezes at the joy in her voice. "New York is amazing. We're going to have so much fun."

I take another deep breath, willing myself to stay calm. "We are," I say, but I'm not entirely sure if I believe it.

2

_____

What the hell was I thinking?

I roll over, flipping my pillow to the cool side and pressing my cheek to the soft cotton, but it doesn't help me relax enough to sleep. *Why* did I say I'd fly to New York? It was all fine and good when I was standing in that dark parking lot, still feeling the sting of Steph and her friends' words, but now I'm wound tighter than the bun I wear on top of my head.

I know they think I'm hilariously boring, but I hadn't realized how predictable my life had gotten until that conversation. It's not like I set out to live a boring life, but I can't deny that I like to feel as though things are within my control, otherwise I spiral. It's kind of scary what happens when I feel overwhelmed, despite all the work I've done to manage my anxiety. This is why I don't take risks; I can't be certain of the outcome. The only place I'm prepared to take risks is in board games, which I've loved playing for years. Just as well I didn't tell Steph's friends *that*.

By morning I've hardly slept. I rub my bleary eyes, reaching for my phone to silence the alarm. There's an

email from Alex and I unlock my phone to read it, shocked to find she's suggesting I get on a flight in two days.

Two days.

Fuck. I know she asked if I could come soon, but that's a *lot* sooner than I was thinking.

Nerves tumble through my belly as I shower and dress for the day. I always follow the same basic routine: moisturizer with SPF30+, a light brush of bronzer to warm up my pale complexion, a swipe of mascara, and my long brown hair pulled up into a tidy bun. I slip on my glasses—black, with a subtle cat-eye shape—and wander back into my room to pack my bag for work. First thing in is my current read—I'm rereading the entire *Harry Potter* series for the millionth time and I'm currently on *The Chamber of Secrets* —to enjoy during my break. I pull on my daily "uniform" of slim-fitting jeans and a plain black T-shirt, and pop tiny gold studs in my ears.

I try to forget about Alex's email as I head off to work, walking the ten minutes it takes to get to the cafe from our flat. Our town is small, sort of blink-and-you'll-miss-it small, a few hours out of Auckland. You can walk anywhere in town within fifteen minutes.

Arriving at work, I push the glass door open. I'm greeted by the familiar smell of roasting coffee beans and it perks me up. I've worked here since I was eighteen, splitting my time between barista and waitress, and I love it. We roast our own coffee, which is fun. The regular customers are lovely, and my boss, Paula, is the best. She's owned the cafe for years and creates the most amazing baked goods, always coming up with new ideas. She's one of the friendliest people I've ever known—almost like a second mum to me, except one I can talk about sex with. You know, if I had much sex.

I drop my bag behind the counter and tie on my apron, looking around the empty space. Sometimes I dream about opening my own cafe, but with a unique twist: a board game cafe. Great big shelves, heaving with every game you can imagine, line the walls. The counters are stuffed with yummy treats and my own brand of coffee, and the air is rich with the scent of cinnamon and croissants. The tables are set up so you can grab a coffee and spend hours getting lost in a game of *Scrabble* or *Settlers of Catan* or *Uno*, with friends or alone. That's what makes it so cool; it's like an introvert's paradise.

On really slow days, I sketch on a napkin I keep in my bag. It started with a simple floor plan, but now there's a list of games I'd love to have, ideas for themed games nights, and even notes on the decor—a warm, golden yellow on the walls, dark-stained hardwood floors, and cozy leather sofas.

But, whatever. I haven't given it a lot of thought. Would it be amazing to create this magical space? Sure. Is it really practical? Probably not. In fact, I should probably throw that napkin away.

"Hey chick, how are you?" Paula appears from the kitchen and turns on the coffee machine. On the counter beside her is a plate of her trademark vegan brownies. I'm not a vegan but she does the best vegan baking, and while I'd usually be dying to have one, I can't stomach the thought right now.

"Good. Um..." I smooth my moist palms over my apron. May as well talk to Paula about this now, though I'm sure she won't be able to give me several weeks off at such short notice. Part of me is already relieved. I want to be there for Alex, but the thought of getting on a flight in two days feels too soon. We'll have to figure out a compromise.

"What's up?"

"Alex called last night. She was a little unhappy." I decide not to mention the part about Mum, given Paula knows her well. "We got to talking, and..." I swallow, willing myself to say the words. "I ended up agreeing to fly to New York for her wedding."

Paula's eyes light up. "Oh, wow! That's fantastic!"

My pulse jumps. She is a *lot* more excited about this than I anticipated. "Right. I wanted to make sure you were okay with it, because I know this is last minute."

"Absolutely! When are you thinking of going?"

"Oh, well..." I emit an awkward laugh. "She sent me an email with a flight in two days time, but I know—"

"Okay," Paula says, and my mouth opens in surprise.

"*Okay*?"

"Yep. I can move some shifts around on the roster. We'll manage without you."

"Good to know I'm so valued here," I say wryly, and she laughs.

"Of course you are. But come on, wouldn't you rather be getting on a plane to New York than wiping down tables here?"

No, I want to say, but it's too bloody late now.

"I know I would," she adds with a chuckle. "If you go sooner, you'll have more time away to see your sister and explore the city. Think of all the sightseeing you can do!"

A cold sweat prickles along my brow at those words again. "Are you sure?" I ask, making one last-ditch attempt to get out of this. My stomach is churning and I'm starting to feel itchy. "Because I don't have to—"

"Totally sure." She gives me a gentle pat on the arm. "I think this will be good for you, chick. I can't remember when you last took time off. You could use a little more excitement in your life."

I frown, thinking again about Steph and her friends' words from last night. Does *everyone* think I'm boring?

"You should head home now to get your visa sorted and pack," Paula says, handing me my bag and waving me towards the door. "I'll cover your shift for the day."

"Oh, um, okay," I mumble, untying my apron. This did not go at all how I expected. "Well... thanks."

"Of course! I wish I could come too, I'm dying to see New York. You'll have to tell me every detail when you get back!" She grins and I send her a weak smile in return.

Guess I'm heading home to pack.

"I still can't believe you're doing this." Steph hauls my suitcase from the car and hands it to me.

"You don't have to sound so surprised," I respond, trying to quell the nerves clawing through my gut as we head across the parking lot at Auckland International Airport. She insisted on taking the afternoon off work to drive me up here. I get the sense she was worried I might not go through with it if she wasn't here to push me through the gate.

"I'm sorry if we were a bit harsh the other night," Steph says. "It's just... sometimes I worry you're letting life pass you by, Harri."

I sigh. "You might have had a point. I could probably make some changes."

I've been thinking about this a lot over the past forty-eight hours. Between the conversation in the bar and Paula's words, it's become painfully obvious to me that my life needs jazzing up. Nothing too outrageous—it's not like I'm about to sign up for skydiving or shag a bloke on a cricket pitch—but it wouldn't hurt to get out of my routine. I know

I'm at the crucial point of the hero's journey—the point that all characters in my favorite fantasy stories come to, where they have to decide if they'll accept the quest—and I'm accepting my quest with enthusiasm. Well, maybe not *enthusiasm*, given I did fly into a panic after Paula gave me the green light and I haven't slept since, but I'm accepting it, and that's what counts.

Of course, accepting it and feeling okay about it are two different things. But... baby steps.

"Well, this trip is an excellent start," Steph says as we enter through the glass doors. "And it kind of gave me an idea."

We step onto the airport concourse and my anxiety level ratchets up a notch. It's teeming with people and I don't have the first clue where to go. I've never even set foot in here.

Steph catches my bemused expression and guides me towards the check-in line. "So, I had an idea..." she repeats, eying me expectantly.

I stand my suitcase as we join the line and turn to her. "What?"

"You said you want to make some changes, right?"

I nod.

"And you're going all the way to New York. Besides Alex, no one even knows you there."

"Uh-huh." I turn my attention back to the line in front of me. God knows what she's rambling on about now.

"So why not play a little game? Participate in an experiment?"

"Sure." I inch forward in the line, only half-listening. The guy in front of me has a curved neck pillow dangling from his bag. Should I have bought one of those?

"You could try out what it's like to be more adventurous."

I glance at Steph again. "Adventurous?"

"Yeah. I want you to have a blast over there. It's a different environment, miles away from home, so why not have fun with it? Take a few risks, be more outgoing?"

I blink. "You want me to go to New York and pretend to be someone else?"

"No, not someone else. Still you, just more bold. Kind of like... Harriet 2.0."

I can't help but chuckle at her words. *Harriet 2.0.*

"Here." She digs into her bag and pulls out a small package. "I got you a going-away present."

I smile, touched. "Aw, you didn't need to do that." I take the gift and unwrap it to find a lipstick, which she knows I don't wear. I give her an odd look.

"I thought it could help you be more confident."

"A lipstick?"

"Open it."

I pop the lid off and peer inside. It's a vivid, crimson red —definitely not my style—and I tuck it into my bag, wondering what to say. Does she even know me at all?

"I know it's not a color you would've chosen," she says. "That's the point. It will make you feel sexy and bold. It's for Harriet 2.0." Before I can respond, she whips something else out from her bag. I recognize the tiny square wrapper immediately and my face warms. Typical Steph to brandish a condom in a public place like it's no big deal. There are *children* nearby.

"Steph—"

"And I have a feeling," she continues, tucking the condom into my bra with a devilish grin, "Harriet 2.0 will need this."

"You're being ridiculous." I move forward in the line again and try not to let her see me blush. When I said I wanted to shake things up, I did *not* mean red lipstick and condoms. But when I glance back at her, she looks disappointed and I feel bad. The condom is a joke, of course, but she must have gone to a lot of trouble to choose the lipstick shade for me.

I soften, smiling. "Thanks for the gift. It's really thoughtful. And I'll think about the whole Harriet 2.0 thing, okay?"

"I hope so," she says, putting an arm over my shoulder and giving me a squeeze.

3

I swirl the gin around in my glass and breathe a deep sigh of relief.

It's been a rough night and I desperately need this drink. You see, the thing I didn't realize as I boarded the flight from Auckland to Houston for the first leg of my journey, is that I'm afraid of flying.

No, not afraid. *Terrified.*

I should have seen that coming, but I was so focused on how scary the New York part of this trip is that I didn't even stop to think about the flying part. And once I was on the plane, it was far too late to reconsider. I only made it through the hideous ordeal thanks to the kindly older lady seated beside me, who offered me an Ambien. I didn't want to take it, because I have a staunch don't-accept-drugs-from-strangers policy, but I kept thinking of Steph's suggestion to take more risks. And when we hit an especially bad patch of turbulence and I had to clutch onto the lady's hand for emotional support—like I'd done during take-off, by the way—I thought *fuck it*, and accepted the drugs.

But then I slept for twelve straight hours, through breakfast and landing, and was the last one off the plane. By the time I ran through the airport, went through the TSA line and located my terminal, I thought I'd missed my connecting flight. I arrived at the gate, breathless, only to discover the next flight had been delayed, and I now had a couple of hours to catch my breath and prepare for once again launching my body into the sky.

At first, I sat and gnawed on my nails, unable to even think about grabbing a snack because my stomach was all tangled again. But then I thought, what would Harriet 2.0 do? She wouldn't be sitting with one knee bobbing up and down so much that the whole plastic row of seats shakes and the woman beside her keeps shooting her daggers. No; she'd grab a drink and relax, ready to enjoy her trip to The Big Apple. And not just any drink. She'd probably drink a martini or something super classy.

So here I am, cocktail glass in hand as I sit at a bar near my gate, about to drink a martini. I've never tried one before, but here's to new things, right?

I take a big gulp and wince as it burns all the way down the back of my throat.

Holy hell, this tastes like pure alcohol. It's like I'm swigging straight from the gin bottle. Why on earth do people drink these?

I glance down at the liquid in the glass. Just as I consider pushing it away, a warm sensation spreads through me and the knot in my middle loosens.

Wow, okay. There might be something to this.

I hold my breath and down the rest of the martini. While I wait for it to work its magic, I rummage in my bag and pull out my compact to check my appearance. Steph talked me into trying the red lipstick and it's still stuck fast to my lips. As a sign of commitment to my exciting new self, I reapply a thick, glossy coat, before adding some mascara and spritzing myself with perfume. I slide my glasses back on as I hear them calling for my row to board.

The airport sways when I push to my feet. I adjust my cotton jersey dress as I wobble towards the gate, and it occurs to me that perhaps knocking back a martini on an empty stomach wasn't the best idea. I'm trying to walk in a straight line but I'm not sure it's working. God, what if they don't let me on? What if I look like a drunk and they think I'm going to start a riot on board?

No, don't be silly. They wouldn't have alcohol at airports if you weren't supposed to drink. I bet it's how half of these people can face boarding this death machine.

Besides, I feel quite good now. My limbs are buzzing, my head is warm and fuzzy, and my whole body feels more relaxed. Maybe I'll make it through this flight with my dignity intact.

I show the attendants my boarding pass, doing my best to stand straight and not give away the fact that the room is swimming around me, then teeter down the gangway to the plane. Once on board, I weave between passengers, giggling. I can't remember the last time I felt this loose. Turns out Harriet 2.0 is pretty fun!

My seat is by the window, in the very back row. I turn to my right, about to clamber to my spot, and notice there's someone sitting in the middle seat.

Not just someone. A guy. He must be in his mid-thirties and he's tall, his long legs awkwardly folded in behind the seat in front. He's in a pale blue business shirt with a navy colored tie around his neck. His eyes are closed, his head rests back against the seat, and his short, dark hair is a little ruffled. He looks so peaceful, I don't want to disturb him.

I glance at my seat by the window. I'm quite sure I can squeeze over him.

Hoisting my bag up onto my shoulder, I creep into the row, grabbing hold of the headrest beside his to steady myself. Then I turn and face him, carefully lifting one leg over his lap and hoping he doesn't open his eyes at this exact moment.

Okay, halfway there.

Ooh, he smells quite nice. What is that? Some kind of aftershave? I lean in closer and inhale the spicy, woody scent, noticing how lush and dark his eyelashes are against the creamy skin of his cheek.

I'm just about to lift my other leg up over him when I lose my balance and fall forward, landing in his lap with a thud.

Shit.

His eyes fly open, his head jerks up, and there we sit: face to face, mere inches apart, me literally straddling his lap as my dress rides up my exposed thighs. Boy, am I glad I shaved my legs.

He stares at me without saying anything, his chocolate-brown eyes wide with surprise. I'm still feeling so out of it with the gin racing through my veins that it takes me a second to react. My body responds first, doubling my heart rate and sending a flurry of butterflies into my abdomen. Before I can say anything, his eyes crease in amusement and he chuckles.

"Well. Hello there."

His deep American accent rolls over me and my gaze drops to his mouth as it curves into a bewildered smile. When I run my eye along his sharp jawline, a wave of heat rushes up my body, catching me off-guard. It's such an unfamiliar sensation that I almost don't recognize it.

Oh. *Oh.*

"Would you like a hand to your seat?"

"Oh my God," I mutter, my cheeks flaming as I come to my senses. Here he was, enjoying a quiet moment in the middle of the afternoon, and I go and hurl myself into his lap. "I'm so sorry. I didn't want to bother you." I pick myself up and, with as much grace as possible, hold down my dress as I haul my other leg over him. Then I sink into my seat, pressing my eyes shut in mortification.

So much for making it through the flight with my dignity intact.

He chuckles again. "That's quite alright."

Stuffing my bag under the seat in front of me, I try to stop my head from spinning. I busy myself with the safety instructions while the plane fills and we wait to take off, but my pulse is erratic and the images all blur together. No one else joins our row and I can't bring myself to look at the guy next to me in case I blush all over again. By the time we are heading down the runway, I'm no longer sure if it's the alcohol that's making me so light-headed, or something else entirely.

ONCE THE PLANE is in the air, I release my vice-like grip on the armrest. At least I didn't grab the poor guy's hand during take-off, but that's little consolation after giving him a lap dance.

I'm still buzzing from my martini but the humiliation has really taken the fun out of it. On the plus side, this whole thing has served as a welcome distraction from flying.

Then, as I'm about to put my earphones in and try to

forget it all, I drop them. On the floor. Between this guy and me.

Oh for *fuck's* sake.

I look down at the narrow crack between our almost-touching knees and sigh. I don't want to spend the next three hours sitting here in silence and I'm too wired to read. I was hoping to watch a film.

I sneak a glance out of the corner of my eye and notice the guy beside me has leaned his head back and closed his eyes again.

Right. Good.

Slipping my right hand down between our knees, I lean over, acutely aware that my head is hovering over his crotch as I grope at the floor.

Where are the damn earphones? I could have sworn they were down here...

A muffled laugh comes from above me, just as my hand grasps the cord on the floor. I snatch it up and curl back into my seat, afraid to make eye contact. I might burst into flames.

"Don't you think we should at least exchange names first?"

Oh *God*. Why doesn't my seat come with an ejector button?

"Sorry," he mumbles, when I don't respond. "Inappropriate joke."

I hazard a glance at him and notice his cheeks are crimson. Good to know I'm not the only one finding this situation so awkward.

I summon a smile. "It's okay. Sorry, I dropped my earphones. And sorry, er, about earlier."

He smiles back, the color disappearing from his cheeks

and his confidence restored. "No problem. It's not everyday a pretty lady throws herself into my lap."

I bite my lip and look down at the tangled cord in my hand. Is it my imagination, or is he flirting?

It's been so long since I've flirted. Most of the time I don't think it's worth the effort, but when I glance up again into his twinkling eyes, my heart skips a beat. I want to flirt back. Except, I think I've forgotten how. Is that possible?

This is so typically me. I have this guy captive for three hours, giving me the sexiest smile, and I have no idea what to say to him. I'm reminded of this game I used to love at my board game club a few years back, where you'd play a card depending on what trait or special power you needed in the moment. Right now, I find myself wishing there was a *Flirt Effortlessly With a Hot Guy* card I could throw down.

Then I realize something: *I* might not know what to say to him, but Harriet 2.0 would. And she'd be confident and sexy. She'd probably end up shagging him in the bathroom or something. Ha!

I take a deep breath, put my earphones down, and twist in my seat to face him. "I'm Harriet."

His smile widens. "Luke. Nice to meet you, Harriet." He tilts his head. "Is that a New Zealand accent?"

"Yes." I grin, letting his relaxed manner put me at ease. I'm about to say more but the flight attendant arrives with the drinks trolley. When Luke orders a whiskey, I order one too, and before I can stop him he pays for both. "Thank you. That's very kind."

"You're welcome," he says with that disarming smile of his. "I haven't met many women who like whiskey."

"I've never tried it," I admit, watching as he pours it over the ice in his plastic cup, then doing the same. "But I like to try new things." Well, *I* don't, of course, but my alter ego does. He doesn't need to know that there's a difference.

"What else do you like?"

I think for a minute as I sip the smoky liquid. It's not bad, actually. Maybe Harriet 2.0 is onto something.

Hmm. What else would she like to do? She's outgoing, so she'd like adventurous things.

"I love anything that takes me out of my comfort zone or gives me a rush. You know; skydiving, zip-lining, spontaneous road trips, skinny-dipping, trying exotic new foods..." I pause as I rack my brain for more wild examples. My mind lands on the earlier thought I had about this lovely gentleman taking me in the airplane bathroom and my cheeks flush.

I push my glasses up my nose as he contemplates me over his whiskey. I half expect him to burst out laughing at my outrageous lies because, let's face it, with my bookish looks I don't seem the type to be throwing myself from an airplane or running naked down a beach.

Instead, he raises his eyebrows, impressed. "Wow. I wish I did more things like that."

Relief sweeps over me. The whiskey works its way into my veins, relaxing me even more, and I smile. I quite like being this new version of myself. Especially when he looks at me like that.

"So what brings you to New York?"

I falter. I don't want to tell him I didn't actually *want* to come—that I made a snap decision to prove I wasn't boring and then felt like I couldn't back out. I think of the reasons everyone else was so excited about me going on this trip. "I'm just coming to explore the city and do some sightseeing."

"Alone?"

I nod breezily, as if I always travel alone because I'm so independent and worldly and confident.

He looks impressed again as he takes a drink.

"What about you?" I ask.

"I live in Manhattan. I was just in Houston for business."

"What do you do?"

"Oh..." He hesitates. "I work in entertainment."

I'm about to ask more when the plane jolts violently. Despite the alcohol coursing through my system, my heart throws itself against my breastbone in fright. I inhale slowly, watching the liquid quiver in my glass as the plane shudders. Somehow, I'm not freaking out. I don't know if it's because I'm in Harriet 2.0 mode, or because the whiskey has taken the edge off, but I feel okay. I can do this.

The plane jerks again and there's a sharp intake of breath beside me. I glance at Luke to find his face is pale and his eyes are pressed shut. His cup wobbles on the tray table in front of him while he grips the armrests tightly, his knuckles white. He looks terrified and there's a tug in my heart.

Without thinking, I place my cup down and take his hand, squeezing. He doesn't open his eyes, but his fingers tighten around mine and squeeze back. I let my gaze linger on his face, taking him in properly. His skin is perfectly smooth apart from a tiny round blemish on the upper side of his left cheek that looks like a chicken pox scar. His dark hair is a little longer on top but cut closer on the sides, his jaw filling in with five o'clock shadow. And that mouth: full and soft as he bites down hard on his bottom lip. He really is beautiful. Perhaps if the guys back home looked more like *this*, I'd be following Steph's advice more readily.

The plane steadies and he exhales, blinking. Time suspends for a split second as our eyes lock, and it feels like... I'm not sure what. Like there's electricity or something crackling between us, concentrated in our joined hands. Like neither one of us wants to let go.

God, it's such an odd situation, being this close to a stranger on a plane when you feel like you could plunge to your death at any moment. So odd, I'm starting to imagine things.

He gives me a sheepish smile as I release his hand. "Thanks. I'm a terrible flier. My ex used to tell me it was pathetic." His gaze slides away and he shakes his head. "But then, she complained about a lot of things I did."

I'm surprised to feel a stab of jealousy at the mention of his ex, at the thought of someone else getting to kiss those lips.

Jesus Christ, I'm losing it. I've only just met this guy. I *never* get like this around men. It must be a combination of the stress of flying and the alcohol, not to mention the altitude up here. I need to get a grip.

I tear my gaze from his and force a laugh. "That's rough. My ex complained I wasn't pretty enough." The words tumble out of my mouth and I cringe. Why the hell did I tell him that?

When I look back at him, he's studying me with a frown. He must be struggling for something to say that doesn't hurt my feelings.

"Anyway," I mumble, "tell me about New York. What should I do there?"

He sips his whiskey, listing off some of the tourist spots around the city—Empire State Building, Times Square, Brooklyn Bridge—but then he tells me about some of the less well-known places he prefers, like the bakery that makes the best donuts, and his favorite coffee shop. When he mentions a bookstore called Strand that apparently has eighteen miles of books I nearly swoon into his arms. I think back to the last guy I dated and how lame he thought it was that I spent so much time reading, yet here Luke is, pointing out the best bookstore in the city. I didn't even ask, but somehow he seems to know to tell me about it, and that, more than anything, makes me revisit the thought of dragging him off to the bathroom and having my way with him.

Well, not me, obviously. *I* would never do anything as outrageous as that. But my new alter ego certainly would.

"And there's a great ice cream place on Bleecker Street," Luke says as he finishes his drink. "They won an award for the best mint chocolate chip."

I wrinkle my nose. I've never understood why people like mint as an ice cream flavor.

"I don't know if it lives up to the hype," he admits. "I've never tried it. To me, the only place mint belongs is in—"

"Toothpaste," I finish, nodding.

"Yes!" He grins. "And gum."

"Agreed. It's fine in gum and toothpaste, but as an ice cream flavor it's—"

"Gross."

"Have you ever tried peppermint tea?" I ask, thinking of when I have to make it at work. The smell makes me gag.

"No." Luke screws up his face. "That sounds disgusting."

The flight attendant appears with her trolley at that moment. "Can I get you any more drinks?"

"I'll take another whiskey, please," I say, before I can wonder whether it's a good idea. I'm having too much fun to care.

"Sure thing. And for you, sir?"

I can't help myself. "He'll take a pot of peppermint tea." Luke glances at me, mirth flickering in his eyes, and I have to press my lips together to subdue my grin.

"I'll take a *whiskey*," he amends, speaking to the attendant but watching me. "And do you serve ice cream?"

A laugh shoots from my mouth. I try to cover it with a cough but it's too late. It doesn't matter—it was worth it to see Luke's face light up at my reaction.

"Sorry, no..." We both turn to see the flight attendant looking perplexed as she hands over our drinks.

"Too bad." Luke pays for the whiskey. The attendant moves on with her trolley and he fixes his attention back on me, a wry smile curling his lips. "You're trouble."

"I don't know what you're talking about," I say, giving an innocent shrug. "And you never know, you might have liked it." My belly flips at his husky laugh, at the way he leans a little bit closer.

Over the next hour Luke and I chat as we sip our drinks, and I marvel at the way it feels almost like we're old friends. I've heard people say they have "chemistry" with someone and thought that was an unusual expression, but for the first time I think I get what they mean. The conversation flows effortlessly, punctuated with laughter, steeped in a sort of kindred familiarity I can't quite put my finger on. We keep interrupting each other—but in a good way, because we know what the other is going to say.

I think he's at ease with me too, because he loosens his tie and unbuttons his shirt cuffs, rolling the sleeves up to his elbows. That's where the wheels fall off because, fuck, he has delicious forearms. Is that a thing? I've never noticed forearms on a guy before because I'm not some kind of weird perve, but these are distracting. They're muscular, with a light dusting of hair and the faintest lines of his veins. I'm all restless with them on display, *right there*. It also doesn't help that every time Luke looks at me his eyes are warm and sparkling, and that we're sitting so close our arms keep brushing. The whole combination makes me feel electric, like a live wire with nowhere for the current to go.

After a while, he excuses himself for the bathroom, much to my relief. I watch him squeeze his way along the aisle up the plane, all long limbs and height, trying not to bump into anyone.

I stand and shuffle out of our aisle, stretching as I step into the little galley area at the back, behind our seats. There's a small kitchen counter, an exit door and a bathroom. I didn't even know all this was back here, and I don't think any of the other passengers do, either. No one has come back to use the bathroom. Even Luke went further up the plane somewhere.

I'm pleased to have a little space to myself, to shake the build-up of energy from my body. By this stage on the last flight I was antsy and desperate for it to be over, but now I'm disappointed at the thought of landing soon. In fact, this flight has been delightful, even with the turbulence earlier. I can't believe I'm thinking that, but Luke has distracted me from flying. He could probably distract me from anything, which is an even *more* absurd thought. The last time I felt this attracted to a guy was... er, never? Perhaps the gods of flying decided to give me a break on this one.

I chuckle to myself as I slip my glasses off and place them on the counter behind me, massaging my temples. My bun is starting to hurt my head as it always does when I have it up for too long. I pull off the hair-tie, letting my brown hair tumble down my back. It's really long—just below my waist—and a mousy sort of brown, the kind that isn't shimmering or exotic or anything, it just *is*. I've never given it a great deal of thought, but as I run my hands through it now I wonder if maybe I should dye it or something. The new me would do that.

The more I think about this Harriet 2.0 plan, the more I like it. I feel empowered, like I could do anything. I'll have to thank Steph for pushing me to try this.

"Wow." I glance up to see Luke in front of me, his eyes wide. "Your hair."

I cock my head in confusion. "What?"

"It's..." he trails off, taking another step closer to me. He shakes his head, a smile building on his lips. "Harriet, whoever told you that you weren't pretty was way off. You are. You're beautiful."

Oh.

There's a flutter behind my ribcage. Is he serious? No one has called me beautiful before. Once a guy said I was "kind of cute," but that was years ago. And he was drunk.

I gaze at Luke, with that gorgeous smile on his mouth, and all of a sudden I'm hot everywhere. I just want to reach out and grab—

The plane jerks and Luke's smile vanishes. He presses his eyes shut again, one hand gripping the edge of the counter, the other instinctively reaching for mine. But the second he touches me, I lose all rational thought. My body takes over and I push up onto my toes, brushing my lips over his. The electric current inside me sparks, zapping right down through my center.

Wow.

Then I come to my senses and stumble back, grimacing with horror.

Oh my God. What the hell is *wrong* with me? I've never done something so brazen in my life.

I open my mouth to apologize, but stop when I see Luke's face. His eyes are open, and even though the plane is still rocking, that smile is back. He lets go of the counter and grabs me by the waist, pulling me hard up against him, pressing his mouth back onto mine.

Holy *shit*.

"Is this okay?" he asks against my lips.

My brain is short-circuiting. I can barely reply, I'm so breathless. "Yes," I manage, kissing him harder.

Oh, yes.

4

I close my eyes and submit to the desire sweeping through me. I cannot believe I'm kissing a stranger on an airplane, but I can only blame Harriet 2.0.

Luke turns me and nudges me up against the counter, angling his head to deepen the kiss. When I part my lips, I feel his tongue lick against mine and fire burns hot through my veins. I'm overcome with the urge to jump up onto the counter and pull him between my legs, and that's when I remember that we're in public. A flight attendant could come back here at any moment. Shit, would we get in trouble?

I spy the bathroom door over Luke's shoulder and before I know what I'm doing, I take his hand and lead him towards it, slipping inside and turning back to face him. He hesitates in the doorway, eying me, and I wonder if I've gone too far.

I mean, what the hell am I doing? My pulse is ringing in my ears, my body is vibrating with adrenaline, my thighs are squeezing together with want. I don't even recognize myself.

But after a quick glance down the aisle, Luke steps into

the space and shuts the door, locking it. The dim light pings on and he turns around, his gaze colliding with mine. And in that shared moment of understanding, everything shifts into high gear.

Our mouths crash together. He kisses me with a new kind of hunger, biting down on my bottom lip, tasting me. My hands move over his back, feeling the firmness of muscle under cotton. I tug at the bottom of his shirt, loosening it from his pants. I'm not sure how long we have and I don't want to waste a second.

"God, you're hot," he growls, dragging his mouth over my neck and raising a hand to cup my breast. His fingers tighten on my nipple through my dress and goosebumps race across my skin.

"You're not too bad yourself," I whisper back with a giggle. I slide my hands up the front of his shirt and grope for his buttons, dying to see his body, to touch him. I've never needed to touch someone so badly in my life.

"Shit." Luke draws back, his forehead pinching. "I don't have a condom."

Disappointment is a sharp, jagged tear right through me. Of *all* the times to not have a condom—

Wait.

I reach into my bra and fumble awkwardly, praying it's still there, that I didn't lose Steph's silly gift, that—

Jackpot!

I whip the square wrapper out of my bra and present it to him with a laugh. I'm about to explain that my friend gave it to me as a joke, but stop. It's pretty on-brand for my new self to carry a condom in her bra. Steph will *die* from shock when I tell her I've actually used it.

Luke takes the condom with a surprised grin. It's the

sexiest lop-sided smile I've ever seen. "Are you sure you're okay with this?"

I look at him like he's crazy. As if I haven't been clear enough. As if I'm going to say *No, take your sexy forearms and leave*. "Fuck, yes. Now come back here." I grab his tie, tugging him towards me.

His eyes darken and he lets me pull his mouth back onto mine, groaning when our tongues meet. God, he tastes good —like whiskey, but also like, well, I can't even describe it. Like sex. Like I just want to fuck his brains out.

I don't think I've *ever* had that thought in my life. I must be losing my mind.

My fingers grasp at his tie and he takes over, untying the knot without removing his lips from mine. Finally his shirt is open and I slip my hands inside, over the patch of hair across his chest, onto his muscular shoulders still tucked inside his sleeves. I haven't touched a man in a long time, and I haven't touched a man this beautiful, ever. I can't get enough.

My lips move along his stubbly jaw, down his neck, onto the smooth, hot skin of his shoulder. I pause when I notice the edge of a tattoo on his bicep, a curved pattern disappearing into the sleeve of his shirt. Before I can ask what it is, he drops his hands to my butt and pulls me up against him. I can feel how hard he is, and need blasts through me, obliterating all other thoughts.

He slides my dress up, his hand brushing against my inner thigh, and I whimper helplessly. When his fingers slip inside my underwear, he moans at how ready I am for him, so soon. I think I have been since I sat down in my seat nearly three hours ago.

He tugs my underwear off and lifts me up onto the sink. I bang my head against the wall in the tiny space, and we both pause, breathless, waiting for someone to pound on the door and tell us to stop. When that doesn't happen, he captures my mouth with his again.

I undo his belt and let his pants fall, digging my hands into his boxer-briefs and smiling when I feel the rigid length of him. As I slide my hands up and down, a guttural sound comes from his throat. My touch spurs him on and he thrusts into my hand, moving his thumb in little circles over the sensitive spot between my legs. No one has done that to me before and the sensation is unbelievable. I bite down onto his shoulder, quivering against him.

"Do you like that?" His voice is rough against my ear and I can only nod, I'm so dizzy.

I have to have him. Now.

I draw away and gaze at him desperately. "Please," I whisper, and he gives me a filthy grin as he tears the condom wrapper open with his teeth. He slides his boxer-briefs down and I devour him with my eyes, watching as he rolls the condom on and feeling like I'm about to starve to death in front of a feast if he doesn't hurry up.

He bunches my dress over my hips and I wrap my legs around him. Pleasure pours through my bloodstream when he sinks into me, and I tug him by the shoulders, inviting him deeper. We share a moan as he fills me to the hilt, then draws back to drive into me again, harder.

"Fuck," he growls, kissing into my neck. "Fuck, Harriet." He takes hold of my calves and leans his upper body away from me, his gaze dropping between us to the meeting of our bodies.

I glance down too, and— "Oh my God," I breathe, watching him slide in and out of me, marveling at the way it feels, the way it looks. I've never seen anything so hot in my life.

Luke brings his thumb to his tongue and licks it, lowering it between my legs. He keeps it there as he builds up his pace, watching me through half-lidded eyes. "You're amazing," he rasps, his thumb swirling in just the right spot.

Holy hell. The way he's touching me like that—the way he's fucking me like he has to give me everything now because we'll never see each other again...

I dig my fingernails into his arms as heat wraps around my spine and builds below my navel. The feeling is so good I have to fight a scream. It's a relief when he covers my mouth with his again, containing the animalistic sounds escaping from my throat. I forget that I've ever had sex before, because this is unlike *anything* else I've experienced. This is... this is...

Something urgent and instinctive grips my core, increasing in intensity, until it feels like I'm going to break. It takes me a moment to realize what's happening, and I can't believe it—

My mind stops working as waves of pleasure crash through me and stars explode behind my eyes. For a split second I'm out of my body—I'm just bliss and ecstasy and perfection. I'm nowhere and everywhere at once. Then I drop back into my skin, shuddering against Luke and gasping for breath.

"Ohhh fuck," he groans, his body tensing as he slams deep. His face contorts with release and I try to mentally record it, so I can watch it back over and over again.

He's still for a moment, his chest heaving against me. Then he cups my face and draws my mouth back to his, brushing his lips over mine. "That was... wow," he murmurs, gazing at me intensely. "You really *are* adventurous, aren't you?"

I giggle, trying to process what has just happened. Did I

really just have the best sex of my life—the first *orgasm* of my life—in an airplane bathroom with a stranger?

We stay frozen, neither of us daring to move. We're suspended in time and space, the only two people on the planet, gazing at each other in disbelief at what we've done, at how earth-shattering it was.

A loud rap on the door breaks the spell and we spring apart. "Please return to your seat, we're preparing to land," a curt voice says.

I glance at Luke wide-eyed, panic simmering in my stomach. He raises a finger to my lips.

"Alrighty," he replies through the door in a casual tone.

We scrabble around for our clothes, trying not to bump into each other in the cramped space. Everything feels suddenly awkward; me pulling on my underwear, him discarding the condom and yanking his pants back up, hastily buttoning his shirt and redoing his tie.

He drags a hand through his hair and looks at me again. "You should, uh, wait here for a few minutes. You know, so it's not obvious."

I nod, wondering how on earth I'm going to face him when we're back in our seats.

He gazes at me for another second, then slips out of the bathroom. I'm left standing there, my heart beating wildly and my head spinning, reeling with astonishment over what I've just done.

5

"There must be something you can do?"

I stand at the customer service desk, fiddling with the strap of my bag. I'm trying my best not to freak out but it feels like all the events of the past few hours are crowding in and suffocating me.

I mean, it's not like I *planned* to sit beside a handsome stranger on the plane. Or to share a whiskey and tell him how spontaneous I am. Or to, erm, have sex in the bathroom.

Jesus. I don't even know who I am right now.

In case things weren't messed up enough, my luggage has gone missing. So I'm standing here, in my dress that still has the faint smell of Luke's cologne on it, desperate to put on something—anything—else. And I can't.

"I'm sorry, I've done all I can," the woman behind the desk says. "We just have to wait for the bag to turn up."

My stomach plunges at the finality in her tone. "So... that's it?" She nods and I wring my hands as my pulse escalates. How am I supposed to survive without my luggage? Why didn't I pack a carry-on suitcase?

It'll be okay, I tell myself. *You can buy new clothes, that's easy. You're just overwhelmed.*

I draw in a breath, all the way down to my belly, and my heart rate begins to slow. Right, I can handle this. I just need to get to Alex's place and I'll feel better.

"Okay, thank you," I mumble, tugging my bag onto my shoulder. I turn and trudge across the airport concourse and, despite myself, I glance around one final time. Just in case. In case he's here.

He's not, of course. He's long gone.

I shake my head at myself and plod towards the exit. It's dark when I step outside. The air feels cooler than home. I pull my phone out to text Alex and find a message waiting from her.

Alex: Welcome to New York! I booked you a car service, just find your name. Can't wait to see you!

Relief washes through me and I quickly fire off a reply that I'll be there soon. When I spot my name on a sign, the driver greets me with a smile, holding the door open. I slide into the car and, for the first time since we touched down, I feel some of the tension drain from my body. I'm so exhausted after everything that's happened, I can barely process the fact that I'm here, in America. I slump in the backseat, sliding my phone away, and that's when I notice the paper tucked into the front pocket of my bag. With a frown, I pull it out to find unfamiliar handwriting. Using the light from my phone, I read the scribbled words.

Harriet, that was incredible. I wish things weren't so complicated with me right now, because if they weren't I would love to see you again. I'm sorry that I can't. Take care, Luke.

I clutch the paper in disbelief. I had no idea he'd written that, I'd thought...

After he had left the bathroom, I stared at my reflection,

waiting for the flush in my cheeks to disappear, for my heart to stop racing. The red lipstick still hadn't budged, and as I tidied my hair and composed myself, I tried to make sense of what I'd just done—who I'd just been. My wild eyes reflected in the mirror showed me just how exhilarated I was, and the throbbing between my legs where he'd been only moments ago assured me that I hadn't imagined it.

When I finally slid the bathroom door open, grabbed my glasses from the counter and turned to our seats, Luke wasn't there. I stood for a few moments, stunned, wondering where the fuck he could have gone. My eyes desperately roamed the cabin, expecting to spot him *somewhere*, but I couldn't. I was about to wander further up the plane when a flight attendant appeared beside me and told me in no uncertain terms that I'd better get into my seat and do up my seatbelt or there would be trouble. So I buckled myself in, numb with shock as I thought about what had happened: I'd had amazing sex with a stranger in an airplane bathroom.

And he'd vanished.

Actually, that was what bothered me the most. It's just plain rude, right? It's not like I was expecting to stroll into the sunset together after we landed, but didn't I at least deserve a goodbye—maybe an "it was nice to meet you," or a "thanks for the hot sex," or something? I couldn't bloody believe it.

Now, as I sit here in the car and read the handwritten note he must have scrawled while I hovered in the bathroom, I chuckle. At least he didn't *completely* disappear then.

I exhale, tucking the note into the bottom of my bag, then turn to look out the window. It's already after midnight, and as we head over a bridge I notice the city lights glittering in the distance. It's such a familiar sight from television and films that I almost feel like I know it myself. In spite of my strange mood, a gasp catches in my throat.

New York is *stunning*. And while only a few hours ago it scared me shitless, I now feel an unfamiliar thrill zip through me. After everything I've been through over the past twenty-four hours, I think I might be able to handle this whole thing.

I smile as I watch the city unfold before me. I'm thrown by the fact that we're driving on the wrong side of the road, and I try to figure out whether or not I'm supposed to tip the driver. Time to get into the American mindset.

Alex is waiting on the front step as the car pulls up and my heart swells with joy when I see her. It's been a year since she moved here, and while we never spent much time together when she was back home, I realize I've missed her.

Guilt twists through me. I should never have said no to being her maid of honor in the first place. I can't believe how selfish that was. I *must* make more of an effort with her. Spending time together over the coming weeks will be a good place to start, and hopefully that will bring us a lot closer.

The driver opens the door and I step out onto the street, offering him what I assume is a reasonable tip. Then I turn and take in the building that Alex calls home. It's a redbrick apartment block in the West Village, with a black fire escape zig-zagging up the front. This street is lined with trees, and with October's arrival some of the leaves are changing color. Stone steps lead up from the footpath (or "sidewalk" as they say here, must remember that) to an arched doorway where Alex stands, clasping her hands together in excitement.

I grin, pulling my bag onto my shoulder. I can see why Alex likes it so much here. I feel like I'm stepping onto a movie set.

"Harriet!" she squeals as I climb the steps.

"Hi!" I shiver in the cold night air, wishing I had at least brought a jacket in my handbag.

Alex tugs me into her arms and squeezes. Tears prick my eyes and I blink them away, squeezing her back. What an overwhelming few days it's been.

She releases me with a smile, then freezes. "Wait. Where's your suitcase?"

"Oh." My gut pitches but I force myself to be nonchalant. "It got lost."

"What?" Her face creases in concern. "Did you talk to them at the desk? Because—"

"Yep. I just have to wait."

"Ugh. That sucks." She links her arm through mine and pulls the front door open, leading me into the lobby. "You'll have to borrow some of my stuff. Or we could go shopping!" She does an excited hop and it makes me giggle.

We pause halfway across the lobby and Alex points to an apartment door. "That was my apartment with Cat when I first moved here, but she lives with Myles now. You'll meet her tomorrow. I'm upstairs, with Michael and Henry." She pulls me along again and we start up the stairs to the second level.

"Thanks for waiting up for me," I say, stifling a yawn.

"Of course! I couldn't wait to see you. But Michael's gone to bed, sorry. He has an early meeting with his agent tomorrow so we have to be quiet."

She opens the door to the apartment and leads me inside. It's warm, and the first thing I notice are the bookshelves lining the far walls of the living room. As soon as I'm rested I know I'll be browsing them. The walls are dark red, and there's a tan leather sofa in the middle of the room, worn in that comfy way that only leather can be. Off to the left is a desk strewn with papers and a hallway. To the right there's a small wooden dining table, which leads around a corner to the kitchen.

"This is lovely," I say. "Very cozy."

Alex beams. "Thanks. You'll be staying in Henry's room. I hope that's okay?"

"Of course." I'm grateful to be staying with them and not at a big, impersonal hotel, but I do feel a bit bad that Alex's soon-to-be stepson won't get to sleep in his own bed. "What about Henry?"

"He's with his mom while you're here," she says, and I hear the faintest American accent creeping into her voice, especially on the word "mom," which I didn't notice over the phone. "Unfortunately, you'll meet her at some stage, too."

Alex has mentioned once or twice how much she dislikes Michael's ex, Mel, and I can't say I'm looking forward to meeting her. I guess that's the problem when your guy has a kid with someone else: there's no way to avoid the ex.

Alex heads down the hallway and I follow, into a room filled with *Star Wars* posters and toys. She gestures to a stuffed Yoda in one corner. "Sorry about the decor."

"Well, it's a lot nicer than the swamps of Dagobah," I joke, and she gives me a funny look.

"What?"

I put on my best Yoda voice. "Much to learn, you still have."

I expect Alex to roll her eyes, but she grins. "I've missed you. You're going to get on so well with Henry."

"I'm looking forward to meeting him," I say, turning to the bed. It's made with fresh sheets and there are towels folded on the end.

"Yeah, he's really sweet. You guys can geek out over *Star*

Wars together." She glances at my bag, then at the bed, before turning to the door. "I'll grab you some PJs."

"Thanks." I sit on the edge of the bed, letting my eyes wander around the room. They land on a framed art print of the Millennium Falcon hanging on the opposite wall. I inspect the round curve of the ship, thinking of the sliver of Luke's tattoo I saw. I don't know why I make that connection. It's a similar shape, sure, but I highly doubt he has Han Solo's spaceship tattooed on his arm—as awesome as that would be.

Alex enters the room. "We'll go shopping tomorrow, okay? I can show you some of my favorite stores." She hands me a pair of pajamas and pulls me into another hug. "I'm so glad you're here."

"Me too." I smile, surprised to realize I mean it.

We say goodnight and Alex heads off to bed. I try to unpack the whirlwind of emotions I'm feeling as I change into the pajamas. Now that I'm finally here, alone in the silence of Henry's room with my thoughts, everything is catching up with me. I'm anxious at not having my suitcase, but my mind keeps coming back to Luke. Memories from the plane flash through my head and my cheeks flush as I think about his kiss, his body against me, his hot breath on my ear. God, that was so hot—*he* was so hot. I wouldn't have minded seeing him again, but his note said things were complicated with him. Whatever that means.

Actually, what *does* that mean? I frown, mulling this over —but I catch myself. I won't over-think this. I won't ruin this for myself like I always do.

I settle into bed, making a decision. I'm going to appreciate what I had with Luke for what it was: fun, sexy, and impulsive. He was gorgeous, and I'm still in awe that he managed to do what no other man—or myself—has done before, but I'll never see him again and that's that.

It's for the best. The last thing I need is to get hung up on a guy. I've managed just fine without them.

But as I drift off to sleep, I can't deny the unfamiliar ache that's tugging at me. I've had a taste of something I didn't even know existed, and I'm not sure I can forget that now.

6

I glance at the shopping bags splayed out at our feet as we jostle along. I didn't want to take the subway (I thought New Yorkers were all about cabs?) but Alex insisted it was easy and much cheaper than a taxi.

I, on the other hand, feel like we're about to be mugged at any second.

My eyes dart around the train carriage, making sure no one is approaching us while we're unawares, but everyone seems to either have their headphones in or their eyes on their phones. Still, I'm rigid with nerves. My hands are so sweaty I can hardly grasp the rail to steady myself. I don't know how Alex does this alone. She's so much braver than me.

"It was fun shopping with you today," she says, gesturing to my bags.

After going through Alex's wardrobe this morning, it became clear that most of her clothes wouldn't work for me. She's taller and curvier than me, and while I managed to find a dress of hers I could wear for the day, I knew we'd have to go shopping. Alex talked me into trying on some pretty dresses, and when I saw my reflection in the fitting room mirror, all I could hear were Luke's words: *You're beautiful*. I remembered the way he looked at me, the way he sent heat searing through my whole body, and in that moment I decided I'd like to put a little more thought into my appearance. So, as well as buying my usual jeans and sweaters to replace the ones currently missing in my luggage, I also got a handful of dresses, following Alex's advice.

And—I can't really believe this—I got some sexy underwear. It's not something I've ever owned in the past, but today I felt inspired. The whole time I looked at lingerie—God, I know it's stupid, but I couldn't help myself—I kept thinking, *would Luke like these?* And when I tried on a red lacy bra with matching panties and felt pleasantly surprised at my reflection, I heard his voice in my ear again, murmuring, *God, you're hot.* I got so flustered I had to quickly dress and get out of there—after buying the set in several colors, of course. I might not be seeing Luke again, but it won't hurt to have some sexier bits and pieces, just in case, well... I don't know. But I'm quite certain Harriet 2.0 would wear sexy underwear.

I smile at Alex. "It was fun. Thanks for your advice. I would never have tried on half of that stuff otherwise."

"Happy to help. I can't believe you listened to me! I don't think I've seen you in something so girly before."

"I know," I say, chuckling. "But I'm trying to get out of my comfort zone and try new things."

The train pulls into the next stop and Alex helps me gather my bags. I follow her onto the platform and up the steps until we reach the street, the tight coil of anxiety inside me slowly unwinding as we leave the subway. We walk for a few blocks until we come to a bar called Bounce where we're meeting her friends, Cat and Geoff, for a drink.

It's been a day of sensory overload out in the city, with the sounds and the sights and the smells (oh, the smells—everything from the pungent odor of garbage and car fumes to the sweet scent of bakeries and coffee. It was... a lot). I was looking forward to getting home and recharging my introvert batteries, but Alex has been so excited for me to meet her friends, I could hardly say no.

She smiles at a blond guy behind the bar as we enter, then points us towards a booth at the back.

"Who's that?" I ask, following her.

"Cat's brother, Cory. He owns the place, so we get cheap drinks." She flashes me a grin as we slide into a booth.

I shove my shopping bags under the table, leaning forward to look at Cory. He's got a short beard, dirty-blond hair cut longish on top and shaved close on the sides, and he's well over six feet tall. He's chatting with a petite, dark-haired woman behind the bar as she pours drinks. Then his brown eyes return our way and he waves.

"He's cute," I murmur.

"Oh, yeah. He's hot. But he's kind of a player. He hit on me my first night in town and Cat says he's always taking girls home from here." She tilts her head, regarding me curiously. "Since when are you checking out guys?"

"What?" I blush, shifting my weight. She's right, I wouldn't normally notice a hot guy. I think Luke flipped some kind of internal switch in me or something, because I noticed a few while we were out shopping today. Or maybe it's just American men. "I'm thirsty," I say, in a feeble attempt to distract Alex.

"Isn't that the truth," she mutters, laughing. "Okay, I'll get us drinks while we wait for the others. What do you want?"

"Um, I'll have a whiskey."

Her eyebrows rise. "You drink whiskey?"

"I've just started. I'm trying new things, remember?"

"I guess," she says, shaking her head as she wanders over to the bar. I watch her chat and laugh with the dark-haired woman as she pours our drinks. When Alex returns to the table, I take my whiskey with a smile.

"Thanks."

"Guys! Over here!" She waves an arm and I follow her gaze to see a guy and a girl enter the bar. The girl is short, with cotton-candy pink hair and a cute floral dress, and she waves to Cory as she makes her way to us. I'm guessing that's Cat.

Behind her is a guy with dark hair, square-rimmed glasses, and a warm smile. His slightly-pudgy frame is squeezed into a blue cashmere sweater and chinos. He hugs Alex when she stands, then turns to me. "You must be Harriet!" He leans over and pulls me into a hug, before sliding into the booth. "I'm Geoff. I've heard so much about you."

"Cat Porter," the girl says, hugging me as well. "It's so good to finally meet you."

"It's nice to meet you too," I say, touched by the welcome.

"Geoff is my boss at the bookstore," Alex explains. "And Cat used to be my roommate. Though it won't be Cat *Porter* for long!" She gestures to the ring on Cat's left hand. "Soon it will be Cat Ellis."

Cat glances down at the ring with a smile.

"Congratulations," I say. "What's your fiance's name?"

"Myles." When she looks back up at me, I can tell she's trying to temper her grin. "He used to be a bartender here."

"Yeah, and you kept him in the friend zone even after he declared his love for you," Geoff says with a chuckle.

"Whatever." Cat pushes to her feet. "I'll get us drinks." She heads off to the bar and Geoff turns to Alex.

"How's the writing going?"

"It's good," she says, sipping her wine. "I took today off to go shopping with Harri."

I twist to face her. "Do you have a lot of work to do?"

"Yeah, I still have about a quarter of my manuscript left to write. My editor is expecting it a couple of weeks after the wedding, so—"

"Your editor?" I interrupt. "I thought you were self-published?"

"I am, but I still work with an editor. And this one cost a small fortune, but it will be worth it. I'm lucky she could fit me in because she's always booked."

I frown, concerned. "If you have work to do, I understand. You don't have to spend time—"

"Harri," she says, placing a hand on my arm. "You flew all the way over here! I'm enjoying hanging out with you. I will have to work at some stage, but I can fit it all in." She smiles, then rises from the booth. "I need to go to the ladies' room. Back in a sec."

Geoff fixes his attention on me. "She's so happy to have you here. Ever since you decided to come, she's been talking about it nonstop."

Guilt weaves through me. Now that I'm here, spending time with my sister, I can't believe I wasn't going to come. "I'm glad I'm here too," I say. "I've missed her. And I've never been a maid of honor before."

Geoff chuckles. "I'm sure she'll have a lot of wedding tasks for you."

Actually, there's an idea. If I help her get some of the wedding stuff sorted so she can focus on work, that might make up for me being such a crappy sister in the first place.

"Great," I say, and the guilt dissipates slightly.

"Have you met Michael yet?" Geoff asks as Alex returns to the table.

"No," Alex answers for me. "He's had loads of meetings because he's pitching a new book, but we'll have dinner tomorrow."

I smile. "Sounds good."

"Okay, a toast," Cat says as she settles back into her seat. She raises her glass. "To Harriet, for coming all the way to New York and meeting Alex's fabulous friends."

I laugh as we all clink glasses, thinking back to the last time I was out drinking, with Steph's friends. I didn't feel nearly as welcome as I do here, and it's only been five minutes. I replay that night in the pub—and the conversation that started this whole thing—and curiosity gets the better of me. "I have a question," I say tentatively. They all lean forward with interest, so I continue. "What's the most outrageous thing you've ever done?"

"Ooh, that's a fun question!" Alex says. I wait for another raunchy story, but she surprises me. "I think it was moving here after Travis dumped me."

Admittedly, when Alex first announced she was moving to New York less than twenty-four hours after Travis ended things, I was shocked and pretty sure she'd come back home with her tail between her legs. But she created a life for herself over here; she built a writing career, which she's always wanted, and she met a lovely man, which, well... ditto. I admire how she went out and made her dreams a reality, regardless of what anyone else thought.

I think of my own dream—of that napkin stuffed into my bag with all my board game cafe ideas—but push the thought away. It's not the same thing.

"And, maybe," Alex adds, her face breaking into a

wicked grin, "the time Michael and I had sex in the back of his truck on the way up to the cabin a few months ago."

I can't help but laugh. There's the Alex I know.

Cat stirs her drink. "For me it was probably when I stole my mom's car. I was seventeen and didn't even have my license. I wanted to visit a guy I liked upstate. Then she called the cops when she found it was missing, and I got pulled over and arrested. It was pretty bad."

"I think I know mine," Geoff pipes up. "I slashed my ex's tires when I found out he slept with someone else."

"Geoffrey Howard," Alex says with exaggerated shock. "You didn't."

"I did. But he deserved it, obviously."

I sip my whiskey as I listen to their stories. I want to share my own story, now that I have a good one, but I don't know if I can. I've only just met Geoff and Cat. What will they think of me?

Geoff turns to me with a grin. "And what about you, Harriet?"

Before I can answer, Alex flaps a hand, chuckling. "Harriet doesn't really do crazy things."

There it is again: that ripple of irritation I felt when Steph dismissed me too. I know Alex is trying to save me the embarrassment of having to admit that to her friends, but this time, she's wrong.

"Actually, I have done something outrageous."

Her eyebrows shoot up. "Really? What?"

"Okay. Don't judge me, but..." I push my glasses up my nose and stare at the table. I can't look at anyone while I confess this. "I kind of, um, had sex with someone I met on the plane."

"What?!" Alex nearly drops her drink. "Where? How?"

My face burns as I focus on my whiskey. "Erm, in the

airplane bathroom."

"You had *sex* on the *plane*?!" Alex exclaims and a guy at the next table glances over.

"Shh!" I hiss, raising my hands to my flaming cheeks.

"Sorry." She leans closer. "But... are you serious?"

With a deep breath, I finally look up. "Yes."

"Oh my God!" Geoff's face splits into a grin. "I'm *so* jealous. I've always wanted to do that."

"I think congratulations are in order." Cat clinks her glass against mine. "That's a bucket list item, right there."

I drain my whiskey with a chuckle. At least this seems to have impressed rather than appalled them.

"I can't believe it." Alex shakes her head. "How did it happen?"

I shrug. "It just kind of happened. We talked for a few hours, and then we were at the back of the plane alone, and the next thing I knew we were kissing, then we were in the bathroom..." I trail off, biting my lip as the images come flooding back to me.

"Well, was it any good?" Geoff asks.

I bite my lip harder, heat swirling through me at the memories, and nod.

"Really?" Cat leans forward, intrigued. "It's such a tiny space."

"I know, but it worked. It was actually..." I look around at the three of them, wide-eyed as they hang on my every word, and feel an unusual swell of satisfaction. "It was the best sex I've ever had."

"Holy shit." Alex's jaw is on the floor. "You really *are* trying new things."

"You know," Geoff says, his green eyes twinkling behind his glasses, "you're going to fit in quite well with us here."

My mouth tugs into a grin. I think he might be right.

7

"I'm beginning to wonder if you've made Michael up," I say, watching as Alex takes the casserole dish out of the oven and sets it on the counter with a flourish.

She laughs. "I swear, he's real. He had meetings yesterday and today, but he'll be here tonight, I promise."

I smile, leaning against the fridge. I notice a list of wedding to-dos stuck under a magnet, and pull it off to inspect more closely. Alex still has to organize a seating plan, create place cards, get her ring sized, make wedding favors, and more. It's a lot to get done in just over two weeks, especially if she has to write, too.

"So as your maid of honor," I say, holding up the list, "is there anything I can do to help with the wedding?"

"Well, you've already got Mum off my back."

I called Mum after finalizing my flight and told her I was coming over to meet Michael and check up on Alex. I'm pleased that seems to have calmed her down—for now, at least.

"But there are probably some other things you could

help with," Alex adds. "I've been feeling a bit overwhelmed with everything that still needs to get done."

"I'm happy to help. Tell me which tasks to do, and I'll take care of them." I stick the list back to the fridge and she smiles, clearly relieved.

"Thanks. We have a dress fitting tomorrow, then I'll see what you can do after that." She hands me some plates and I carry them over to the table, setting them out. I'm momentarily transported back to our dinner table as kids, laying the plates out while Mum fussed in the kitchen. Except in that version, Alex wasn't at the stove. In fact...

"When did you start cooking?"

"What? I've always been able to cook."

I snort. "I don't think you can call microwaving a frozen pizza 'cooking'. This is a proper meal. You used a recipe and everything."

She chuckles. "Yeah, I figured I should step my game up when I moved in here. Michael's a good cook, but he can't cook all the time. And if I'm cooking it's for both him and Henry." Her smile wobbles and her gaze slides from mine. "And now that I'm marrying Michael, I'll officially be the stepmother of an eleven year old boy."

"Are you okay with that?" I don't know if I could do it; sometimes I still feel like an eleven year old myself. Should be getting my Hogwarts letter any day now.

Alex fixes her smile back in place. "Yes. I love Michael so much. He's an amazing guy—I actually can't believe I've found someone like him. And Henry is such a sweet kid. He's been so welcoming and lovely and I can honestly say I love him too."

This makes me smile, because I know she means every word. She's always been the mushy kind. But I can also sense that there's something she's worried about, so I just keep setting the table quietly, waiting in case she wants to say more.

She gives a weighted sigh. "It's just, sometimes I worry—"

There's a sound at the door and she stops, turning to me with a grin. My stomach quivers and I smooth my new dress down. I'm kind of nervous to meet this guy. He will be my brother-in-law, after all. I hope he's good enough for my sister.

The door closes and a tall man with broad shoulders, dark hair, and a short beard enters the kitchen. He pulls Alex close, kissing her on the lips. It's such a sweet and intimate gesture that I immediately feel weird and busy myself with the table-setting again, pretending I didn't notice him come in. Which is absurd, because of course I did. He's very tall, and I can see why Alex fell for him—he's gorgeous.

What *is* it with these American men? Why don't we have them like this at home?

He turns to me, extending a hand to introduce himself, and I feel a flicker of recognition. There's something about him that's familiar, somehow.

"You must be Harriet. I'm Michael," he says in a deep accent, his mouth curving into a smile. "It's so nice to meet you, finally."

I smile back, trying to hide my confusion. I know I've never met him before, and I've only seen a handful of photos, but for some reason it feels like I *know* him already. I shake my head to clear the odd sensation. "Yes, you too! Thanks for letting me stay with you."

"Of course." He reaches a long, muscular arm up to grab a bottle of red wine from a shelf and opens it. "Sorry I haven't been around the past couple days. I had to prepare a pitch for my new book and I've been super busy, especially with the wedding coming up." He pours a few glasses and hands one to me.

Alex places a dish of green beans on the table and takes a glass from Michael's outstretched hand. She leans her head against him as he slips an arm around her. There's a bit of an age-difference between them—I think about eleven years—but I have to admit: they are *adorable*.

"How was your flight over?" Michael asks, taking a sip of wine.

Alex's eyes light with glee. "I think it was *very* good, wasn't it, Harriet?"

Heat rises to my cheeks and I shoot her a look of horror.

But her mouth hooks into a wide grin as she turns to Michael. "You won't *believe* what Harri did on the plane," she says, barely able to contain herself.

Oh God. It was one thing to tell Geoff and Cat, but what will Michael think of me?

Sweat springs to my brow and I raise a hand to my burning cheek. Michael gazes at me, his face a combination of amusement and curiosity. I'm just contemplating fleeing the room when there's a knock at the door and it creaks open.

"Hello?"

"In here," Michael calls. He turns back to me and Alex, waiting to hear the rest of the story. But I'm focused on the table again, straightening the knives and forks and avoiding his gaze, praying Alex doesn't say any more.

I hear someone else enter the room and Michael speaks again. "Harriet, this is my brother."

I glance up to see a tall, dark-haired man in the kitchen. His jaw is lined with dark stubble, his eyes are a deep brown, and I get a whiff of spicy, woody cologne. His gaze hitches on mine and it takes my brain a second to process who's standing in front of me.

My heart stops.

I watch as his face contorts in confusion, then realization, then dismay. "Luke Hawkins," he says awkwardly, extending his hand.

I blink, frozen to the spot, trying to piece everything together.

Why is he here? He can't be...

"Luke is also Michael's best man," Alex adds.

No. Please, no.

I extend a limp hand and he shakes it while I stand there, mute with shock. His eyes are carefully trained on me and, straight away, I can tell the way he wants me to play this.

I swallow hard, making my face as expressionless as possible. "Hello, I'm Harriet. It's so very nice to meet you." My tone is overly-formal and I cringe.

This is... I can't. This is too much.

"Will you please excuse me?" I say stiffly, trying to ignore the way my stomach has plummeted off a cliff. "I just need to go to the bathroom." I turn and dash up the hall, locking the bathroom door behind me with trembling hands.

What the fuck is happening right now?

Perching on the edge of the bathtub, I force myself to slow my breath, but my heart continues to rattle against my ribcage, my thoughts in free fall.

How is this even possible? How did I not realize...

I shake my head. This cannot be happening. I'm having some kind of jet-lag-induced hallucination, surely.

I spring to my feet, a ball of anxious energy, unable to sit still. Wringing my hands, I make myself take another deep breath.

I have to calm down.

But I can't.

Because I just realized I had sex with my sister's fiance's brother.

The best man.

Holy fuck, this is bad.

And—God, I'm ashamed to admit this—but that isn't even what's striking me as the worst thing about this situation. What's really bothering me right now, if I'm being honest, is that he didn't seem pleased to see me.

I shake my head again, unable to even believe myself.

Who cares about that?!

But I can't help it. I turn to the mirror and survey my reflection, relieved to see that at least I don't look like garbage. In fact, with my dark red lips, my hair half-up and half-down, and my cute new dress, I look quite pretty.

So ha, Luke. Joke's on you. Look at what you're missing out on.

Oh God. I need to get a grip. This is bad. This is really bad.

My pulse begins to climb again and I clutch the edge of the sink, aware that I need to remain in control. I cannot have a panic attack right now.

Sliding my glasses off, I lean over and splash cold water on my face. It jolts me out of my head and back into my body. I count to ten while inhaling and exhaling, then I do it again.

Okay. Okay, maybe this isn't so bad. In fact, maybe it's kind of funny.

I mean, not right now. Right now it's mortifying. But after the wedding, when I'm back home and the whole thing is behind us, we can all have a good laugh at the crazy coincidence. And hopefully, after tonight, I won't even have to see him again until the wedding day. I just have to get through tonight.

Yes. Everything will be fine.

I smooth my hair down and check my makeup, pushing my glasses back up my nose. With another deep breath, I open the bathroom door. Luke is hovering in the hallway and my heart catapults into my throat when I see him.

No. This will not be fine!

He glances over his shoulder then nudges me down the hall, into the shadows.

Jesus. Does he think we are going for round two or something? Not that I wouldn't consider it, because it's all I've been thinking about since the plane, but... here? Now?

I trail my eyes over his knitted sweater and jeans. He looks so different out of his shirt and tie—even better, if that's possible. My gaze catches on his lips and heat races up my body. I can't believe that mouth was on me. I shove the thought away before I lunge at him.

He looks at me hard, keeping his voice low. "Did you tell them?"

"Well, hello to you too."

He shakes his head, glancing down the hall, then back to me again. "Seriously, Harriet," he hisses. "Did you tell them what happened?"

"No!" I hiss back, not bothering to keep the irritation out of my voice. Then I remember what I told Alex and the others at the bar. "Well, I told Alex that something happened on the plane, but I didn't mention your name or anything. I didn't even know you were—"

"Okay." His posture relaxes. "Okay, good."

"But *this* looks a bit suspicious, doesn't it?" I gesture down the hallway and glare at him.

"Shit, yes," he mutters. "I just had to check."

There's a sound in the living room and without stopping to think, I yank open the door to Henry's room and hurl myself inside, my heart pounding.

This is insane. Why is he here? And what the fuck am I supposed to do now?

8

This whole Harriet 2.0 thing was a ridiculous idea. I can't believe I let Steph talk me into it.

I scrub at my lips in the bathroom mirror, willing the lipstick to disappear, but it's one of those long-lasting, color-stay ones that won't budge.

Dinner was awful. Five minutes into it Alex suggested that since Luke is the best man, he and I could work on the wedding tasks together, at which point I blurted out that I was feeling unwell and had to go lie down. She was obviously disappointed and now I feel terrible.

But I couldn't just sit there, opposite him, pretending nothing had happened. I couldn't pretend I hadn't tasted the soft curve of his lips, felt the silky hardness of him in my hand, heard the way he moaned *Ohhh fuck* when he couldn't hold back any longer. I couldn't stop thinking about his fingers, working their way up my thighs, slipping between my legs, touching me eagerly.

And I couldn't pretend that I was okay with the way he behaved when he saw me. He wasn't the least bit happy, while all I wanted to do was drag him up the hallway and do it again.

So I hid in my room like a coward until I heard Luke leave, and Alex and Michael go to bed. Now I'm in the bathroom, trying to get this stupid lipstick off my mouth, my mind working overtime.

I am *not* cut out for doing outrageous things; just look at how spectacularly this has backfired. The *one* time I do something wild and it comes back to bite me in the ass. It's karma, that's what it is. Of all the men in all the world I could have shagged, how did it end up that I slept with Michael's *brother*? And not just that—he's the best man at their wedding, which *I now have to organize with him*.

Unless... maybe I could tell Alex I'm unable to help with wedding stuff after all? That I'm here to see the city, and...

No. I can't do that. Not after everything I've already put her through with refusing to come over here in the first place. I'm not that selfish.

Maybe I can do it without Luke's help. That could work, right?

But what if Alex asks why I can't work with Luke? What will I tell her then?

Fuck. This is a nightmare.

I tiptoe from the bathroom across the hall and snatch my phone up off the bed. It's after eleven but I'm too wired to sleep. I grab a key and pull Alex's jacket off the back of the door, trying not to think about the fact that my luggage is still nowhere to be found. Every time I do, I feel sick.

I guess that's the least of my problems now.

When I step outside the building, the cool air hits me in the face and I pull the jacket tighter. I spot a tiny coffee shop across the road with the name *Beanie* on the glass. Warm, yellow light spills from the front window onto the dark street, and I head over and push inside. I'm enveloped by the smell of espresso and cinnamon, and for the briefest moment I forget my troubles as my eyes feast on the glass cabinets filled with rows of delicate pastries and colorful macarons, topped with a gleaming espresso machine. This place is just like the sort of cafe I want to create, but with stacks of board games lining the wall and sumptuous sofas to sink into.

I order a chamomile tea—God knows I need to calm down—and find a table near the window. After doing some timezone calculations, I find Steph's name in my contacts and press the call button, popping my earphones in. She answers after only three rings.

"Hey! How's it going?"

I lean back in my chair, rubbing my temples. "Not great, Steph."

"Uh-oh. What happened?"

"Well, for starters, I accidentally slept with the best man."

There's a pause on the other end, and I glance down at the screen to check the call is still connected. "Are you there?"

"Yes. Sorry, I don't think I heard you properly."

I draw a breath and repeat myself, more calmly this time.

"Okay, I did hear you." Another pause. "So... how did that happen?"

"It was bloody Harriet 2.0! You and all your talk about being more adventurous." The barista places my chamomile tea on the table and I send her a strained smile.

"What?" A laugh bursts down the line. "I never told you to bone the best man!"

"I didn't *know* he was the best man, did I? Or I wouldn't

have..." I can't even hear myself over the roar of Steph's laughter, and I'm trying to keep my voice low in the quiet coffee shop. "You and that stupid condom you put in my bra, I swear—"

"Oh my *God*!" She's howling now. "You actually *used* it?!"

"It's not funny, Steph! This is an absolute disaster."

More laughing. I hear her gasping for breath, and it's a full minute before she calms herself down enough to speak. "But... why?" she manages at last.

"Because—" I falter. I'm not totally sure why, but it is. I mean, he certainly wasn't pleased to see me. And if Alex finds out I had sex with her fiance's brother, won't that be kind of awkward? It's almost a bit incestuous, isn't it? I know it's not *really*, but it feels wrong, and the last thing I want to do is make her uncomfortable at her own wedding. "It just is, Steph. The best man is Michael's brother—Alex's brother-in-law-to-be. We hooked up before I knew, and then tonight I saw him again, and... Ugh, it's just weird."

"Yeah, okay. I see what you're saying. This does put you in a tricky situation."

I reach for my chamomile tea and inhale the fragrant scent before taking a sip. I might need something stronger.

"Maybe you're overreacting," Steph says. "Alex will understand. It's not like you did it on purpose—you didn't even know who he was. And it's not like it will happen again, right?"

I cradle the steaming cup in my hands. Before I can stop it, my mind slingshots back to the plane. I think of the way Luke growled my name, the way he touched me and made me feel pleasure I didn't even know was possible. A delightful thrill runs up my body. I don't want to make things awkward for Alex, but *God*, if he wanted to do it again, would I be able to say no?

"Harriet?" Steph's voice cuts into my thoughts.

"Er, well... no."

"You don't sound so sure."

I set my teacup down with a sigh. "Steph, he is *so* sexy. The chemistry and connection between us was amazing. You know me—I'm *never* like this with guys."

"Yeah, that's true."

I chew my lip for a moment, wondering if I should tell Steph what, exactly, made this particular time so momentous. I kind of want to tell someone, and she's the only one who knows the details of my lackluster sexual past. "And, um, you know that little issue I've always had?"

"You mean the elusive big O?"

Heat suffuses my cheeks and I glance around the coffee shop, even though no one can hear her. "Yeah."

"Wait." Steph's voice is suddenly sharp and alert. "Are you saying—did he give you your first orgasm?"

"Um, yeah."

"Oh my God! Harriet! This is huge!"

Now it's my turn to laugh.

"Seriously! Congrats, girl!" She giggles. "Have you had one since?"

"Well I haven't slept with him again, have I?"

"What? You know you can give yourself one, right?"

"Oh." I hadn't really thought of that. "Yeah, I don't know if I can." And I'm not sure I want to. It wasn't the orgasm, so much. It was *him*. "Anyway, you can see why this is making things a lot harder. And then seeing him again tonight, I remembered just how good it was."

"Yeah," she murmurs. "Harri, it sounds like you want it to happen again. I know this is an awkward situation, but is there any way it could? Because this is kind of a big deal."

I imagine Alex discovering I've slept with her husband's

brother and my stomach curdles. It doesn't matter how sexy he is; no man is worth upsetting my sister or compromising her wedding. I can't believe I was even considering it. I've gone years without sex and I've been just fine, why would now be any different? What the hell has happened to me?

"We can't do it again," I mutter, reaching for my cup. "I need to put Alex's feelings first." It doesn't matter, anyway. Luke was uncomfortable seeing me tonight, so it's unlikely that he would want anything to happen. And what did he say in his note, that things were complicated? What does that even mean?

"I'm sure everything will be fine," Steph says. "But don't blame Harriet 2.0. If it weren't for her, you wouldn't have had hot sex. If anything, I'd thank her."

We end the call and I mull over Steph's words as I finish my tea and climb the stairs to the apartment. I don't know if I agree; without Harriet 2.0's antics, things would be a whole lot easier right now.

But if I'm being honest with myself, I don't want to take back what I did on the plane. It wasn't just the sex, or the chemistry, or the life-altering orgasm. It was who I was when I was with him—a glimpse of who I could be.

It was the feeling of coming alive.

9

The dressing room curtain opens and Alex glides out, her cheeks pink with happiness. I know it's a cliche, but there's no other way to describe her: she is radiant.

Her gown has a fitted bodice that shows off her waist, then flares out into a full skirt, layers of silk and lace and tulle tumbling to the floor. It's an off-white, champagne color, and it's breath-taking. It will go perfectly with the indigo-blue maid of honor dress I just had fitted.

"What do you think?" She steps up onto the pedestal and turns to look at her reflection. "Will Michael like it?"

"Uh, yeah." I chuckle. She could turn up dressed in a garbage bag and he'd still adore her, he's that smitten.

"I hope so." She smooths her hands over the bodice of her dress, studying her reflection, and her expression clouds. When she catches my eye in the mirror, I tilt my head to one side in concern.

"You okay?"

She turns back around and heaves out a sigh. "I'm worried about Henry."

"Henry? What about him?"

"I'm going to be his stepmom. I'm going to help raise him. I love him, but I'm just... I don't know." She gnaws on a fingernail.

"Don't know what?"

"I don't know if I can be a parent. I skipped over the part when they're young and you kind of figure it all out and it doesn't matter if you mess up. He's eleven—there's no time for me to figure it out. When I mess it up, he's going to know and it could be really bad."

"You're not going to mess up!" I say, laughing. "Why would you think that?"

She shrugs and pulls in a shaky breath. I soften when I see she's close to tears.

"Have you spoken to Michael about this?"

"No, I don't want to freak him out. He has so much going on at the moment with his book pitch. And—" She pauses, fingering the lace on her dress. "There's something else. I've told you about Mel, right?"

I nod.

"I'm worried that I won't be able to hold my own with her. She causes so much drama and what if she does something to make Henry hate me? Or to break Michael and I up? She's already insisting on coming to the wedding, which—"

"Wait." I raise my hands, frowning. "Michael's ex-wife is coming to your wedding?"

Alex nods.

"But... why? Isn't that awkward?"

"Yes! That's what I said! She insists she has to be there for Henry, that it will show him we can all be adults and have a harmonious relationship, blah, blah, blah." She lifts her gaze to the ceiling. "But I wouldn't put it past her to pull some stunt on our wedding day."

My mouth falls open. "Really?"

"She's bad, Harri. But if I tell her she can't come, that will piss her off even more and she'll probably show up and cause drama anyway."

I exhale slowly, turning this over. Poor Alex. It's bad enough still having the ex in the picture, but now she's coming to the wedding? This is supposed to be the day where Alex is blissfully happy, not the day where she has to keep one eye out to make sure her groom's psycho ex doesn't burn the place down or poison the guests.

No wonder Alex is feeling overwhelmed about the wedding. I definitely need to relieve some of the pressure for her. After talking with Steph last night, I realized how silly I was being about the Luke situation. It doesn't matter if I'm feeling awkward—it's not about me. I owe it to Alex to help with the wedding, and if I can, I should try and manage Mel so Alex can actually enjoy her day.

Except... I'm terrible at confrontation. I hate conflict and avoid it at all costs, while it sounds like Mel is someone who thrives on it. What if I can't stand up to her?

Then it occurs to me: *I* might not be able to stand up to her, but my alter ego could, no problem.

I glance up at Alex again, her face etched with worry. "I'll take care of Mel," I hear myself say.

"That's really sweet, but she's a nightmare."

"It's okay," I say resolutely, standing. "I'll handle her. She won't ruin the day, I promise." I take a step towards Alex. "And as for everything with Henry, you're going to be fine. I think you'll be a great stepmother. You have a good relationship with him and you care. That's what matters. He's lucky to have you when he could be stuck with just Mel." This brings a small smile to Alex's face. "But you should tell Michael what you're thinking. He'd want to know, and I'm sure he'll say the same thing as me."

She nods and reaches out to pull me into a hug. "Thanks. I feel so much better."

I squeeze her tight, relieved. Maybe Harriet 2.0 will come in handy after all.

WHEN WE STEP OUTSIDE the bridal boutique, the sky has darkened into a deep pink, streaked with wisps of cotton candy. I pull my jacket tighter around my shoulders and survey the busy streets of Midtown. This part of the city is what I think of when I picture New York: iconic sky-scrapers, yellow cabs, pavements crowded with people, a cacophony of traffic and honking horns. On our first day out shopping, it felt chaotic and claustrophobic, and I spent the whole day in a knot of anxiety.

But I'm coming to see there's a way to handle this place. Having Alex with me is good, and it also helps if I research where we are going in advance. Then when we're out, I can focus on breathing and staying present in my body, and I don't get quite so overwhelmed.

The West Village, where Alex lives, is so different to Midtown. It really does feel like its own village, with smaller townhouse-style apartments in rows, boutique shops, and single-lane streets lined with trees. I didn't know New York had such quiet neighborhoods, but I like it there.

Alex turns to me as we head down Seventh Avenue. "I forgot to ask, how are you feeling today?"

"What?"

"Because last night at dinner—"

"Oh, yes," I say hastily. "I'm feeling much better."

"What was it, anyway?"

"It was, erm, a migraine. You know how suddenly they can come on."

She nods as we pause at a street crossing. "Yeah. So you're feeling better now?"

"Yes. Totally fine now."

"Good, because Michael texted me and asked if we wanted to meet him and Luke for dinner. What do you think?" She looks at me hopefully and I swallow against the sudden swell of nerves in the pit of my stomach. "It would be good for you to get to know him, because—well, I don't want to pressure you, but if you are happy to do some wedding prep, then Luke could help."

I give a mute nod as my pulse ticks up. I wasn't expecting to have to see him so soon, but I can hardly tell her no, can I? I can hardly say, *I'd rather not work with Luke because we had mind-blowing sex and I can't stop thinking about it even though it's wildly inappropriate.* In fact, I can't come up with a single good reason not to go to dinner.

This isn't about you, I remind myself. *It's about Alex.*

Drawing in a calming breath, I paint on a smile. "Sure. Let's have dinner."

"Great." She links her arm through mine. "We'll head back to the Village. Luke is just finishing up work downtown and will meet us in half an hour."

I rake a hand through my long hair, then rummage in my bag for a brush. I haven't worn my hair in a proper bun since the plane and it's nice to have it out, but I'm sure it's become a bit windswept since we've been out today, and not in a sexy way. At least I'm wearing something different from last night, but I wouldn't mind a chance to refresh my makeup...

Oh God, what has happened to me? I can't remember the last time I cared about how I looked in front of a guy and now I want to fix my hair and makeup? For what? It doesn't matter how sexy Luke is or how vivid my fantasies of him might be. Nothing is happening. I need to remember that.

"Sounds good," I say, shoving my hairbrush away. "Let's go."

We take a cab back to the Village at my insistence (I *cannot* face the subway right now) and Alex leads me into the restaurant where we are meeting the guys. It's nice: warm and intimate, with tiny tables, dim lighting, and candles dotted about the place. But that doesn't stop the roiling in my belly.

Right. The only way I'm going to make it through tonight is with copious amounts of alcohol.

As soon as we're seated, I order a whiskey. We sip our drinks as we wait for the others to arrive, chatting about the wedding. Or rather, Alex sips her drink. I down mine as fast as I reasonably can without raising her suspicions, and wait for its relaxing spell to work. I think back to the magic cards in my favorite board game. Where's a *Calm the Fuck Down* card when I need one?

I'm just about to go to the bar and order another drink when the door swings open and two men stride in. Seeing them now, side-by-side, it's so obvious they're brothers. The same towering figures, dark brown—almost black—hair, espresso-colored eyes, broad shoulders. Luke is slightly taller and isn't as built as Michael, plus he's a good five or six years younger, but the similarities are uncanny.

My breath catches at the sight of him. Somehow, he's better looking than last time. Is that possible?

"Hey, honey," Michael says, leaning down to kiss Alex. He folds himself into a chair beside her.

"Hi, guys." She grins and slides menus across the table.

Luke pulls his suit jacket off and hangs it over the back of the chair, smiling at Alex. His eyes glide over to me and linger. My stupid heart somersaults and I do my best to give a distant, polite smile. As he takes a seat I notice he's wearing the same tie he wore on the plane. He reaches up to loosen it now, scanning the menu on the table in front of him. An image of me grabbing that tie and pulling him towards me appears in my mind, and I feel my cheeks color.

"I'll go grab us some drinks," Michael says, standing again.

Yes. More alcohol, please.

He places a hand on Alex's shoulder. "Another wine, sweetheart?" She grins and he turns to me. "What are you drinking?"

"Whiskey, thanks."

Michael nods and looks to Luke.

"Uh, whiskey too. Thanks." His eyes meet mine and a tentative smile touches his lips. I feel the color in my cheeks deepen.

God, how am I going to do this?

Alex pushes to her feet and slips her hand into Michael's. "I'll come help. You two get to know each other."

I stare at the grain in the wooden table top. If only she knew.

As the two of them head to the bar, the ball of nerves inside my gut tightens. I pick up a menu, trying to ignore the way my palms are sweating, trying to think of anything other than Luke sitting right beside me.

"Hey," he says, keeping his voice low. "I'm sorry if I was weird last night."

When I lift my gaze to his, I have to remind myself to keep breathing. "Well, it is a weird situation. But I don't really get why you're desperate to keep it a secret."

His jaw tightens. "We just have to. Okay?"

"Why?" I ask, annoyed by the pang I feel. "Was it *that* terrible? Do you regret it that much?" And then it dawns on me. "Wait, oh my God, is that why you left? It was so bad that you couldn't face me afterward?"

His lips part in shock. "No! Is that really what you think?"

I shrug, peeking over his shoulder to check that Michael and Alex are still out of earshot. They're standing at the bar, kissing, for God's sake.

"No, Harriet. It wasn't... that's not it at all. Didn't you get my note?"

I level my gaze back at Luke. "Yes, but it was still humiliating."

At least he has the decency to look ashamed. "I'm sorry. I didn't mean to humiliate you, but I knew that if I sat down beside you again, if I looked at you again..." He shakes his head. "I didn't trust myself not to ask for your number."

My heart skitters. In his note he did say he wished he could see me again, but I guess I hadn't really believed it until now. This is not helping things.

He looks over his shoulder then back to me. "But my life is really complicated right now, and that wouldn't have been the right thing to do either." He pauses, his brow furrowed as his eyes search mine. "You're right, though. I shouldn't have left without saying anything. I guess I thought it would be easier if we just... never saw each other again."

I fiddle with the menu, processing this. I'm tempted to

laugh at the irony, with us now being stuck together over the following weeks, but what comes out is a sigh. "Look, it's fine. It was a crazy, impulsive thing to do, and it was really fun..." I trail off when his frown is replaced by a grin that makes my mouth go dry. *Get it together.* "But now we are in this awkward situation, which neither of us saw coming, and—"

Shit.

I spot Alex and Michael heading our way and lean back, whipping the menu up in front of me. I will my slamming heart to return to normal, hoping Alex can't read my face.

Michael places my whiskey in front of me and I mumble a "thank you." As Alex and Michael take a seat again, I tune out their chatter and focus on the menu. The waiter appears shortly after and we order. I'm relieved by the distraction of it all, but once he's taken our menus I feel naked, with nothing to focus my attention on except the others.

"So," Luke says casually, "have you done any sightseeing, Harriet?"

"Um, not yet." I chew on my lip. "To be honest, I'm not really into the crowds and everything."

"But you'll want to see some of the main places, right?" Michael asks. "Go up the Empire State Building?"

Alex turns to Michael. "I think Harri is kind of intimidated by the city, and I totally get that. I was terrified when I first came here, remember?" She nudges Michael and he nods.

I glance down at my hands, embarrassed.

"If you've never been here before it can be overwhelming," Luke says, and I send him a grateful smile.

"There are a few places I'd like to show you." Alex twirls her glass thoughtfully. "The only thing is... I haven't done any writing since you arrived, and it's starting to stress me out."

"Why don't you give me a few wedding things to do while you get some work done, and we can hang out later?" I suggest.

"Really? That would be so great. Maybe you and Luke could work on the seating chart."

Despite myself, pleasure swoops through me at the thought of seeing Luke again soon. Spending time with him might be fun.

No. That's a dangerous thought.

"Is that okay?" Alex asks.

I meet Luke's gaze and hesitation flashes in his eyes. For a second I think he's going to say no, and hope and dread mix into an uncomfortable cocktail in my chest.

"Well..." I begin, feeling the need to let Luke off the hook. "Do I need Luke to do that?"

"Uh, yeah," Michael says. "He knows all our family and friends, so he should know who to sit by whom. Plus," he adds with a chuckle, "he loves puzzles. You should take advantage of that."

"Shut up." Luke shoves his brother, his cheeks tinged with pink.

"I can email you the guest list," Alex says. "I'd love to get this sorted so we can make the place cards and things. Michael and I could probably look at it soon, but he's working on his pitch for the next few days, and we—"

"No problem," I interrupt, seeing the stress line Alex's face. I glance pointedly at Luke. "We can do that. Right?"

He blows out a breath and nods. "Yep. We can go to my place."

"Great!" Alex beams. "Thank you, guys. That will help a lot."

The way her shoulders relax with relief reminds me what really matters here. I pat her arm, smiling. "Of course. We're happy to help."

Our meals arrive, along with another round of drinks, and we eat in silence for a while. It's good to have something else to focus on and, finally, the tension inside me starts to ebb away. Maybe, just maybe, I will be able to do this.

After dinner, Alex goes to the bathroom and Michael insists on going to pay, and I have a second alone with Luke again.

He leans in to speak to me. "I'm sorry that this is so awkward. If I'd known who you were when we met..."

"What, you wouldn't have had sex with me?" Whoops, probably shouldn't have said that. But he's close enough that I can smell his cologne and it's doing something to my brain.

Amusement dances across his features, then he looks serious. "No, not... Well, it would have been very hard to say no." The intensity in his eyes makes my blood heat, and desire surges through me.

I open my mouth to say something, but I don't know what. If only—

"You ready?" Alex appears at my side, grabbing her bag off the table.

I nod and tear my eyes away from Luke, trying to steady my breathing as we file out the door onto the pavement.

Remembering my manners, I turn to Michael. "Thank you for dinner."

He smiles warmly as he slips an arm around Alex. "No problem. You flew all the way over here for our wedding, it's the least we can do."

"Oh, that reminds me," Alex says, angling herself to face Luke. "Is Dena coming to the wedding? You never RSVP'd for her."

Luke stiffens. "Um... yeah."

I glance at him, puzzled. "Who's Dena?"

He keeps his gaze fastened on the sidewalk and an uneasy feeling settles over me.

"Oh," Alex says breezily, "she's Luke's wife."

10

I feel like I've been punched in the gut. All the oxygen around me has vanished and I stand there, blinking in shock.

His wife? He's *married*?

Alex is chatting about the wedding but I can't hear a word. I stare at Luke, waiting for him to say something. After what seems like an eternity, he drags his gaze back to mine. I silently beg him to tell me it's not true, but his face tells me it is.

Fuck. I feel sick.

"We could try that place a few blocks over for dessert?" Alex's voice cuts into my thoughts.

Michael kisses her on the head. "That's a great idea."

They turn to us and I wrench my gaze from Luke's, trying to find my voice.

"Sure," Luke says, as if the whole world isn't tilting on its axis.

I swallow hard. My head is spinning and dinner is about to end up on the sidewalk.

God, I have to get out of here. I don't want to do this to

Alex again, but I cannot be around him right now. I don't know what I'll say or do while I feel like this.

I lift a hand to my forehead, pressing my eyes closed to avoid Luke's gaze. "Alex, I'm so sorry but I think my migraine might be coming back." It's not a complete lie. Now I really do feel ill.

Her face falls, but she nods. "Okay. We'll go home."

"No! You guys go and have your dessert. I'll head back, it's only a few blocks. I'm sure I'll feel better tomorrow," I add, still unable to look at Luke. Because I'm not sure at all.

Alex hesitates. "Okay, if you don't mind?"

"Let me at least walk you home," Luke offers, and it takes all my strength not to punch him in the mouth and tell him to fuck right off.

Instead, I turn as calmly as I can and fake a syrupy smile. "No, thank you. I'm fine." Then I spin on my heel and stride off down the street before I do or say anything that will get me into trouble.

I stalk along for a block in a daze. I have to be careful to watch where I'm going, which streets I need to turn down. I'm so worked up, I could walk all the way uptown without realizing.

I mean, Christ. He's *married*? That's his version of *complicated*? That's not complicated at all. That is, in fact, pretty damn straightforward.

"Harriet! Wait."

I pause, then continue my furious pace when I recognize the voice.

"Please, wait." He's beside me now. "I wanted to tell you. I didn't know how to explain—"

I stop, spinning to face him. "Explain what? That you're married?" I shake my head, my nerves raw. "How could you have sex with me? What kind of an asshole are you?" My heart is juddering against my ribs and my breathing is shallow. I hate confrontation but I just cannot let this one slide.

Harriet 2.0, have at it.

"Here I was thinking that maybe you were a nice guy, but you're not. You're a total sleaze."

His eyebrows slant together and he rakes a hand through his hair. "It's not like that, you don't understand. Things are complicated—"

"Ha!" I huff, incredulous. "Stop using that bloody word! Because it's not—it's very clear cut. You're *married*." I turn on my heel and start walking again, ignoring his voice calling my name. Nausea slams into me as my words ring in my ears, and I think of his poor, unsuspecting wife. No wonder he wouldn't let me say anything. And Michael and Alex are friends with her! I can't believe I did that to another woman, to Alex's friend—and, oh God, no...

I whip around. He's still standing where I left him and I stride back a few feet. "Do you have kids?" I demand, dreading the answer. I cannot be a home-wrecker, I cannot live with myself if—

"No! Of course not. It's not even—"

"Well that's something," I mutter. At least I haven't torn a family apart. My stomach clenches like a fist as I move my eyes over his handsome face. Of course he's married. He's far too good-looking to be single. In fact, I bet this isn't even his first affair. He's probably hooking up with women all the time—he could certainly have his pick of them. The only problem is that *this* one came back to haunt him and now he has to face it.

"Please, let me explain." He looks desperate, and for a single second I feel sorry for him. "Dena and I—"

"Stop," I say, raising a shaking hand. "There is nothing you could say that would possibly justify—"

"We're getting divorced, Harriet."

I freeze. "Divorced?"

Oh. I get it.

"Is that because of your—" I break off, searching for the right word, and he narrows his eyes at me.

"My what?"

"Your..." What's the best way to put this? "Er, philandering."

His mouth pops open. "What? No!"

I eye him doubtfully.

"I'm serious, Harriet. I don't know what kind of idea you have of who I am, but you are the only person I've slept with since Dena and I got together in our twenties. When I met you on the plane, my lawyer had just phoned to tell me she'd signed the divorce papers."

I study him for a moment, unsure if I should believe him. People will say anything to get themselves out of a bad situation, and this one is quite the pickle. But as I take in his slumped shoulders and tortured expression, I can't help but think he might be telling the truth. And when I cast my mind back to the man I met on the plane—the man who didn't have a condom, who told me things were complicated before he ever knew he'd see me again... Hell, the fact that he left a note at all...

Everything in me wants to believe him.

"Why didn't you tell me last night?"

He gives a hollow, humorless laugh. "I wanted to, believe me. But we haven't told my family."

"What? Why not?"

He glances down the street to double check we're still alone. "Dena moved out five months ago, on a trial basis, but we both knew that it was over right away. We want different things. I was going to tell Mike, but then he asked me to be his best man and I didn't want to be a bummer when he was so excited about his wedding. And then as the wedding got closer it just got more awkward."

In spite of everything, sympathy tugs at me. "I'm sure he would understand."

"Maybe." Luke shrugs. "It's not just that. You don't know how difficult our dad is. When Mike got divorced, Dad was so disappointed and it blew up into this big thing. And then with my job—" He glances at me, and I can tell he's deciding how much more he wants to share. "Anyway. Dad will *not* be happy when I tell him, and I didn't want to cause drama by fighting with Dad at the wedding, so it just seemed easier to keep playing happy families until after they were married."

"But aren't they wondering where Dena is? Why she didn't come to dinner tonight?"

"I told them she's out of town until the wedding," he mumbles. "That she's at some insurance conference for work."

I let my breath out in a long stream, trying to make sense of the situation. "If Alex and Michael believe you're married, and you're not going to tell anyone, why have you told me? Why not just let me keep believing it too?"

"Because I can't stand the thought of you hating me for the next two weeks. And I want you to know..." His eyes return to mine from under low brows. "I'm not some cheating asshole."

"So you *are* divorced?"

"It's being finalized over the coming weeks."

I frown. "But it's not final yet." It's a statement, not a question, but he nods in confirmation anyway. He offers me a hopeful smile, but I shake my head. "It doesn't matter what papers you've signed, or what is *going* to happen. The fact is, you're still married. You were on the plane."

"Okay, yes, but that's just a technicality—"

"No, Luke." Irritation bolts through me. "If I'd known you were still legally married, then I wouldn't have slept with you. But you didn't give me that information, and now I've done something I can't undo."

"I didn't think I'd ever see you again! And it's not like you asked if—"

"*Don't* put this on me," I snap. I rub my temples, picturing the coming weeks where Luke and I have to spend time together, pretending nothing has happened between us. Right now, all I want to do is get on a plane and go home.

But... I can't do that to Alex.

God, I'd give anything for a time machine so I could go back and take a different flight, so I could tell Steph that *no*, I won't pretend to be some outgoing, sexed-up version of myself, thank you very much.

Don't blame Harriet 2.0, thank her.

Steph's words come back to me, and as much as I want to push them away, I realize she has a point. Not because of the sex, or because of meeting Luke, but because of the person I'm becoming. I'm standing up to someone when I'd usually let myself be pushed around, and I'm going to need to do that soon with Mel.

Besides, I like this new side of myself. I like feeling prettier in my clothes, being a little more confident and bold. I'm not going to let some guy ruin that.

I force my gaze back to Luke. "Look, I'm sorry about what's happening with Dena, but until everything is finalized, you're still married. We should never have done what we did, and we can't let it interfere with anything."

He sighs.

"Okay?" I take a step closer and put my hands on my hips. "I need to hear you say it. My relationship with my sister is important, and this wedding means everything to her. We can't let our mistake get in the way. We need to forget anything ever happened between us."

He begins to protest but I cut him off.

"I'm serious. We need to completely forget about it. No more secret conversations when Alex and Michael aren't listening."

"Okay," he mumbles. "Okay, we'll forget all about it."

"Good. Now I'm going home, to scrub the memory of it from me. And when I see you next, we'll play nice for their sake."

He nods again, his face solemn.

In the spirit of moving on, I try to muster a smile. "Goodnight, Luke."

He stares at me for a second, then squares his shoulders and fixes his gaze across the street. "Goodnight, Harriet."

And with that, I turn and head back to the apartment.

11

I slide the book back onto the shelf with a sigh. Things must be bad if even a trip to the bookstore isn't making me feel better.

This place is lovely, though: a small, street-level store in the West Village, with narrow aisles and stacks of books that reach all the way up to the ceiling. There's soft music playing, cozy armchairs, and that indescribable smell of books that just feels like home.

I wasn't going to go out today, but Alex wanted to get some work done and I felt bad moping around the place. And, you know—when in doubt, go to the library. Or... the bookstore where your sister gets a great discount.

I know I'm going to have to face Luke and get on with things, but I needed a day to myself, to get over how shitty I feel about what happened. I'm not sure what it is I feel so shitty about; if it's that he lied to me, that I am stuck in this situation with him now, or that—perhaps worst of all—I let him get to me. I let myself develop a little crush on Luke, simply because he was sexy and a good shag, only to discover—whoops—he's got this huge complicated secret.

In some ways, though, learning he's married has made things a lot easier. It's stopped my escalating fantasies about what could happen between us and freed me to focus on Alex. Which, I keep reminding myself, is what matters most here.

I let my gaze wander across the shelves. It's then that I notice a pair of eyes peeking through the stacks, watching me.

Jesus. Who is this creep?

I poke my head around the end of the aisle and spot Geoff, pretending to dust a shelf. "Hi, Geoff."

"Harriet!" He turns to me with an expression of exaggerated surprise. "I didn't see you there! How are you?"

I chuckle. "I saw you watching me."

His cheeks color. "What? Oh, well—"

"It's okay. Alex suggested I come here and use her staff discount."

"Great! See anything you like?"

I shrug.

"Maybe I could help you find something?" When I don't respond, Geoff sets the duster down. "Are you okay?"

"Yeah, just having a crappy day. I discovered something last night that kind of bummed me out."

He smiles kindly. "Do you want to talk about it?"

I open my mouth to say *Yes, please, help me feel better about this* until I realize, of course, I can't talk to him about it.

"I'm guessing it's about a guy?"

My face warms and I push my glasses up my nose, inspecting the carpet.

Geoff chuckles. "That's a yes."

I emit an uncomfortable laugh, wishing he wasn't one of Alex's best friends, so I could just spill it all to him.

"Look," Geoff says when I don't elaborate, "I can tell you

don't want to talk about it and that's okay. Maybe you should do something nice to make yourself feel better."

"Like what?"

"I don't know, what normally cheers you up?"

"Buying books." I gesture to the stacks of books around us—usually one of my favorite sights—and feel a fresh wave of misery. For as long as I can remember, books have been an escape for me. They became my lifeline in high school, as I struggled to find my place in a world that felt increasingly hostile. I spent the majority of my spare time at the library, escaping into fantasy worlds where I didn't have to think about my own life. Which is exactly what I could use right now, but... I glance at Geoff and hike up a shoulder. "For some reason I'm not feeling it today."

"Okay. What about something like, I don't know, getting your nails or hair done?"

I give him a doubtful look. He doesn't know me well so it's not his fault, but that's hardly my style.

He laughs at my expression. "I was just thinking of something different from books, since that's not working. When was the last time you got your hair done?"

I chew my lip, casting my mind back. "I think I had it trimmed a couple of years ago?"

His eyes widen. "Seriously? Please let me take you to my friend Casey, he's great. What do you say?"

I consider this for a moment. It's not like I've got anything else planned, and it might be nice to have a little pampering. Plus, I was thinking the other day that the new me might like to do something with her hair. In fact, I'm quite sure she *would*.

"Okay."

Geoff clasps his hands together. "Yay! I'll just give him a call and see if he can squeeze you in."

I slump down in a chair while he makes the call, picking at a fingernail.

Ugh, I need to get out of this funk. I'm in New York City, for crying out loud. I'm hanging out with my sister, not to mention her lovely friends. So I accidentally slept with a married guy, is that the worst thing in the world? He was already getting divorced—it's not like I've ruined a marriage.

But the irony of this situation is not lost on me. I'm over here for Alex's wedding and I've just slept with a married man. And now I have to lie to Alex—not only by hiding the fact that Luke and I slept together, but also by going along with the charade of his happy marriage. I hate that he's put me in this position.

Geoff appears in front of me, his jacket already on. "Casey had a cancellation a few minutes ago, so if we hurry we can see him now." He reaches for my hand and pulls me to my feet.

"What about work? Don't you have to…"

He waves my protest away, dragging me out of the store. "It's fine. I've got a lunch break and I can tell you need cheering up."

He glances at me over his shoulder and I smile. Gratitude courses through me at his kindness. I knew I liked him.

"Okay, are you ready?"

I nod, my stomach squeezing with apprehension. Maybe this wasn't the best idea. I don't pay much attention to my hair, but I also don't want to look ridiculous. And Casey has spent the last hour and a half doing God-knows-what back there. He covered the mirror so I couldn't see and just told me to "trust him." I wasn't sure I wanted to trust this random guy, but Geoff swore he's the best. Which was all fine and good, except Geoff then took off back to work, leaving me stuck here at Casey's mercy.

I take a deep breath as he uncovers the mirror, revealing my new hair. And all I can do is stare at my reflection, dumbfounded.

Oh.

I turn my head, watching my locks shimmer under the salon lights.

This is... I mean, this is just...

"Wow," I breathe.

"You like?" Casey asks, tilting his head to one side. He reaches out to fluff my hair a bit, then stands back to admire it.

I nod again, speechless. *Like* is an understatement. It's gorgeous. He's kept most of the length, tidying the ends and adding a few shorter layers, and dyed it a deep, glossy, cranberry red. And he's given me a fringe! Well, "bangs" they call them here. It's long and floppy and sweeps off to one side. And on top of all that, he's done something to make the length fall in long, straight sheets.

"How is it so straight?"

"Straightening irons," he says, holding up a device.

I take them and turn them over in my hand. I knew he was using some contraption back there, but I had no idea what. "Do you sell these?"

He grins. "We sure do."

"Good. I'll take some." I look back at the mirror in awe. I can't believe I've never done this before. In fact, if you'd told me he was going to dye my hair red—and give me a freaking fringe—I would have run screaming from the salon. But this looks amazing.

Gazing at my reflection, with my dark red lips and now

my red hair, I feel empowered. There she is, in the mirror: Harriet 2.0. And she's badass.

I always found it kind of baffling when Steph told me she feels better after getting her hair done, but now I think I get it. I feel like a new person.

I practically skip the few blocks back to the building, the crisp autumn air making me feel alive. Well, that and this fabulous new hair of mine. I stride into the apartment, ready to tackle the wedding planning head-on. Who cares about Luke and his nonsense? I'm here for my sister, and nothing is going to get in my way.

12

"Hey." Luke opens the door to his apartment with an easy grin, but I stand in the hallway, clutching my bag.

After my time in the salon yesterday, I decided to jump in head first with the wedding stuff. So here I am at Luke's place, ready to knock out this seating plan. The only problem is, I forgot what it feels like to be around him. I may have underestimated how challenging this will be.

When he steps aside for me to enter, I hesitate. I take in the half-tilt of his lips, the scruff shading his jawline, the knitted gray sweater fitting snugly over his arms. There's a flicker of heat in my body, and I feel annoyed at it for betraying me.

Right. Time to get back to the plan: acting like nothing ever happened between us.

"Hi." I force a polite smile, skirting around him through the doorway.

"Wow," he says as I pass. "Your hair."

I place my bag down on his front table, pretending I don't hear him.

"It looks beautiful, Harriet."

I make the mistake of meeting his gaze. I swear I spot something in his eyes, but as quickly as I notice it, it's gone.

I blush and glance away, ashamed that I'm still letting myself get flustered by his attention. "Thanks," I say with a casual shrug, trying to keep my tone indifferent. "It was time for a change."

He closes the door and I follow him into the kitchen, my breath stuttering. I might not know much about New York real estate, but this place must be worth a small fortune. A massive loft apartment in Chelsea? Small. Fortune.

Luke gestures to the fridge. "Would you like a drink?"

"Sure," I murmur in a daze, wandering further into the enormous space.

This is the kind of apartment you see on TV: high ceilings with exposed steel beams, and a whole wall of windows, giving the place a light, airy feel. The living room, kitchen and dining room are all in one open-plan space. The kitchen is gleaming chrome and white shiny surfaces, separated from the dining space by an island with a white granite countertop. The whole vibe of the space is industrial chic; the kind of effortless look that can only be achieved with careful consideration. And money.

Woah. He must be rich. I rack my brain, trying to remember what he said he did for work.

Wandering around the corner into the living space, I cast my gaze over the pristine interior. Then my whole body freezes.

Holy shit.

Stretching the length of the entire back wall, completely at odds with the rest of the decor, is a deep metal bookshelf, stuffed with, well, I don't even know where to begin.

I step forward, my jaw hanging open as I take in the

sight before me. The first thing that catches my eye is the Lego Death Star, nearly two feet wide. On the shelf above it sits a model of the DeLorean from *Back to the Future*, and a bunch of figurines—some from *Star Wars*, some from *Teenage Mutant Ninja Turtles*. Then I notice the board games and my heart does a little flip. He's got loads of them, carefully stacked. I scan the titles, recognizing a few I love and a few I've never played. I want to pull them out and examine them further, but my eye is drawn to the books on the next set of shelves, and I tilt my head to skim the titles. They're mostly sci-fi and fantasy—and a limited edition boxed set of the entire *Harry Potter* collection.

My heart is thumping hard as I turn back to him, seeing him through new eyes. I can't believe this. He's... fuck. He's a total nerd. As I see his cheeks color under my appraising gaze, it occurs to me that maybe he's embarrassed he's such a geek. And for some reason, that's kind of adorable.

Nope. I quickly catch myself. It doesn't matter that he's being cute, that he likes all the same stuff I like, that he's the only guy who's made me orgasm. *He's* the reason I have to spend the next two weeks lying to my sister.

He holds out a can of Coke and I take it with a sigh. "I... like your apartment," I mumble, at a loss for what else to say. Although if I'm honest, I don't love the ultra-modern, shiny look. With the white carpet and walls, and the gleaming surfaces and LED lighting, everything feels kind of sterile. I prefer wood and soft fabrics, warm yellow lighting and squishy sofas you can sink into, somewhere to drink red wine without feeling like you might destroy everything in sight if you're not careful. I glance at his angular white leather sofa. It doesn't look like it's even meant for sitting on.

Luke cocks his head to one side. "Really? I can't stand it."

"What?"

"Well," he says, dropping down onto the sofa, "it's not really decorated to my taste."

I gingerly lower myself beside him, letting my eyes drift over the decor again. This must be Dena's taste, then.

"Apart from the TV," he adds with a grin. He reaches for a remote and presses a button. A gleaming white wall panel slides aside to reveal a giant screen and a cabinet with several gaming consoles.

I have to laugh. "You're big on gaming." Though after seeing his bookshelves, it doesn't surprise me in the slightest.

He chuckles. "It's part of my job."

"Right," I say, turning to face him on the couch, being careful not to somehow rip the leather. Knowing me, I'll probably slash a hole in it with my keys and end up owing him thousands. "What do you do, exactly?"

He draws a breath, eying me. "Do you really want to know?"

I frown, puzzled by his hesitation. "Well, I did. Now I'm not so sure." An awkward laugh escapes me, then I feel all the blood drain from my face. "Oh, God. It's not something to do with porn, is it?" I screw my nose up, recoiling. Come to think of it, he did say he works "in entertainment"—everyone knows that's code for porn. Why is that only occurring to me now?

He barks out a loud laugh, taking me by surprise. When I don't laugh with him, his face twists in horror. "You're not serious?"

I shrug, my eyes darting around the apartment looking for... I don't know, video cameras? Whips? Economy-sized bottles of lube?

"Jesus. No, Harriet."

"Okay. Good." I laugh with relief. "Then in that case, yes, tell me what you do."

"It's not going to sound all that exciting now," he says wryly. "I create video games. We released a game on PC earlier this year, and soon we're putting out a console version."

"Wow, that's so cool!" I crack open my can of Coke. "You're not working today?"

"No, I'm off for a couple weeks with the wedding coming up."

"Work doesn't mind you taking all that time off?"

"One of the perks of being your own boss, I guess."

I pause, my drink halfway to my mouth. "You're the boss?" He nods, and I don't know why, but that knowledge sends a little thrill through me. "It must pay very well." As soon as the words leave my lips, I cringe. I know it's not classy to talk about that stuff.

He shrugs, leaning back on the sofa. "We're doing alright. I've only been at it a few years. I bought this place back when I was in software development and making a lot more."

Well, that makes sense. You can make loads doing that sort of stuff, can't you?

"I was going to redecorate when—" he breaks off, glancing at me. "Anyway, I just haven't gotten around to it. It's been like this for years."

"I like the bookshelves."

His eyes rest on mine for a second, as if trying to read me, then his mouth tugs into a lop-sided smile. "They're a new addition."

I adjust my glasses, glancing back at the shelves. "You just... went out and bought all that stuff?"

"No. Well, some of it. A lot of it had been in storage for

years, and last month I just decided—fuck it. I live here alone now, I should be able to have my stuff out."

I sip my drink, reading between the lines. Dena didn't want him to have this stuff out. I mean, it doesn't go with the rest of the space, but what kind of wife won't let her husband have his possessions in his own home? Sympathy trickles through me and I push it away.

"What's your favorite book?" I rise to my feet, perusing the titles. He has everything from Neil Gaiman, George R. R. Martin, and Tolkien, to George Orwell, Ray Bradbury, and Arthur C. Clarke. It makes sense that he loves fantasy and sci-fi if he spends his days creating video games. I wonder what his games are like.

"Do I have to pick just one?" he asks. But before I can answer, he adds, "I guess if I had to choose, I'd say *Ready Player One*. Oh, and *Ender's Game* is good, too." He gives me a sheepish look. "You must think I'm a total geek."

"I do." A grin stretches across my face before I can stop it. "But *Ready Player One* is good."

His eyebrows spring up. "Wait, you've read it? Or have you just seen the film?"

I raise a hand to my chest in offense and turn back to the shelves. "I've *read* it, thank you."

"Really?"

I touch the book spines, debating how much I want to share. After the way I was teased in high school, there are some people I don't share this side of myself with. But I'm sensing I won't be judged here. My gaze lands on a small stuffed badger with a yellow scarf around its neck and my heart softens. Of course he's a Hufflepuff, like me. I think back to the plane—to the way I felt a sense of connection to him, even as a complete stranger—and suddenly understand why. We're cut from the same cloth.

"Yes," I say, sinking back down onto the sofa. "And *Ready Player Two*. I've read most of the books on your shelves. That *Harry Potter* box set is awesome."

Luke gazes at me with a funny expression and I swallow hard. I've been so full of anger about this situation we find ourselves in, but the longer I sit here, talking to him about the things he loves—the things *I* love—the more I let my guard down.

And that is not good.

"We should get on with the seating plan," I mumble, peeling my gaze away.

"Yes. Right. Hold on." He stands and wanders out of the room. I lean across the couch, craning my neck to catch a glimpse of his bedroom or—is there an office back there?— but all I can see is darkness beyond the door. He appears a moment later and I scramble back to where I was, hoping he didn't notice.

"So, I was thinking we could use these." He places a large piece of card down on the glass coffee table, along with a stack of Post-Its. Then he holds out a bunch of pens in different colors. "We could color code the plan, to make it easier. Like, blue for the wedding party, red for family, green for friends. That sort of thing."

Oh, fuck. Is this gorgeous man talking to me about stationery and color-coding? Forget the plane; *this* is the sexiest thing to ever happen to me. How am I going to make it through this in one piece?

Luke mistakes my silence for reluctance and his cheeks flush. "Sorry, that might be too much. Whatever you think."

"I think that's a good idea." I gulp in some air, trying to stop the traitorous surge of heat flowing through me. I've always loved stationery but I had no idea it could be so... *erotic*. I guess when it's in the right hands. My gaze drops to his big hands, clutching the pens, and my breathing quickens.

I shake my head, desperate to snap out of it. Grabbing my phone, I pull up Alex's email with the guest-list, then hand it to Luke.

"Okay, so we know there are tables of eight, plus the bridal table." He draws some circles on the card, and sticks some of the Post-Its down.

I try not to feel disappointed when he places Dena's name on a table. At least she isn't seated at the bridal table with us, but does she *really* have to be there at all?

I reach for the Post-Its, feeling my irritation return. "You didn't put my date down," I snap.

He's surprised for a second, then I catch a spark of amusement in his eyes. "You have a date to the wedding?"

"Yes," I say forcefully, glaring at him.

"He's not on the list."

Shit. Of course he's not on the list, he doesn't bloody exist. But there's no way I'm going to sit through this entire wedding while Luke feigns marital bliss without at least having a date on my arm.

"Well, leave a space for him."

Luke narrows his eyes. "What's his name?" His lips twitch as he watches me, and if I didn't know any better, I'd think he was enjoying this.

"I don't know yet. But I will have a date, don't you worry."

He snorts, then writes "Harriet's weirdo" on a Post-It and places it onto the board with a dramatic eye-roll.

That's something for Harriet 2.0 to do: find a date to Alex's wedding. Fast.

Battery Operated Boyfriend.

"Alex," I say, staring at the sex-toy on the shelf in front of me with a frown, "when I asked you to help find me a date for your wedding, this is *not* what I meant." I turn to look at her. "Why are we here?"

She grins, glancing at Cat and Geoff beside me. After two days in "the writing cave" as she calls it, Alex decided she'd done enough work for the time being, and brought me out to see some of her favorite places in the city.

Apparently, one of her favorite places is a sex shop in the East Village called *O-Land*. If I'd known that when we left the house this morning, I can assure you I would have protested.

"You said you want to try new things," Alex explains. "I still can't believe you dyed your hair! It looks so good."

Geoff nods vigorously. "It really does."

"Anyway," Alex continues, "that made me wonder what *else* would get you out of your comfort zone, and I thought you might find something here." She gestures to a row of multi-colored vibrators on a stand beside us.

I glance between the three of them, all watching me with interest, and shift my weight. What are they expecting me to do? Wander over and flick one on, give it a whirl?

Look, it's not like I haven't been in an adult store before. Steph dragged me to one in Auckland once. I just didn't, you know, *buy* anything.

"Well... thanks," I mumble. I'm trying my best to act mature and knowledgeable, to show how at ease I am in this type of environment, but I can feel the flush on my neck.

Geoff wanders off to survey some devices along one wall, and Cat disappears to the lingerie section. When I turn back to Alex, she takes my arm and steers me towards the row of vibrators. I had no idea my sister was so comfortable in sex shops. But then I think about the sex in her romance novel and bite my cheek. She's pretty comfortable all-round in this arena.

"See anything you like?" she asks, motioning to the display. Far from trying to embarrass me, she actually seems to be wanting to help.

I shrug, looking at the vibrators. They're all different colors and sizes, but some of the shapes have me a little perplexed. There's the standard, erm, anatomical style, but then there are these curved ones shaped like the letter C, and some have a little bit that sticks out the side. I think I know what those are for, but the curved ones have me flummoxed. Who has a vagina shaped like that? Should *my* vagina be shaped like that? No one has complained about the shape before, but gazing at these curved devices I suddenly wonder if I've got some kind of defective vagina.

No, that doesn't make any sense, does it? Otherwise guys would, well, they'd have to be that C shape. And we all know they're not.

"What about this?" Alex picks up one with a little bit sticking out. "A rabbit."

"What?"

She hands it to me and I tentatively lift it up to inspect it. The shaft of it is long and thick, covered in a silicon-type material that is blue and glittery. The bit that sticks out is shaped like a bunny-rabbit, with a little face and ears and everything. Poor bloody rabbit, being shoved face-first down there.

I shake my head, handing it back. "No. I cannot masturbate with a plastic rabbit," I say matter-of-factly, and Alex snickers.

Bunnies aside, I will admit part of me is curious. I think back to what Steph said on the phone the other night—*you know you can give yourself one, right?*—but then I remember the handful of failed attempts in the past and push the idea aside. Besides, it's not the orgasm I'm craving, it's... something else. Some*one* else.

"Ooh, this one comes with a remote control," Alex says, gesturing to a bright pink one.

"Remote control?" I repeat, bemused. Why on earth would I want a remote control? It's not like I'll need to switch it on from the other room or something.

"Oh my God." Alex clamps a hand over her mouth in an attempt to suppress her mirth. "Look at this." She reaches for a box up on a shelf. There's a picture of John Stamos on the front and I take it from her, squinting at the image. John Stamos makes vibrators now? That can't be right.

I read the description aloud to Alex. "*Anatomically modeled on John Stamos. An exact replica of John Stamos for your pleasure.*"

Alex howls with laughter and Geoff and Cat appear

beside us, dissolving into giggles when I hold the box up in disbelief.

"You *have* to get that," Alex says, wiping tears from her eyes. "Didn't you used to love John Stamos?"

"No, I didn't *love* John Stamos. I liked *Full House*." I mean, what nineties kid didn't? And besides, I always thought Bob Saget was more handsome, if I'm honest. But I'm hardly going to tell Alex that.

"*Full House*?" Cat frowns in confusion. "Aren't you a little young for that?"

Alex shakes her head, grinning. "We had these VHS tapes of the show that Harriet used to watch over and over. She had such a crush on John Stamos."

I huff, exasperated. "I did not—"

"Wait," Geoff says, leaning over to scrutinize the box with sudden interest. "Do you think this is *actually* modeled on him? Like, did he make a mold of his—"

"I don't think so, Geoff." Cat chuckles. "It's a gimmick." She points to the bottom of the box where there's small text in a language I don't recognize. Yeah, this is definitely *not* official John Stamos merchandise.

I reach to put the box back but before I can, Alex snatches it from my hand and wheels around, heading for the counter. "I'm getting this for you," she calls over her shoulder.

"What? No!" I trail after her but she's already handing her credit card across to the salesperson.

"Oh, come on! I wanted to thank you for helping with the wedding, and now, John Stamos can help *you*." She waggles her eyebrows and chortles at her own joke. Before the sales assistant can even wrap the item, Alex hands it to me with a flourish. "Enjoy!"

I stare at her outstretched hand, recoiling. But she

thrusts the box towards me and I stuff it in my bag, trying to ignore my burning cheeks. "Thanks... I guess."

When we exit the store, to say I'm relieved is an understatement. "Where are we going next?" I ask Alex warily as we step onto the sidewalk. "A strip club? Or maybe a pole-dancing class?"

"That sounds fun," Cat says and Alex laughs.

"Oh, shit." She reaches into her bag and pulls out her phone, looking at the screen. "I have to take this. I might be a minute." She steps away and Geoff turns to me with a smile.

"You seem to be feeling better today. Have you sorted things out with that guy, then?"

Cat glances between us. "What guy?"

"No one," I mumble. Geoff gives me a knowing look and I sigh. "Okay, there was someone, but nothing is happening. Even if—" I pause, eying them both. I *cannot* reveal any details about Luke; these are Alex's best friends.

"Even if?" Geoff prompts.

"Even if... I sort of wish there were." Oh God, what's wrong with me? I'm supposed to be *angry* with Luke about this mess we're in, so why am I still letting myself replay our time on the plane in an endless loop through my head? I've tried to stop but it's a losing battle. Yesterday I saw a different side to him—a geeky, color-coding, book-and-game-loving side I didn't know was there—and it's making things difficult.

"I knew it!" Geoff leans closer, lowering his voice conspiratorially. "Spill."

A laugh chuffs out of me. "Okay, fine." I glance to check that Alex is out of earshot. "There's this guy I kind of like, even though he's off-limits."

"Right. First up, define 'kind of like,'" Geoff says.

I chew my lip, watching a passing car as I think of the way I get all hot and flustered whenever I'm around Luke. "I can't stop thinking about him," I mutter. "Every time I see him—"

"So he's here in the city?" Cat interrupts.

Shit. I've said too much.

Geoff lifts an eyebrow. "How do you know him?"

Shit, shit, shit. I've definitely said too much.

"Oh, well..." My heart is stammering now as I steal a glance at Alex. She's engrossed in a heated conversation on her phone and I turn back to the others. How can I explain this? How on earth would I know a guy over here? Unless... "It's the guy from the plane."

"Oh!" A wicked grin splits Geoff's face. "Mister hot plane lover."

I blush furiously.

"So, what's the problem?" Cat asks. "What do you mean he's off-limits?"

I fold my arms across my chest and study the sidewalk. There's no way I'm going to tell them that the guy I shagged on the plane turned out to be married. God knows what they'd think of me if they knew that. And that's before we get to the fact that he's Michael's brother and the best man at their wedding.

God. I should never have said anything.

"It's... complicated," I say, to borrow Luke's woefully inadequate terminology. I remind myself of my decision to prioritize Alex and the wedding, and straighten up. "Anyway, it doesn't matter. That's not why I'm here."

Geoff grins. "No reason you can't still see him."

I shake my head. "No, Alex needs to come first." Thinking of Alex, I glance at them in alarm. "Please don't say anything to her. I don't want her to think—"

"We won't." Cat gives me a reassuring smile. "It sounds like there isn't much to tell, anyway."

I exhale. "No, there isn't."

"We'll see," Geoff says with a wink.

I look back just as Alex shoves her phone into her bag. Then she heads over to us, her expression twisted with worry.

"Everything okay?" I ask.

"No." She massages her temples and my stomach dips. I step closer, touching her arm.

"What is it? What happened?"

"That was my editor. Remember how I was glad she could fit me in a few weeks after the wedding? Well, I got that wrong. Turns out she can only fit me in if I send her the manuscript in a week and a half."

I blink in shock. "A week and a half?"

"Yep." Her face crumples and she slumps down onto the steps of O-Land, dropping her head into her hands. "I can't do this. I can't finish a novel, plan a wedding, show my sister the city..."

My heart clenches and I sit beside her. "Hey, don't worry about me. I'm here to help you, not be a burden."

She looks up, sniffing. "I know. I'm sorry, that's not what I meant."

Cat leans against the stair railing. "Could you work with a different editor?"

"I've already paid her." Alex wipes her nose. "It was my mistake. I've been so distracted with the wedding that I got the date wrong."

"You said you only had a quarter of the book to finish, right?" Geoff asks. "Can you do that in a week and a half?"

"Normally yes, but with everything else—"

"Don't worry about everything else." I squeeze her arm.

"I don't need to go sightseeing. Seriously, it's not..." I trail off, unsure how to explain that I'm actually relieved at the thought of not visiting Times Square or the Empire State Building with throngs of tourists.

Her forehead creases. "But I promised you, Harri."

"I really don't mind. I'm here for *you*. That's what matters. And as for the wedding stuff..." I swallow, knowing that if she's spending the next week and a half focused on her writing, I'm spending more time with the one person I should be avoiding. "Luke and I will take care of everything."

Because if that's what Alex needs, that's what I'll do.

14

I smooth my red hair down over one shoulder and key in the code Luke gave me to enter his building. When the door pops open, my heart jumps in my chest.

I climb the stairs, lugging a bag filled with art supplies I picked up earlier today. I thought it might be nice to hand-letter the place cards because I learned calligraphy a few years ago. Though as I reach Luke's door, I can't help but wonder if this is a bad idea. His pristine apartment hardly seems the right place to pull out a pot of India ink and a calligraphy pen. But then, I can't do this in a coffee shop, and Alex needed her place quiet so she could focus. Plus, I thought it might be a nice surprise.

I knock on the door, trying to quell the anxiety rising from my belly. *There's nothing to be nervous about*, I remind myself. Last time things were fine. Well, apart from when I got unreasonably aroused as he discussed color-coding the seating chart, but that won't happen again.

The door swings open, and there on Luke's face is a pair of black, square-framed glasses. "Hey," he says, like this is no big deal.

But it is a big deal. It's a huge deal. He's every possible nerd fantasy come to life. Before I can stop them, my eyes sweep down his body, taking in his gray sweats and black T-shirt. Anyone else wearing this would look like a slob, but on him it's sexy as hell. The shirt fits his shoulders and chest perfectly, clinging to all the right bits, and the pants are slung low across his hips. I bring my gaze back to his glasses, which he adjusts self-consciously, and I have to swallow down the saliva pooling in my mouth.

Shit, this was a terrible idea.

"Uh, hi," I mumble, stepping into his apartment. "I didn't know you wore glasses."

"Yeah, sometimes my contacts irritate my eyes."

When I turn back, his cheeks are pink. I hold up my bag of supplies, forcing myself to look away. "Where should I put these?"

He leads me to the dining table. "Is here okay?"

I glance at the perfectly white, glossy table, seated atop a perfectly white, plush rug. I guess this spot is as good as any.

"Sure. Thanks." I take a seat and unload my supplies, focusing on setting up. I haven't done any hand-lettering in a while, so I'm going to need to do a few practice rounds first.

"Can I get you a drink?" Luke offers as he wanders into the kitchen.

"That would be great." I busy myself unscrewing the lid to the India ink and setting it down, then doing some practice strokes on the paper.

"Whiskey?" he asks, and there's a hint of a smile in his voice. I ignore it.

"Sure." Except, it's been several hours since I last ate and drinking whiskey on an empty stomach, while alone in this apartment with him, is probably not such a good idea.

"Actually..." I swivel around in my chair and he pauses mid-pour.

"Everything okay?"

"Well, I haven't eaten, so I probably shouldn't—"

"Me neither. Want to order something?"

I hesitate. Eating dinner here with him seems, I don't know, intimate somehow. But my stomach rumbles as if on cue, and I nod. "Yeah."

"Do you like Thai food?" Luke pulls a menu from a drawer and hands it over.

"Sure." I run my eyes over the list, then hand it back, pointing to chicken Pad Thai.

"Is that all? Come on, you want more than that."

"Well..." I nibble my lip and he laughs.

"I'll order that and a bunch of other stuff. Trust me, it's good."

"Okay." I smile and turn back to my lettering.

He orders the food then brings me my whiskey, peering over my shoulder. "Wow, that's really cool."

"Thanks," I mumble. "I haven't done it in ages. I'm a bit rusty."

"Really? I think it looks great."

I try to hide my smile, hoping he can't see it from where he's standing behind me.

"Are you sure you'll get them all done tonight?"

"Yep." I dip my pen back in the ink then stop, hyper-aware of the way he's hovering. I turn and throw him a pointed look.

"What?"

"I can't do it with you right there!"

"Fine, fine. I'll leave you to it." He laughs and wanders over to the sofa, hitting the button to reveal the TV. Then he sets his whiskey down and pulls out one of the game controllers, slipping on his headset and loading up a game.

I smile to myself as I feel my body relax. For some reason, things are feeling easy between us tonight and I'm relieved. If I could get my attraction to him under control, things might even be good. And I can do that; attraction is nothing more than a chemical response in the brain that I can just ignore. I'm a grown woman with self-control, for Christ's sake. I'll simply... stop being attracted to him. Easy.

I manage to get a whole bunch of the cards done before dinner arrives. The first couple are a little wonky, but by the end they're looking good. Luke is so involved in his game he doesn't notice the door buzz. I have to call out to him to get his attention.

"Sorry." He removes his headset with a chuckle. Then he flicks the screen off, the TV sliding out of view. I reach for my bag to hand him some money but he shakes his head. "It's on me," he says as he lopes to the door. He returns a moment later and when I go to clear the table, he gestures to the sofa, so we settle in there with the food.

And he's right; it is good. I eat quickly, washing it down with my whiskey, and he pours me another one.

"So I told you about my job, but I don't think you've ever talked about your work," he says over Panang curry. "What do you do?"

"Oh." A whisper of embarrassment passes through me. I mean, my sister and his brother are both writers, and he has his dream job, whereas I...

He tilts his head to one side, watching me curiously, then amusement colors his features. "Wait," he says, fighting off a smile. "It's not something to do with porn, is it?"

It takes me a second to realize he's teasing me, and I let

out a laugh. "Oh, yes," I joke. "Surely you're familiar with my work?"

The side of his mouth kicks up in a sexy grin, his eyes burning into mine as he pushes his glasses up his nose. "Yes," he murmurs. "I am."

My heart stumbles against my ribs and I glance down, mentally kicking myself. I need to be more careful.

"I, er, work in a cafe," I mumble. "Making coffee, clearing tables, whatever." I shrug. Then out of nowhere I hear myself saying, "But one day I'd love to open my own cafe. One that has board games you can play while you drink coffee and eat delicious baked things." I jab my chopsticks into my noodles, surprised at myself.

Luke's eyes brighten with enthusiasm. "That would be so cool! Tell me more about it."

I smile, buoyed by his response. And then—I can't quite believe myself—I set my food down and stand, grabbing the napkin from my bag and handing it over. I sink down onto the sofa again, feeling slightly ill and wondering what the hell I'm doing, showing this to him when I've never showed it to anyone else.

He sets his own food aside, carefully unfolding the worn napkin. It's probably nonsense to him, given how many random ideas are scrawled on there, in no real order. But he turns it different ways, tilting his head as he examines every scribble. Then he folds it and hands it back without saying anything. I tuck it into my bag and pick my food up again, avoiding his gaze.

"I know it's silly." My face is hot as I stare down at my noodles. "It's just—"

"It's not silly at all." He studies me for a moment. "You know, there are a few board game cafes here in the city."

"Oh. There are? Well... never mind then." I stuff a spring

roll in my mouth. I thought it was an original idea, but if people are already doing it, then I'm too late. Disappointment lodges uncomfortably in my solar plexus. I didn't realize quite how much I wanted this.

"No," Luke says with a kind smile. "What I mean is, it's obviously a concept that can work. If you do it right, it could be really cool."

I munch my spring roll, thinking. Even though I dismissed the idea as unrealistic, it's been blossoming inside me for years now. It would be the perfect way to combine my skills from working in the cafe with my love of games. But then I remind myself that our board game club back home closed due to lack of interest, and sigh. "I don't think it would take off in my town," I say. Thinking about home now stirs an odd feeling inside me. Despite it being little more than a week since I left, it seems almost like a different lifetime. "And I don't know anything about running a business," I add.

Luke nods, reaching for another carton of food. "Well, you could take classes in business."

My shoulders slump as I think about university. I never went, not like Alex. After high school and all the drama, all the anxiety it caused me, I just couldn't face the thought of going to university.

"Yeah, maybe," I murmur, wishing I'd never brought it up. "So, um, what game were you playing?"

His face lights up and he starts off on an impassioned spiel about the game and the designer of it and how groundbreaking it is. I nod along, half listening, half thinking about my board game cafe and trying to ignore the sense of defeat that's settled over me.

I'm just about to reach for my whiskey when, out of the

corner of my eye, I see something moving across the floor. Not just something—a turtle.

What?

I rub my eyes then check again—and yes, there is a turtle on the floor. What the hell?

"Is that... a turtle?"

Luke turns to look and heaves out a sigh. "Shit," he mutters, setting down his food and pushing to his feet. "Not again." He steps over and scoops up the turtle, shaking his head in disapproval.

"I'm sorry, what is happening right now?"

He gives me a sheepish look. "This is my turtle, Donnie."

"Donnie?"

Somehow, he looks even more sheepish when he clarifies, "Donatello."

I gulp down the giggle rising up my throat. "As in—"

"Yes."

I try to flatten my lips but it's no use; they pull into a wide grin. He's named his turtle after the nerdiest of all the *Teenage Mutant Ninja Turtles*—and yes, I know, the fact that I know that makes me nerdy too. But we've already established that about me. He is *so* much worse.

Luke's cheeks turn red when he sees my grin. "Shut up," he mumbles. "Ever since I got his new tank, he keeps escaping. I can't figure out how he does it. I have to hire a full-time house-sitter every time I leave town in case he gets out."

"Seriously?"

"Yes. I have a lady who comes and watches him."

Oh, God. I can't stop the laugh that squeaks from me at this point. He has a *turtle lady*? This is absurd; a man held captive by a tiny turtle.

"Let me guess, her name is April?"

Luke gives me a withering look. "Her name is *Andrea*,

and she's really good with him. She feeds him and changes his water and gives him his treats..." He shrugs, like this is perfectly normal and we all have turtle ladies.

I raise a hand to my mouth to hide my chuckle, but Luke doesn't notice. He's too busy holding Donnie up and speaking to him in hushed tones, softly scolding him for escaping. My laughter dies away as I gaze at this tall, gorgeous man, being so gentle with this tiny creature. And not just any creature; a miniature *Ninja Turtle*. There's a flutter between my legs at just how fucking adorable this is.

He goes to put Donnie back in his tank, and when he returns beside me on the couch, his cheeks are still crimson. He picks up his food to continue eating, but I can't stop staring at him. There goes any hope I had of curbing my attraction to him. Because there's nothing sexier than a man who's kind and loving to little creatures—and who also happens to love the *Ninja Turtles*.

It's not just that, though. He's different when we're here, in his apartment—more awkward, almost nervous. I've never seen a guy blush so much. For some reason, it's *really* working for me.

I turn back to my food with an almighty sigh. Goddammit, I'm in trouble.

When we're done eating, I return to the table to keep working on the place cards while he continues his game. It only takes me another thirty minutes to finish, and I survey my work, pleased. I hope Alex and Michael like it.

I stand and stretch, wandering towards the couch, apprehensive about interrupting Luke's game. But he hits pause and turns to me, slipping off his headset with a smile. "How's it going?"

"All done. Can I use the bathroom? I just want to wash some of this off my hands."

"Sure. Second door on the right," he says, turning back to his game.

When I'm finished in the bathroom, I sneak a glance into Luke's home office. In the corner is Donnie's tank, and I spot him tucked safely inside, soaking up the warmth from the UV lamp. I giggle as I head back into the living room, imagining Luke finding him in random places all over the apartment. Little Donatello, the escape artist.

Luke pauses his game, looking up. "What are you laughing about?"

I shake my head. "Nothing."

He flicks off the TV and rises to his feet with an amused grin. "Nothing?"

"Just... Donnie. I can't believe you have a *Ninja Turtle*."

The smile slides off his face and he drops his gaze to the floor. I realize he thinks I'm making fun of him and my chest squeezes.

"No," I say, placing a hand on his arm.

Shit. I should *not* have done that. I'd forgotten how lovely his forearms are, and when my fingers brush his skin and his gaze snaps back to mine, darkening behind those sexy glasses, my breathing turns shallow.

But my stupid mouth continues without me. "I think it's cute. I think you're—"

What the hell are you doing? Don't tell him you think he's cute!

I yank my hand away and take a step back, sucking in some air. My heart is hammering, but I force myself to pretend everything is normal. Luckily, I manage a smooth subject change. "Um, is it okay if I leave the place cards here to dry?"

Luke gives a slow exhale, glancing away as though he has to collect himself. "Sure." When his gaze returns to me, he smiles. "They look great. I'm surprised you got them all done tonight."

I chuckle. "I find your lack of faith disturbing."

He stares at me, silent. He has the strangest expression on his face when he finally says, "Did you just... quote Darth Vader?"

"Yeah." Why is he looking at me like that?

He swallows, so loud I can hear it. Fire kindles in his eyes as they move over my face. It makes me feel light-headed, because he's looking at me like he did while I quivered against him on the plane. Heat flashes through me at the memory.

Jesus Christ. *Get ahold of yourself!*

"I should go," I mumble, turning back to gather my things. My hands are shaking and I knock the jar of India ink, sloshing some out onto the table.

Shit.

I spin towards the kitchen, searching for paper towels, but his modern cabinets have everything stored away out of sight. Spotting a stack of napkins from dinner, I throw myself across the kitchen island to try and grab them. There's a groan behind me, and I glance back over my shoulder to find Luke's eyes fixed on my ass, his hands balled into fists at his sides.

Okay, that's on me. I *am* bent all the way across the kitchen island and, yes, my ass is right up in the air. But that is the least of my problems right now.

I grasp the napkins and straighten up, turning back to him. His gaze meets mine and he blinks. A muscle pulses in his neck.

"Uh—" I gesture past him to the ink on the table, but he's oblivious.

"Fuck, Harriet," he rumbles, and my thighs squeeze together.

And then I hear a sound that makes my blood run cold.

Drip. Drip, drip, drip.

We both whirl around to find black ink, trailing over the edge of the table and pooling onto the white rug.

Oh my God. No.

My hand flies to my mouth. I stand, frozen with horror. Luke glances from me to the ink on the carpet and a frown knits across his brow.

"I'm so sorry," I blurt as panic closes like a hand around my throat. "Is there a way we could somehow—"

"No." His jaw tightens. "I think it's ruined."

My stomach dissolves. Sweat prickles on the back of my neck. "Shit, I'm sorry. It was an accident. I can get it cleaned, or I'll replace it. I didn't mean—"

"Forget about it."

"No," I insist. "If we can't clean it I'll buy you a new one. You just have to tell me—"

"It doesn't matter." He lets out a long breath, removing his glasses and rubbing his eyes. He might be *saying* it doesn't matter, but I can tell that it does. The way he's looking at me makes something sharp twist through my middle, and I'm horrified when I feel tears sting behind my eyes.

"I'm sorry." I glance away, blinking rapidly and trying to hold myself together. Then I grab my things and race out the door.

15

I stare at the ceiling, willing my brain to switch off. I've been in bed for three hours and I can't stop replaying what happened at Luke's—how one moment he looked like he wanted to take me right there on the kitchen island, the next like he couldn't stand the sight of me. Every time I picture his face after I spilled the ink, my heart sinks. I'm sure it's an expensive rug, but it was an honest mistake.

My phone buzzes on the nightstand and I roll over, blinking at the bright light from the screen in the dark room. My pulse accelerates when I see who the message is from.

Luke: Harriet, I'm sorry. Are you okay?

I prop my head up on my hand, reading his words over again. Am I okay? I'm not sure, but I type out a reply anyway.

Harriet: I'm fine. Sorry again about the rug.

I expect to receive another text, but Luke's name lights my screen with a call. I hesitate, checking the time. It's nearly two in the morning, and I don't know if I want to talk to him.

But I take a deep breath and answer. "Hey."

"Hey." His deep voice comes down the line, rougher than usual. "I wasn't sure if you'd be awake."

"Yeah. I can't sleep."

"Me neither. I had to talk to you. I'm sorry for being a dick about the rug." His tone is heavy with remorse and I feel myself soften.

"It's okay. I overreacted, running out of there, but I was mortified. That rug is probably worth more than my car. I'll replace it as soon as you tell me where—"

"Seriously, no. I meant it when I said it doesn't matter. I don't even like the damn thing. I was just frustrated—I mean, after you..." He's quiet for a moment, and all I can hear is his breathing. "I wasn't thinking straight."

After I what? I want to ask, but he continues.

"I threw the rug in the Dumpster and actually, it felt good. I never realized how much I've been walking on eggshells since Dena moved out. I started to redecorate—I redid the bedroom and put up the shelves—but it was like I was afraid to touch the rest of the place. Then tonight... Really, I should be thanking you. You reminded me that I've never felt comfortable here. Once the wedding is over, I'm going to finish redecorating."

"You should," I say, and he makes a sound of amusement.

"You said you liked my place."

"Yeah, I did, but... I was trying to be polite. Honestly, I kind of feel like..." I fiddle with the blanket, searching for the right words. "Like I can't breathe in there."

"*Yes.* You're right. That's exactly what it feels like." He releases a huge sigh. "Anyway, I'm sorry. I was going to call tomorrow but I couldn't sleep. I just kept thinking about how upset you looked when you left. I hate that I made you upset."

Despite myself, a smile nudges my lips. He was worried about me being upset? The thought drains all the tension from my body, and I settle back onto the mattress. I realize, as I tuck the phone between the pillow and my ear, that speaking with Luke in bed at this time of night feels kind of intimate—almost like he's here with me.

"I feel better now," I murmur.

"Good." He sounds relieved and it makes my heart beat faster. "Can I take you somewhere tomorrow?"

"Where?"

"I've been thinking about your cafe idea, and what you wrote on that napkin. I thought—"

"Oh." I huff a laugh, feeling embarrassed. *Why* did I show that to him? "I just doodle on that when I'm bored. It's like... a fantasy to get me through the workday."

"No way. That napkin—those notes—that's not just a fantasy. That's something you really want. That's a dream."

"Well, you know." I pull the covers up to my chin. "It's not good to dwell on dreams and forget to live."

The quiet chuckle from Luke tells me he recognizes Dumbledore's wisdom. "Trust me when I say, it's also not good to ignore your dreams."

Something warm spreads through my veins. He called me up in the middle of the night to make sure I wasn't upset, and now he's thinking about my cafe and wants to take me somewhere. God, he's being so freaking sweet right now.

"Harriet..." He says my name in a low rumble that shivers right through me. "Just let me show you this place tomorrow, okay?"

"Okay," I hear myself reply. I snuggle under the covers, my

hand resting on my belly. For the first time in a long time, I'm tempted to trail that hand lower, to keep Luke on the phone and tell him that I can't stop thinking about what we did on the plane, to forget about all the things that are holding me back and just live inside this moment. I think of the way he looked at me when I leaned over the kitchen island tonight—the way he ground out the words *Fuck, Harriet*. It makes me restless and hot, makes my breath come in short, quick bursts.

Then I hear a sound out in the hallway and the light flicks on, shining through the crack under my door, and I'm brought to my senses.

What is wrong with me? Why do I keep forgetting that I'm supposed to be angry with him about our situation—not attracted to him?

I clear my throat, forcing a neutral tone. "I'll see you tomorrow, then. Good night."

"Good night, Harriet."

And when the line goes dead, I tell myself it's for the best.

16

"This place is... wow."

Luke grins beside me. "I thought you'd like it."

Like is an understatement. I had a feeling he might take me to a board game cafe after our phone call last night, but I could never have imagined how amazing it would be.

Down the center of the big room is a row of wooden tables and chairs, two of which are crowded with groups playing games. There are sofas and coffee tables down the back, and to the right is the counter with a coffee machine and low glass cabinets filled with treats. The ceilings are high, with light fixtures dangling low, giving off a golden glow. The whole place is cozy, warm, and inviting.

But none of that takes my breath away like the wall to the left: floor to ceiling, lining the length of the cafe, are shelves crammed with every board game imaginable. And it's not just games—there's books, figurines, comics, all kinds of things.

"Oh my God!" I breathe, rushing over to the wall. There are so many games I lose count—loads I've never even heard of. I sense Luke behind me and turn to him with an incandescent grin. "Thank you so much for bringing me here."

He smiles proudly in response. "You're welcome. Coffee?"

I nod, fastening my gaze back on the shelves. There's a whole section with fantasy books and I'm drinking them all in.

He laughs, then I hear him go to the counter to order. But my mind is too busy whirring with the sight before me. It's like I've stepped inside a dream—my own dream, which I'm only realizing right now I want *desperately*.

Luke appears beside me again, gesturing to a table, and I wander over with him in a daze. He pulls my chair out for me, but—oh, shit—my foot catches on something and I stumble, losing my balance. My bag drops from my hand and I slam face-first into Luke's chest. His big hands grasp my shoulders to steady me, and for a second I'm pressed against him, so close my nostrils fill with the scent of his laundry powder and that familiar, woody cologne. My heart is galloping and I'm not sure if it's because I almost fell or because I'm practically in Luke's arms.

"Well, hello there," he says with a chuckle, and heat spreads over my cheeks as I remember falling in his lap on the plane. A sly grin slants his mouth, then his expression turns serious. "Are you okay?"

I nod, wishing my pulse would calm down. "Sorry, yes." A laugh tumbles out of me as I step back. I glance down to see a stack of board games beside the table. That's what I tripped on.

Oh, and there's the contents of my bag, scattered across the floor.

"Shit," I mutter, getting down on my hands and knees, hastily gathering my things.

God, what a way to make an idiot of myself in front of Luke.

I finally take a seat opposite him, the warmth in my cheeks fading as I get some air in my lungs and pull myself together.

That is, until I look up to see a smile playing around Luke's lips. His eyes flit over my shoulder and back to mine, the smirk on his face growing. "I, uh, think you missed something." Before I can respond, he stands, takes a couple of strides, and reaches down to retrieve something from the floor. Then he's back, sitting opposite me, grinning like mad.

And in his hand is the box with the John Stamos vibrator.

My jaw drops in horror. *Fuck.* I forgot that was in there.

I meet Luke's amused gaze. "That's not—"

"*An exact replica of John Stamos for your pleasure,*" he reads aloud, his eyes dancing.

Heat flares up my face. I'm going to kill Alex.

"Really? John Stamos?"

"It's not—I mean, I didn't—"

"I would have had you pegged as more of a Bob Saget girl," he says, lips twitching.

Oh my God.

He turns the box over and reads from the back. "*Let John Stamos fill your house with this anatomically correct model...*" He quirks an eyebrow at me. "Did you pick this up today?"

"No!" I swipe at it but he holds it out of my reach, still inspecting the package with interest. A few tables over, a group of young guys are playing *Settlers of Catan* and they turn to watch us, snickering amongst themselves.

"Will you *stop* waving it around!?" I hiss, shrinking with mortification. At that moment the barista brings our coffee and I can't even make eye contact. As soon as he's gone I reach for the box again, but Luke is still holding it away from me.

"What is it with women and John Stamos?"

"I don't know," I mutter. "Well, he does have great hair. But that's not why—" I cut myself off, trying to get back on track. "Alex bought it for me as a joke. It's not like I'm going to *use* it."

He lowers the box, peering at me. "Really?"

"Really. Given the choice, I'd much rather have—" My gaze collides with his and I stop myself just in time, pressing my lips closed. *Sex. I'd much rather have sex. With you.*

His eyes linger on me for a moment longer, then he slides the box back across the table without saying anything more. I stuff it in my bag, mentally cursing Alex. Then I pick up my coffee and take a long, slow sip, looking anywhere but at Luke and trying my best to pretend that whole thing did not just happen. Because if I allow myself to acknowledge it did, I will *die*.

Luke reaches into his pocket and pulls out his phone, glancing down as it buzzes in his hand. When he sees who's calling, his eyebrows slash together and he stares at the screen, his mouth in a thin line.

I glance between him and the phone. "Are you going to answer that?"

"Yeah," he mutters. "If I let it go to voicemail, I'll never hear the end of it." With a heavy breath, he hits the talk button and lifts the phone to his ear. He gives me an apologetic look and rises from the table, stepping a few feet away.

I know I should mind my own business, but I'm curious about who would make Luke that reluctant to answer. As he speaks, I find myself leaning across the table, straining my ears to listen.

"Yes, I know," I hear him say over the din of the cafe. "I

already—" He pauses, his shoulders tense. Maybe it's a work call. "Okay, but you said to—" Another pause, and when he speaks again his voice is louder, agitated. "Yes. That's exactly —" Whoever it is, he can't seem to finish a bloody sentence. "Fine. Yes, I will." Shit, maybe it's Dena. "I said I will." He lowers the phone from his ear, and I realize that's the end of the call. Not even a goodbye. What the hell?

He pinches the bridge of his nose for a second, then pockets his phone and turns back to me.

"Everything okay?" I ask tentatively as he settles back in at the table.

He shrugs, reaching for his coffee. "Just my dad."

What? That was his *dad* not letting him get a word in? Jesus, what is that guy's problem?

I frown, watching the way Luke sips his coffee as if nothing has happened. Something comes back to me from the night I learned about his divorce—something about his father being difficult. If that phone call is anything to go by, Luke wasn't kidding.

I open my mouth to ask him about it, but when Luke looks at me with a smile, I bite my tongue.

"Want to play something?" he asks, gesturing to the shelves, and I feel a little thrill. "Go pick a game."

"Okay." I rise to my feet and take in the shelves lining the left wall of the cafe. I haven't played a board game with anyone for a while; Steph doesn't like them, and the club hasn't run for a couple of years now. But it's okay, because I know the game I want to play. My lips tug into a smile when I spot it on the shelf.

The game is called *Wisdom Quest* and it relies mostly on strategy—which means the more you play it, the better you get. The object of the game is to take your character on a journey around the board, collecting wisdom and powers.

You can use the powers of the different cards to block other players from moving forward and to steal their wisdom.

Luke watches as I unload the board, the game pieces, and the card deck. Once everything is set up, I walk him through how to play. I kind of expect him to get bored, because it's pretty detailed, and I keep getting distracted and going off on tangents about the characters and their various back stories. But I'm surprised to find he's listening intently, his eyes lit with interest, watching me.

We begin playing, and when I place down my first card —a *Swift Journey* card, to help me on my quest—I'm hit with a wave of happiness. I haven't played this game in so long and I miss it.

Luke plays a card and moves his game piece with a grin. He's picked it up easily and seems to be enjoying himself. I can't explain the strange feeling in my ribcage as I watch him play.

"What is it about board games, then?" he asks, draining his coffee and setting it aside. "Why do you love them so much?"

I play another card, thinking. "I guess there's an element of escapism. For a few hours you're in another world, not thinking about your own life. Plus, it's like a tiny universe that I can manipulate and control. I can use strategy, take risks and explore various outcomes, without worrying too much about how it will end. I want to win, but that's not really the point for me. It's about playing with different outcomes."

Luke nods, moving his game piece forward. "It sounds a lot like video games. Do you ever play them?"

I shake my head, pushing my glasses up my nose.

"You'd like them, I think. Escapism, strategy, adventure." He plays a card, then looks up at me with a secretive little smile. It's not until then that I notice he's attempting to back my character into a corner.

My lips curl wryly. "If you think you can distract me from what you are doing with conversation, you are wrong." I know this game better than him. I set down a card that sends him halfway back around the board and he laughs.

"Not at all. I'm enjoying talking about games with you."

I meet his gaze, expecting to see another mischievous sparkle there, but his expression is genuine and open. He means what he's saying, and that realization creates a warm glow in my chest. He brought me to this place, knowing I'd love it. He *wants* to talk about—to play—games with me. He's having fun.

And that makes me feel something I don't want to acknowledge. Something that isn't purely a physical attraction. Something else altogether.

I shove the feeling away and give an uneven laugh. "It's your turn," I say, gesturing to the board.

We play for another hour and a half, ordering more coffee, talking about board games versus video games. By the time we finish up—I won, of course—I'm equal parts relieved and disappointed.

Luke smiles at me as he tucks the cards back into the box. "You could totally do this, you know."

"Do what?"

"Open a board game cafe."

I cast my gaze over the games and coffee counter again. A cheer goes up from one of the *Catan* guys and I smile.

Could I do this?

A tingle zips up my spine at the thought of owning this place, coming here every day, spending my time surrounded by coffee and books and games. It would be a nerd's haven; they'd come by the dozens, and—

I deflate as reality hits. I mean, what nerds? Only a handful of like-minded people live in my town at best, and somehow I don't think that's enough to sustain an entire business.

I set my coffee down with a sigh. "I don't think so."

"Why not? We already talked about the business stuff. You can learn that."

"I know," I say, tracing my finger around the rim of my cup. "And you're probably right. But there's a lot more to it than that. It wouldn't work in my town. There aren't enough nerds." I watch a group at another table as a heated debate breaks out over the game's rules.

Luke follows my gaze and chuckles. "Yeah, you need the nerds. Have you ever thought about doing it somewhere else?"

I shrug. While I'd spent a lot of time choosing paint colors and imagining the floor plan, I'd never mapped out the practical details of starting this business, because I'd always dismissed it as unrealistic. But now that I'm sitting in this blissful place, I almost can't imagine *not* doing it.

"You could do it in New York."

I choke on a laugh. "You're kidding."

"Why not?"

I study his face. He's serious; he actually thinks I could just move to New York, like, *no big deal.* As if starting a business wasn't daunting enough, I could *also* move to the other side of the planet—to a city that terrifies me—to pursue this crazy idea of starting my own cafe.

Except, it's not *that* crazy, is it? This cafe was once the dream of its owner. People start businesses all the time. And this place is busy; four more tables have filled up since the vibrator fiasco. If they can do it, why can't I?

And as for New York... I feel a nervous sort of exhilaration when I stop to think about it, because I'm not nearly as scared as I was when I first arrived. I might not have conquered the subway yet, but I'm comfortable in the West Village and getting cabs to Luke's place in Chelsea. I'm getting there.

I glance again at Luke, wondering how he's managed to do this—to take something that I assumed was a fantasy and make me consider it as a possibility. Despite the din around us, all of his attention is focused on me, on my dream of running a cafe like this.

"Maybe." Because maybe *I* couldn't do this, but... could Harriet 2.0?

I shift uneasily as realization washes over me. I was so mad at Luke for not telling me he was married on the plane, but I lied too. No wonder he believes I could move here and open a cafe. He thinks I'm my fearless alter ego.

But I'm not, am I? She's a fantasy self I tried on to impress a sexy stranger on a plane because I thought I'd never see him again.

Oh God. I'm a complete hypocrite.

And just like that, all my anger towards him seems unjustified. Especially when I consider how sweet he's been.

"Luke..." I rub my forehead and exhale. "I'm sorry if I've been kind of a bitch to you."

"When?"

"Just, you know, when I found out you were married and all that."

He chuckles. "It's okay. I can understand why you were angry that I didn't tell you."

"Yeah, but you're right—we both thought we'd never see each other again."

His eyes track over my face. "I'm glad we did though," he says, and my pulse surges. We stare at each other for one, two, three beats, the air between us crackling. His gaze ignites with something both foreign and familiar, and my mouth goes dry.

Fuck, I can't take this unspoken thing between us. Not talking about it is making it worse. Surely having it out in the open would be better than this. Anything would be better than this.

"Do you ever think about it?"

Luke's eyebrows rise. "Think about what?"

"The plane."

"Are you kidding?" He grunts a disbelieving laugh. "I haven't been able to *stop* thinking about it." The rough edge to his voice makes my blood rush hot under my skin. "And after last night—" he cuts himself off with a shake of his head. "Never mind."

"Last night?"

"When you were... bent over the kitchen island like that..." He swallows thickly. "I've thought about it even more."

Holy shit.

Molten heat spreads down my limbs, pooling low in my belly. He's thought about me bent over the kitchen island? I almost can't breathe at the thought.

Well, I was wrong. Talking about this is not helping in the slightest.

His eyes search mine, as if looking for some kind of answer from me, but I can't form words. Just when I think I can't take it for another second, he wrenches his gaze away.

"We should probably go," he mumbles.

I suck in a breath, snatching up the game and taking it back to the shelves. He's right—we need to go. I need to get some space from him. Now.

17

Michael and Alex are on their way out when I arrive back at the apartment that evening, and I'm relieved to have some time to myself.

Alex, however, is plagued by guilt. "I'm so sorry we have to leave," she says as I kick my shoes off. "Michael's agent wanted to have dinner with us, and—"

"It's fine! Seriously. I hope you guys have a nice time."

Alex slips her heels on with a grin. "I had an idea, though. Since I'm so swamped with work, I thought I'd ask Luke to take you sightseeing."

My stomach wobbles. "Oh, you don't have to do that. I'm sure he's busy."

"He's off work right now," Michael says, pulling on his dinner jacket. "He can spare a day to show you around. After all, we're about to be family."

Something about those words makes me a little uneasy, but I push the feeling aside. "Are you sure—"

"I just texted him." Alex grabs her bag and leans in to peck me on the cheek. "He said he'll take you tomorrow."

"Great," I mumble as the door closes behind them. I

head into Henry's room and set my bag down with a frown, processing this. It's hardly ideal. Not just because I don't want to play tourist; I also shouldn't be spending extra time with Luke.

After that conversation at the board game cafe this afternoon, I had to get out of there. The chemistry between us was intense and it freaked me out. It's getting harder to ignore how attracted I am to him, despite the fact that he's still technically married and—I seem to keep forgetting—I'm here for Alex. Nothing good can come of pursuing the attraction between us.

But, fuck... I'm so drawn to him. Sure, he's gorgeous—anyone with eyes can see that—but it's not just his good looks. He loves all the same things I do, maybe even more than me. I've never met a guy who is happy to spend hours playing games, or discuss the merits of different game formats, or compare the book version of my favorite stories to the films. He's a nerd, through and through, like me. We're kindred spirits in that way, and I think part of me recognized that on the plane, even before I knew any of that stuff about him. It's like my soul just knew his, or something.

And not only that—he's thoughtful, too. He called me when he thought I was upset, he went out of his way to take me to that cafe today, and he's been so encouraging with my own cafe idea. No one has ever cheered me on like that before and it's really nice.

I know I'm not the only one feeling this thing between us, not after what he said to me today. Every time I replay his words—*I haven't been able to stop thinking about it*—I feel like I'm going to explode.

If I'm going to spend the whole day with him tomorrow, I need to take the lid off this pressure cooker. At least I have the apartment to myself. I wouldn't normally attempt this; I never feel the urge since it's always proven to be fruitless. But ever since I met Luke, let's just say... I haven't been able to stop thinking about it. About sex. About *him*.

My gaze lands on my bag and I reach down, pulling out the John Stamos box. Alex spent good money on this, and I *am* in a bit of a pickle with the whole Luke situation. May as well do the logical thing here. And I'm not going to lie, I am a little curious what all the fuss is about...

With vibrators, that is. Not John Stamos.

I open the box and pull out the plastic, removing the device from the packaging. Then I hold it up to investigate more closely. I'm sure it's a gimmick, as Cat said, but what happens when I turn the base around like—

Oh.

The whole thing starts vibrating in my hand, and even though it's quiet and I'm home alone, I fumble to shut it off, terrified someone can hear.

I glance at the box again, noting the words "Completely Waterproof" on the side, and an idea hits me. At least if I were in the shower, the water would hide the noise of the vibration, should anyone happen to come home, or...

Whatever. It will just make me feel more comfortable.

I change into a robe, tucking the device into the pocket and tiptoeing across the hall. I don't know why I'm creeping about the place like everyone is home and knows what I'm doing. I need to damn well relax.

Once inside the bathroom, I slide the lock and turn the shower on, then strip off my robe.

Okay. I can do this. I can use a vibrator and give myself an orgasm and calm down about Luke. Simple.

I step under the stream of water, feeling strangely nervous, which is ridiculous. Drawing in a deep breath, I tip my head back and let the water cascade over me, thinking of

Luke. I know it's probably not wise to think of *him* while I do this, but... come on. What else am I going to think about? He's the reason I'm in this mess.

I glide my hands down my chest and take my breasts into my hands, finding my nipples hard and waiting. I roll them between my fingers, letting my mind drift back to what Luke said today, about seeing me bent over the kitchen island. I remember the way he looked at me last night, the way his hands were in tight fists at his side, like he was struggling to stay in control. I wonder what would have happened if he'd lost control altogether. Would he have pushed my dress up over my ass? Gripped my hips? Yanked my panties aside and entered me? Heat pulses between my legs at the thought, and I drop my head forward against the shower wall, breathing hard.

I don't know what's wrong with me. I would *never* normally like the thought of being bent over anything, for Christ's sake. It just feels so demeaning, not to mention dangerous. I'd have no sense of control in that position—I'd be completely at his mercy. But the thought of being at Luke's mercy makes me want to do very dangerous things.

I reach for the vibrator and turn it on, leaning forward and bracing one arm against the shower wall, picturing Luke again. Then I lower the device between my legs, touching it to my most sensitive spot, and pleasure zings through me.

Woah. Okay, yeah. There might be something to this.

Closing my eyes, I give in to the fantasy that's been tempting me all afternoon. Instead of being bent over in the shower, I'm in Luke's apartment, face-down on the kitchen island. And instead of this inanimate device between my legs, it's Luke, driving into me relentlessly from behind. He's got his sexy glasses on, and one of his hands grasps my hip as he leans over to growl filthy things into my ear, his other hand fisting in my hair. He fucks me like he did on the plane —hard and fast, holding nothing back.

God, fucking him on the plane was so hot.

Those images come back to me now, one after the other. The way he asked *Do you like that?* as his fingers slipped between my thighs. The way he watched himself thrust into me like it was the best thing he'd ever seen. And when I think of the way he said *Ohhh fuck* when he couldn't hold back anymore, heat rushes up my legs. I collapse against the tiled wall as sensation crashes through me, my mouth falling open around a silent moan, my body riding the waves of pleasure.

I stay like that for a moment: propped up against the shower wall, catching my breath, waiting as I come down from the high.

Shit, that was... wow.

Straightening up, I turn off the device and set it aside, a surprised smile pushing at my lips. A sense of empowerment settles over me as I wash my tired and satisfied body. I don't need a man to experience that kind of pleasure. I can do it myself.

Well, with a little help from John Stamos.

I giggle, thinking about it. This whole time I assumed I wasn't a very sexual person, but I think I've just been doing it wrong—because that was freaking awesome. I might be more like Harriet 2.0 than I realized.

And, if I'm lucky, I've made it a little more bearable to be around Luke for the time being.

18

I'm still in my bathrobe, nursing a steaming cup of coffee, when there's a knock at the front door. After my time in the shower last night I slept amazingly well, and I'm feeling more relaxed about things with Luke. I think it was just built-up tension that needed a release. No wonder I was wound so tightly. No wonder I'm *always* wound so tightly.

I stand from the table and smooth my hair, wishing I'd had the forethought to get dressed when I woke up this morning. What if it's Luke at the door? He isn't supposed to be here for another hour, but—

The knock comes again, louder, and I hurry across the room. This might be for the best, anyway. A fluffy dressing gown, no makeup, and bed hair is sure to smother any flames of attraction between us.

But when I swing the door open, I come face to face with a woman and boy. The woman is stunning and my first thought is that she must be a model or actress or something.

Her perfectly sculpted brows knit together when she sees me. "Who are you?"

"I'm Harriet." I resist the urge to add, *You're knocking on our door, lady. Who the hell are you?*

"Who?" she asks, making no attempt to mask her irritation.

"Alex's sister."

"Oh. Right." She pushes past me into the apartment, dragging the boy in behind her.

"Excuse me——" I begin, but she whips around.

"Is Mike not up yet? I need him to take Henry for a few hours."

Ah. Henry.

I give him a friendly smile and embarrassment paints his cheeks.

"You must be Mel," I say, extending a hand.

She looks down at it, apparently trying to decide if I'm going to infect her with something. Then she gives it a limp shake, wincing with distaste as she does so.

Bloody hell. Alex wasn't kidding about her.

"Yes, yes." She flaps a hand. "Can I leave Henry with you? I need to go."

I glance at Henry, alarmed. What would Alex want me to do? I mean, he lives here, so I don't see why she can't leave him with me. And Alex and Michael will be up soon.

"Er, sure. If you don't mind, Henry?"

He shrugs, heading into the kitchen and grabbing himself a bowl of cereal.

"Great. I'll be back to get him by four," Mel says as she breezes past me.

"But I thought you said only a few hours? I don't know if——"

"Thanks, bye!" The door swings shut behind her with a thud.

I exhale, wandering back into the kitchen. Henry is

seated at the table, tucking into a bowl of Cheerios. His dark hair slants across his forehead, his eyes focused on his bowl. I return to my seat and pick up my coffee, taking a long gulp.

So that's Mel. She's... interesting.

Oh, who am I kidding? She's terrifying. She's statuesque and stunningly gorgeous, with glorious long dark hair and legs up to her armpits. Not only is she beautiful, she certainly seems confident—a little demanding, if not forceful.

Or just plain rude.

Poor Alex. It must be awful having her as the ex.

As if reading my mind, Henry glances up with a grimace. "Sorry about my mom."

I bite my tongue and sip my coffee. "She seems... nice."

He snorts, staring into his cereal. "You're the first person to ever say that," he mutters. Then he looks up at me again. "I'm so glad Dad met Alex. She's really cool."

This makes me smile. See? I knew Alex had nothing to worry about with Henry.

"So I guess you're going to be my aunt," he continues.

"Huh." I hadn't given it much thought, but he's right.

Apprehension threads through me. Am I ready to be an aunt? What does an aunt do? Am I supposed to be a fun aunt, sneaking him booze and teaching him about girls? If that's the case he's going to be seriously disappointed—and *not* because I don't live here.

I chuckle to myself as I realize that this is exactly what Alex is going through right now, except on a much larger scale. She's going to be a mother—a step-mother, but still. It sounds like she's going to need to play a pretty big role in his life.

I hear a door open and a few moments later Alex

appears in the kitchen, yawning. "Henry?" she asks, blinking in the morning light.

"Hey, Alex. Mom just dropped me off. I hope that's okay?"

Alex's face creases with stress. "Well, actually..."

Henry sighs, his gaze falling back to his bowl, and Alex stops herself. She wanders over, leaning down to put an arm around his shoulders and give him a squeeze.

"That's totally fine, bud. This is your home. You know you're always welcome here." She catches my eye and sends me a worried look. I know she was planning to write today and I think Michael has a meeting later.

"Why don't you come out with us today, Henry?" I hear myself say. If I'm going to go sightseeing with Luke, Henry could come along. In fact, that's brilliant! With Henry there, things will have to stay PG-13.

"That's a great idea." Alex looks at Henry with a hopeful smile. "What do you think, bud? A day out with Uncle Luke and Aunt Harriet?"

Uncle Luke and Aunt Harriet. I think back to what Michael said last night about us being family and cringe. I should definitely *not* imagine Luke bending me over his kitchen island.

I glance at Henry, suddenly desperate for him to join us. He happily agrees, and I realize that this could be my chance to show him I'm a fun aunt. This could be good.

I pull my phone out to let Luke know Henry will be coming too, and he responds right away.

Luke: Great! Make sure you bring a change of comfortable clothes and wear contacts.

What? I reread his words, frowning. Where the hell is he taking us?

"THIS IS AWESOME!" Henry exclaims, racing ahead with excitement.

I stare at the ropes in front of us, trying to make sense of the absurd scene. A man swings from a trapeze before releasing his grip, spinning through the air and landing below.

"Do you like it?" Luke asks, turning to me. His eyes are bright and his mouth is curved in an expectant smile. It reminds me of that moment on the plane where he asked me in a rough voice, *Do you like that?* My gaze strays to his navy-blue hooded sweater and jeans as I recall my fantasy from in the shower last night, and a flush creeps up my neck.

I force my attention back to the ropes, relieved he can't read my mind. So far, not off to a good start.

"When Alex suggested I take you out, I knew you wouldn't want to go to any of the big tourist spots," he continues. "But I thought this would be perfect for you."

I blink uncomprehendingly. Why the hell would Luke think this is perfect for me? What does he have planned next? Lion taming? Flame-throwing? Perhaps I'll have to walk on a high-wire over the Hudson River?

"You love this sort of thing, right?" Luke's grin is huge. "It's not exactly skydiving or zip-lining, but it's supposed to be fun."

Oh, right. Of course. My alter ego loves this stuff. She's probably done it a hundred times before and is a complete natural. I bet this is how she warms up for an afternoon of BASE jumping.

I'm about to tell him I can't do this—to shatter this illusion he has of me as some outgoing, adventurous person—but I stop when I see his expression. He's proud and excited; he's gone out of his way to bring me here because he thought I'd love it.

Shit. I'm going to have to go through with this.

I plaster on a smile, trying to ignore the way my gut is turning like a corkscrew. "This is... fantastic. Thank you."

He beams back at me. "I'm so glad you like it! Let's get changed, then we can get started."

I wander into the bathrooms in a daze. My hands are shaking as I change into the leggings and T-shirt I brought in my bag. I can't believe I'm about to climb up thirty feet to a tiny platform and hurl myself off. Sure, I'll be attached to a rope and clinging onto a thin bar, but is that really any consolation?

There must be some way I can get out of this. I could fake a heart attack, or faint, or pretend I've suddenly got intense, uncontrollable diarrhea...

My legs feel robotic as they take me back out to meet Luke, and I realize that if I'm not careful I might have a very real panic attack. I can already feel my lungs tightening and adrenaline spiking through my veins.

Luke isn't there when I get out, so I take a seat beside Henry, making myself take careful, calming breaths.

There's nothing to be scared of, I tell myself. People come here for *fun*. It can't be that bad. If they have a whole business based on this then it can hardly be risky, right? This is America, where everyone sues everyone at the drop of a hat. You couldn't run a business like this if it was dangerous.

Except, what was that waiver I signed on the way in? I might have signed it without paying much attention—*not* because I was looking at Luke's ass in his jeans—but now that I think about it, I'm certain the words "serious injury" and "death" were in there.

Oh God.

Henry glances at me with a grin. "Isn't this so cool?"

I manage a nod, drawing another deep breath to control my spiraling anxiety. Luke appears at that moment in his sweats, but I'm too distracted by the looming trapeze to appreciate how sexy he looks.

He sends me a warm grin and guilt seeps into me. He's gone to all this trouble to organize this, just for me, and here I am being ungrateful. Well, terrified mostly, but also ungrateful.

"You ready?" He gestures to the tiny platform suspended by ropes.

"Yes!" I squeal, attempting to inject enthusiasm into my voice even as it quivers. "Let's do this!"

The instructor runs through a few of the basics with us, before strapping me into a harness and clipping some ropes on. Then I have to rub my hands in chalk and follow her up a rope ladder. My heart is hurling itself against my ribs, trying to escape from my body and what I'm about to do. I don't blame it. And I'm going to need more chalk because I'm sweating this off. I can barely remember to breathe at this point, let alone *control* my breathing. Each rung of the ladder feels like a nail in my coffin. I wish I'd hugged Alex tighter when I said goodbye this morning.

I should just come clean and tell Luke I can't do this. So Harriet 2.0 isn't real, I made her up, and I'm not some kind of daredevil. He'll understand, won't he?

But as I clamber onto the platform and cling to the ropes for dear life, I make the mistake of glancing down at Luke and Henry. Luke's face is lit with joy as he gives me a thumbs-up.

Henry cups his hands around his mouth and yells, "Go, Aunt Harriet!"

Oh Christ.

On wobbling legs, I manage to make it to the middle of the platform. The woman holds me by the back of my waist harness (Why? In case I get too enthusiastic and fling myself off prematurely?) and fiddles with some ropes, while I try my best not to black out. My pulse is deafening.

Then she pulls the trapeze bar forward with a big pole and, somehow, it's in my hands.

"Whenever you're ready," she says.

If I wasn't convinced I was breathing my last breath, I'd laugh. *Whenever I'm ready.* Yeah, right.

Okay, no. I need to take back control here. My therapist years ago taught me to tune into my physical senses to stop myself from getting swept up in my frantic thoughts, so I force my attention back to my body. It's trembling, and my chest is tight, and my head is spinning. I can't feel my legs. But the slower I breathe down into my belly, the more I start to relax. I mean, "relax" is a relative term at this point, but it's helping.

I remind myself of all the ways I've stepped outside my comfort zone over the past week. I flew to New York alone. I had sex with a hot stranger on an airplane. I made new friends and explored the city. I dyed my hair. I now own—and use—a vibrator, for God's sake. I can handle a little swing through the air.

I can do this.

I take a deep, deep breath, close my eyes, and before I can talk myself out of it, I step off the platform.

And just like that, I'm doing it—I'm flying through the air, gripping tightly to the trapeze bar. All I'm aware of is the roar of blood in my ears, the whoosh of the air as I swing. Then I open my eyes and for the first time since we arrived up here, I notice everything beyond the trapeze rig. I notice where we are: by the Hudson River. I notice the Statue of Liberty, all the way down in the harbor, and the skyline around us—the stunning view that I almost didn't see.

Wow.

My body glides smoothly through the cool air and my ears tune in to everything else. I hear Luke and Henry cheering me on and whistling below, and elation and pride burst like a firework in my chest.

Oh my God. I did it. I did this bold thing and it is *incredible*.

As my swing slows, I take another lungful of air and let go of the trapeze bar. I land with a bounce on the net below, then scramble to the edge to find the others.

Henry is already halfway up the platform for his turn, but Luke is right by the net with a mile-wide grin, his arms outstretched to help me down. I reach for his hand, but instead he grabs my waist, lifting me from the net. I'm so amped up that I leap at him, wrapping my arms around his neck and winding my legs around his waist as he spins me in circles.

"That was amazing," he murmurs into my ear, and I squeeze him tight. If it wasn't for him, I wouldn't have done that. I wouldn't have forced myself to do something so daring, and proved that, actually, I *can* do things that scare me.

"Thank you," I breathe. I wait for him to put me down, but he holds me tighter. And I might be imagining it, but I'm sure he just smelled my hair. I huff in his scent too, feeling giddy. And for the first time, I let myself acknowledge the little wish that aches inside me: that he wasn't married, that everything was different—that he could, in some impossible way, be mine.

Eventually, he loosens his grip and sets me down. He gazes at me, his eyes animated and his mouth stretched into the biggest smile. My skin tingles from where his hands still rest on my waist, and my heart is racing again—only this time it's not from the trapeze.

I've never felt more alive. This is better than the plane; this is something else. I'm struck again by Luke's ability to push me out of my comfort zone and make me feel like someone else, and all I want to do is kiss him.

"Uncle Luke!"

Luke's hands drop from my waist and we turn to Henry who's paused on the edge of the platform, ready to jump.

"You can do it, Henry!" Luke calls.

Henry launches himself with ease, calling "Woohoo!" as he goes. We watch as he swings and makes a big leap onto the net, then bounces there, grinning.

"My turn, I guess." Luke laughs nervously, rubbing his hands together. "I'm not sure if I can do this."

"What?" I say, surprised. "You totally can."

"I'm not like you, Harriet. I'm not as adventurous—"

"No." I shake my head, wanting to at least tell him some of the truth. "That wasn't easy for me. If *I* can do this, you definitely can. Besides, you'll regret it if you don't."

"You're right." He straightens up. "I just need to get past my fear."

"Well—" I chuckle, putting on my Yoda voice. "Fear is the path to the dark side."

A low laugh rolls out of him. There's something swirling in his gaze as he takes a step closer, but just as he's about to say something, Henry climbs off the net beside us.

"Are you going, Uncle Luke?"

"Yeah." Luke nods, not lifting his eyes from me. "No regrets, right?"

"Right," I murmur, watching him go.

And as he climbs the ropes, I can't help but wonder if he was talking about the trapeze, or something else entirely.

19

I wander the abandoned subway platform, straining my ears for the sound of approaching trains that I know will never come. It's eerily quiet down here.

Luke strolls past, hands tucked into the pockets of his hooded sweater, head cocked to read the plaques dotted along the platform. Up ahead, Henry ducks into an old subway car.

After we finished our time on the trapeze—I went three more times, each one a little easier than the last—we changed and headed out. When Luke suggested we come to the New York Transit Museum in Brooklyn I wasn't sure what to expect, but I've got to hand it to him; this place is awesome.

Entering the museum was like entering any other subway station: down the steps with the green railing, all the way underground to a disused subway platform, lined on either side by old trains as far as you can see. The difference here is that there isn't the screech of trains coming and going, the press of the crowd to get on board, the feeling that

I could be mugged or pushed onto the tracks at any second. I'm surprised that—as much as I hate the subway in Manhattan—I'm captivated here, walking through these old carriages, thinking of all the people who rode them and what their lives might have been like.

I lean closer to read a plaque that dates the carriage in front of me back to 1907 and utter a reverent "Wow."

Luke stands beside me, reading the information he's probably read a hundred times before. He told me he comes here all the time, and I couldn't help but find that nerdy little fact adorable—even though I know I shouldn't.

"Isn't it awesome?" he says.

I nod, amazed at how old the carriage before me is. People have been riding these trains since the early twentieth century and here I am, a modern woman, scared of the subway. I shrink with shame.

Luke angles his body towards me. "What is it?"

I blush and smooth my hands over my dress. How can he tell something is up?

"You okay?"

I meet his gentle gaze. "When we went to the board game cafe yesterday, and when we came over to Brooklyn today, why did we take a cab and not the subway?"

He shrugs. "I thought you'd be more comfortable. Alex mentioned something about you not liking the subway. I was surprised by that at first—I mean, you go skydiving and do all these wild things." He shakes his head, smiling to himself.

An uneasy laugh ripples out of me as I look across the platform of the museum. No wonder he was confused. Who's afraid of the subway but happily jumps from an airplane?

Luke leads us off the platform into the empty subway carriage, and I glance around in wonder. Unlike the subway cars today, we have to step onto the end to enter. The body of the car is made of wood—no steel or plastic—and the interior is painted a dark red, with windows lining each side and leather handles hanging down along the center. Seats line the walls like the modern cars of today, but many of them face forward and back, like a bus. They're covered with a woven, wicker material, and the whole thing makes me feel like I've stepped back in time.

I check ahead for Henry, then spot him out on the platform further back. As I wander down the middle of the car, I wonder what the people on here were doing, where they were going, a hundred years ago.

"See?" Luke says behind me with a smile in his voice. "What is there to be scared of?"

I sit on one of the seats, thinking of the trapeze I just swung on, and wonder how to explain it to him. "I think, on the actual subway, I don't like all the people. I guess it's the same reason I don't want to go to the major tourist places. I get anxious around the crowds. People are unpredictable, and sometimes I don't feel safe—" I cut myself off with a grimace.

I hate talking about this stuff. It feels like a weakness of mine, like some deeply flawed part of who I am, despite the fact that multiple therapists have told me not to think of it that way. But I've been anxious as long as I can remember, and very few people have been understanding about it. There were some girls at high school who were especially nasty to me during those times I couldn't quite keep it together—one particular panic attack comes to mind. Boyfriends and even friends in the past have been exasperated by it. Steph spends a lot of time trying to push me out of my comfort zone, but it's because she worries I'm missing out on things. She doesn't know how bad it was for me at high school, and I prefer it that way. Because if she *did* know about that part of my life, she might treat me differently for it.

"I know it's silly," I mumble.

"It's not." Luke lowers himself onto the seat beside me. "We all have our thing."

A comforting kind of warmth flows through me at his words. He's not judging me and that's... really nice.

His knee nudges mine. "Remember me on the plane? I was terrified."

Our eyes lock and my heart bumps against my breast-bone as I think of the way I took his hand to comfort him, the way I kissed him and made him forget everything. "I remember," I murmur.

Henry passes outside, waving at us through the window as if we were commuters. Luke and I wave back, watching as he steps onto the next carriage.

"You're so good with him," I say, smiling. Then before I can think better of it, I ask, "Do you want kids of your own?"

Luke's jaw tightens and he sits silent for a moment. "Yes. It's one of the reasons..." he trails off and I fill in the blanks.

"She didn't want kids?"

"No." He lets out a long, weary breath. "It's not entirely Dena's fault. I thought I didn't want kids either. For years I was focused on my career, and it felt like a family would just get in the way of that." He gives a sad shake of his head. "But as I watched Mike raise Henry, and I got to spend time being Uncle Luke... I love it. I realized I do want kids of my own, but she wasn't changing her mind. It was just one of many problems between us, but it was the one I couldn't let go of. I couldn't give that up for her, and I didn't want to resent her for it later."

"That sounds tough." I can't imagine being in that position. I've always known I want kids one day, when I meet the right guy. My mind unhelpfully points out what a great dad Luke would be, but I tell it to *shut up* and focus on the conversation. "It must have been hard to go through your marriage ending without your family's support. I'm sure if you'd told Michael, he would have understood."

"Yeah, he would have. Probably better than most. That's the problem."

"What do you mean?"

Luke sighs. "Mike's been through a lot over the past few years. His divorce completely wrecked him, and when Mel dragged him through court to fight for custody of Henry, he became a shell of a man. I honestly thought he'd never be happy again."

I nod. I remember Alex saying something about him being in a bad place when they met.

"But now he is," Luke continues. "And after everything he's been through, he deserves to enjoy it without worrying about me and my shit, without... I don't know, feeling guilty, because my marriage is over when he's the happiest I've ever seen him." He picks at a loose piece of wicker on the seat between us. "I know it sounds stupid, but I didn't want to do anything to take away from that."

There's a pang in my chest at how selfless that is. "It doesn't sound stupid," I murmur. "It sounds like you just want him to be happy. But... you also deserve to be happy." I reach out and place my hand over his, squeezing. As soon as I feel the warmth of his skin under my palm, I realize touching him was a big mistake.

Suddenly, it's too quiet down here in this old subway car,

without the sound of trains or commuters. There doesn't even seem to be anyone else in this part of the museum. I don't know where Henry has gone. Silence stretches between us and my breathing goes shallow, like I can't suck in enough air. I can feel the weight of Luke's gaze on me, and when I bring myself to look at him, my pulse skips at the question in his espresso-brown eyes. The corner of his mouth lifts in a tentative smile, and for the first time I notice a small dimple in his right cheek underneath his scruff. I move my gaze over his face, from the chicken pox scar under his left eye, to the bristles along his jaw, until they land on his full lips.

God, he is so unbelievably gorgeous. It takes all my strength to pull my hand away again.

"Harriet..." His voice has a gravelly burr to it that makes my thighs quiver. He inhales to say more when Henry appears in the carriage in a frenzy of excitement.

"Did you guys see the big engine down the end?"

Luke drags his gaze from me to smile at his nephew. "Not yet, buddy. Let's go."

Henry dashes off again and Luke stands, reaching for my hand and pulling me up. I try not to notice the way he twines his fingers with mine as we head out of the carriage, the way he doesn't let go until we are back on the subway platform.

AN HOUR LATER, we head out and grab a late lunch, strolling through Brooklyn Heights as we eat. Luke spends the time telling me about the area and Henry shows me some of the places he knows. I'm pleased to have him there as a buffer between Luke and me. Otherwise, who knows what I'd do.

I don't think my time in the shower last night worked quite as well as I thought it did because, fuck, the force is strong in this one. Every time I look at Luke I'm sure he can tell exactly how I feel. He's feeling the same things, too—it's written all over his face. And even though I know that nothing should happen between us, I'm also aware that my self-control is not bulletproof. If Luke were to straight-up tell me he wants me, would I be able to say no?

I don't want to find out.

After walking for some time, we arrive at the foot of the Brooklyn Bridge and Luke turns to me with a grin. "You okay to walk across here?"

I hesitate, glancing at the crowd.

"I know it's a little touristy," he says. "But it's worth it. The views are amazing, especially on a day like today."

We both look up at the azure sky, not a single cloud in sight. It is a beautiful day and I don't want to miss seeing the city from the bridge. Besides, after the trapeze this morning, this doesn't seem so bad.

"Okay."

He leads the way and we start to climb, Henry racing ahead. The wooden walkway takes us up higher than the traffic, with a white line dividing the narrow space. We have to keep to the left, because cyclists come tearing down the right, and the first time it happens I get a fright and lurch into Luke's side. He chuckles and switches so he's walking on the outside of me, and I pretend I don't find that incredibly sweet. I also pretend I don't want his hoodie, which he offers when he sees me shivering in the wind. I know if I snuggle into the warmth and smell of his sweater, it will be all downhill from there. And if I see those forearms of his again? Forget it. I'll be a goner.

He shares things about the bridge as we walk, like when

it was built and how long it took and how many people died in the process. I find the last bit a little morbid and when he catches my expression, he apologizes.

But I have to laugh, because he's trying to make this good for me. I realize again how grateful I am that he's making such an effort, because I'm certain I wouldn't have come here on my own.

We slow our walking as we arrive at the first of the two big towers of the bridge. It's such an iconic sight—the pointed Gothic stone arches and suspension cables stretching out to the deck below like a giant man-made spiderweb.

"Thanks for taking the time to show me this stuff," I say to Luke as we stop to read a brass plaque set into the stone.

"You're welcome."

We wander over to the railing and I glance at him. "To be honest, I was nervous when Alex said you were going to take me sightseeing, but it's been great."

"I'm glad you enjoyed the museum, and the trapeze was really fun. Actually, this week has been the most fun I've had in ages."

"Yeah." I smile to myself. "Me too."

I lean against the railing and look out at the glistening water, watching a water taxi and mulling over Luke's words. Despite our circumstances, this has been one of the best weeks I've had in a long time. In fact, I can't remember a time when I've done so many fun—and challenging —things.

It's not just getting out of my comfort zone. It's Luke. When I'm around him, I feel different. I connect to an inner sense of self I didn't know existed. He makes me feel alive, and sexy, and—hell—turned on, all the time. Ever since we had sex on the plane, he's awoken some dormant part of me and I want to explore that more. Because if I feel like that after ten minutes alone with him in an airplane bathroom, after a few stolen moments between wedding tasks and sightseeing, imagine how it could be if we were actually... together.

God. I'm having some dangerous thoughts today.

I can feel the heat of Luke beside me, and when I turn to look at him, his eyes are roaming my face. "I'm not imagining this, am I? This thing between us?"

My heart kicks and I swallow hard. "No. You're not."

"And we..." He glances along the bridge to check Henry is out of earshot. "We shouldn't act on it, right?"

I give a humorless laugh. "Are you asking me or telling me?"

"I—" He wipes a hand down his face, looking pained. "Ugh, I don't know."

I study the cars as they pass under the metal beams below us, and draw on my last reserves of self-restraint. "No, we shouldn't act on it. You're still married, and even if you weren't, you want Alex and Michael to *think* you're married, so..." I trail off, shrugging.

Luke nods, his brow pulling low. "Yeah. I can't ruin their wedding with my drama."

"Anyway," I say, laughing to try and lighten the mood. "It's weird either way, right? Your brother is marrying my sister and we're essentially in-laws in a week and a half. We'll be like family."

"I guess that is a little weird." His mouth twists in a dirty smile. "Mike would *not* be happy if he knew the things I've imagined doing to his wife's little sister."

He—*what*?

Heat explodes in my core and I tighten my hands around the railing. There's dynamite in Luke's eyes as they sink down the length of my body then slowly climb back to my face. I want so badly to ask him what he's imagined, but somehow, I stop myself. Knowing the details of that would make this impossible.

Instead, I take a fortifying breath and do my best to send him a disapproving look. "You probably shouldn't say stuff like that."

"Yeah." He chuckles softly. "Sorry. I'll try to behave myself." His forehead wrinkles with a frown and he reaches into his pocket, pulling out his phone. "Shit, I need to take this. Is that okay?"

I wave a hand, desperate for some space from him. "Go for it."

He steps away to take the call, and I stare out over the water, replaying his words: *I'll try to behave myself.* That's good, I suppose, though I'm not entirely sure I believe him. And worse, I don't want him to. It will take a million shower sessions with John Stamos to get this out of my system, and maybe not even then. How are we going to make this situation work with the attraction between us? We still have to finalize all the wedding tasks and my self-control is running out fast.

Luke finishes his call and appears back beside me, leaning down onto his elbows on the railing. His whole face is lit up as he gazes over the water, his cheeks rounded into a grin. I know I should look away—should walk away—but I can't. There's something so magnetic about his smile, his energy. And when he turns to me and his smile tugs wider, my insides melt.

"You seem happy," I say.

"Yeah. I just got some great news."

I tilt my body towards him, relieved the intensity from

before has passed and we've returned to the usual ease between us. "What is it?"

He goes to speak again, then spots Henry walking our way. Grinning, he gestures down the bridge. "I'll tell you later. Come on."

20

Alex holds up her glass of champagne, her eyes gleaming with pride. "Congratulations to Michael on his latest book deal."

Luke dropped Henry off at Mel's place earlier and now we're at a bar called Deidrick's in the West Village, celebrating the result from Michael's meeting with his agent today. It's a funky little place: low lighting, large bar, and round, wooden tables along one wall. There's a dance floor off to one side—currently empty—and a DJ playing early 2000s songs in one corner. I bet the dance floor gets packed later.

Michael's cheeks flush with modesty as we all raise our glasses. I meet Luke's gaze and tip my glass ever so slightly in his direction. We might be here to celebrate Michael's book deal, but every time I glance over and see Luke's broad smile, the way his whole posture looks more relaxed than I've ever seen, I can tell something is up with him. Since the bridge he's been different. Lighter, more playful, just... happy. It's infectious.

"So how was sightseeing?" Alex asks over her glass. "Where did you go?"

"I took her to the Transit Museum," Luke says, grinning at me.

Michael groans. "Poor Harriet. I know you and Henry love it, but—"

"No." I shake my head with a laugh. "It was awesome. And it made me reconsider my fear of the subway."

"That's great!" Alex says. "The only way to get comfortable with the subway is to just go on it a lot. After a while, you get used to it."

Huh, kind of like the trapeze. The only way I got comfortable with it was to *do* it. No amount of thinking about it and mentally rehearsing helped. I had to throw myself off the platform.

Of course, I'll need to *avoid* throwing myself off the platform in the subway, but you get the point.

We talk about the museum for a while, sipping our champagne. When the bottle is empty, Alex stands and wanders to the bar, returning with another bottle and a tipsy grin.

"The only thing missing from the Transit Museum," Luke says as he pops open the champagne, "is a Platform Nine and Three-Quarters. Now *that* would be cool."

Alex holds out her glass, scrunching her nose. "What?"

Luke sends me a secret smile and my heart does a funny little hop. Because that *would* be cool, but I'm not thinking about that at all. I'm thinking about the man who would say something like that.

I slide Alex a grin. "It's a *Harry Potter* reference."

"Oh." She rolls her eyes. "You two are such nerds."

Luke chuckles as he refills my glass. "That may be the case, but you should have seen Harriet this morning. I took her to that trapeze school in Hudson River Park, and she was totally fearless."

"Really?" Alex gives me a doubtful look.

"Yeah." Luke nods, his eyes fixed on me. "She just got up there and went for it. I was actually a little freaked out but I figured if she could do it, then so could I."

"Wow," Alex says, impressed. "Harri, you're inspiring me, doing all these new things. Dyeing your hair, swinging from a trapeze, not to mention..." Her words are swallowed by giggles, her cheeks rosy from the alcohol. "Can I tell the guys, please?" I open my mouth to ask what she means, but she turns her attention to Luke and Michael. "You'll *never* guess what Harriet did on the plane ride over here."

Oh. Shit.

I pause, my glass halfway to my lips and my smile frozen on my face, dread rising inside me. I feel Luke stiffen at my side as Michael leans forward curiously.

"She hooked up with some random guy she met, in the airplane bathroom!"

Oh God, Alex.

I press my eyes shut as my stomach turns over. I wait for Luke to say something, or to stand and leave, but he laughs along with Michael. When I cautiously peel my eyes open, I find the three of them looking at me.

"Really?" Michael says with a disbelieving chuckle.

"Er..." I begin, setting my glass down, but Alex is on a roll.

"Oh, come on!" She swats me on the arm before focusing back on the guys. "She totally did. And she said it was the best sex she's ever had!" She thumps a hand on the table, chortling with laughter.

Heat sweeps up my neck and I concentrate on a spot on the table. I can't look at Luke. Or anyone. Ever again.

"Is that right?" I hear from beside me.

I risk a glance in Luke's direction. His mouth is half-tilted in a grin, eyebrows raised, and annoyance sizzles in my gut. He doesn't have to look so damn pleased about it. And he should *not* be encouraging this.

"The best sex you've ever had, huh?"

My cheeks are flaming as I reach for my glass of champagne again and gulp it down.

"I mean, how does that even happen?" Alex muses aloud, topping up my glass. "How do you end up in that situation?"

"Did he comfort you during some bad turbulence?" Michael suggests.

I grumble under my breath. If only I could tell them the truth: that *I* was the one looking after *him*. That might give me a little of my dignity back.

"Or maybe he gave up his seat so you could sit by the window and you couldn't resist such a chivalrous guy?" Alex's eyes become misty as her romantic imagination kicks into overdrive.

"Or maybe you threw yourself at him when he least expected it?" Luke chimes in and the other two roar with laughter. He gives me a knowing grin and I cut him a look of irritation.

"Um, no. That's definitely *not* what happened."

"Really? Maybe you"—he gestures vaguely for effect —"threw yourself into his lap? Or lured him into the bathroom when he was vulnerable?" He nudges my knee under the table and I swing a foot out to kick him, but hit the table leg instead.

Ow.

"Oh my God, Harri, is that what happened?" Alex asks, noticing my grimace.

"What?" I glance at her, horrified. "No!"

"Or maybe you simply begged the poor guy for sex?" Luke says, his lips twitching deviously.

A laugh bursts from Alex. "Harriet's not the type to beg for sex." She wipes her eyes, then turns and leans close to Michael, whispering something to him.

"Exactly." I send Luke a withering look. Honestly, I don't know what's gotten into him tonight.

"Are you sure?" he asks, swigging from his glass. "Are you sure you didn't say *please*?" He cocks a playful eyebrow and my face burns with shame.

Because I did say please, I know I did. I wanted it.

"Well, anyway," I mutter through gritted teeth, refilling my glass so I don't have to look at him. He might think this is hilarious, but two can play this stupid game. "It doesn't matter. I mean, the sex was alright, which is surprising considering how *very* quick it was. The whole thing was over before it could even begin, really."

I challenge Luke with my gaze, watching his smile falter. My mouth pulls into a satisfied smirk as his cheeks stain pink, and we stare at each other hard for a moment, neither one of us wanting to back down. Then his face falls, almost imperceptibly, and regret winds through me.

I suddenly remember Alex and Michael's presence, and when I glance at them in panic, I'm relieved—and not at all surprised—to find they're in a world of their own.

When I look back at Luke, his whole demeanor has changed. He's leaning back in his chair, sipping from his glass and gazing out across the bar, his smile gone. And even though he was being a real dick a moment ago, I just want to go back to the joking and teasing.

"Oh! Harri, I forgot to tell you." Alex leans forward, grinning. "Cat knows someone you might want to take as a date to the wedding."

I offer her a feeble smile. I should be happy about this, I know I should—I did, after all, ask her to find me someone—but I couldn't care less right now. And if I'm entirely honest, I know who I want to go to Alex's wedding with. But I can't.

"What's his name?" I ask, trying to muster some enthusiasm.

"Derek. He's a nice guy."

"Great. And, um, what does Derek do?"

"He's her accountant, I think."

There's a snort beside me, and I turn to peer at Luke. "What?"

"Accountant. What a boring job."

"So? Who cares?" I happen to agree with him, but I'm not exactly in a position to be turning this Derek away. Not when I'll have to spend the whole wedding watching Luke parade Dena around the place.

"What will you even talk about?" Luke asks.

"I don't know. We'll drink and dance. It's a wedding."

"Whatever," he huffs.

Jesus, what is his deal tonight? One minute he's laughing his head off and needling me about sex, the next he's sulking like a moody teenager.

"Is he cute?" I ask, fixing my attention back on Alex.

She thinks for a minute, then nods. "I think you'll like him. Medium height, clean shaven, blue eyes and blond hair."

I try not to cringe. He sounds like the antithesis of Luke, which right now feels like it would be unbearable.

Luke chuckles beside me and I glance at him sharply. "What now?"

He gazes down into his glass, shrugging. "Nothing. He sounds... great. Derek sounds like a great guy." His lips tighten into a smirk.

I stare at him for a moment, trying to understand why he's being such an absolute jerk, then it hits me.

Oh my God. Is he *jealous*?

I tilt my head, eying him, but he just looks down at his glass, brooding.

"Ooh, I love this song!" Alex exclaims as *Hey Ya* by Outkast comes on. She grabs Michael's hand and yanks him up. "You guys want to dance?"

"Maybe later," I mumble, and she bounces away to the dance floor with Michael, disappearing into the crowd. I turn to study Luke as he peels the label on the bottle of champagne, lost in thought. "What was that? All that shit about me begging you?"

He chuffs a quiet laugh, picking at the label. "I'm just in a weird mood, sorry. I got carried away playing along with them. And, er"—he glances over his shoulder, then back to the bottle—"I'm also sorry if the sex was... quick."

Okay, I didn't expect *that*. "It wasn't."

He looks up at me and apprehension lingers in his gaze. I sigh, wanting to soothe his poor, wounded ego. First person he has sex with after his marriage ends and I tell him it was crap.

"I shouldn't have said that," I murmur. "I was annoyed at you for winding me up. But, come on. You know how good it was on the plane."

A husky laugh escapes him as he appraises me, and for some reason, I find myself wanting to tell him just how significant the plane was to me.

"If I tell you something, will you promise not to judge me?"

"Of course."

"Alright." I slug back some champagne, checking we are still alone. "On the plane with you was the first time I ever..." I trail off, waiting for him to connect the dots, but he looks mystified. "It was the first time I ever, um"—I clear my throat—"climaxed."

His mouth forms a small O shape. "You hadn't climaxed during sex before?"

"No, I hadn't—" I shake my head, cringing. God, why did I mention this? "Um, I hadn't *ever* before."

His eyebrows shoot up. "*Never?*"

"Never."

"Until..."

"Yep."

His eyelids fall to half-mast and a breath gusts out of him. "So... I gave you your first orgasm."

I suck my bottom lip between my teeth, nodding.

"Holy—" he breaks off with a little growl. "Harriet, why are you telling me this?"

I lift a shoulder. "I don't know. It was a big deal for me, and you made it happen. I thought you might like to know."

A scowl drags his eyebrows together and he reaches for his glass. "You shouldn't have told me," he mutters, knocking back his champagne. Then he sits there, seething at me.

I frown. "Why are you being such a dick?"

"Excuse me?"

"Tonight, Luke. What's going on with you?"

He drains his glass and sets it down. After contemplating me for a moment, he forces the air from his lungs. "Fine. You know that call I took on the bridge?"

"Yeah?"

"That was my lawyer. He told me my divorce has been finalized. I am officially no longer married."

My lips part in surprise. "Really?"

He nods.

Right. Well. I'm not sure what to do with this information. And as I watch the way he twists his champagne glass on the table in front of him in agitation, I get the sense he isn't either.

"And you're... unhappy about that?" I venture. But that doesn't feel right. He seemed thrilled when he got the call.

"No. That relationship died a long time ago. If anything, I'm relieved."

"Then what's going on? You've been all over the place tonight."

"I know." He stares into his empty glass. "I'm just... struggling with something."

"With what?"

When he brings his gaze to mine, I can see the frustration smoldering in his eyes. "With the fact that there is something I want, right in front of me, and I can't have it."

Oh.

My pulse quickens, because I know he's talking about me. Desire spills through my veins and my hands tingle with the urge to grab his collar and yank him towards me, despite the fact that Alex and Michael are only a few feet away.

Goddammit. Why did his divorce have to be finalized *now*? Everything was fine when he was still married, when he was off-limits.

But with every heated glance he gives me, my self-control evaporates. Now that I know he's available—that he's feeling as desperate about this whole thing as I am—how much longer will I be able to keep resisting him?

I flush the toilet and reluctantly step out of the stall. I know I can't hide out in the bathroom all evening, but I had to get away from Luke. I'm not thinking straight. I'm going to need a *Keep Your Pants On* card to survive this.

Washing my hands, I gaze at my reflection in the mirror above the sink. I haven't been home to change since being out with Luke all day, and my makeup needs a touch-up. I redo my red lips, smacking them together at myself in the mirror. Then I remove the hair-tie from my bun and shake my hair loose, letting it tumble down over my shoulders. With a deep breath, I leave the bathroom.

It's fine, I tell myself. *You can do this. You can resist Luke.* So he's not married anymore. Big deal. Even though—if I'm being entirely honest—that was the main thing keeping me away from him.

God. I am the worst sister in the world.

Luke appears in the corridor as I'm closing the bathroom door behind me. "There you are. You were gone for a while and I wanted to make sure you're okay."

"Oh." A smile sneaks onto my lips. "I'm fine. Where are the others?"

He lifts his gaze to the ceiling. "On the dance floor, all over each other like they're sixteen."

I snort a laugh. So it's not just me who thinks they can be a bit much sometimes.

Luke sighs. "Listen, I'm sorry about tonight. I don't think I'm doing a very good job of dealing with what's going on between us here. It's just... this past week, I've felt more alive than I have in forever. I haven't had this much fun or connected with someone like this before, and—" he cuts himself off. "Anyway. I'm sorry."

"It's okay. It's not just you." I run a hand through my hair and pull it over one shoulder, watching the way Luke's eyes follow.

"You seem to be handling this much better than I am."

I get a flashback to the shower last night and warmth tinges my cheeks. "I'm really not, trust me. And now that I know you're not married anymore—" *Shit. Stop.* Luke's eyes darken and I attempt a laugh, wanting to break the tension. "I guess I only made things worse when I told you that you gave me my first orgasm." I mean it to be a joke, but he doesn't laugh.

"Yes." His voice is like sandpaper. "Do you know how hot that is? All it makes me want to do is give you a hundred more."

Well, *fuck*.

I can't stop the little whimper that comes from me. Luke's jaw flexes, his Adam's apple bobbing as he swallows, and my self-control dwindles a little more. I step closer, lifting a trembling hand and placing it on his chest, feeling his heart thump against my palm. We stare at each other for a long moment, neither of us daring to move.

Finally, he reaches out to tuck a strand of hair behind my ear.

"You're gorgeous, Harriet."

His fingertips graze my earlobe and my heart rate accelerates violently. I close my eyes, shivering as his touch trails down from my ear and along my neck. Goosebumps erupt across my skin and a heavy throb begins between my thighs. When I open my eyes, his gaze is hungry, desperate. Slowly, I slide my hand down his chest, over his firm stomach, listening to the way his breath catches. I reach his belt buckle, and the hunger in his eyes intensifies as I hook a finger into it and tug.

Fuck, who *am* I right now? What I wouldn't give for an invisibility cloak, so he could pin me against the wall, push my dress up, and—

"Excuse me."

We leap apart, both of us knocking into the walls behind us. For a split second I think it's Michael, catching us millimeters apart from kissing. Or more; God knows what I would have let Luke do to me back here.

But it's just some guy trying to get to the bathroom.

"Yes, sorry," Luke mutters, turning sideways so the guy can squeeze past in the narrow corridor.

I stare at Luke, my breath coming in little pants as I fight the urge to put my hands on him again. When Alex appears in the corridor a moment later, I nearly faint.

Oh my God. What if that had been her, a few seconds earlier? How the hell would we have explained *that*?

I tear my gaze from Luke and suck in a lungful of air, willing my pulse to slow down. I think I'm going to be sick.

"Hey guys!" Alex says merrily. "Luke, can I steal her for a minute?" She links her arm through mine. "Come to the bathroom with me."

Overwhelmed with relief that Alex has rescued me from myself, I follow her back into the ladies' room. I lean against the sink and take slow, controlled breaths while she ducks into a stall. I need to stop shaking, or she'll know something is up.

"I'm so glad you had fun sightseeing with Luke today," she says, flushing the toilet and coming back out. "I'm not surprised you guys are getting on so well. You have such similar interests."

"We're not getting on *that* well," I blurt. Heat climbs my neck. Why is my voice so shrill all of a sudden? "We're just working on wedding stuff for you."

"Speaking of the wedding," Alex says, pulling out her lipstick and applying a fresh coat in the mirror, "Mum called me today."

"What did she say?"

Alex sighs, tucking her lipstick back in her bag and turning to me. "The usual. But she really dialed it up this time. I think because it's getting closer to the wedding, she's panicking. She keeps telling me that I haven't known Michael that long, and asking if I'm *sure* I want to marry him. At one point she said she and Dad were worried I was getting carried away with some fantasy of Prince Charming..." Alex trails off, lowering her gaze to her hands. "I just wish, for *once*, they would be happy for me. You know?" Her voice cracks and guilt rips clean through me.

I have never been so appalled with myself as I am right now. I flew all the way over here for Alex, but what am I doing instead? Fixating on Luke and his divorce and the extremely inappropriate feelings I seem to have developed for him.

What is *wrong* with me? I need to do better.

Slipping my arm around her, I give her a squeeze. "I'm

sorry. I know that sucks. But you love him and that's all that matters, right?"

She nods, saying nothing.

"The wedding will be perfect and they'll see how happy you are. They'll know you're doing the right thing."

Alex wipes her cheek. "I'm just stressed. Between them questioning everything, and Mel coming to the wedding, and all the stuff that still needs to be organized..." She draws in a shaky breath. "Then I've got this deadline coming up—"

"No," I say, squeezing her again. "You focus on the deadline and I'll take care of the rest. I'll make sure Mel doesn't pull anything. I'll keep an eye on Mum and Dad. And the rest of the wedding stuff..." Shit, Luke and I have been really slack the past couple of days, with the board game cafe and sightseeing. Where has my head been at? "I'll get that sorted too. All you need to do is get your writing done and show up to the wedding. Okay?"

She gives me a watery smile. "Okay. Thank you so much, Harri. I don't know what I'd do without you."

I hand her a paper towel to dry her eyes, hardening my resolve. It was fun to flirt with Luke, but it needs to stop. Alex and Michael's wedding is the most important thing here. I need to focus.

We leave the bathroom together, finding Michael and Luke at the table, chatting. Michael frowns as we approach, clearly able to see Alex has been upset.

"Hey," he murmurs as she lowers herself onto a chair beside him. "What's going on?"

She buries her face in his shoulder, saying something I can't hear, and I surreptitiously gesture for Luke to join me at the bar. He glances from Alex and Michael to me, then pushes to his feet and follows me to a bar stool.

"What's wrong?"

I slide onto a stool beside him. "Nothing can happen between us. Seriously."

"What?" His eyes flare in alarm. "Did she know we were—"

"No. But, God, if she'd come into that corridor any sooner..."

"Yeah. Yeah, I know." He stares down at the bar with a deep groove etched between his brows, then drops his head into his hands. "Ugh, this sucks." When he looks back at me, his agonized expression makes something hot tangle in my chest.

"It's not like I don't want to, Luke. Everything you said about this past week being amazing—I feel that too. I am *not* handling this well, trust me. You have no idea how much time I'm going to have to spend with John Stamos—" I break off as his eyebrows hit his hairline.

Christ, how much did I drink?

"You actually used John Stamos?"

I grimace. "I had to. I was going crazy. I didn't *want* to, I wanted—" I stop myself from saying "you" because I know there's no point. I glance back at the table and my stomach pinches as I watch Alex and Michael talking. "But... it doesn't matter that we *want* this." I turn back to Luke, forcing the words out. "We can't have it. I can't do anything that could ruin their wedding."

"Yeah, the wedding is important to me too. It's probably not worth the risk."

"No. It's not." I'm wringing my hands now. It doesn't matter what my mouth is saying—the rest of me knows I'm lying to myself.

"And you're leaving anyway," he mumbles, as if to himself. "So even if..." He motions towards me vaguely. "Nothing could come of it."

I meet his gaze and an unspoken realization passes between us. This—whatever this is—will all be over, soon. My chest hollows out at the thought.

"For what it's worth," Luke says, his expression softening, "I wish everything was different."

"Me too," I whisper. My throat feels tight. I dig my nails into my palms but it doesn't help.

Luke notices and places his hands gently over mine. "We're doing the right thing."

I nod. He's right. I can't risk hurting my sister and losing the relationship we've been building since I arrived here. That's how I know it's the right thing to do.

But if that's the case, why does it feel like I've just lost something?

22

Okay, so Luke and I are on the same page. We're going to put the wedding first and forget about the attraction between us. It might not be the page I *want* us to be on, but at least we're both there. That's what matters.

I set down the huge bag of supplies in Luke's hallway and glance over my outfit. I wanted a break from Harriet 2.0 today. She's the one who shagged Luke on that flight, who's been fantasizing about him nonstop, who told him last night—cringe—she was wearing out her vibrator dealing with her sexual frustration. I mean, *I'd* never do any of those things.

So I figured it might be a good idea to step away from the trouble she's causing and be my old self, just for a bit. I put my jeans and a simple sweater on, and tied my hair up in a bun.

But I still wore my red lipstick. That's really grown on me.

I wipe my sweaty hand on my jeans, then raise it to knock on Luke's door. Nerves writhe in my belly as I wait.

I'm not religious, but I silently pray that things are cool, that the intensity and chemistry that's been woven into every glance, every word between us lately, is gone. I put off coming over here all day because I'm a coward, but I can't put it off anymore. We need to get started on the center-pieces for the wedding.

"Hey," Luke says when the door opens.

Oh for fuck's sake. He's wearing his glasses again and they look sexy as hell. It feels like some kind of cruel test from the universe.

His lips tip into a warm smile and he gestures for me to come inside. Despite everything, my shoulders relax down from my ears. I forgot how much being around him actually puts me at ease. It's only when I get caught up in my thoughts that I start to spiral.

"Hey." I reach for the bag of supplies but he grabs them for me, hauling them inside.

"What's this?"

"Stuff for the centerpieces." I follow as he sets the bag down on the white table. I begin unpacking everything and he heads into the kitchen, returning a moment later. When he hands me a can of Coke with a smile, things feel purely platonic and I'm relieved.

Definitely not disappointed.

"Thanks," I say, taking the drink, pretending I don't notice the way his fingers brush mine.

"You're welcome." His gaze rests on me for a second and I hold my breath, wondering what he's going to say next. But he turns to the table, keeping us on task. "So, what are we doing here?"

We spend an hour assembling candles in wooden bowls with fake sprigs of fern. They're going to be stacked on top of secondhand books—since Alex and Michael are both writers—with table numbers on little wooden stands. We work in silence and I manage to relax enough to focus on assembling the items, while Luke stacks the finished pieces into boxes for us to transport to the venue later.

"Can we take a break?" he asks as he seals up one of the boxes.

I nod, pleased with what we've done so far. "Sure." We both lean back in our chairs and stretch. My gaze strays across the table and collides with his. I clear my throat. "So, er, how's Donnie? Any more prison breaks?"

Luke laughs. "No. I think I've figured out how to keep him in his tank. But then, I thought that the last time, so..." He shrugs, the corner of his mouth lifting into a smile. His eyes glide over to the TV, then back to me, and he stands. "Want to play a game?"

"What kind of game?"

"A video game. The game I designed."

"Oh," I say, a little taken aback. I can't deny that I've been curious about his game, and games feel like a safe space for us—something we can do that won't lead to us battling the impulse to rip each other's clothes off. Especially if I'm staring at a screen instead of his face. Or his arms. Or any part of him, really.

I rise to my feet. "Sure. I probably won't be very good, but I'll give it a go."

His face splits in a grin and we both take a seat on the leather sofa. "Normally you'd play this on a computer, but I'm testing the console version because we're releasing it soon. I hope you like it." He hands me the controller and the headset, looking kind of nervous.

I smile, wanting to reassure him. "I'm sure I will."

He spends a few minutes explaining the concept, which controls to use, until—to my surprise—I'm eager to play.

So I jump in and, after a few false starts, I pick it up with ease.

And actually, it's really fun. I'd always assumed video games were sort of mindless, shoot-em-up type games, but this is quite sophisticated. It's set in outer space, and there are all these different planets you can visit and spaceships you can purchase. There are missions and rewards, and all kinds of different things your avatar can do. The graphics are amazing. Once I figure out all the controls, I'm hooked. It's got all the things I love about a good book—total immersion, the feeling of being outside yourself and living a different life for a while—with the strategy and participation required for playing a board game, but on another level.

Luke offers tips at the beginning, then sits back to watch me play. After a while I almost forget he's there, I get so involved in the game.

And, God, it's nice to be out of my own head for a bit. I haven't picked up a book in ages and I miss the escapism. I'm used to reading for hours a day and I only now realize I haven't been doing that at all lately.

"Should we order some dinner or something?" Luke says, interrupting my game.

I hit the pause button and glance away from the screen, shocked to find the afternoon light has given way to the darkness of early evening. "How long have I been playing?"

He chuckles. "An hour and a half."

"Seriously?"

"Yeah. Do you like it?"

I pull off the headset. "I *love* it. It's so much fun. I can't believe I've never played video games before. And—okay, I don't have anything to compare *your* game to—but it's awesome. I would totally buy it."

Luke beams. "Thanks, that means a lot. Because Dena
—" he stops himself, his grin fading as he looks down at his
lap. "Never mind."

"Dena what?"

He releases a hard breath, eying me cautiously, apparently deciding whether or not to continue. "She hated it," he
says at last.

"She *hated* it? How? What did she hate?"

He shrugs, picking at a piece of lint on his jeans,
avoiding my gaze. I've never noticed before how much he
shrinks when he talks about her. "She hated video games in
general. She was so pissed when I left my job to pursue
creating this."

"Wow. That's..." I shake my head, truly dumbfounded,
and empathy rushes through me. "Well, I think it's really
cool."

His posture straightens, almost as if pride is lifting him
up, and for some reason that makes my chest ache. When
he looks down at his hands, trying to hide his smile, I have
to fight the urge to pull him into my arms.

I shake the feeling off, setting the controller aside. "Dinner," I mumble. "Let's eat."

We order pizza and settle onto the sofa, and I ask him
more about his game—how he came up with the concept,
what the different spaceships can do and how many
planets you can visit, what the plans are to develop it going
forward. Every time there's a gap in the conversation I
wedge another question in, so we can't stray into other
territory. As long as he's talking about his game, I'm safe.
Well, it kills me to see him so animated and inspired
because it's sexy as hell, but I also love seeing him like that.
I get the sense he could use someone to cheer him on
more.

"So if I wanted to get into video games," I ask, swallowing my last bite of pizza, "what console should I buy?"

He laughs. "It's not that simple. It depends what kind of games you want to play."

"Well, I like this." I gesture to the screen. "It's really detailed. I always thought video games were about guns and shooting bad guys."

"There are loads of those too, and they can be just as fun."

I wrinkle my nose. "Really? How?"

Luke wipes his hands on a napkin with a wry smile. "Sometimes you just want to blow shit up. It can be a good way to relieve stress. I guess it depends on what you want out of a game. Like, sometimes I play the game to escape and explore, and other times I want to compete and fight. My game has a battle mode to do that."

"Battle mode?"

"Yeah. It turns it into a multi-player game and you battle other players for control of a ship or a planet. That can be fun too."

"Can you show me that?" I ask, wiping my hands.

His mouth ticks up in a lop-sided smile and he stands, reaching into the cabinet under the TV to retrieve another controller. "Want to play together?" He holds out the controller, and for some ridiculous reason, the idea of playing with him makes my heart bounce against my ribs.

"Sure." I take the controller and turn to the screen, listening as Luke walks me through how to play in battle mode.

We play for a while and, naturally, I lose a bunch of rounds. He did *invent* the game, after all. But it doesn't take me long to pick up on what he's doing, and next time I take a gamble and try something different. He doesn't see it coming, and when his avatar is blown to bits, he turns to me, slack-jawed.

"That was brutal."

I giggle. "You just shot me three times in a row. It's about time I won."

He grins, loading up the game again. "It's okay. I know how to get you back."

Somehow—don't ask me how—I already anticipate what his next move will be. I wait until he's about to execute it and—BAM! I take him down again. "Okay, yeah, this is pretty fun," I say, chuckling.

He glances at me, half frowning, half smiling. "You're a natural."

Luke wins the next round, but I win the following two. He's getting increasingly frustrated that I've picked it up so easily, but I'm not going to lie—after the way he needled me last night, it's fun to wind him up.

"Whoever designed this game needs to make it harder," I tease, and he grumbles something to himself.

Aw, now I feel bad. He was so excited to show this to me and I've taken all the fun out of it. But he's so easy to read—I can always guess which way he's going to go. It's not about the game, it's about his body language. This wouldn't be so easy if he wasn't right beside me.

On the next round I purposely fumble my move. He does exactly what I think he's going to do, so it's easy to hit the wrong button. I watch my avatar blow up and raise my hands in surrender, giving Luke a look that says "whoops!"

But his eyes narrow behind his glasses and he sets the controller down. "What was that?"

I place my controller on the coffee table, doing my best to look disappointed. "I messed up. You won."

He shakes his head, eyes dancing as they move over my face. "You did that on purpose."

"What?" Maybe I'm easy to read, too. I rise and gather the pizza boxes, heading into the kitchen so I don't have to look at him. "It was an accident."

Luke jumps to his feet, following me. "No, it wasn't."

I set the boxes down and turn to see him standing there, arms crossed, amusement crinkling his brow. At least he's not annoyed, but that would be easier. It's much harder to resist him with that playful expression on his face—and don't get me started on those forearms, corded with veins as they're folded over his chest. *Fuck me.* Who knew a plain white T-shirt could make a guy look so freaking good?

"Fine." A grin pushes at my mouth. "I let the Wookiee win."

The smile drops off Luke's face. Lightning flashes in his gaze and I falter, wondering why it feels like the atmosphere has shifted all of a sudden.

"I mean—" I aim for a carefree chuckle, desperate to lighten the mood again. "It's not like I *actually* thought you'd pull my arms out of my sockets if you lost, but—"

"Stop." Luke holds up a hand, pressing his eyes shut as though he's in pain. "You have to stop quoting *Star Wars* to me."

The rough scrape of his voice makes me hesitate. "Why?"

"Because it's *torturing* me, Harriet."

"What?" A nervous laugh whistles out of me. "How?"

His jaw is tight and he shoves a hand through his hair, letting out a low growl. "Do you know how fucking sexy it is? How sexy *you* are? Playing video games with me, talking about this stuff?"

My heart takes off in a sprint. Maybe he's not that easy to read, because I didn't see *that* coming at all.

"Well, do you know how sexy it is that you actually get the reference?" The words rush from my mouth before I can stop them. "That you took me to that board game cafe? That you played my favorite game with me? That you—"

I'm cut short as Luke steps forward and captures my mouth with his. Shock hits my system first, making me freeze. But it only takes a split second for me to realize what's happening, and... *fuck.* I sink into the warmth of his mouth, parting my lips and welcoming his tongue with my own. He moans and presses me into the kitchen island, and I don't fight him.

God, I'm so weak. I can't do anything but let him slide his hands into my hair and take me. Need floods my bloodstream and my body arches against him, my hands fisting in the front of his T-shirt. How is it possible that we've resisted doing this for the past week? It feels like finally breathing after not having enough air. Like I won't be able to survive without this now.

He's the first to break the kiss, stepping back and straightening his glasses to stare at me with dark eyes. "I'm sorry," he manages, his breath ragged like he's just sprinted up the stairs of The Empire State Building.

I press the pads of my fingers to my tingling lips, wondering how I'm going to stop myself from wanting to do that again. To do that forever. I'm breathing hard too, and my pulse is off the charts. "It's okay," I whisper at last, not sure what else to say. Because it is okay—it's *more* than okay. It's everything I want.

Everything I *shouldn't* want.

"Harriet..." He pushes his hands into his hair and tugs in frustration, until it's sticking out at crazy angles. "This is killing me. I've done everything I can to fight my attraction to you and it's not working."

I nod, wanting nothing more than to take his agitated hands in my own and soothe him, kiss him. I should look away, but I can't. I'm pinned in place by the desire burning hot in his eyes.

And just like that, the final thread of my self-control snaps.

23

"I think we should have sex," I blurt.

Luke's eyebrows spring up. "What?"

I repeat myself with less certainty. "I, er, I think we should have sex."

"Are you serious?"

"Yeah." I push away from the counter, pacing as I think aloud. "There's so much sexual tension between us and it's making things impossible." I recall Alex upset in the bathroom at the bar last night. I can't let her down, but I also need to be practical here. I turn back to Luke. "Maybe if we sleep together—just once," I add, raising a finger for emphasis, "it might help to... I don't know. Defuse it. Then we can get on with the wedding."

"*Defuse* it?" Mirth colors his tone. "You make it sound like a bomb."

"Well—" I huff a laugh. "I do kind of feel like I'm on the brink of exploding when I'm around you. And I know it's not just me."

"It's not." We share a loaded glance, then he scrubs a hand over his jaw, considering my words. "So... just once?"

"Yes. We've agreed that the wedding is what matters most."

"Yeah, and I want that to be our number one priority. But..." He steps closer, heat simmering in his eyes. "I also want *you*."

I breathe out in sheer relief. "I want you too, Luke. You have no idea how much."

"God, I love hearing you say that." He takes my face and tilts it up to his. When his lips meet mine, all the nerve endings in my body tingle with anticipation. I relax against him, sliding my hands up his chest, gripping onto his shirt again.

Then I pull back enough to meet his gaze, narrowing my eyes. "Just to be clear," I say, thinking of him teasing me last night, "this is *not* me begging you for sex."

He chuckles, dropping his hands from my face and taking his glasses off, placing them on the counter. I'm about to protest when he turns back to me. "Okay. How about I even the playing field a little bit?"

"What?"

He forces a serious expression. "Harriet, can I *please* kiss you?"

"Well, alright," I say with mock reluctance, when what I really want to say is, *Fuck yes, do it now and don't stop.*

I wait for his mouth to land on mine again, but he buries his face in my neck. "Harriet, can I *please* have sex with you?"

My knees weaken as his lips move over the sensitive skin below my ear, and I giggle, feeling woozy.

"*Please* let me touch you. *Please* let me take your clothes off. *Please* let me do dirty things to you."

My giggles die away as heat trickles down through my

middle. Now I'm not laughing; I'm practically gasping for breath.

He draws back to gaze at me. "Please?"

"Shut up," I mutter, standing on my tiptoes and circling my arms around his neck.

He grins, lowering his mouth back down to mine. He kisses me softly, teasingly, nibbling my lip, grazing my jaw, kissing the corner of my mouth—all while keeping his mouth closed. I grumble against his lips in frustration, wanting nothing more than to thrust my tongue down his throat.

"Shhh," he whispers between chaste kisses. "I'm trying to kiss you."

Oh, I know what will do the trick. I'll channel Yoda. "Do or do not, there is no tr—"

"Don't." He puts a finger over my lips, a sexy grin tilting his mouth. "If you keep that up, I'll fall in love with you."

Happiness swells in my chest like a balloon and I quickly pop it. *Just once*, I remind myself. *You are only doing this once. He's being silly.*

I go to kiss him again but he pulls back, sliding his hands down and squeezing my butt. "I love these jeans."

I gaze at him desperately, on the brink of begging again. Why has he stopped kissing me? I've been thinking of nothing else since the plane and it feels like he's dangling it in front of my face.

He slides my glasses off and places them on the table. Then he runs a fingertip along the bridge of my nose. "You have the cutest freckles there."

"Luke!" I finally cry. "Why are you moving so slowly?"

He laughs at my exasperation. "I'm just taking my time."

"Why? On the plane we were halfway done by now."

"This will be nothing like the plane," he says, seriously

now. "If we are only going to do this once, I need to make it count. So quit your complaining."

I snap my mouth shut, suddenly understanding. He's trying to savor it. And I should be too. Except, God, now that he's touching me, now that I'm close enough to smell his spicy, woody aftershave and his soap, my legs are practically trembling with my need for him.

He takes my hand and guides me across the living room, into his bedroom. He flicks the light on and I stop in the doorway, taking it in. It's nothing like the rest of the apartment, with its white, gleaming, sterile surfaces. Instead, the walls are painted navy blue, so dark they're almost black. A collection of framed retro comic book and Star Wars prints hang above the bed. There's a worn, brown leather armchair in one corner, a wooden dresser, and a charcoal-gray rug. The only color is a red throw across the foot of the bed and a mustard-yellow lamp.

He flicks another switch and the lights dim slightly. He motions for me to look up and when I do, my breath catches in my throat. The ceiling is dotted with tiny lights, like stars, against a dark background.

"Wow," I whisper. It's amazing in here; so out of place with the rest of the apartment. I open my mouth to say something but he smiles, getting there before I can.

"I got this room redone a few months ago because I was having trouble sleeping."

"I love it. You should do the rest of the place like this."

He nods, slipping his hands into his pockets. "Yeah, that's what I'm going to do. I decided that when you destroyed the rug."

I turn my hands up. "You're welcome?"

He chuckles. Then he steps towards me, almost nervously. "Still want to do this?"

I bite back a smile. I love it when he gets self-conscious like this. "No, actually. I think I'm going to head off."

His brow furrows and I giggle.

"Oh my God, I'm kidding!"

He lets his breath out in an embarrassed laugh, his posture relaxing. "Sorry. This feels kind of surreal. I didn't think I'd get lucky enough to be with you again."

My heart swoops. "Me too."

He reaches for the bun on my head and slides the hair tie off, letting my hair tumble down over my shoulders. "Oh," he says on a sigh, tucking a strand behind my ear. "I love your hair."

He takes me by the waist and tugs me close. His gaze drops to my mouth and, impatient, I push up onto my toes to steal a kiss. When he parts his lips, I can't help myself—I flick my tongue against his. He responds by tightening his hands on my hips and pressing his arousal into my belly. And when he kisses me back, this time he's not pacing himself. He strokes his tongue over mine in a wet, dirty kiss —a promise of what we're going to do to each other. Lust spirals down my limbs, emanating out through every nerve in my body, and I push him back onto the bed, climbing on top of him.

I don't think I've ever done that with a guy before. With Luke, though, I can't make myself behave. This is what it was like on the plane: he made me want to do things I would never normally do. Kissing him is a different kind of intensity that makes me feel like I'm someone else.

But he doesn't seem to mind. In fact, he lies back happily, his pupils wide and dark with anticipation, his mouth curved into that gorgeous grin of his. I pull his shirt up his body and he wriggles it off over his head, tossing it aside. He's in good shape for someone who spends so much time playing video games.

I touch his firm stomach, asking, "Do you work out?"

"Yeah. Sometimes it's the only thing that keeps me sane."

I nod in understanding. When I'm feeling especially anxious, I go for long walks to burn off the excess energy.

"This past week, when I wasn't with you I was at the gym," he says. "I would have snapped a lot sooner otherwise."

I smile wryly. "So, this is you managing this situation well?"

His laugh morphs into a grimace. "No. Obviously." He draws my mouth down for a kiss. "I think you know what you do to me, Harriet. I slept with you two hours after I met you. I've never done anything like that in my life. You just... have this effect on me. I can't explain it."

"Yeah," I whisper. "I know the feeling."

We gaze at one another in the dim light, and I brush my mouth over his, savoring the way his bottom lip feels so soft against my own. I'm vaguely aware of a thought hovering at the edge of my mind—that I'm going to want to do this more than once—but I shove it away, focusing on Luke. His hair is ruffled and I push my hands into it as I kiss along the hot skin of his shoulders and chest. Then I lean over to inspect the tattoo on his left bicep, and my mouth widens into a grin. I can't believe it.

"Oh my God," I tease. "What kind of super-nerd gets the Millennium Falcon tattooed on his arm?"

Luke's cheeks streak with crimson and I kiss them both. He goes to speak, but I cover his mouth with mine.

"It's fucking hot," I say, dragging my teeth gently over his bottom lip. "I love it."

His brows rise, then he shakes his head with an evil grin. "Oh, you're going to pay for that." Before I can respond, he flips us over so I'm on my back and pins my hands above my head.

I shriek, pretending to squirm, but I'm surprised to find I'm completely at ease with him taking charge. I trust him. And perhaps even more surprisingly, I don't just feel *comfortable* with him holding me down—it's kind of turning me on. I'm at his mercy, and that thought thrills me. I spend so much of my life trying to stay in control, but right now I feel like I can let go.

I gaze up at his strong, muscular arms, pinning me in place. How is it possible that something as normal as forearms can be so damn erotic? Why on earth—

"You okay?" Luke is watching me, hesitant. "Do you want me to let you go?"

"No, I like it. It's just..."

"What?"

I chew my lip. "Okay. Don't judge me, but you have such nice forearms. I'm kind of... obsessed with them." My cheeks warm. "Is that weird?"

He shrugs. "You know I'm obsessed with your hair." He releases a hand to stroke it over my head and gather my hair to one side, caressing it tenderly, reverently. I smile, feeling adored. Then he wraps it around his fist and gives the tiniest tug, and heat detonates inside me.

Christ. I didn't expect to like that so much.

I wriggle, feeling restless, wanting his body on mine. He drops down to kiss me hard, pressing his hips between my parted legs and grinding against me. The friction is divine, but there are far too many clothes in the way. He must think so too, because he peels my sweater off and unhooks my bra. When he dips his head to suck my nipple into his mouth, I gasp at the shocking surge of electricity through me. He continues over my stomach, unzipping my jeans and tugging them down my legs, discarding them on the floor. My underwear follows, and he lowers himself to his elbows, sliding his hands up my thighs and guiding them open.

I think of past boyfriends who didn't like doing what Luke's about to do, how annoyed they got because I wouldn't orgasm in five seconds. Then I have a brief moment of insanity. "You, um, don't have to..."

Luke stills. "You don't want me to?"

I prop myself up onto my elbows, glancing down at him. "Well, yes," I say, laughing awkwardly. "But usually guys don't... I mean, don't feel like you have to." *Stop. God.*

"Usually guys don't what?"

I cringe. "They don't want to. They just want to get on with it." *Why are you talking him out of this?*

Luke gives me a strange look. "You're dating the wrong guys, Harriet. Do you think I'm down here out of some sense of obligation?"

I lift a shoulder.

"I'm not." He urges my legs further open, letting his gaze settle between them. "This is for *me*. I want to taste you. I want to feel you come on my tongue."

God, that's hot. But uncertainty stirs inside me. "What if I... *can't*?"

He looks up at me and his face softens. "Well, I'll be down here all night trying." He hooks his mouth into a filthy grin, then sweeps his tongue over the wet heat between my thighs. A soft groan escapes him. "Fuck," he murmurs, tasting me again. "So sweet."

Holy mother of God. I'm going to pass out, I'm so turned on. I'm not sure if it's from his words or what he's doing with his mouth, but hell, I want it all. No one has ever said anything that sexy to me, and no one has gone down on me purely because they want to—because they want *me*—that badly.

I'm dazed with pleasure as he works his tongue on me, slowly and skillfully. My hands go to his head and thread into his hair, my hips rocking up to meet the movements of his mouth. When I look down, he lifts his mouth away and slides two fingers into me, watching as they move in and out, before lowering his tongue again.

I nearly combust. Heat licks across my skin, concentrating in a ball of burning energy low in my abdomen. My hands grasp at the sheets, tightening into fists, my thighs pressing together around his head. But he pins me down, holding me in place while he brings me to the edge. I let out a broken whimper, throwing my head back on the bed as I'm lost in sensation.

It takes me a moment to come down from the high and catch my breath. How on earth did he manage to do that to me so quickly when no other man has even come close?

He pulls himself up until he's sitting back on his heels, admiring me spread out on his bed. His eyes drink in my naked skin, absorbing every freckle, every curve, every scar —there's a few of those. I've never been in this position, this exposed—not with the lights on—but I actually feel okay. Under Luke's gaze, I not only feel comfortable, I feel good. I feel alive.

"You are so unbelievably sexy," he says, unbuckling his belt. Delight sings through me at his words.

"So are you." I drag myself up to sitting, reaching forward to unzip his jeans. "Especially like this," I add, loving the way his breath hitches as I wrap my hand around the hard heat of him. I want to give him what he just gave me. I want to get down on my knees and take him into my mouth until I make him incoherent with pleasure. But the truth is, I don't know how to do that. Not well, at least. And I'm too scared to try.

Instead, I watch as he stands, shucks his pants, and rolls on a condom. He climbs back over me and positions himself between my legs, pausing to lean down and press his lips to mine. As he kisses me, my need for him grows again until I'm physically aching to feel him inside me. I've never felt a need so intense, and it's only made worse as he continues to take his damn time.

The word "please" flies out of my mouth before I can stop it and I wince, waiting for him to laugh.

But he just gives a sexy grunt, his eyes hazy as he pushes into me. His low moan reverberates against my lips and I wrap my legs around him, drawing him in as deep as I can. Every atom in my body pulses with ecstasy.

"God," Luke rasps. "You feel even better than you did on the plane."

I give a satisfied sigh in response. This isn't like the plane at all—it's slower, more intentional. I'm trying to map the feel of every muscle in his back as he moves over me, the delicious scratch of his scruff against my collarbone. I want to memorize every one of his sounds, the way his skin tastes salty but his mouth tastes sweet—tastes like, well, *him*.

He's taking his time, too; lips traversing my neck, my jaw, then coming back to mine. His movements are careful and measured, his expression is one of concentration. Maybe he's trying to mentally record everything as well.

Once will never be enough.

The thought I was fighting earlier comes back in full force. I try to push it away, but it's insistent. I need to make every second count.

My tongue slips out and traces the shell of his ear. He

groans into my neck, pressing himself deeper, so I do it again before sucking his earlobe into my mouth.

Lifting himself up, he draws all the way out of me. I'm hollow with the loss of him, surprised by the sudden and shocking sense of emptiness, and a little gasp of frustration escapes my lips.

He looks away self-consciously, his cheeks turning pink. "I, uh, just need a minute."

Oh.

I take the chance to enjoy the view of his sexy chest and sculpted shoulders. He's just pure, firm muscle under smooth, soft skin. I could kiss every single inch of him and never get enough.

I glance away, trying to ignore the disappointment building behind my breastbone. Once this is over, that's it. That will have to be enough.

Before I can dwell any more on that thought, Luke leans down and slowly sinks back inside me. My body eagerly welcomes him, as if he's been gone for an eternity rather than only a few seconds. Then he holds himself over me, giving a cautious roll of his hips, watching as I writhe beneath him.

"Deeper," I urge, wrapping my legs around him, tugging him down against my skin. I grab his ass and pull until he's buried inside me.

"Oh my God." His breath rushes out against my lips. "Do you know how amazing you feel?"

I don't get the chance to answer, because when he grinds into me hard, my mind empties. His hips move again in strong, deep thrusts, and something primal awakens inside me. I claw at his back, panting into his skin and biting his shoulder as heat blazes down through my center.

His lips move to mine and his kiss becomes urgent, his

moans spilling right onto my tongue. He slides one hand down to the slickness where our bodies are joined, touching me until I'm frenzied and whimpering. And when he rasps, "Come for me, Harriet," the inferno inside me erupts. Pleasure bursts from my core—nuclear, white-hot. I cry out, but it's swallowed by his mouth, by his own raw, gasping groan as he joins me in release.

When I finally come to, we're a mess of tangled limbs and broken breaths and sweat. My heart is going a million miles an hour, and as Luke withdraws and rolls off beside me, I feel hollow.

I try to stay in my body—to focus on the warm, pleasant sensations humming through me—but my mind won't obey. My thoughts come crashing in, reminding me what Luke and I agreed.

Just once.

We've done that now. It's over. It was amazing—hell, if I thought the plane was good, that was nothing compared to this—but that's it. Mission complete, return to base. We did what we said we'd do, and now we go back to focusing on the wedding. We go back to how things were before.

Even if that's the last thing I want to do.

"That was..." Luke begins beside me, and I tilt my head to look at him.

"Yeah."

There's a tiny crease in his brow as he assesses me. "Better than John Stamos?"

I choke on a laugh. "Better than *anything*."

His eyes smolder in agreement, and I have to fight the urge to climb onto his lap and beg him to take me again.

I wrench my gaze away, my mind spinning. It's slowly dawning on me that us having sex again might not have been the best idea. When I hazard another glance at Luke, I see the same realization on his face—in his gaze, in the way he's worrying his bottom lip between his teeth. That beautiful bottom lip.

I can't help myself. I reach over, stroking my thumb over his lip, his cheek, his jaw. He closes his eyes, pressing a kiss to the inside of my wrist, and my heart twists.

Fuck.

We didn't defuse the bomb. We just lit the fuse.

24

I set my phone down on the table in front of me and secure my earphones, tilting the screen up so the front camera catches my face. I got out of Luke's place quickly, making a lame excuse about being tired. I'm pretty sure he saw through that, though. He saw me for the scared little liar I really am.

But I need to process everything. I convinced myself that having sex with Luke would somehow get it out of my system, but how bloody delusional am I? The more I think about it, the more I realize there *is* no getting Luke out of my system. And the more I think about *that*, the more I panic.

So I caught a cab home to the Village, stopping in at Beanie to call Steph. She's the only person I can speak to about this. My stomach is swirling as I press her name in my contacts, and when the call connects, relief engulfs me.

"Oh my God, your hair!" Steph gapes at me through the screen on my phone. I haven't spoken to her properly since our last call and I miss her like mad. Seeing her now, I feel myself begin to relax. She'll help me figure this Luke stuff out.

"You like it?" I turn my head, showing off my red locks for her.

"I love it! I can't believe you dyed your hair. A week and a half ago you were worried about wearing red lipstick. And now..."

A grin creeps onto my lips. "That's not the only new thing I've done; I went on a trapeze the other day." I'm tempted to tell her about John Stamos, but that might be too much.

"A *trapeze!?*" Her eyes widen with shock. "Harriet George! What the hell has happened to you?"

I chuckle, amused by her response. I guess she has a point; two weeks ago if you'd told me I would be saying these things, I wouldn't have believed you for a second.

"Honestly, Harri. I know you said you were going to be more adventurous, but this is next level. Dying your hair bright red, going on a trapeze—not to mention sex in an airplane bathroom. Ooh, speaking of, are you getting on alright with the best man?"

Heat rises up my neck as I examine my cup of tea. "Erm, yeah. We're getting on *really* well."

"What does *that* mean?"

"It means..." I take a long sip of tea, bursting with my need to tell her everything. "It means I, um, slept with him again."

"*What?*"

I set my cup down, resisting the urge to grin like an idiot. "I know. It just sort of happened."

"Wow." Steph arches an eyebrow and I grimace, thinking back to our last conversation.

"I know I said I wouldn't, but—"

"Don't ruin this for yourself," Steph says, holding up a

hand. She knows me too well. "You're only human. Besides, I'm loving this wild new Harriet!"

This time I can't hold in my grin. "Me too."

"Was it as good as last time?"

"Um... yes." *Understatement.*

She lets out a little shriek. "Well, what's happening with him then? Are you going to do it again?"

My smile slips. "Oh, no. We probably shouldn't."

"But you want to?"

My head nods without my consent and I curse myself for being so weak. A week and a half ago I didn't even know this guy, and I didn't spend most of my waking minutes picturing his lips on mine. I was perfectly happy in my own bubble, disappearing into make-believe worlds in my books, existing only to go to work and come home, living a life that was safe and predictable, perhaps a little boring, but comforting in its own way. I was perfectly happy.

But... was I really? I thought I was, but after this past week —after tonight—I'm not sure. Meeting Luke has changed me. I've never connected with someone like this, I've never felt this kind of chemistry—and we've already covered the other thing he's helped me with. But it's not just sexual, it's everything. When I'm with him, I feel like someone else. Someone who isn't quite so afraid, someone full of life. I feel like a better me.

"If you want him," Steph says, interrupting my thoughts, "you should go for him."

I trace my finger around my teacup, thinking about this —about what it would be like if I showed up at his place tomorrow and told him that I want to do it again. And again. That I don't want to stop.

A thrill shoots up my spine at the thought. It's the same sensation I felt after going on the trapeze, the kind that was equal parts terrifying and exhilarating. The kind that tells me to do it.

But guilt is tugging at me, reminding me how important it is that I get everything organized for Alex, that I don't do something stupid and ruin her wedding. After all, Luke is going to be there with Dena and he's insistent he has to pretend to be married. I might wish that wasn't the case, but it's what Luke wants to do and I'm going to respect that.

I rub my face, exhaling. "It's not that easy, Steph. With the wedding and everything... it's risky." And as much as I hate to think about it, I'm leaving in a week. After the wedding is over, I have to go home and pretend that none of this has happened.

I swallow, feeling empty at the thought of going back to my old life. My life without Luke. If anything, that makes me want to make every moment with him count, to do everything I can with him.

"Well, think of it this way," Steph says. "Would you be okay if this was it? If you never kissed him again?"

My chest constricts. "No."

"Exactly. So what if it's a little risky? I'm sure you can manage the wedding at the same time. You'd never let this get in the way."

"Maybe," I mumble, unconvinced.

"Besides, what did Hermione say?" Steph pauses, thinking. "Something about how it's exciting to break the rules?"

I laugh. "I can't believe you remember that."

"You've made me watch those films with you a hundred times. I know *way* more about Hermione than I'd like." Steph rolls her eyes, but her lips twist with a little smile.

"Right. But you're forgetting one thing—they got caught. So..."

"Oh shit, yeah. Okay then, think about it as Harriet 2.0

—*she* wouldn't let anything stop her." Steph peers close at the screen for a moment then frowns. "Shit, my boss is calling. I'd better take it. But I want a full update on this soon, okay?"

"Okay." I end the call with a sigh.

When I get back to the apartment, my suitcase is sitting inside the front door. I haven't seen it since I checked it into the airport back in New Zealand, and it takes me a second to recognize it.

"Hey." Alex glances up from her spot on the sofa where she's working on her laptop, her face lit by the glow of the screen.

"My suitcase," I say flatly, slipping my boots off.

"Yeah. It came for you this evening."

I look at it, feeling an odd sensation behind my sternum. So much has happened since I got on that flight, it feels like it doesn't belong to me anymore.

"You must be relieved," Alex says, tapping away on her keyboard. "You've got all your stuff, finally."

I don't reply. Instead, I drag the suitcase into the bedroom and close the door behind me. Hauling it up on the bed, I enter the code to unlock the padlock on the zipper and pop it open. Inside are all my things, undisturbed, as if frozen in time: my jeans, my simple T-shirts, my plain cotton underwear that doesn't match, my sensible shoes—and of course, several books.

And as much as I recognize all of the items, I'm not sure I recognize the woman who wore them anymore. The objects that I carefully selected to bring with me, the things that once comforted and defined me, no longer have the same meaning. They feel like relics of a bygone era, props from an old movie I once starred in.

I was waiting for my suitcase to arrive and now that it's

here, I don't want it. I don't want to be that person anymore. I don't want to dress in clothes that make me feel invisible, to bury my nose in a book and forget about my actual life.

No. For the first time, I want to live my own life out loud, in my fun new clothes with my red hair and a man who rocks my world in bed. I know it's risky to pursue something with Luke, but Steph's right: my alter ego would take the risk. And I want to be her. I want to be brave enough to try.

I contemplate the suitcase for another second, then zip it back up and stuff it under Henry's bed. I won't be needing it after all, because now I know what I want. I want Luke, and tomorrow, I'm going to tell him just how much.

25

L uke's expression is apprehensive when I arrive the following afternoon. I sent him a text this morning saying that I'd be coming over to finish the center-pieces and I wanted to talk. I deliberately kept it vague, because I want to feel him out. I'm pretty sure we're on the same wavelength, but I'd rather have this conversation face to face.

I enter his apartment with a smile, going straight to the centerpieces on the table. Setting my bag down, I pull out the ring Alex gave me this morning and place it on the table, so I remember to do it. It's her wedding band—an heirloom passed down through the Hawkins family, or something. It needs to be resized today because it's the only opening the jeweler has for six weeks. She was going to take it herself, but I leapt at the chance to take another task off her hands. I guess I felt like it might help assuage some of the guilt I've been feeling about what I did with Luke—and what I plan to do again. Because while I'm feeling strangely relaxed about things between Luke and I now, I'm sick with nerves at the thought of doing anything to jeopardize the wedding.

Luke's eyes land on the ring box. "Is that what you wanted to talk about? You're proposing?" He emits a self-effacing laugh, shifting his weight.

Oh God, he's being cute and nervous again. It makes me want to kiss him.

I shake the feeling off, trying to stay focused. "It's Alex's ring. I need to take it to the jeweler to be resized today."

He nods, slipping his hands into his jeans pockets. Then he pulls his bottom lip between his teeth and rocks on his heels, watching me like he's waiting for me to say something more.

"I, um, want to talk about what happened last night. But..." I motion to the unfinished centerpieces on the table. "Can we get all of today's wedding tasks done first? That way I can relax."

He lets his breath out slowly. "Okay, yeah. That's a good idea."

We settle at the table and get to work, and the tension in my stomach slowly dissipates. *See, you're not a terrible sister. You're getting these things done for Alex's wedding because you know that's what matters most.*

As we work in easy silence, occasionally sneaking glances at each other, I realize that I *can* have my cake and eat it too. As long as Luke and I make sure the wedding runs smoothly, the rest of it should be fine. What difference does it make if we're having sex, as long as nothing interferes with the wedding?

Luke sets the last centerpiece in the box with a grin. "Those look great," he says, closing the lid, and pride fills my lungs. He lets his gaze slide back to me and opens his mouth to say more, then closes it again. His eyes drop to his hands and he inspects his knuckles. I know he wants to talk and he's trying not to push me. It makes me want to put him out of his misery.

I glance at the ring box on the table, then check the time on my phone. I still have an hour before the jeweler closes. Plenty of time to clear the air with Luke. Except... how the hell do I ask for this? I've never been in this position before.

"So..." I bite my lip. "Last night was fun."

Luke's gaze swings back to mine. "It was."

Silence settles over us. And even though we were just working in complete silence a few moments ago, this feels different. Loaded.

Eventually, Luke exhales, scrubbing a hand over his face. "Look, Harriet... about last night. I know we said we'd only do it once, but I'm just going to come out and say it: I don't think that helped. At all. If anything, I feel like it's only made things worse." He pauses and I nod my agreement. "I know you're worried about the wedding stuff, and that still needs to come first. But... I'm not sure I'm finished with you yet."

My lips curl in amusement. "*Finished* with me?"

He shrugs, his dark eyes glittering as they appraise me. "You can't tell me you don't feel it too—what we have here."

"Yeah." My heart thuds harder. "I don't think I'm finished with you, either. And I don't want to stop doing..."

His eyebrows lift. "Doing what?"

"Um..." How do I phrase this? "You."

A laugh rumbles out of him. "Is that right?"

I nod. Warmth blossoms in my chest at the way his eyes light with affection as they move over me. He stands and walks around the table, taking my hands and tugging me to my feet. When his arms slide around my waist and pull my body against his, I sigh as if the weight of the world has been taken from my shoulders.

He tucks his face into my neck, breathing me in. "Good," he murmurs against my skin.

I shiver with desire, having him pressed so close to me again. His hands slide into my hair and he draws my lips to his, taking my mouth with hungry strokes of his tongue.

Holy hell. I love that he's not wasting any time. It's been less than twenty-four hours since he kissed me but it feels like forever.

"I love kissing you," Luke rasps against my lips. "Do you know how hard it was to sit there and not kiss you just now?"

I can't help myself. "How hard?"

"This hard." He takes my hand, molding it to the thickness of his arousal through his jeans. When I stroke him, he groans, pressing himself against my palm, and lust rockets through me. I grab his hand and drag him into the bedroom.

"I need you now," I say, climbing onto his mattress like I own the damn place. I don't know who I become when I'm in bed with him, but I like it. I like not over-thinking, just letting my body take over. I like that he likes this version of me.

"Fuck yes," he says, watching me yank my dress over my head, then whip off my bra and panties. I should have brought more than one pair of underwear, because these are ruined. He hasn't even touched me and I'm *beyond* ready for him. As he urgently strips off his clothes, I realize I'm not the only one who needs this. He rolls on a condom, but when he goes to climb on top, I shake my head. I nudge him back onto the bed, straddling him. Then I ride him until I see stars.

AFTER, we sit side-by-side against the headboard, the room lit only by the tiny lights on the ceiling above us. Luke slides his arm around my back and pulls me close to him. I lean my head into his shoulder, still recovering.

That was amazing. It's like every time we have sex it gets better. And now, as he presses his lips to my temple, I find myself wishing I didn't have to go home tonight. Or any night.

I push the thought away and look up at the ceiling. "I love these little lights."

I feel Luke smile beside me. "Yeah. I'm a total space nerd, as you probably guessed, so I wanted to have the stars over my bed."

I turn to him, mock-surprised. "You're a space nerd? Wow, I had no idea. All the *Star Wars* stuff, the sci-fi books, your video game... I really should have seen this coming."

He surveys my face in the dim light, as if trying to read something I'm not saying, and I kiss his shoulder.

"It's just who you are, Luke. It's my favorite thing about you."

With a rueful laugh, he lets his gaze fall. I notice the slight downturn in his mouth, wondering if I said something wrong.

"You okay?"

He nods. "You're just... I think you're the first person to say that. You like me not in spite of all that, but because of it."

I shrug. "It's the same with me. Most people see the things I love as a nerdy side to me that they have to put up with. But you... you like that side to me."

"Yeah. I think it's fucking cool. I think *you're* cool." He kisses the tip of my nose and I grin.

"I've never been called cool before, but I'll take it."

He laughs. "I've never been called cool either, if that helps."

"Oh, you're definitely cool. And you have the coolest job."

Luke snorts. "Tell that to my father."

I twist to face him properly. "He doesn't like your job?"

"He doesn't care much for anything I do."

I frown, thinking back to the phone call he took when we were at the board game cafe. "What do you mean?"

"Dad is... not an easy man to please. Never has been. Growing up, he was always on my case about something. I didn't play enough sports, I didn't get good enough grades, I spent too much time playing video games or reading about space. It was like, no matter what I did, he was always disappointed."

"What about now? You're so successful, how can he be disappointed with that?"

Luke lifts a shoulder, a muscle ticking in his jaw. "I think for a while he was starting to come around. I worked hard in my previous job, and yeah, I was pretty successful. I had a wife, and a great apartment..." he trails off and lies there quietly for some time. I'm bursting with questions but I force myself to be quiet, to wait for him to say more, because I know that's not the end of the story.

"I was really unhappy at work," he says at last. "For a while it was okay and I could handle it, but it got worse. Every time I had to get up and go to the office, a little part of me died. I felt like I was living someone else's life. I was, of course—I was doing what I thought would make my father proud, not what I actually wanted to do. But then something happened. I modified a really popular game and my mod went viral. The creators of the game contacted me and asked if I wanted to collaborate with them on something new, and it was like a dream come true. I had more than enough money so I decided to go for it. But Dad..." Luke rubs a hand over his chin, his eyes narrowing. "He just thought I was throwing everything away. He told me he was so disappointed in me for 'giving up' on my job. He never saw it as me following my dream."

"That sucks." Sympathy weaves through me and I touch his arm. "I know another Luke who had a complicated relationship with his father."

Luke makes a small, amused sound. "Dad's not *quite* as bad as Darth Vader. But yeah, he doesn't get me at all. And Dena's even worse. Your parents don't always love your life choices, but you at least expect your wife to stand by you. She put up with my gaming for the most part, but when this opportunity came up, she told me what she really thought —that gaming was juvenile and pathetic. You know what she said when I told her I wanted kids? That I was an overgrown child and she didn't want *more kids*." A bitter laugh leaves him. "She kept saying it was immature to give up such a good job to pursue a career in gaming, but it felt more like... like finally doing what was right for me helped me grow up and find my place in the world. It wasn't long after that I realized we'd never be right for each other, and asked for a divorce."

I absorb his words, tracing my finger in a figure eight over his forearm. I can't for the life of me understand how she could tell him his passions were pathetic. My heart hurts at the thought of him being shamed for the things he loves, because I know all too well what that's like.

After a while Luke adds, "And she hated Donnie."

"What? How can someone not love a tiny *Ninja Turtle*?"

"I know, right? Dena wanted me to get rid of him, but I've had him since I was eighteen. He's my buddy. Turns out he's going to outlast her. Ah, well. He's nicer than her anyway."

"Why did you guys get married then, if you were so wrong for each other?"

"It wasn't all bad, and when you're with someone for so long, you get comfortable. We were turning thirty and everyone around us was getting married. It just sort of seemed like the next step, you know? In hindsight, I don't think we really thought it through. Because if I had, I'm sure I would have realized it was a mistake. It became clear after we moved in together, though. For a start, she made me keep all my games and books in storage. And the TV—she considered it a huge compromise that I had my gaming consoles in the living room, even though they were out of sight. When we went to dinner parties, she used to tell people I worked in 'entertainment.' She kept it vague because she was embarrassed that I design video games."

I tilt my head. "That's exactly what you told me on the plane."

He chuffs an ashamed laugh. "I know. It just slipped out. But honestly, I think I was embarrassed to tell you the truth. You were this beautiful woman and I worried, I don't know, maybe you would think it was lame."

I kiss his jaw. "No way."

"Well, that's before I knew you were obsessed with board games and had read all my favorite books," he teases. Then his expression softens. "You're so comfortable with who you are, Harriet. You just accept yourself and the things you love. It's really inspiring."

Huh. I've never thought of myself like that. After the way

I was tormented in high school, there are some people I definitely don't share this side of myself with. But Luke's right, I have let my geek flag fly around him. I guess that's just what Harriet 2.0 is like. She's confident enough to be herself.

"It's weird, when I think about it," he continues. "I didn't know any of that stuff about you when we met, but I was so drawn to you. Almost like I knew we had those things in common, without actually knowing it. Does that sound insane?"

"No," I murmur, smiling to myself. "I had the same thought."

"Then the more I learned about you..." He shakes his head, leaning back to look at the ceiling with a sigh. "I can't explain it. I've never connected with someone like this. It's not just physical, it's..." He pauses as if searching for the right words, and I take his hand and thread my fingers through his.

"I know. I feel it too."

He rolls his head to the side, looking at me. Something wordlessly passes between us and my heart tumbles. Suddenly, it feels like we are straying into dangerous territory.

Luke swallows, glancing away. "Have you thought any more about your board game cafe idea?"

I let my breath out in a long trickle, gazing up at the stars on his ceiling. "I have. I really want to do it—and, who knows? Maybe it could work in New York," I say, remembering my decision last night to be braver. "But... every time I think about it, I feel overwhelmed. There's just too much I don't know. I would have a lot to learn about business and it just feels so intimidating."

Luke nods, his expression gentle as he contemplates me.

"Yeah, I get that. But you're intelligent; you could pick all of that up easily. If you really want it, you can make it happen."

I consider his words, wondering how, after all the trouble with his dad and his wife not supporting or encouraging his dreams, he still manages to be this positive and optimistic. As I gaze at him, I realize he means what he's saying—that I could actually do it. And I almost believe him, too.

"I'll think about it," I promise, tilting my face up so I can kiss him.

"Good." He slips his other arm around me and pulls my body close to his.

Our kiss deepens and I slide my hands up his back, surprised to find I'm aching to feel him inside me again, so soon. But he feels the same, and it's not long before he's on top of me, nudging my legs apart and entering me with a groan. This time it's slower, and we kiss passionately, taking our time to relish every sensation, fleeting as it is, before the whole thing comes to an end.

As I'm dressing afterward, he watches me from his spot under the blanket. "Do you have to go?"

"It's late." I pull my dress on, fighting the urge to crawl under the covers with him and snuggle into his arms. As much as I love being with him, I know that spending the night would be crossing a line—a line I don't want to go anywhere near. At least if I leave now, I won't be waking up next to him, cementing him in my brain as some kind of permanent fixture.

No; if I go now, I can wake up alone, as I usually do. It's much safer.

Not to mention Alex would wonder where on earth I'd got to overnight. How would I explain that one to her?

"Yeah, okay," he mutters, staring at his hands. He wraps

the red throw around his waist as he follows me out of the bedroom.

I pad over to the table and pick up my handbag with a smile, pleased we got the centerpieces finished. But when I turn to go, my gaze snags on the ringbox. My heart plummets.

Fuck.

I was so distracted by Luke, I forgot to take that to the jeweler. And Alex stressed that it had to go *today*.

Panic tunnels through my middle. God, I am the worst person in the world. I'm over here fucking the best man instead of doing the things Alex is counting on me to do.

Luke notices the ring too and chuckles. "Whoops. Guess we got a bit distracted there."

"It's not funny," I snap, and he looks at me, surprised.

"We can take it tomorrow."

"No, we can't. She said it had to go today. It's some specialist jeweler she had booked, or something. I don't know, but—" My breathing turns shallow and my vision narrows. "She's expecting me to pick it up tomorrow. *Tomorrow*, Luke. What am I going to tell her—"

"Hey," he says, concern written into his brow as he steps towards me. "It's okay—"

"It's not okay!" My lungs are tight. I've let Alex down and I only have myself to blame. How could I have been so stupid?

Luke reaches for me. "We'll figure something out, Harriet. Just breathe."

I shake my head, stepping away. Alex's tear-streaked face appears in my mind and my gut lurches. "You don't get it! You don't understand the stress Alex is under right now! She's expecting me to do this for her and I'm being so selfish, with you—" I gesture to him. He looks shocked but I'm too distressed to care.

I need to get out of here. I can't breathe. I can't believe I've done this.

I turn for the door and run.

26

It's early when I wake, and I take my coffee back to bed and crawl under the covers, cradling the steaming mug in my hand. I can't face Alex yet, so I'm hiding in here like the coward I am.

I stumbled out of Luke's last night in such a state, I'm surprised I was even able to remember Alex's address for the cab driver. I was trying to focus on breathing and avoiding a panic attack, and when the cab finally pulled up at the apartment I couldn't recall how we'd got there. Thankfully, Alex and Michael were in bed when I got in, so they didn't see me losing it. I went straight to my room and spent hours researching jewelers online, but you have to make an appointment which means it wouldn't be ready in time, and only a handful work in the specialized antique style of Alex's ring. After that, I crawled into bed. Luke texted to ask if I was okay, but I was too exhausted to reply. Not that I could sleep; every time I was on the cusp of dozing off, my mind would remind me that I might have fucked up my sister's wedding and ruined everything.

I tap the hot mug in my hand now, feeling calmer in the

cool light of morning. There has to be a way to salvage this. I'll call a handful of jewelers today and take my chances. If I offer more money I might be able to elbow my way to the top of the list. Surely it doesn't need to go to that specific jeweler. Gold is gold, right? Even if it is a Hawkins family heirloom, there must be someone who can resize it without having to know all about the style, or whatever. And what was so special about that style, anyway?

Setting my mug down, I reach for my bag to inspect the ring. My hand roots through its contents, landing on tissues, my wallet, lipstick, hairbrush, headphones...

Dread snakes through me as my hand fails to touch a small, velvet box. I force myself to take a calming breath, praying I'm overreacting. *It's here. Of course it's here.* I dump the contents of my bag out onto my lap and stare at it.

The ring isn't here.

My chest seizes as I frantically check the lining and pockets of my bag.

Still no ring. My stomach turns inside-out.

Where the fuck is it?

I know I grabbed it from Luke's last night. At least, I'm sure I did. I was so distraught, I barely remember leaving. Is it possible I dropped it in the cab? Or when I climbed onto the sidewalk?

Please. This can't be happening.

I whip the covers off, stuffing my things back into my bag with trembling hands. I need to retrace my steps. I need to see Luke. He'll know what to do, how to fix this. He has to.

I throw on my clothes and dash out of the room, relieved to see Alex isn't up. I scrawl her a quick note to say I'm doing wedding things all day, then scramble down the stairs and outside.

The cab ride to Luke's is a blur. Adrenaline is pumping

through my veins and I can't breathe properly. The only thing keeping me sane is the same thought on repeat, over and over: *Luke will know what to do. He'll make this okay.*

When I get to his building, I key in the code and practically sprint up the stairs. Then I pound on his door with my fists, my heart drumming in my ears.

Come on, Luke. I need you.

He opens the door in sweats, groggy and yawning. "Harriet?"

"I've lost the ring," I blurt, pushing past him into the apartment. My eyes scour the table where I last remember seeing it, but it's not there. A cold sweat beads along my brow as I turn back to Luke. "I had it when I left and now I can't find it." My breathing is so shallow I feel faint.

Luke closes the door. "It's okay, I've—"

"It's not!" Hot tears sting my eyes but I don't care. "I don't know what to do, Luke. Alex—"

"Harriet, I've got it."

"What?"

He crosses the room, reaching for me. "I've got the ring."

My chest caves in. I suck in a faltering breath and my body goes limp as Luke gathers me into his arms.

"You left it here last night."

"Oh my God." A tear escapes down my cheek and I bury my face in Luke's T-shirt. "I thought I'd lost it." His palm moves in a gentle circle on my back, and I stay like that, nuzzled against him, letting my pulse slow and my hands stop shaking.

"I'm sorry," Luke murmurs after a while, and I draw back to look at him, adjusting my wonky glasses. "I thought you knew you'd left it here. Plus, I wanted to surprise you."

"Surprise me?"

"Yeah." His mouth slants into an uncertain, lop-sided

smile. "I have an old college friend whose wife is a jeweler, and I only thought to call her after you left. I dropped it off late last night and she promised she'd have it ready for me later today."

"Are you... are you serious?"

Luke nods. His brow pinches as he examines my face. "Are you okay?"

"I..." I inhale slowly, feeling exhausted. I probably *look* exhausted, too. "Yes. Fuck, I'm so sorry. I completely overreacted." This is one of the worst parts of having anxiety. In the moment the panic feels so real, but others don't see it like that. They just see you losing your shit, and then looking stupid after everything you worried about turns out to be fine. I dip my head, ashamed, but he tilts my chin back up to him.

"You didn't overreact." He presses a soft kiss to my mouth. "I know how much this wedding means to you, and you didn't want things with us to get in the way."

"You must think I'm ridiculous."

"No." He shakes his head, gazing at me tenderly. "I think you care about your sister and her wedding."

"I just feel so guilty, Luke. Being with you when I know the others wouldn't like it, keeping it from Alex..."

"I get it. I'm not crazy about keeping this from Mike either, especially with Dena coming to the wedding." He grimaces. "But I can't—"

"I know," I say when I see the anguish line his forehead. I think of what he told me last night about Dena and his difficult relationship with his dad. "It's okay. I know."

"Look, do you want to stop?" He tucks a loose strand of hair behind my ear, then takes a big breath and steps away. "I'll understand if you do."

I gaze at the man in front of me—the handsome,

thoughtful man who took me to a board game cafe, who encourages my idea, who talks about games and books with me for hours, and gives me the greatest pleasure I've ever known. When I thought I'd lost the ring this morning, the only person I wanted to see was him. He felt like the only one who would know how to comfort me, how to make everything better, and he did. Even though he saw me for the anxious mess I really am, he's still showing me nothing but kindness. Not just kindness—acceptance. Affection. Desire. He saw me fall apart and he still wants me.

And that makes me feel things that are well beyond my control now.

"I don't think I can," I whisper.

His eyes soften with relief and a rush of air leaves his lungs. Then he reaches a hand to the nape of my neck, stroking his thumb over my cheek. "If you'd said yes, I would have respected that and tried to make it work. But..." He pauses, and his voice is edged with emotion when he finally says, "I'm so glad you didn't."

I step forward, lifting my mouth to his. The tension in my body ebbs away as his lips brush mine and his hands slide up my back.

"We won't let anything else interfere with the wedding, okay? I promise you that. I can't stand seeing you so stressed out." He rests his forehead against mine. "What do we still need to do?"

"We need to get the ring and collect mine and Alex's dresses, as well as the tuxes. We have to make wedding favors for everyone, and put together some welcome gifts for people coming from out of town. Then it's just setting things up in the reception hall when we arrive and making sure the day goes smoothly."

"I'm going to help with all of that, okay? This isn't just your job. It's *our* job."

Gratitude sinks into my bones. "Thank you." Even though he's taken so much weight off my shoulders, I feel myself droop. After the stress of last night and this morning, I'm suddenly so tired I could collapse.

He smooths a hand over my unruly hair, half twisted up into a bun, assessing me. "Did you get any sleep at all?"

I chuckle wryly. "Do I look like shit?"

"You could never look like shit." He kisses my forehead. "But you do look tired. It's still early, why don't you come get some sleep?"

I nibble my lip, glancing down at the dress I threw on in a rush. "I don't have anything..."

"You can borrow a shirt. Come on." He takes my hand and guides me into the bedroom. Then he goes to the dresser, pulling out a black T-shirt. "Here," he says, grinning when he hands it over.

I hold it up to see a picture of baby Yoda—or Grogu, as he's actually called—and smile sleepily. "Aw, I love *The Mandalorian*."

"Of course you do, baby. You think I didn't know that?"

I stare at him, blinking. He just called me "baby." Like I'm... *his*. It makes my insides all hot and messy with so many emotions I'm too tired to process.

But one thing is clear: I fucking love it.

Luke cringes. "Sorry," he says, his cheeks coloring. "That was... I don't know why I called you that."

I shake my head, pushing up onto my toes to kiss him. "I don't mind it. I think I quite like it, actually."

His fingers curl into my waist. "I think I like calling you that. I've never called anyone that."

I'm too sleepy to really think about what this means—

Luke calling me baby when I'm leaving and everything feels so complicated. And I don't *want* to think about what it means. I just want to sink into the beauty of this moment with him. All these tiny moments we have together before the wedding happens, and I have to leave, and everything goes away.

I pull off my dress and Luke spins around so he can't see. It makes me laugh. "You've seen me naked, what are you doing?"

"I don't trust myself not to touch you," he says, raking a hand over his scalp. "I want to let you sleep."

I giggle as I remove my bra and tug the shirt over myself. I undo the bun on my head and set my glasses on his night-stand, then climb into bed. "Will you touch me later?"

"Uh, yeah," he says, turning back to the bed and slipping under the covers beside me. "I won't be able to stop myself after snuggling with you."

He brings his arms around my back and draws me in close, so my nose is tucked right into his chest, against his warmth. I can hear his heart beating, and in the cocoon of his arms, the stillness of his room, a feeling of utter tranquility settles over me.

Wow. I haven't felt this calm for...

Actually, I'm not sure I've ever felt this calm.

Luke presses his lips to my head, stroking his fingers over my back in slow circles, and I decide that in this moment, nothing else matters. Right now, all that matters is the way he's holding me. The way it feels like the best thing in the world.

27

There's bright light spilling into Luke's bedroom when I wake later that morning. I stretch and yawn, feeling a hundred times better. Not just from getting some rest, but from being snuggled in Luke's bed. I roll over to see he's gone, but I can smell coffee and something cooking through the partially-opened door, and I peel the covers off eagerly.

When I pad out into the kitchen, Luke is facing away from me, doing something at the stove. My eyes meander over his shoulders and down his muscular back. Man, I must have been in a right state when I arrived here this morning, because I didn't even appreciate how good his ass looks in those gray sweatpants. Or his crotch, I notice, as he turns to catch me staring.

Whoops.

"Hey," he says, the corners of his eyes crinkling. He's got his glasses on and it makes me want to kiss him senseless. He switches off the stove and sets the pan aside, then pours me some coffee. "Here."

"Thanks." I take the cup with a smile and hold it under my nose, savoring the malty scent.

His gaze drifts down my body. "Damn, you look hot in my shirt."

I hide my grin behind my coffee cup.

"I made pancakes."

"Oh." That's adorable. Nobody has ever made me pancakes before. Nobody's ever made me breakfast. I take a big sip of coffee and set it down, trying to pretend that doesn't make me ridiculously happy. "Sounds good."

"Mm," he says, stepping closer. "Are you hungry?"

"I'm starving." I run my tongue out over my bottom lip.

Luke's eyes linger on my mouth, the espresso-colored irises turning an inky black. "Good." He expels a heavy breath. I think he's fighting the urge to kiss me, and it makes me hot all over.

"Luke," I say, closing the gap between us, bringing my mouth an inch from his.

"Yeah?" he chokes out.

"I want some pancakes."

His brow dips and I giggle.

"I'm kidding. Kiss me."

He narrows his eyes, a mischievous smile nudging his lips as he shakes his head. "Nope. Not after that."

I ponder him for a second, then decide to call his bluff. "Okay." I hike up a shoulder and turn for the counter. "I'll just—"

"Fine." He takes my arm and hauls me against his chest. "You win." His mouth covers mine and I sink against him. "As if I could ever say no," he murmurs, kissing me again. His kiss starts gently, with slow strokes of his tongue, dipping into my mouth, teasing me. Heat sparks in my abdomen, spreading out along my limbs and settling heavily between my thighs.

It only takes a minute for our sweet kisses to escalate. The soft flick of his tongue against mine becomes rough and demanding, his mouth urging mine open further so he can take more. He presses his body into me against the kitchen island. I can feel him hardening for me, and I groan right into his mouth, lowering my hands to stroke the bulge in his pants. I can't help myself. I want to feel exactly what I'm doing to him, because he's having the same effect on me. He's been kissing me less than five minutes and I'm already giddy.

He removes his glasses and sets them aside, then he drops his hands to the kitchen island, caging me between his arms. He contemplates me with dark eyes as I stroke my hand over his straining sweatpants. I love the way it pulls a rough sound from his throat, makes his eyes flutter closed in pleasure. Seeing how good it makes him feel sends waves of wet, molten heat right through my center.

"God, you drive me wild," he rasps, grinding himself against my palm. His cheeks are flushed, and I lean into the curve of his shoulder, pushing his shirt aside to press my lips to his skin. Then I raise my mouth to his ear, grazing my teeth over the curve of his earlobe, and he forces a groan out through his teeth. "Come with me," he says gruffly, turning for the bedroom. But I tug him back by the arm and push him up against the kitchen island.

"No." I fall to my knees in front of him. "We're doing this right here."

His eyebrows inch up, but I don't hesitate. I *am* hungry, but it's not pancakes I want. I replay his words—*you drive me wild*—and they make me feel wild myself. No man has ever said that to me before. Not even close. And the more he shows how much he wants me, the less I stop to think about what I'm doing.

I push his sweatpants down his hips and his erection springs free. While I've never found the male anatomy especially nice to look at, I'd be lying if I said this wasn't one of the most beautiful things I've seen. I think I get what he means about going down on someone not for them, but for you. Because right now, I want nothing more than to take him into my mouth.

I close my fist around his thick length, wetting my lips. When I flick my gaze up to his, he's watching me with hooded eyes. I lick the moist tip of him, deliberately taking my time as I relish his musky, salty taste. A hard breath shudders out of him as I do it again, swirling my tongue.

"Fuck," he growls. "You look so good down there, baby."

Hearing him call me that again makes my heart thunder in my chest. I'm on my knees in front of him and he's calling me baby and I never want to leave his apartment again.

No. I can't think that thought. I know I can't.

Instead I wrap my lips around him, drawing him into my mouth. He throws his head back on a long moan and his knees buckle. He has to grip the counter behind him.

Good. I want to make him lose his mind.

I focus on my task, paying attention to the way he responds. How he loves it when I use my hands too, when I suck harder, when I drag my tongue up the underside and over the tip.

His hand moves from the counter to grab my hair and pull it to one side, out of the way. Then he holds it like that as his hips thrust forward. I look up, locking my gaze with his as I let him fuck my mouth, and he grits out a string of incoherent words. I can't believe *I'm* doing this to him, I'm making this gorgeous man come undone. I feel like a goddess, drunk on the power I have over him. It makes me take him deeper, until he abruptly stills.

"Shit—stop," he says, and I pull my mouth off him with a pop. He's breathing heavily, his eyes pressed shut like he's in pain.

"Everything okay?"

After a beat, he opens his eyes. "Uh, yeah." He takes my face gently and pulls me to my feet. "I just didn't want to finish in your mouth. I want to be inside you when I do that." He kisses me and I smile against his lips.

"You want to be inside me?"

He nods, his glazed eyes making him look drugged with lust.

"Okay." I take a deep breath, summoning my courage. I know what I want, and I'm going to damn well ask for it. I want him like I fantasized in the shower. I want him to take me right here.

Sliding my underwear down, I kick it off and turn so I'm facing the kitchen island, just like in my fantasy. Then I reach for Luke's hand, placing it on my hip. "Like this." I lean forward, lowering my top half across the counter. The granite is cool through Luke's T-shirt, my breasts pressed against the hard surface, my ass up in the air. I can't believe I'm here, with the bright light of day streaming in through the sheer curtains, exposing myself in such a vulnerable position. But I don't feel vulnerable or exposed. I feel bold. I feel exhilarated.

Behind me, Luke lets out a low groan. "Jesus Christ, Harriet. Do you know how many times I've imagined doing this to you?"

My breath comes out in a stutter. I've wanted this ever since my time in the shower. Ever since he stood behind me here a week ago, on the brink of losing control. Maybe I can make him lose control now.

He drops to his knees behind me, hands on the backs of my thighs, spreading me. Then he slides his tongue over the slick heat between my legs.

Oh—my—

My knees collapse beneath me. No one has done that from this angle before. It feels so much naughtier for some reason, and that makes me love it more.

He works his tongue over me until I'm a panting, heaving mess on his counter, then he rises to his feet and ducks out of the room. A second later, he's back—sweatpants gone, shirt off—rolling on a condom.

He steps behind me, lifting me up off the counter a little, slipping his hands up under the shirt I'm wearing to grasp my waist. Then he leans forward, speaking softly into my ear. "You okay?"

"I'll be better once you're inside me," I mutter, squeezing my thighs together with impatience. I reach across the counter and grab his glasses, handing them back to him. "Wear these."

"Seriously?"

I turn to look at him. "Seriously."

He hesitates, then takes the glasses, sliding them up his nose.

Hell yes—there's my sexy nerd.

"You look so fucking hot with those on." I turn back to the counter and lift my ass up for him.

"Good to know," he says with a chuckle, positioning himself at my entrance. His hands skate around to cup my breasts and he pinches my nipples between his forefinger and thumb. Heat zips down my middle, culminating in a hot pulse between my legs.

Then, without warning, he pushes into me.

"Oh—fuck," I cry. Pleasure invades me, rolling through me in a wave that pulls me under. I can't breathe, I can't think—I can only feel.

Luke lets out a harsh breath behind me, placing his hands on my lower back and nudging so I fall forward again. Then he grasps my hips and draws all the way out before thrusting back in. We both moan as he fills me perfectly.

"Ever since you bent over this counter last week," he growls, building up his pace, "I've wanted you here. Just like this."

"Me too," I admit, closing my eyes and giving into the sensation of him taking me just how he wants me. I can't explain it; even though he's in control of me right now, I've never felt more free.

His hands squeeze my hips. "You really thought about it?"

"I did," I pant. "I made myself come thinking about it."

He makes a rough, guttural sound. His thrusts become more shallow and when I glance back at him, he's looking down, watching himself fuck me.

Holy... I can't even...

"Oh my God." My eyes roll back and I let my head drop again. "This is..."

"I know," he grits out behind me. "You make me crazy, Harriet. You make me want to lose control."

"Do it." My voice is a throaty whisper. "Lose control with me."

"I shouldn't—"

"Please." I don't care that I'm begging now. I'll beg all day for him. "Please, Luke. Please—"

Smack.

I hear the sound first, chased by the stinging sensation a split second later, burning on my ass cheek. I jolt with surprise, but that feeling is quickly replaced with another: arousal. Luke just smacked me on the ass, and I *liked* it.

I look at him over my shoulder and he grimaces. "Shit, sorry. That was probably—"

"That was so hot."

His eyes flash behind his glasses and he does it again, harder.

Smack.

I groan, pressing my forehead to the cool granite of his counter as heat devours me. *Why* do I like that so much?

"Fuck." He presses himself deep, leaning over me so his chest is flush with my back. Sweeping my hair to one side, he kisses the back of my neck. "You turn me on so much. I love how you have no inhibitions with sex."

I'm too aroused to really process his words. I know I have inhibitions—or rather I did once, before him. But I can't recall them now. I can't recall why, or who I was, then. All I can do is try to remember to breathe while he rolls my nipples between his fingers and grinds into me.

"Tell me what you want," he says against my ear. His voice is so low and commanding it makes me clench around him.

"This. You."

"No." He tweaks my nipples harder. "I know you want more. Tell me, baby."

"I want..." What do I want? "Pull my hair." The words spill from my mouth without my permission and I cringe, waiting for him to object, to tell me I've gone too far. But instead, he grunts in approval.

"Fuck yes." He straightens up, sliding his hand into my hair at the scalp, tightening it into a fist. "Like that?"

"Yes," I gasp out. The pain that prickles across my scalp somehow makes the pleasure he's giving me that much more intense. When he slams into me again, tugging with his hand, heat pours through me from head to toe. "Yes, Luke, yes."

He keeps one hand on my hip, the other one twisting in my hair as he drills into me, fucking me with abandon. I'm losing track of time and space, feeling myself climb higher, burn brighter, and then—

"Oh, baby—" Luke buries himself deep inside me, releasing a hoarse, broken moan as he reaches his limit. That pushes me over the edge, and I free-fall into oblivion with him. Ecstasy explodes through my body, my legs shake uncontrollably, and I cry out in surrender.

I'm not sure how long it is until I become aware of my surroundings again, but when I do, the kitchen island is digging hard into my stomach and I half laugh, half groan.

Luke untangles his hand from my hair and withdraws from me, disposing of the condom. When I finally straighten up and turn around, he pulls me into his arms, smoothing a hand over my head, tucking a lock of hair behind one ear. "Did you... I mean, I'm sorry if I got there before you..."

"I did," I say, squeezing him.

He sighs, pressing a sweet kiss to my forehead. "You're amazing, Harriet."

"So are you." My legs are weak and I sway against him. "I can't even stand now."

He chuckles and scoops me up into his arms. "Have a shower. I'll warm up breakfast, then I'm taking you out."

"Out?"

He carries me through to his bathroom, then sets me down on the tiled floor. "Yeah. We need to get the ring, and there's something I want to show you." He passes me a clean towel, pausing to examine my face. "Are you... all good?"

"Why wouldn't I be?"

He lifts a shoulder. "I hope you feel okay about everything we just did."

"Oh." A smile pushes at my mouth. "Uh, yeah, I'm okay."

His brow wrinkles uncertainly and I slide a hand up the back of his neck, tilting his head down so I can kiss him.

"Luke, that was..." I try to find the words to describe how I'm feeling. Satisfied, yes, but it's more than that. I feel empowered. I feel strong. I feel like I've tapped into a new inner power I didn't even know was there. "That was unlike anything I've ever done. That was the hottest sex I've ever had." *By fucking light years.*

His face relaxes into a grin. "Okay, good. I just wanted to check. And for the record, same here." He leans in to turn on the shower, then kisses me again before leaving me alone in the bathroom.

As I step into the warm water, it feels like a baptism. I can't explain it; all I know is that I'm not the same person I was when I woke this morning. I feel like I've been reborn.

28

L uke takes me somewhere on the Lower East Side, and when our cab pulls up he opens the door with a secretive little smile. In his hand is a folder he grabbed from his office before we left, but he hasn't told me what's inside. In fact, he hardly said anything on the drive over and I'm not sure what to make of it.

We step from the cab and I glance around, trying to figure out what he has planned, but nothing catches my eye. I'm even more confused when a guy in a shirt and tie grins at Luke and wanders over to clap him on the shoulder.

"Hawkins!" he says, then turns to me, extending a hand. "You must be Harriet. I'm Isaac."

"Er, hi." I shake Isaac's hand, bewildered.

"Isaac is in real estate," Luke explains, but that only raises more questions than it answers.

"Here's the ring." Isaac pulls a familiar velvet box from his pocket and I lunge on it, relief rushing through me. I pop it open and check all is as it should be, then turn back to Isaac.

"Thank you so much. But..." I glance at Luke in confusion.

"It was Isaac's wife, Julia, I took the ring to last night," he explains. "And when I was over there chatting with them, I had an idea."

I draw a breath to ask for more information, but Luke gestures for me to follow Isaac, who's pulling out some keys. He leads us to an empty shop and fiddles with the lock before swinging open the glass doors and guiding us inside. It's dark, then I hear a switch flick and a row of lights along the ceiling illuminates the space.

I wander down the length of the store, taking it in. It's long, receding back from the street, with exposed ceilings. The walls are a mess, with peeling paint and half-demolished drywall in places. There is what appears to once have been a bar, stacked with crates, and a door behind it that I can only assume leads to a kitchen or something. In one corner is a stack of chairs and tables.

I turn to Luke, wondering why on earth we are here. He says something to Isaac, his voice low, his eyes on me, and Isaac nods.

"Okay, well, I'll leave you guys alone for a while," he says with a smile, and heads back out the door.

Luke wanders towards me with a half-smile on his lips, and for a second I think he's going to kiss me, that he's brought me here to have sex. I'm not saying I wouldn't consider it, but it does seem a bit odd.

Unless... Oh God, maybe this is some kind of kinky sex club? Maybe it's like those secret speakeasies you hear about, where it looks like nothing and you have to do a special knock somewhere and a door opens leading you to a basement. My mind floods with images of sex dungeons, walls lined with whips and chains, and my stomach knots with apprehension. I might have loved our adventurous time in the kitchen this morning, but there are only so many sexual achievement badges I want to unlock today.

I watch Luke warily, but he pulls up a couple of chairs and motions for me to sit. So I do, setting my bag down beside me.

"What do you think?" he asks, placing the folder on his lap.

"Um..." I glance around and back at him. "For what?"

"For a board game cafe."

What?

Surprise steals my breath. I open and close my mouth, but no words come out.

Luke chuckles. "I've been thinking about what you said, that you wanted to do it but didn't know where to start. When I saw Isaac last night, I remembered he works in commercial real estate. I ran the idea by him, and he had a look through his listings to see what might work." Luke grins as he gestures to the space around us.

I stare at him, stunned. First of all, he went out of his way to get the ring sorted for me because he knew I was freaking out. And now, he's brought me here...

When I don't say anything, his smile recedes. "I know it doesn't look like much right now, but there's a lot of potential here. I don't think it would take much to do it up. You would have to invest in some stock, but"—he taps the folder —"I did some initial projections, and I think after about six months you should be able to turn a decent profit."

I swallow, trying to process this. He thinks this could work. He thinks this is possible.

His face is uncertain as he watches for my reaction, but I don't know what to say. My heart is doing something strange inside my chest. I can't believe he did this. It's one thing to say a few encouraging words about my dream, but he went out of his way to show me that it's *not* just a dream. That it could be real.

"Luke," I murmur. "I can't..." I trail off, searching for the right words. He looks crestfallen and I shake my head vigorously. "No—" A laugh tickles my throat. "I mean, I can't believe you did this." I rise from my chair and sit in his lap. I probably shouldn't, given we aren't in private, but at this moment *nothing* could stop me from touching him.

A grin breaks across his face and he wraps his arms around me, visibly relieved. "Oh, shit. I thought you were mad at me or something."

"No." I take his face in my hands and press my lips hard against his. "How could I be mad? You went to all this trouble."

"So what do you think?"

I look around the place, seeing it through new eyes. It is a great space, and I could absolutely see it working. My body buzzes with excited energy as I visualize how my floor plan would work in here, what the walls would look like painted a warm, golden yellow. All those details, scrawled on that napkin in my bag... I can see them coming to life in this space.

Luke places the folder in my hands and I flick it open, running my eyes over the contents. There are pages of numbers and notes, some typed, some hand-written, all—more or less—unintelligible to me. There are a few numbers I can make sense of, though, and I'm pretty sure I'd have enough money to set this place up and get it running. One of the good things about having next to no social life over the past decade is that I've accumulated a very healthy savings account.

"This is great, but..." I glance up at Luke and sigh. "There are already board game cafes in the city."

"There are, but none in the East Village or Lower East Side. I think it would do really well around here." He pauses before adding quietly, "You could totally do this, Harriet. I'm happy to loan you the money to get set up if you need."

I glance at him in surprise. He would loan me the money? Why would he do that for me?

I shake the thought away, not daring to let myself think it. "That's really sweet, thank you. But I have enough."

His eyebrows shoot up. "That's fantastic," he says, squeezing me. "Did you ever think of what you might call the place?"

"Not really. But I like the idea of a play on words. Like... Cakes and Ladders."

He looks puzzled. "Cakes and Ladders?"

"Yeah, like the game Snakes and Ladders, where you go up or down depending on—"

"Oh, right. We call it *Chutes* and Ladders here, so it would have to be something else. Like..." He rubs his chin, thinking. "Chutes and Lattes."

"I like that! What about Noughts and Coffee?" I'm pretty pleased with this one, but Luke looks confused again. "Seriously? Noughts and Crosses! It's the game with the crosses and zeros, and—"

"You mean Tic-Tac-Toe."

I huff in mock indignation. "You Americans and your weird names for things."

A warm laugh rumbles in his chest, and he presses his mouth to mine.

"Game of Scones," I murmur against his lips.

He draws away with a chuckle. "I think that's the one."

"I know you're kidding but I kind of love it. Game of

Scones," I repeat to myself, looking around the place again, imagining it as my own. When I glance back at Luke, his mouth is curved in an affectionate smile. "Why have you gone to all this trouble for me, to show me I could do this?"

He shrugs. "I guess I know what it's like to not have someone support your dream. It's pretty soul-destroying. I wanted to give you what I didn't have."

"You really believe I could do this."

He tilts his head to one side, raising a hand to tuck a strand of hair behind my ear. "Absolutely. I think you *should* do this."

I look down again at the folder, feeling my heart swell. I'm struck by a sudden, powerful sense of how much I want this. *Really* want this. Not just that I *want* this, but that I could *do* it. I could.

But...

I release an uneasy breath and stand from Luke's lap, clutching the folder. "You do realize I live in New Zealand," I mutter, inspecting a wall to avoid looking at him.

"Well, yes. But you could move." He pushes to his feet. "Your sister already lives here. She'd love to have you here permanently."

I smile to myself, because he's right. Even though she's been busier lately, I've enjoyed getting to spend time with her. Things feel different between us over here, and I'm sad at the thought of going home without her.

"And, you know," he murmurs from beside me, slipping his hand into mine, "Alex isn't the only one who might like you to stick around." I turn and meet his gaze—tentative, searching, hopeful—and my heart trips and stumbles. When he breathes a tiny self-conscious laugh and looks down at his feet, I have to bite back a grin wider than the East River.

Is he for *real*? Is he seriously suggesting he wants me to move to New York, and that he and I could—

"So, what do you think?" Isaac's voice makes me jump and I drop Luke's hand.

He laughs, turning to Isaac with an easy smile. "She'll take some more convincing, I think."

"Fair enough." Isaac hands me his business card. "Call me if you change your mind."

I take the card and turn it over in my hand. They head out onto the street, chatting and laughing, and I stand there staring after them, my mind racing.

29

"Okay... nude, I guess."

Alex gives me a strange look. "Are you sure you don't want to go for something more exciting?"

I shake my head, and the manicurist reaches for the nude polish. I've already had these ridiculous gel things put on my nails, making them twice as long as they should be. It's bad enough I won't be able to use my hands for anything now; the last thing I need is for them to be bright orange or something. Even Harriet 2.0 has her limits.

I relax back against my seat as the manicurist sets about painting my nails. It's been a busy few days and it's nice to unwind and be pampered a little.

"You know," Geoff chimes in from where he's getting his feet scrubbed, "you could argue that going nude *is* the most exciting option." He tosses us a cheeky grin and we all laugh.

"So, are you feeling ready for the big day?" Cat asks Alex, blowing on her scarlet nails.

"Mostly." A smile brushes Alex's lips. "Once I get this

draft to my editor tonight, I'll feel better. The only reason I'm not totally stressed is because Harri and Luke have worked so hard to get the wedding sorted. I don't know where I'd be without them."

My body tenses ever so slightly and I steal a quick glance at Alex. After our minor detour into New York real estate three days ago, Luke and I have spent a lot of time together. We haven't spoken about the cafe again, or Luke's suggestion that I move to New York, and I'm glad that he's given me some time to process it.

Instead, we've spent our time in bed, under the pretense of completing wedding tasks. We actually managed to finish the wedding stuff in one day, and I've been terrified that Alex would figure it out. Every night I've come home from Luke's, anxious that her and Michael would be suspicious, but they've both been so distracted by their work they haven't noticed a thing.

"And is Mel still coming?" Cat asks.

"Ugh, yes." Alex makes a face and Cat glances at me.

"She's told you about Mel, right?"

"Yes. I'm on it. My job on the day is to make sure she doesn't do anything."

Geoff snorts. "Good luck."

My eyes dart between the three of them. "You don't really think she will pull something, do you?"

"I don't know." Alex's brow knits. "I wouldn't put it past her. I'd hate for Henry to get caught up in something, and I want Michael to be able to relax."

Right. I need to absolutely stay on top of the Mel situation. It doesn't matter what's going on with Luke, or Dena, or anything else—Mel needs to be kept in line so Alex and Michael can enjoy their wedding.

"Don't worry about it," I assure Alex. "You can count on me."

"Thanks, Harri. Are you still okay to go up to Indian Lake early?"

"Uh-huh." I focus on my nails, careful to suppress the excited smile I feel forming on my lips.

As nice as it's been spending the past few days with Luke, every evening I've had to come home. But Luke had a great idea; the wedding and reception are taking place at some lodge at Indian Lake, a town in the Adirondacks where his family has had a cabin for years, and he thought we could go up to the lodge a day early to "get everything ready" (read: spend a whole night alone together in the cabin). I was nervous when I floated the idea to Alex, expecting a raised eyebrow at least. Instead, she was overcome with relief and thanked me for being "so thoughtful," then turned back to her laptop without a second thought. I couldn't believe it.

But the fact that she doesn't suspect anything—that she trusts me so implicitly—has made the guilt I feel about lying to her so much worse. It's not just that, though. Growing up, Alex and I never talked about boys or that kind of stuff. I finally have something so juicy to share, and I can't. I've never wanted so badly to tell my sister something, and it's killing me.

Anyway, at least the wedding is organized, so I know that will go smoothly. Now Luke and I can go to the cabin for a night alone before our families arrive. Anticipation rushes my bloodstream at the thought of spending an entire night with Luke.

"...so he'll just see you the morning of the wedding..."

I sigh happily, letting my mind drift off as I picture curling up in Luke's arms, kissing his—

"Harriet!"

I startle, causing the manicurist to smudge my nail. She gives me a disapproving look and sets about cleaning it up.

"What is going on with you?" Alex demands, her eyes narrowed to slits.

My cheeks grow warm. "What?"

"I've just spent the past five minutes talking to you about Derek and you've been somewhere else the whole time."

"Derek?"

"Your date for the wedding."

"My date?"

"Yes!" she says, exasperated. "Remember, you asked me to find you a date for the wedding. Cat asked Derek, and now—"

"Oh. Yes. Derek." Shit. I completely forgot about him.

"You still want to take him to the wedding, right?"

"Er, well..." I don't *really* want to take this random Derek character to the wedding, even if Luke will be there with Dena. I never wanted to take him at all, but I can't say that now.

"Oh for God's sake." Alex puffs out a frustrated breath. "Why have you changed your mind?"

From the corner of my eye, I catch Geoff sending me a knowing look. For a moment I wonder what's going through his mind, if—fuck—has he figured it out? Then I remember the conversation with him and Cat where I told them I'd been in touch with the "guy from the plane." And I realize that maybe, if I'm careful, there is a way I could share some things with Alex.

"Okay." I give Geoff a conspiratorial smile, then turn to Alex. "I... uh, I've kind of been seeing someone."

"What?" she squeals, and Cat chuckles at her response.

A grin streaks across Geoff's face. "I knew it! Is it your hot plane lover?"

I nod, finally letting myself beam like I've been wanting to all afternoon.

"Wait, what?" Alex cocks her head. "You've been seeing the guy you hooked up with on the plane?"

"I have," I say cautiously. Relief rolls over me at sharing —well, if not the whole truth, some of it.

"Oh my God!" She smacks a hand on the table and the manicurist pauses, giving her a look, but Alex doesn't notice. "Why didn't you say something? How did this happen?"

I shrug, trying to be nonchalant. "It just kind of... happened."

"Wait." She sits upright, concern flickering across her face. "So you *haven't* been working on the wedding stuff?"

"Of course I have! That's all sorted."

"Oh." She settles back in her chair, going quiet for a moment. "I guess I did notice you'd been staying out pretty late. I just figured you were at Luke's."

"No!" I say, a little too quickly. My pulse jumps and I stare intently at my nails as heat spreads across my neck. "I was with... Liam." *Gah! That's too close to Luke!*

"Liam," she repeats, as if testing the name out. I glance at her in worry, but she's grinning. "Well, tell me about him! I want to know everything."

This time I do blush, properly. I haven't had a chance to share this with anyone, and I'm dying to. I know I probably shouldn't say anything, but surely a few, vague details would be okay?

Before I can help myself, I'm gushing. "He is *so* sexy— but it's more than that. He's been really supportive about this idea I had to open a cafe. And he's so cute with me, always holding my hand, kissing me, and he does this sweet thing where he tucks my hair behind my ear." I smile, picturing the adoring way he looks at me when he does that, and a little sigh escapes me. "He's just... he's amazing."

"Wow," Alex breathes, her eyes wide. "You really like this guy."

My skin prickles uncomfortably at her words. She's right —I *do* really like this guy. I like this guy who is pretending to be married to someone else and lives thousands of miles away from where I live.

"Yeah," I mumble, my shoulders slumping. Across the salon I see Geoff watching me curiously, but I ignore him.

"So you'll bring him to the wedding then?" Cat asks.

"Oh, no." I shake my head and a heavy feeling settles over my heart. "It's... no, it's not like that."

"What?" Alex asks, puzzled.

I shrug, blowing on my nails. "It's complicated." I think back to when Luke first used that word, and how much more complicated it is now.

"You mean it's just a fling?" Cat says. "Because you're leaving?"

"Yeah," I mutter. A fling. I hadn't thought to label it but I guess that's what it is.

"Are you *kidding*?" Alex blinks at me, incredulous. "I've *never* heard you talk about a guy like that before. That's not just a fling, Harriet. It sounds like you're in love."

"I'm not in love," I reply, chuckling. That's such an Alex thing to say. "It's only been a couple of weeks." But she's right about one thing: I like him a lot. So much that I can't bear the thought of leaving. And that's before I remind myself that I'll have to see him pretending to be in love with his ex-wife soon. But there's no point dwelling on that right now.

I push the thought from my mind, and by the time we

finish up and head out of the salon, I'm back to being excited about spending the night at the cabin alone with Luke. It's going to be delicious.

The four of us wander through the East Village, talking and laughing in the pink blush of early evening. There's a cool nip in the air, and I smile when we step into the warmth of Bounce. Alex and Cat head for a booth, but Geoff grabs my arm.

"We'll get drinks," he calls to the others, then drags me up to the bar.

I open my mouth to ask Geoff what's going on when a tall, bearded bartender appears in front of us. Cat's brother—I remember him from the last time we were here.

"Hey!" He runs a hand through his messy, dirty-blond hair. "You're Alex's sister, right?"

"Yes," I say, smiling. "I'm Harriet."

"Cory Porter." He extends his hand and I shake it, feeling a little flustered. I'd forgotten how cute he is.

Beside me, Geoff rolls his eyes at Cory. "Don't even think about it."

Cory laughs, raising his hands innocently. "Just being friendly."

"Sure." Geoff adjusts his glasses, then gestures behind the bar. "Can we get a round of strawberry rosé mojitos?"

"Seriously?" Cory scrunches his nose and Geoff chuckles.

"Yes. It's a bride thing."

"Fine." Cory lets out a resigned sigh. "I'll get Josie. She knows how to make them." He heads to the other end of the bar, speaking to a petite brunette woman, and she grabs a pitcher to make our drinks.

Geoff turns his attention to me. "I told you something

would happen with your plane man," he says with a self-satisfied grin. "So you figured everything out?"

I play with a cardboard coaster on the bar, overcome with the sudden urge to tell him everything. Steph's been busy at a work conference and hasn't had time to chat, and when I think of the last time I talked to Geoff, he was so encouraging.

"Well," I say, dropping my voice, "kind of."

He quirks an eyebrow. "What does that mean?"

"He's—" How do I explain this? "He's recently divorced. He still has some loose ends to tie up, but—"

"Loose ends?"

I glance over to check that Cat and Alex are still in the booth. "Yeah. He hasn't told everyone he's divorced yet."

"Why not?"

"Oh, um..." I stall, thinking. I can't very well tell him about the wedding situation, can I? "That's the complicated part."

Geoff's brow furrows in a frown. When he catches my worried expression, he shakes his head. "I'm sorry. It's probably nothing."

Unease threads through me. "Geoff, tell me what you're thinking."

"Well..." He hesitates, holding his breath, then exhales. "I find it strange that he's divorced, but hasn't told everyone."

"He has a good reason. And... he will. It's just not the right time."

"Right," Geoff says, unconvinced. "I hope you don't take this the wrong way, but surely, if he likes you as much as you like him, *now* would be the right time? Why would he want to hide what he has with you? I know you said this is just a casual thing or whatever, but you do seem to be quite... invested. I'd hate to see you get hurt."

A pitcher appears on the bar in front of us. "Strawberry rosé mojitos," the brunette bartender says. Her green eyes are bright with a smile.

"Great! Thanks, Josie." Geoff takes the pitcher then turns back to me, his face softening. "Look, I'm sure it's fine. If you say he has a good reason, then..." He shrugs, nodding towards the others. "Come on. Let's have a drink."

I watch him head to the booth, my gut twisting like a rag. I know what Geoff is saying and it makes sense. But... Luke isn't hiding *me* so much as he is keeping up appearances to placate his father. After the wedding, all that will be over. He still has to tell his family, of course, but he *will* tell them, I know that. He won't pretend to be married forever, otherwise why would he suggest I move to New York?

"Harriet!" Alex calls.

I scuttle over to the booth, shoving Geoff's words away. It might have only been a couple of weeks, but I know Luke. I know this is not something I need to worry about.

30

The door thuds closed behind us and I expel a long, relieved breath.

We are *finally* at Luke and Michael's family cabin after a four and a half hour drive through torrential rain. It wasn't so much the drive or the weather that was the problem, it was that I couldn't have my hands on Luke while he was driving. Every time I leaned across to kiss him or touch him, he batted me away. When he caught my hurt expression he explained that he *wanted* me to touch him but I probably shouldn't, in case he careened off the road and killed us both. I guess that's a justifiable reason, but still.

I turn to Luke impatiently, thrusting my hands up into his damp hair and pulling his mouth down onto mine. He drops the bags he's carrying and laughs against my lips, setting his hands on my waist and walking me backwards towards the bedroom. As he drags my sweater up, I shiver in the cool air.

"Okay," he says, drawing away from me. "We will enjoy this a lot more if we're warm."

I pout and his cheek twitches with a suppressed smile.

"Why don't you unpack the groceries while I make a fire, then we can, *you know*." He wiggles his eyebrows in a suggestive manner like a cartoon character, which earns him a giggle.

"Fine." I waited four and a half hours, what's a few minutes more?

Agony, that's what.

I tear my hands off him with a long-suffering sigh and pad over to the kitchen, looking around the cabin. It has big round log walls, high peaked ceilings, and a stone fireplace in the main living area. There's a comfy sofa and two armchairs, and a small kitchen with wooden cabinetry and simple wooden bench tops.

I unpack the groceries, listening to the rain whip against the windows. I'm not sure what we'll do if it doesn't ease up; the wedding ceremony is supposed to be outside. I make a mental note to secure an alternative location first thing in the morning if it's still raining. That way, Alex can rest assured that everything will still go ahead.

It only takes me a few moments to unpack and when I'm done I head back into the bedroom, looking for Luke. He said he was going to make a fire, but he hasn't been out to the living room. Why is he—

Oh. There's a fireplace in the bedroom and he's kneeling in front of it, coaxing little flames across the kindling, staring into it thoughtfully. Damn, he looks sexy making a fire. He's pushed back the sleeves of his sweater to expose those delectable arms of his, and when he places another log onto the growing flames, it sets off some kind of primal response in my brain. Next thing I know I'm beside him, pulling him up so I can get his lips on mine again.

"Can I have you now?" I ask, trying and failing to keep the desperation out of my voice. My fingers find their way to his forearms and stroke over the muscle, squeezing gently. "Fuck," I groan as I feel the tendons flex under my fingertips. Who needs foreplay when I can just do this?

He looks down at where I'm touching him and his mouth hooks into a sinful grin. Then he nudges me back onto the bed, climbing over me. "Take your hair down," he growls, and I immediately obey.

We spend the next forty-five minutes making up for that unreasonably long car trip, and when we finally relax onto the mattress, I take a moment to soak in the surroundings. The room is lit by the glow of the fire in front of us, while rain and wind pound against the windows outside. It's the most romantic setting I've ever seen.

"This place is amazing," I say as Luke pulls me in close to him.

"Yeah, I love it. Mike and I have been coming here since we were kids."

Something occurs to me suddenly. "Will Donnie be okay while you're away?"

"I have the turtle lady, remember?"

"Oh, right." I chuckle. "Of course." I rest my head against his bare chest and listen to the thrumming of his heartbeat, smiling to myself.

"It's so nice having you here with me," he murmurs, running a hand down my body. His finger swirls tenderly over my stomach, trailing lower, pausing to move back and forth over the row of tiny scars along the top of my thigh. Propping himself up on his elbow, he gazes at the little ridges, etched into my skin many moons ago. "What are these?"

I shift uneasily. I have the fleeting impulse to lie, but when I think of how Luke has seen every part of me—including the messy bits—and still wants me, I know I don't have to. "Scars," I say at last. No one has ever asked about them before, because I haven't been comfortable letting others see them. I guess that's why, in the past, I've only ever had sex in the dark.

"I know." Luke gives me a gentle smile. "But what are they from?"

I study his face, the way his forehead is creased in concentration as he traces his fingers back and forth over the tiny stripes. His curiosity is endearing; it seems he really doesn't know.

"I used to cut myself," I say, hearing the words from my own mouth for the first time in years. The only other person I've shared this information with is my therapist, and she gets paid not to call me crazy. Despite the fact that Luke has shown me nothing but kindness and acceptance, I half expect him to recoil in disgust.

But he just slips his arms tight around me and tucks my head against his chest. "Oh, baby," he murmurs, stroking a hand over my hair. He doesn't ask any more questions, but his embrace is so comforting, so—dare I say it—*loving*, that I want to tell him more.

"It was in high school. I haven't done it since. But back then... it was not a good time."

He leans back, his eyes regarding me with concern.

"I was bullied. A lot."

"For what?"

I can't help but chuckle at his genuine bewilderment. "Well, I wasn't always the super cool, sexy lady you see today."

He doesn't laugh. He just leans down and presses his lips against mine, running his thumb over my cheek.

"I don't know," I mumble. "For being a nerd. I liked

things that weren't cool. I read a lot, I wore glasses, I was awkward and I guess I was just easy prey."

He gives a little nod, tucking a lock of hair behind my ear.

"This was just one way of dealing with it," I say, gesturing to my scars. "I know it wasn't healthy, but I was a teenager. I didn't know how to handle everything. It got so bad—" I break off, wondering how much to share. I hate revisiting this period of my life and I *never* share it with others.

Before I can stop them, the images rush back to me and my chest burns. I'm back in the girls' bathroom at high school, the sound of cheap plastic heels clicking on the filthy linoleum as Tracey Merritt backs me into a corner, flanked by two girls—Jade and Meredith.

"Where do you think you're going, *Harriet*?" Tracey always said my name in a mocking sing-song, just to emphasize how much she hated me. "Off to play another one of your board games?"

I tried to move past them, but they stepped closer. Trepidation climbed my spine as I realized I was alone with them in the bathroom. I clutched my books tighter, like a life preserver in a stormy sea, hoping someone would come to my rescue.

"Or maybe it's book club today?" Jade asked, arching a menacing brow.

Meredith joined in with a cackle. "It will be something completely nerdtastic. You're such a dork, Harriet." She took a step forward, sneering, and panic zipped through me. My pulse scrambled and suddenly, it felt like I was treading water and only just staying afloat.

"She can't even talk," Tracey said, snickering. "It's pathetic. You're pathetic, Harriet."

I tried to take a breath, determined to prove them wrong. "I'm not—" I choked out, but I couldn't find the air I needed to speak. My lungs seized and my vision blurred. I didn't know what was happening to me.

"*Pathetic*," Tracey hissed. "No wonder you can't get a boyfriend." She jabbed a finger into my chest, sending me stumbling back into the wall. My heart slammed in my ears as I cowered under her, and when I tried to grip onto the wall for support, my hand slipped. My books crashed to my feet. The room spun around me and I couldn't fill my lungs. I wasn't afloat anymore—I was drowning.

I don't remember much after that. I think someone found me and took me to the school nurse, but I can't be sure. It took this happening a few more times before I learned what was happening to me. Panic attacks, they called them. *Attack* certainly felt right—like my body just turned on me when I needed it most.

The doctor recommended therapy to help me manage everything. I resisted going at first. Living in such a small town, I worried everyone would know I had these issues, that I would be labeled as "that girl." But I also didn't want to keep feeling that way. I wanted to get past it. Not just being taunted for who I was and what I loved, but for the way everything felt sort of... dangerous. All the time. The way I couldn't trust my body not to betray me. The way it felt like there was no way to be safe.

Eventually, once I learned how to manage things in a healthy way, I found some semblance of a normal life. I decided I wouldn't let those girls and their nasty words stop me. With hindsight and maturing, I came to see that people's behavior is usually a reflection of how they feel about *themselves*, and has little to do with others. I embraced my inner nerd and learned to love myself. I got a job, I had friends, and I had my board games and my books. I had a life.

Well, I'd thought I had. But after these two weeks with Luke, I can see very clearly that the life I'd created for myself was so safe, so insulated from the outside world, that it had become a sort of prison. I hadn't even been aware that I was afraid—afraid of another panic attack, of all the things that could go wrong if I didn't keep a tight grip of control over every aspect of my life. I had my books and games, but that was all I had.

And now, as Luke gazes at me with compassion, a realization starts to crystallize in my mind. In the past, I'd thought I wasn't all that interested in men, but now I'm wondering if I was actively avoiding them. Those few times that I *did* attempt anything, my inability to let go, to give up control, to be vulnerable, meant that nothing real ever developed. I was afraid to share my full self, scars and all, with anyone because I thought they'd think less of me for not always being able to keep it together. They never saw me at my worst—they never even *knew* about my worst—and I preferred it that way. Even Steph doesn't know about my panic attacks.

But Luke has seen me worry, he's seen me afraid, he's seen me confront my fears, and he still wants me. It's only been two weeks but it feels like he knows me better than anyone. That's how I know it's safe to share these things with him, too. I know he won't run away.

"Wow," Luke says, after I tell him everything. "That must have been so hard."

"It was." Tears prickle in my throat at the way he holds me tighter, and I take a controlled breath, waiting for them to pass. "Anyway. It was a long time ago, and I haven't had a panic attack since, so... that's good."

"You're such a brave, amazing woman, Harri. You know that?"

I give him an odd look. How on earth does that make me brave?

"Even after everything you went through in high school," he continues, "you're still this outgoing, adventurous person. You still do things most of us are too afraid to do. I mean, I've never been skydiving and I'm not sure I could. And what about the trapeze? You're pretty much fearless."

I swallow the frustrated groan threatening to rush from my mouth and close my eyes, unable to look at him. It's true that I feel more like my alter ego than I ever have, and I know I'm not the same person I was when I stepped on that plane in New Zealand. I've surprised myself with the things I've done over here. But each of those victories was hard-won; I had to consciously work through my anxiety and push myself to do them. That's a far cry from the thrill-seeking adrenaline junkie I've led him to believe I am. The only place I've naturally felt adventurous is in bed—and the plane, and the kitchen—with him. I'm still trying to figure out why I feel so free with him sexually. I think it started with the plane—the close proximity and unusual circumstances, and the fact that I thought I'd never see him again. I just totally let go, and I've been that way with him since.

I know I should come clean about Harriet 2.0, but I'm worried that telling him the truth might make him see me differently. He's been so accepting of my anxious side, but that's because he *also* thinks I'm brave and outgoing. Once he knows I don't have a wild side, he'll realize that my anxiety isn't just a part of me—it's *all* of me.

"I'm not fearless," I say, glancing up at him. "*You're* fearless, Luke. You left a job to follow your dreams, even when your wife and father told you it was stupid. That was really brave. I admire you so much for that."

He sighs, fiddling with a strand of my red hair. "No, I'm not brave. If I was, I would have told everyone about my divorce five months ago. Instead, I've been living a lie."

My heart squeezes for him, and I press a kiss to his warm skin. "Don't be so hard on yourself. Sometimes it's difficult to tell people the truth if you think it will make them look at you differently."

"Yeah," he murmurs. "I just can't stand the thought of Dad having yet another reason to be disappointed in me."

"You really think he'll be disappointed?"

Luke utters a bitter laugh. "My parents love Dena. They're going to think I did something to drive her away, that it's all my fault. I'll be surprised if Dad even talks to me after this."

I'm quiet, processing this. Surely he's overreacting? Surely they could see their son was unhappy with her, and now, with me...

My thoughts grind to a halt. Because, of course, they won't see him with me—and soon, I won't be here with him anyway.

"But you will tell him?" I ask, and I find myself holding my breath as I wait for his reply.

"I'm going to have to eventually. She won't play along forever."

"Why *is* she going along with it?"

Luke grimaces. "I really hoped you weren't going to ask me that."

Dread crawls across my skin and I pull my hand away.

"We..." He scrubs a hand over his face, reluctantly meeting my gaze. "We have an arrangement."

I inhale sharply as my stomach nosedives. If he's still sleeping with her, I'm going to—

"God, no!" he exclaims, reading my face. "It's just financial."

"Oh." My breath rushes out in a whoosh, followed by a laugh of relief. "Sorry. I thought maybe you and her were still..."

He reaches for me again, gathering me into his arms. "You really think I'd be here, doing these things with you, if I was still doing things with her?"

I shrug, awash with jealousy at the thought of the two of them together. This isn't a feeling I'm familiar with and it's very unpleasant.

Luke sighs, dragging his nose up my neck to my ear. "There's just you, Harriet."

Just you.

I soften into him, letting his words soothe me. "So, what do you mean when you say you have a financial arrangement?"

"She wanted the Mercedes in the divorce settlement and I agreed, as long as she went along with this."

"It really means *that* much to you that she's at the wedding?"

"Well, I never liked that damn car. She chose it. But it wasn't just that." Luke's gaze drops to his hands. "I didn't want Mike's wedding ruined because I was arguing with Dad, and I knew they'd all wonder why she wasn't there. I thought it was pretty harmless—she knows my family and it will keep everyone happy and allow them to enjoy the wedding, rather than getting caught up in my drama. It seemed like the perfect solution." He rakes a hand through his hair, his eyes returning to me. "But then I met you."

My lips tug into a tentative smile. I'm brimming with

questions, like how soon after the wedding he's planning to tell them, if he's considered telling them sooner now that he's met me, if, after the wedding and he's told everyone, if I did consider moving here and opening my cafe, would he... could he and I be together?

Because as I lie here, nestled into the warmth of Luke's side, listening to him talk about the things that have hurt him, I'm forced to confront just how much I care for this man. I care that he's been hurt, that he's still hurting. I care that he feels trapped, that he feels like he can't tell his family the truth. I want nothing more than to kiss him and take his hurt away, but I know it's not my place. And worse than that, I'm not sure if he wants me to. I'm not sure if he's feeling what I'm feeling.

"Anyway," Luke says with a strained laugh. "Let's talk about something else."

I wriggle onto my side to look at him properly. There's one thing I *can* do right now to distract him from all of this. I lean in and graze my lips over the shell of his ear. "Or we could *do* something else."

His gorgeous mouth tips into a grin. He grabs my waist and flips me onto my back, diving down to take my nipple into his mouth. And for a few hours, we both forget the things that have hurt us.

31

I 'm in big trouble. I knew there was another reason I didn't spend the night with Luke, but I let myself forget it.

He's a really cuddly sleeper, and we spent the whole night in each other's arms. I never thought *I'd* be a cuddly sleeper, if I'm honest. It just seemed impractical, and a little suffocating. But snuggled close with Luke, I slept better than I have in a very long time.

And now, as I roll over in bed and see him dozing beside me, I realize what a mistake I've made. I'll never be able to wake up alone again without feeling like something —*someone*—is missing.

I run my eyes over him: the scruff that has now grown into a short beard, dark and coarse against the smooth creaminess of his cheek; the tiny round scar below his eye; his lush lashes and his full, soft lips. He is truly the most handsome man I've ever laid eyes on and I still can't believe he kisses *me*, he wants *me*.

With a yawn and a stretch, he blinks awake. "What a beautiful sight to wake up to," he murmurs, his sleepy, smiling eyes moving over my face. They flicker with interest. "You know, I've never seen you without your red lipstick."

Shit.

My hand flies to my mouth, self-consciously touching my lips. I haven't applied it since we left the city and, well, I used my mouth a *lot* last night. All that friction must have rubbed it off.

He gives a little chuckle as he reaches out to stroke a thumb over my cheek. "I'm not complaining. It's nice to see the real you."

The real you.

He has seen the real me—more than anyone has—and he's still here. The things I've shared with him haven't sent him running. If anything, they've brought us closer. And while I'm feeling brave for sharing those things, there are still some things I can't bring myself to say—like the fact that the past two weeks have been the best two weeks of my life, that I'm feeling things for him I've never felt for anyone, and now I'm scared that once I go home, I'll never feel like this again.

But all those thoughts die away as he tenderly trails his hand over me. He brushes past my nipple, setting off fireworks across my skin, then tucks his hand around my back and pulls me against him. I nuzzle into the warmth of his chest, closing my eyes and breathing in his spicy, woody smell. I don't want to think about any of that. I just want to enjoy the time we have together.

I feel something hard digging into my hip, and reach down eagerly, grasping him and taking him by surprise. He gives a sharp, delighted grunt, pressing himself against my hand, and I begin to move in slow, gentle strokes.

"I just cannot get enough of you," he murmurs into my

hair, his fingers tightening on my back. "It doesn't matter how many times we have sex. It's never enough."

A thrill runs through me and I nuzzle further into his chest so he can't see how delirious I am.

"It's not really about sex, though. Just being with you, Harri, talking with you..." he trails off, his eyes fluttering closed as my hand continues to work. And then he says something I'm sure he doesn't mean to say, something that probably just tumbles out because of the way I'm touching him: "I wish I could wake up to you like this every morning."

I swallow hard, my breathing going all funny. Because, God, I'm wishing that so much right now.

I don't know what to say. But I do know what I'm feeling, because it makes me do something I've never done: I kick my underwear off, roll on top of him and go to slide him inside me without a condom. I pause at the last second. "I'm on the pill," I say in a rush. I've been on it for years to help regulate my periods, but I've never used it for, well, *this* purpose.

Luke's eyes widen. "Are you sure you're okay with this?"

I nod. "I'm healthy."

"Me too."

"So... is this alright?"

A smile slowly curls along his lips. "Yeah. *Yes.*"

I grin. Glancing down, I position him at my entrance, and we both watch as he sinks inside me, nothing separating us.

He groans, pressing himself deeper and throwing his head back on the pillow as he's overcome with sensation. I move my hips in a slow, gentle rhythm, my hands on his chest, studying his face for every single sign of pleasure. I don't want to miss any of it. He's right—we could have sex a million times and it would never be enough.

"Come here, baby." He reaches for me, pulling me down close. His hands slide over my back, palms spread flat and wide, hot against my skin. It feels like he's trying to hold every inch of me, to possess me, and heat rockets through me at the thought.

"I love having your hands on me," I whisper against his lips, and he hums his agreement.

His lips make a trail along my jaw, my collarbone, teeth grazing my ear. "I could fuck you like this forever," he murmurs into my hair, and my breath sticks in my throat.

Forever?

No, I must have misheard that.

But—

His hands tighten on my ass, holding me in place as he thrusts up into me from underneath, hitting a spot that wipes every scattered thought from my mind. When he lowers his thumb between my legs, I moan and clench around him, moving my hips to match his rhythm. The silky feeling of him inside me, knowing there's nothing between us, quickly pushes me over the edge, so that I'm heaving against him and panting into his mouth.

Bloody hell. I don't know how that happened so fast.

Once I've caught my breath, he wriggles up the bed, sitting back against the headboard with me still straddling him. I like this so much more, because now I can wrap my arms around him and bury my face in his neck and breathe him in. God, I feel drunk. But it's not just the pleasure, it's him. It's his salty skin on my tongue, fistfuls of his hair in my hands, all of him filling me deep. I've never wanted to consume so much of one person.

His hands skate down to grip my hips, and he dips his head to take my nipple in his mouth. I arch forward, dropping my head back in ecstasy.

I cannot live without this man now.

The thought appears in my mind, lit like a bright neon sign, and it scares me so much that I try to shove it away.

I crush my lips to his, willing my stupid mind to shut up. "Luke," I breathe, kissing along his rough jaw, sucking on the soft flesh of his earlobe. I force myself to bite my tongue —physically bite my tongue—in case I say something I can't take back.

He draws away to gaze at me, raising a hand to stroke my hair, my cheek. "Harriet, I..." His movements slow as his eyes trace my face. There's something about the way he's looking at me that makes my heart explode behind my ribs, as if it knows something I don't. I hold my breath, waiting for him to go on.

But he doesn't. Instead, he takes my mouth in a bruising kiss, digging his fingertips into my hips and holding on for dear life, moaning as he falls apart inside me.

We stay like that for a long time, holding each other close, neither one of us daring to move.

32

Later that afternoon I stand outside the lodge, fighting the urge to cuddle into Luke's side in the cold autumn air. Alex and Michael arrived at lunch time and we offered to greet people at the lodge so they could have some time out together before the madness of the weekend begins.

Both our families are arriving today and spending the night before the wedding at the lodge, and the other guests are arriving tomorrow. And tonight, I think, Michael will stay at the lodge, while Alex stays at the cabin with me, Luke and... yeah. Dena. She's not here yet, but every time a car passes, my stomach capsizes and I feel like I'm going to be sick. I don't know how I'm going to do this.

"Harriet!" Mum calls out as she and Dad crunch up the gravel driveway, suitcases bumping along behind them.

I turn away from Luke to wave at my parents. I know Alex has been stressed about Mum and Dad arriving, because she thinks Mum is going to try and convince her to come home. One of my top priorities is making sure Mum doesn't spoil this whole thing for Alex.

"What have you done to your hair?" Mum leans in to inspect my head, frowning in disapproval. She reaches a hand towards me, but I duck out the way and give her a bright smile, ignoring the comment. We haven't seen each other in weeks and now we're catching up on the other side of the planet for Alex's wedding. You'd think my hair would be the least of her concerns.

"Hi, Mum. Good to see you got here okay." I pull her into a hug then turn to Dad. "How was your flight?"

"Long," Mum mumbles, and Dad shoots her a look. She straightens and smiles. "But we are glad to be here for Alex's big day."

When I glance at Dad, he nods. Right, he must have had a word to her about behaving appropriately. That will make things a little easier.

Dad extends a hand to Luke. "Hello, I'm Clark—Alex and Harriet's father." He gestures to Mum. "This is Audrey."

Luke smiles broadly, shaking Dad's hand. "So nice to meet you. I'm Luke—Michael's brother, and the best man."

My gaze pings back and forth between Luke and my parents, an uncomfortable sensation stirring inside me as my two worlds collide. I'm not sure I like this.

"This place is lovely," Mum says, taking in the lodge. Christ, if she can keep this positive attitude up the whole time Alex will be ecstatic.

I turn to look at the lodge. Mum's right, it is lovely. One main building that has a restaurant, a small hall where we'll have the reception, and log cabins scattered around the grounds. It has beautiful views of the lake, and there's a little courtyard where the ceremony will take place, which is going to look stunning with the glorious display of red and orange foliage surrounding us. Thankfully, the awful weather of last night seems to have cleared and should be gone for the rest of the weekend.

"It is, isn't it?" Luke motions towards the entrance. "Let me help you inside."

They glance at me and I wave a hand. "I'll catch up with you soon. Go get settled in."

Luke wheels their suitcases into reception. Mum's face lights with a genuine smile at this gesture, and relief sweeps over me. She's going to be the least of Alex's problems.

Luke pops back out to join me a moment later. "They seem nice."

I shrug. They're perfectly nice, really. Alex has been butting heads with them since moving over here but I think they just worry about her. As parents go, they're not bad. Maybe I should make more of an effort to see them. They only live ten minutes away from me, after all.

An odd sensation hollows out my chest. I do *not* want to think about going home and hanging out with my parents. That's the last thing I feel like doing.

I look over to find Luke's gaze resting on me, his expression wistful. "Harri," he says, in a quiet voice. "You know, I really wish..." He drags a hand through his hair, his eyes roaming my face. "Dena will be here soon. And I wish..."

I nod, wrestling my gaze from his, and swallow down the lump forming in my throat. "I know," I murmur. "Me too."

As if on cue, a white Mercedes SUV pulls into the parking lot and glides into a spot. Luke gives me a pained expression, forcing out a resigned breath.

My gut clenches into a tight ball, my breathing shallow and rapid. This is it. I'm going to meet Luke's ex-wife.

The car doors open and two older people get out, ambling up the gravel towards us with their bags. When I glance at Luke in confusion, he seems puzzled too.

"Mom? Dad?"

"Hello, darling." A blond woman in her late sixties smiles at Luke. She's dressed in a tan pantsuit, her hair pulled back in a tidy chignon.

My eyes flit over to a tall man of a similar age with silver hair. His expression is clouded, a slight scowl on his handsome face. "I don't know why they insisted on getting married all the way up here," he mutters to no one in particular.

The woman pulls Luke down into a hug, and when she releases him he gives her a bemused smile. "Why are you guys—"

Another car door slams and footsteps crunch up the gravel. I know who it is, and I can't bring myself to look. My stomach is turning over now, crashing in on itself like a raging sea, and I have the intense urge to cling onto something before I drown.

"Hi, honey."

She's right in front of me and I can't avoid her anymore. My eyes take in her tall, slim figure, dressed in black pants and a tan trench coat. Her hair is black, cut into a chin-length, poker-straight bob, parted squarely down the middle. Invisible hands clutch at my throat as I watch her lean into Luke and plant a kiss on his cheek. For a brief second he looks uncomfortable, then he seems to remember his manners and turns to me.

"Harriet, this is my mom, Annette, my father, William, and"—he sucks in a breath—"my wife, Dena."

Oh God. I can't breathe.

"This is Alex's sister, Harriet."

Dena smiles in my direction and slips her hand into Luke's. My chest is taut with agony but I ignore it, forcing a radiant smile. Because if I don't, I'll either scream or burst into tears.

"I didn't know you two were coming up with Dena," Luke mumbles to his parents.

Annette touches her hair. "It seemed silly for her to drive up on her own, darling."

"I'm still not sure why she didn't come up with you in the first place," William adds, giving Luke a peculiar look.

Luke and Dena exchange a quick glance, then a laugh slides from her throat. "I told you, Bill. I was away on business and only just got back, otherwise *of course* we would have come together. But it seems he couldn't wait for me to get home." Her eyes trail curiously over me and I glance down, pretending to study the gravel, checking for signs that the earth might be opening up to swallow me.

With a harrumph, William pats Dena on the arm. "I don't know why you put up with him."

Her hand squeezes Luke's. "Oh, I have my reasons." She gives him a knowing grin and he half grimaces, half smiles, avoiding my gaze.

"Am I carrying these all by myself, then?" William mutters, grasping their bags.

"Sorry." Luke reaches for them, shamefaced. Ever since this lot got here he's been different, his usual bright and playful expression gone. It makes my heart ache.

They all head into the lodge and I hover. At this point, given no one else is arriving today, I'm not sure what else to do but follow them to the reception desk where we wait for someone to help us.

"Hello?" William barks, smacking a hand on the bell with unnecessary force. He turns to Annette with a deep groove of annoyance between his brows. "Where are the staff?" His eyes flick to Dena and back to Luke. "Why is Dena carrying her own bag?"

Luke reaches for her luggage, shrinking even more. He's now carrying three bags and I almost reach out to help him. It takes all my self-control not to. He sends his father an expression of *happy now?* and William just shakes his head.

Jesus. This guy is a nightmare.

"Thank you, honey," Dena purrs, leaning her head against his arm. My heart claws up my windpipe at the sight.

And then something happens that makes my blood turn to ice in my veins. Luke glances at his father, then his mother, then turns to Dena and kisses her on the top of the head and smiles. He doesn't once look at me.

My vision blurs and I look away. Why am I even here right now?

I'm about to leave when my parents appear out of nowhere and Dad begins introductions with William, Annette, and Dena. Everyone is talking and laughing but I just feel nauseous. I can't look at Luke. I can't be around this anymore. I just want to slip away.

While everyone is busy I take the opportunity to creep towards the door. I'm just about to make my exit when I run smack into Alex and Michael.

"Oh, there you are!" Alex says, her arm linked through Michael's. "We were just talking about doing dinner tonight. It will give everyone a chance to get to know each other."

Alarm spikes through me. "I thought we weren't doing a rehearsal dinner?" That's one thing I haven't organized.

"No," Michael reassures me, "but an informal thing might be nice."

I glance desperately between their hopeful faces and slap on a smile. "Absolutely."

Extra time with Dena and Luke playing happy families? Why not?

33

I try everything I can to get out of dinner, but ultimately, I know I need to be there. This is about Alex and Michael, not me. And who knows how long Mum's cooperation is going to last.

So that's how I end up wedged between Mum and Alex, opposite Dena, Luke and Michael, while Dad, Annette and William are further down the table. William takes care of everything, ordering champagne for the table before anyone else can order, insisting we all must drink it to celebrate. I try not to be irritated, but there's something about this guy that rubs me the wrong way.

It doesn't matter. I'm just waiting for the evening to hurry up and be over so I don't have to keep seeing Luke with Dena. In his defense, he looks bloody miserable. And she's hardly paying attention to him anyway; she's engrossed in a conversation with William about insurance premiums, or something. Yawn.

"Everything ready for the wedding then, Alexis?" Mum asks. I stiffen, waiting for her to say something that might ruffle Alex's feathers, but she just smiles over my head like I'm not even there.

"Yes, thanks to Harriet and Luke's tireless work." Alex gives me a nudge. "Thanks so much for everything, Harri. You've been a lifesaver these past couple of weeks. So selfless. You're the best sister I could ask for."

I give her a meek smile, swallowing down the guilt rising inside me like vomit. *It's fine*, I keep telling myself. So I'm lying to her about Luke. It's not going to interfere with the wedding, and that's all that matters right now.

"I always wanted a sister." Michael grins at me across the table. "I'm glad to have you as a sister-in-law, Harriet."

I can't help but smile back, because that's really sweet. But hearing him refer to me as his sister makes me feel even more queasy, because it forces me to confront the fact that he's now kind of my brother. And—gulp—does that make *Luke* kind of my brother?

Shit. It's definitely weird that we've been sleeping together. And it's even worse that now it's gone *way* past the point of just sex.

"You must be looking forward to getting back home after all this," Alex says.

Against my better judgment I let my gaze slide to Luke, but his eyes are riveted to his glass. I give Alex a mute nod, trying to ignore the way my heart feels strangled. I guess I thought Luke might be, I don't know, at least a *little* bummed about me leaving. But after seeing him with Dena, everything feels off. Her presence has totally thrown me. Before, it was like Luke and I were inside some kind of invisible forcefield, safe from the chaos of the outside world. We had this shield around us, protecting us from all the shit that could be thrown our way. But Dena has broken the spell and now shit's flying everywhere and I have to be extra vigilant in case something suddenly spears me through the heart.

"We saw Paula the other day," Mum says, glancing at me. "She mentioned something about selling the cafe."

I twist in my chair to face her. "What?"

"She said something else too. What was it, Clark?" Mum leans towards Dad, tugging on his sleeve.

"What?"

"What did Paula say? She was selling the cafe, but she said something else."

"Audrey," Dad says, his eyes bouncing between Mum and me, "she asked us not to say anything until she'd had a chance to talk to Harriet."

Mum's cheeks flush and she turns back to me. "I'm sorry, sweetheart. I didn't think."

Okay. Well. This is unexpected.

Anxiety pools in my empty stomach as I process Mum's words. If Paula is selling the cafe, am I out of a job? My pulse climbs as I stare down at my plate, trying not to panic. Maybe the new owners will keep us on. They could keep running the place as it is, with us there—that's also possible, right? But for some reason, that idea doesn't reassure me any more.

I glance at Mum again, twirling her glass, eyes dancing as she listens to the others talk. Her cheeks are pink from champagne and I make myself take a deep, soothing breath. She probably misunderstood Paula. Anyway, Paula loves the cafe. She wouldn't sell it. Although she did mention something about wanting to travel when I told her I was going to New York, didn't she? But—no, she was excited for me, that's all. I can't let myself worry about this now.

I catch Luke watching me from across the table and send him a brittle smile as our meals are served.

"Didn't you mention something the other day about an idea you had for your own cafe?" Alex asks me, her fork in the air. "When we were at the salon. I'm sure you did."

My eyes stray to Luke's again and he nods, his expression encouraging.

"Er, well... I have had some ideas," I admit, taking a bite of my steak.

"Really?" Mum chimes in. "You want to run your own cafe?" There's a hint of disbelief in her words and my shoulders slump. Even my own mother thinks it's unrealistic. But I shouldn't be surprised; she didn't believe Alex could become an author, either.

"I think it's a great idea," Luke says. He gazes at me warmly and, for a moment, I feel the forcefield there again. "I've been trying to convince her to do it, helping her come up with ways to make it work."

Oh, shit. I suddenly remember what I told Alex at the salon—that my mystery man has been encouraging me with this—and glance at her in alarm. But she's oblivious, gazing at Michael across the table.

"Well, you know a thing or two about working for yourself," Michael says. His voice is tinged with brotherly pride, and Luke grins.

"Speaking of work, how's *that* going?" William asks, joining the conversation with sudden interest. He has one eyebrow cocked, his question underlined with what almost sounds like sarcasm.

My irritation ratchets up a few notches. What is wrong with this guy?

But Luke ignores his tone, smiling. "It's good, actually. I've had the past couple of weeks off, but before that I had a meeting in Houston with a company we're looking to partner with, to expand into virtual reality. I'm just waiting to hear back from them." His whole face is animated now. "It's a big shift, but if we can incorporate VR into the game, we can—"

"Ugh, isn't Houston airport the worst?" Dena says, cutting Luke off mid-sentence.

He sighs and stuffs a piece of steak in his mouth. I make a mental note to ask him more about virtual reality and this opportunity with the Houston company, if I get the chance. He seems really excited about that.

Dena continues, oblivious. "I was there for work last year and had the *worst* layover." She shakes her head to emphasize what an absolute *tragedy* she endured at Houston airport.

"Didn't you fly into Houston, Harriet?" Michael asks.

I nod, crunching on a green bean.

"That would have been around when Luke was there," he adds thoughtfully.

There's a nervous twinge in my abdomen, as if from that information alone he's figured out everything that's been going on and is about to reveal it to the whole table. I focus diligently on loading my fork with more beans.

"Hey," Alex says with a giggle, her cheeks rosy from the champagne, "wouldn't it be funny if you guys had been on the same flight and not even realized?"

My neck is hot as I shove the beans into my mouth, keeping my gaze averted from Luke.

"Oh, I think she was too busy on that flight to look for my kid brother," Michael says, mirth glimmering in his eyes.

Alex chortles, then her face grows serious as she glances across at Michael. "Oh, I didn't tell you, honey. She has actually been *seeing* this mystery plane man."

I take a long slug of champagne. I can feel Luke's eyes on

me, and sweat gathers on my top lip. I wipe at it discreetly, willing my erratic heartbeat to settle.

Michael tosses me a grin. "Well, I hope he's good enough for my new little sister," he says affectionately, and I grimace so hard I nearly break a tooth.

"Actually," Alex adds with a smug little smile, "I think she might be falling in love with him."

Oh *God*.

Michael's grin widens. "Really?"

"It's not..." My face is in flames. "I don't think... It's only been a few weeks." I can't bring myself to even so much as glance in Luke's direction. If only these two knew what kind of trouble they're causing.

"Oh, come on," Alex needles. "You're so smitten."

Luke's gaze is boring a hole into me now and I raise a hand to my burning cheek, shaking my head.

My mother leans closer beside me, angling to speak to Alex, her voice brimming with excitement. "What's this about Harriet being smitten?" A shadow crosses her brow. "It's not another American man, is it? Because if I have to fly over here for another wedding—"

"Jesus," I mutter, pushing my chair back with a scrape. I snatch up my champagne glass and drain it. "I'm going to go and make sure the reception hall is all set for tomorrow." And I stalk out of there, refusing to look at Luke.

34

I enter the empty reception hall and click the door shut, letting the darkness of the room swallow me.

Bloody Alex. I can't believe she said I was falling in *love* with Luke. That's absurd. Even though I didn't see his face, I know that would have freaked him out. We've only known each other for two and a half weeks, for Christ's sake. That would be enough to freak any man out. Compared to me, Dena is probably looking like a far more reasonable option right now. And let's face it, he didn't seem too fussed about her being here, what with all that head kissing at reception earlier.

I fumble along the wall for the light switch and find a whole panel. I flick one, which floods the room with bright light. Blinking, I glance at the panel and press the one labeled "dance floor," turning off the rest. The room goes almost dark, except for a few colored lights over the dance area and a spinning ball that ricochets light around the room. Without music playing it feels kind of surreal, which matches my mood perfectly.

Heaving out a sigh, I wander around the reception hall,

absently checking the place settings and the table decorations, making sure everything is as it should be. It looks
really good, and the hand-lettering on the place cards adds a
nice touch. All our hard work has paid off.

I hear the door open and glance up in surprise. Luke's
tall figure is illuminated by the light outside, then the door
clicks shut and I see his shadow moving between the tables.
My pulse ramps up as he nears, a roller coaster of nerves
crashing through me. No doubt he's come to tell me that we
need to cool off, that it's all over. He must be terrified by that
nonsense Alex was spouting.

He stops a table away from me, hesitating. I can see the
outline of him and the spinning light flicks over him, briefly
revealing his features, but I can't make out his expression.

It's probably just as well. I'm not sure I want to see the
horror on his face. Unless he finds the whole thing hilarious, like that time he teased me for begging him. Or he
might even pity me. That would be the worst, I think. See,
this is the problem with letting your guard down—

"Hey," he says softly, interrupting my spiraling thoughts.

"Oh, hi." I keep my voice light, reaching to straighten a
place setting.

"You okay?"

"Yep." I swallow, hoping he'll get this over with and not
drag it out.

He takes a step around the table towards me and,
instinctively, I step in the other direction, inching away from
him. I can't get too close in case I lose it.

He's quiet for the longest time, just standing there as the
lights spin around us in the dark.

God, I have to say something.

"Sorry about Alex." A shrill laugh trickles out of me.
"She's ridiculous."

He doesn't say anything and I shift my weight. *Come on Luke, get it over with.*

"The place cards look really good," he murmurs at last. "You've done a fantastic job."

I glance around us and pride swells inside me. I really hope Alex and Michael like them.

"Have you tested the sound system?"

"No," I say. But that's a good point.

He wanders off and I exhale, fiddling with a centerpiece on a table. A few minutes later there's a rustling sound over the speakers and a song comes on. It's a slow, romantic song, and I stiffen. I don't know what Luke's up to, but I don't like this at all.

Before today, I felt like I knew him so well, like I could read what he was thinking and feeling. But that was only when it was just the two of us. Now that we're around all these other people, I don't know what to think. I keep coming back to Geoff's warning after the salon—about how if Luke really liked me, he'd want to tell the others—and it's messing with my head. Maybe I misread everything and he doesn't like me as much as I thought. Maybe, after all that shit Alex was saying, he's realized it's gone too far.

Someone comes up behind me and I nearly leap out of my skin. When I whip around, Luke is right there, gazing down at me.

"Have you tested the dance floor?" Up close I can see his expression is gentle, but for some reason that makes me even more anxious, like he's trying to soften the blow that's about to come. He takes my hand, tugging me onto the dance floor, and foreboding spirals down through my gut.

I get the message, Luke. Just say it.

He takes my other hand, so that he's holding them both, and I stand there as he sways awkwardly to the music. He huffs a sheepish laugh, but I'm rigid, waiting for it to happen.

Finally I mutter, "Just get it over with, Luke."

"What?"

I shake my head, looking down at our joined hands. "I know you're here to end things. I know Alex freaked you out. She was *way* off, what she said, but you probably—"

"She didn't freak me out," he says. I glance up to find his brow knitted, and he sighs, dropping my hands.

Oh God. Here it comes.

But he reaches for my waist, drawing me close. He lowers his mouth and brushes his lips over mine, and I melt against him, limp with relief. He's not ending things. This isn't over. I'm an idiot.

My hands tighten on the lapels of his dinner jacket. "She didn't freak you out?"

"No. It's *you* that's freaking me out a little."

"Me?"

"You thought I came in here to end things with you."

I look up at him, nodding.

"And you keep insisting that Alex is wrong." His gaze burns into mine and my heart launches like a skyrocket. Is he suggesting... I mean, is he saying he *wants* me to be in love with him?

Before I can respond, he leans down again, capturing my mouth with his. He slides his hands up to cup my face, his tongue licking against mine. It's soft at first, but it only takes a moment for desire to spark between us. Soon, our tongues are tangling and my hands are sliding down to his ass, pulling him against me. When I feel his arousal press into my belly, I whimper with need and take his hand, turning for the door.

"Let's go."

He hesitates, chuckling. "Where are we going to go?"

Reality hits me like a bucket of cold water. Of course, where *are* we going to go?

And then a wicked, truly outrageous idea blossoms in my mind and I mentally high-five Harriet 2.0. I lead Luke down the back of the reception hall, into a dark corner behind a speaker, deep in the shadows where even the spinning light from the dance floor isn't reaching. I can't see Luke's expression in the dark, but I don't need to. I feel his urgent kiss, his hands claiming my tingling skin, the hard bulge in his pants urging me on as he presses against me. Before I know what's happening, he's lifting me up and pinning me against the wall, entering me with a low groan, grunting in my ear as he drives into me, murmuring my name over and over again.

And all I can think is, *I can't let this man go.*

WE SLIP out through a side door onto the courtyard. The night air is crisp and invigorating as I fill my lungs and release it in a giggle. The moon is high, three quarters full, and the lights from the lodge flood out onto the courtyard, but we duck back into the shadows behind a pergola heaving with ivy.

Luke grins from ear to ear. "That was amazing. I've never done anything like that."

I raise a brow and he laughs.

"Well, apart from the plane." He runs his eyes over me in the half-light. "You have a way of making me do crazy things."

It's funny, because he has the exact same effect on me. I

was hardly shagging strangers on planes or in dark corners before I met him.

He steps closer and slips his arms around me. I snuggle into his warmth, realizing how cold it is out here.

"There's something about you, Harri," he murmurs, and I remember what he said inside—that he didn't like me insisting Alex was wrong. What did he mean by that? I think I know, but I don't dare let myself believe it.

"There's something about you too," I whisper in reply, unable to bring myself to ask all the questions swirling in my head. He checks the time on his phone and I draw away. "I guess you need to head back," I mumble. Displeasure crashes through me at the thought of him getting into bed with Dena tonight.

No, that's not right. It's straight-up jealousy. Perhaps a little rage.

"No way." He pulls me close again. "I told Dena I'd be busy for a few hours setting up the hall and wouldn't be back until late."

"Did she buy that?"

He tucks a strand of hair behind my ear. "I don't care."

Oh God. He doesn't care. He doesn't care about her. I knew it. His words from last night come back to me: *There's just you, Harriet.*

"So, what does my wild girl want to do now?" he asks, his eyes glittering playfully.

My heart flutters. He called me his girl. I'm *his* girl.

Well, he called me his *wild* girl. I feel the familiar thud of guilt as I think about the lie that led him to believe that's who I am. As much as I've grown into my alter ego, there's still one thing I'm too scared to do, and that's be honest with him. Not just about what I told him on the plane—about everything. I want to tell him what I'm feeling, which is, I don't know—not love, *obviously*—but that I'm so devastated at the thought of going home and not seeing him again, I'm so miserable to think of going back to my life as it was, and I can't imagine not having him with me all the time. That I don't know who I am without him anymore, and I don't want to be that person, anyway.

What's the word for that?

I wrench my gaze from Luke, afraid that he can see everything in my eyes. I spy the lake down below us, shimmering in the moonlight, and suddenly I want nothing more than to plunge into that icy water, to see if I can wash these intense feelings away.

"Can we get to the lake from here?"

Luke's eyebrows push up. "I think so. Why?"

"I want to go skinny-dipping."

He emits a disbelieving laugh. "It's freezing!"

"So?" A smile plays on my lips. He wants wild, he's getting wild.

He studies me for a moment, perhaps trying to figure out if I'm serious. "You're a little scary sometimes, you know that? Beautiful, but scary."

The Ron Weasley quote makes me laugh, especially because he intentionally butchered it. Still, being compared to Hermione is a freaking honor.

"Okay." Luke's mouth stretches into a grin. "Let's go."

We step out of the shadows, checking to make sure no one can see us, and I follow him to a path. Once we're out of sight of the lodge, he spins around and grabs me, kissing me hard. Then he turns and continues down the path, picking up his pace, and I follow breathlessly.

There's a rustle in the leaves beside us and my pulse goes haywire. It occurs to me that we're out in the wilderness, in America, where there are bears and snakes and things. But—and I know this is stupid—with Luke's hand snug in mine, guiding me along the path, I feel secure and safe. I feel okay.

The path opens out onto a small, pebbly beach with a jetty, tucked down below a line of trees, out of sight of the lodge. Our shoes crunch over the stones as we approach the water. The air is much colder down here, and I look out at the cool, smooth lake stretching ahead of us in the moonlight, wondering if this is a good idea. Are we going to get hypothermia or something?

My gaze finds Luke's, and uncertainty flickers back at me. Before I can change my mind, I grab the hem of my dress and pull it up over my head. I shiver as the cold air rushes over my bare skin, but don't stop. I kick off my shoes and give Luke a challenging stare.

He shakes his head with a smile, hastily removing his jacket and unbuttoning his shirt to catch up with me. I focus on his delicious arms to distract myself from the cold. He toes off his shoes, drops his pants, and stands there in his boxer-briefs.

We are now standing a few feet apart, in our underwear, hesitating.

I glance at the water again and drag in a lungful of the icy air. Surely this is insane? Surely he's going to stop me at any moment?

But he just grins, his sharp gaze daring me to undress further and get in the water.

I reach behind and unclasp my bra, then wriggle my underwear down my legs, not taking my eyes off him. Goosebumps dot my skin, the air chilling me to the bone. Even watching Luke slide his boxers off can't distract me now.

He holds two hands in front of himself for modesty. "It's

very cold," he breathes, clutching his hands to his crotch. "So, you know…"

I chuckle and step closer, pressing my chest against him. My nipples are like rocks, and as they brush over his skin he lets out a low groan, his eyes falling closed.

He snaps them open and looks at me. "Are we doing this or what?"

I nod and turn to face the water, reaching inside for all the courage I can find. On a rush of energy I start to move, one foot in front of the other, over the stones, towards the water. Luke's hand catches mine, and as our feet hit the lake I have to stifle a shriek. My toes are instantly numb but I don't care. Without stopping, we wade all the way in, until our heads go under and we pop up and stare at each other, eyes wide, breathing ragged. Then we're laughing and racing back to the shore, Luke's hand gripping tightly onto mine, the madness of what we've done hitting us.

But I don't care. I'm high on adrenaline and I realize that I've never, in my whole life, felt more alive.

BY THE TIME we get back to the cabin, I'm shivering. I don't want to go in there, don't want this amazing night to be over and for him to climb into bed with Dena—*God* how I wish that wasn't going to happen—but I need to get into a hot shower.

Luke pauses right outside the door, taking my hand. "I need to tell you…" He hesitates, then swallows hard. "I'm so crazy about you, Harriet. You make me feel alive, like no one ever has."

His words make my heart soar, and I try to contain my massive smile. "Luke…" I search his face, wanting so much to tell him what I'm feeling, but I don't know where to start. And as I hear my teeth begin to chatter, all I can manage is, "Shit, I'm freezing. We have to get inside."

Something shifts in his expression, and he rakes a hand through his damp hair, then reaches for the door handle. It's quiet when we creep inside; both Dena and Alex are in bed. The only light comes from the flickering fireplace, and I rush over to it, holding my hands out to soak up the heat.

Luke grabs a thick blanket off the back of the sofa and wraps it around my shoulders. I stand there for a moment, gazing up at him in the firelight. I know I can't touch him now, I can't kiss him in here, but I try to find some way to explain what I'm feeling.

"Luke," I begin again, keeping my voice quiet. "You're—"

The door to Alex's room opens and I leap away from Luke as light spills into the living room.

"I thought I heard you guys!" she says, grinning. "How is everything looking? Is it all set up okay?"

My pulse is frantic but I quickly pin on a smile. "The hall looks fantastic. It's all set."

She beams, clasping her hands together. "Great!" She takes a step closer to me, her face softening. "Listen, Harri, I'm sorry about what happened at dinner. I didn't mean to give you a hard time about that guy."

"Oh." I flap a hand. "That's fine, don't worry. I over-reacted."

"No, I got carried away. I know you've never been in love before and when you were talking about him I honestly thought it sounded like you were."

I slide a nervous look to Luke, wincing with embarrass-ment. My wet hair is dripping down my back and I'm silently pleading with Alex to just *shut up* and go back to bed so I can say goodnight to Luke and get into the shower alone with my jumbled thoughts.

"Anyway," Alex continues, "if you say you're not, then I believe you. But I just wanted—" She stops mid-sentence, her brow pinching. "Why do you have wet hair?"

Shit.

Panic zips through me and my gaze bolts to Luke. He looks back at me, frozen.

"I fell in the lake," I blurt. My ears are ringing and my icy hands somehow feel clammy.

"What?" Alex says, her nose wrinkling in confusion. "*How*?"

"Well, er—" I glance at Luke again but he stares at me blankly. "I went for a walk, on the jetty, to get some fresh air after setting up the decorations. You know, it was quite hot in the reception hall, and I was still a bit annoyed after dinner, and I was walking along the jetty, and, well, these shoes aren't that good, then I tripped, and—" I stop as Luke throws me a look. *Too much, Harriet.* Everyone knows that a good lie doesn't have too many extraneous details.

Alex's eyes flit over to Luke and narrow in suspicion. "And what happened to *you*?"

"Uh..." He clears his throat. "I jumped in to help her, of course."

"He did," I assure Alex. "I probably would have been fine, because I can swim, but he was very concerned."

"Right." Her eyes move between us. "But... your clothes are dry."

"Oh, well," I begin, not sure where I'm going with this but hoping like hell something good comes out when I continue. "We, erm, popped back up to the lodge and dried them under the hand driers in the bathroom."

She gives me a bizarre look. "You took your clothes off in

the bathroom and dried them? Why didn't you just come back here?"

"Uh…" I flounder, my stomach in free-fall.

This is it. We're done for.

"Because we still had work to do in the reception hall," Luke says, and I could just *kiss* him.

"That's right." I nod vigorously. "We didn't want to come home before we had everything just perfect."

"Oh." Alex stares at us both for a moment, her brows slanted together, and I hold my breath. Then her face breaks into a smile. "You guys have worked so hard on this wedding. Seriously, I can't believe all you've done for us. Michael and I are so grateful."

"You're welcome," I manage. "It's been our… pleasure." My cheeks heat with awareness and I yank my gaze away from Luke.

Thankfully, Alex doesn't notice. "I love you guys. Now go to bed so you're ready for tomorrow!" She gives a little squeak of excitement and slips back into her room, plunging the living room into near-darkness.

I almost collapse with relief when her door closes. As my eyes adjust to the firelight, I see Luke raise a hand to his forehead.

"That was close," he mutters.

I gaze into the fire, trying to ignore the guilt bleeding through me. "I wish I could tell her the truth."

When I glance back at Luke, his expression is agonized. "Look, we will. Just… give me some time, okay?"

I scrutinize his face. Time? For what? And either way, I don't *have* time. I'm leaving in a few days, and that's it. I'll never see him again.

No. I shove that thought away, into the deep recesses of my brain where I can ignore it. Instead, I give Luke a little nod and simply say, "Okay." He said we'll tell her, after all. If he says we will, I trust that.

A shiver works through me and I glance at the bathroom. "I'm going to have a shower. I guess you should go and hop into bed with Dena," I add, unable to keep the bitterness out of my voice.

He shakes his head, speaking in a low voice. "I'll sleep out here, say I wanted to be by the fire or something."

"You don't want to be in there?" I press, even though I'm quite sure I know the answer.

"Are you kidding? If I could be anywhere, it would be with you." He exhales wearily, reaching out for me then thinking better of it and dropping his hand. "I know this isn't easy for you, with her here. I just need some time, okay?"

There's that word again: *time*. The one thing I don't have.

But I give him another nod and say goodnight. Then I pad off to the bathroom, trying to convince myself that, somehow, we'll find a way to work everything out.

35

The ceremony is absolutely beautiful, and the weather is perfect: sunny but crisp and cool, with the blaze of fall colors surrounding the courtyard making for a stunning setting. I can see why they chose this time of year.

Everything goes smoothly, but it's not until we are milling in the reception hall, waiting for Alex and Michael's entrance and sipping champagne, that I start to relax.

"This is such a wonderful venue," Geoff says, glancing around the hall.

He, Cat and Myles arrived at lunchtime today. Myles is really nice, and exactly the kind of guy I imagined Cat to be with: medium height, chestnut hair and scruff, a tattoo snaking up his right arm into a dress shirt with rolled back sleeves. He's smitten with her; he hasn't left her side since they arrived. Cat strikes me as being tough and fierce, but there's something about the way Myles makes her soften that tells me he's a good guy.

It's been great having these three here. They came early to see how Alex was getting on and to check if we needed help with anything. Geoff has been on parent patrol since he arrived—making sure they're happy and not letting Mum bother Alex. I have it on good authority he's been talking Michael up so much that even Mum is starting to come around.

My eyes meander around the room and land on Luke. He's standing dutifully beside Dena, but she's enthralled by another conversation with William. I can see what Luke means about those two getting on well. No wonder he's afraid to tell his dad.

He sends me a tiny smile, bouncing his eyebrows ever so slightly and tipping his champagne glass in my direction. He doesn't do anything more, but the sparkle in his eye— the one that's reserved only for me—sends pleasure melting right through me. I know he'd much rather be over here on my arm, and the thought makes a satisfied little smile nudge my lips.

And boy, does he look good today. He's wearing a tux, which highlights everything that's gorgeous about him: his tall frame, his broad shoulders, his dark hair. Okay, I can't see his forearms, but the rest of it is divine enough that I can live without them for a few hours. He groomed his short beard for the day, so the dark edge of the bristles emphasize his Adam's apple and the lines of his jaw. I never thought I'd be the type of woman to like a beard on a man but it's so incredibly masculine and sexy. Every time I look at him there's a rush of heat between my legs that makes my thighs squeeze together. I'm desperate to drag him into a broom closet somewhere, to hike up my dress and have him press me against a wall from behind. God.

He was pretty forthcoming with compliments for my dress, too. We had a brief moment alone in the hallway this morning while Alex and Michael were getting ready in their separate rooms, and he pulled me to one side.

"Harriet, you look so beautiful," he'd murmured, checking the hallway for others. "Seriously, that dress, your hair..." His gaze swept over me and his fists flexed at his side, like he was fighting the urge to touch me. When his eyes met mine, they speared me with a look that was pure lust. "I wish we could be alone."

I wanted to tell him how orgasmic his tux was, but Mum appeared in the hallway asking if she could see Alex, and I knew I couldn't let her go into Alex's room alone. I had no choice but to give Luke a faint smile and walk away. It nearly bloody killed me.

And now, as he basically eye-fucks me from across the room, I have to force myself to turn my attention back to the others in case the raw, primal need on my face gives everything away.

"Ugh," Cat says as she takes a glass of champagne from Myles and casts her gaze across the room. It's teeming with guests, only a handful of whom I actually know, but they all seem very friendly. Except Mel, of course. I follow Cat's gaze and see she's staring right at Mel, who's wearing a floor-length, off-white gown that plunges low. It's the most inappropriate thing I've ever seen anyone wear to a wedding, but thankfully Alex has been too busy making heart eyes at Michael to care.

Mel is even more terrifying than I remember. And, I've noticed, she seems to be quite close with Dena. I didn't see that coming but I guess it makes sense. They were, after all, married to brothers. They probably spent summers at the lake and had Christmas and holidays together. In fact, I wonder if Mel knows they've divorced?

So much for Mel coming to support Henry, though;

she's barely spent two seconds with her son, who has been sitting with Michael and Luke's Nana—Henry's great grandmother—the whole time in the corner. I checked in with him to make sure he was okay, but he seemed happier away from the commotion. I don't blame the poor guy.

"I can't believe Mel is here," Geoff murmurs. "And she *had* to bring Mark."

"Who's Mark?" I ask, passing my eyes over the guy she's with. He's tall and lean, with short brown hair and a silver chain glinting around his neck from under his dress shirt. Mel has one hand protectively on his bicep, her nails blood-red against his white shirt.

"Cat's ex-husband." Myles's gaze narrows in their direction as he tucks Cat into his side and presses a kiss to her pink hair.

"Wait," I say, slowly playing catch-up. "Michael's ex-wife is dating your ex-husband, Cat? How do they know each other?"

Cat twirls her champagne glass, releasing a sigh. "Mel and I used to be friends. Good friends, or at least I thought we were. We were neighbors when she lived upstairs with Michael, before their divorce. Then I found out she was hooking up with my ex not long ago, so"—she shrugs—"that was the end of our friendship."

I glance back at Mel and Mark, shaking my head in disbelief. "Wow."

"You have no idea." Geoff pushes his glasses up his nose with a humorless laugh. "Not only did she screw Cat over with Mark, she also tried to run her out of business. And she tried to get Alex fired."

"Really?" Alex never mentioned any of this.

Geoff nods.

"What is *wrong* with this woman?" I mutter. "Someone needs to put her in her place."

"*Yes*," Myles says fiercely, and we share a frown.

Cat snorts. "It's not worth it."

I'm about to say something more when a hush falls over the room. We collectively turn to the doorway, where Alex and Michael enter. The room explodes into applause and I join in with whoops and cheers. Emotion wells up inside me as I watch them, glowing with love and happiness.

Before I can stop myself, my eyes veer over to Luke. He's gazing right at me, his eyes shining, and I have to glance away in case I start blubbering like a fool. I don't know where all this sudden mushiness has come from. I must have had too much champagne.

Alex and Michael do the rounds, greeting everyone and being congratulated, before we all sit down to dinner. I'm thrilled to find Luke is sitting right beside me—he must have switched the seating arrangements, and given we're maid of honor and best man it's not exactly suspicious—but it makes it hard to focus on eating. Well, that and the fact that I can feel Dena watching us from two tables away.

After dinner, there's the clinking of a glass and we turn our attention as the toasts begin. I know I'm Alex's sister and the maid of honor, but I'm not making a toast and neither is Luke. Alex told us that after all the work we'd done, we didn't need to give toasts. I think, actually, she knew I would be uncomfortable getting up and speaking to a room full of people. Either way, I'm more than happy to not be the center of attention.

Michael stands with his glass and we all settle down to listen. "I just want to say a few words. First of all, Alex and I have to thank my brother, Luke, and her sister, Harriet, for taking care of a lot of the last-minute wedding details. Both

Alex and I have been really busy with work and these two stepped up, without a word of complaint, and made sure everything was perfect."

Pride bubbles up inside me. I glance at Luke with a grin, so pleased that after everything, they got to have the wedding they wanted and nothing got in the way. It's all been worth it.

"They worked tirelessly," Michael adds, "day after day, late into the night."

Heat blooms in my cheeks and I peel my gaze from Luke's. I mean, we certainly were up for all hours of the night, but...

"We are so very grateful," Michael continues, raising his glass. "Thank you, guys. We'd also like to thank all our friends and family for making the trip here, especially Alex's family who have come all the way from New Zealand. We'll be coming for a visit very soon." He grins, tipping his glass in the direction of my parents who beam back at him.

Oh bless, Geoff. You've done it.

Michael turns to Alex, his eyes twinkling. "And I have to say something about my beautiful bride." He gazes at her and they exchange a secret smile. "A year ago I was trying to buy a sandwich when a girl spilled coffee all over me." He shakes his head with a chuckle. "When she turned out to be my new neighbor, I wasn't happy. Things in my life had been..." He pauses, running a hand over his beard. "They'd not been very good, for a while."

I glance at Mel. She shifts in her seat, lifting her chin defiantly.

"But it didn't take long for me to fall in love with Alex," Michael continues. "She's beautiful, she makes me laugh, and she's the sweetest, most optimistic person I've ever met. She accepts me for who I am and supports me in everything

I do. And she's an amazing step-mother to Henry. She loves him as if he were her own son, and we are both so lucky to have her in our lives."

I squirm in my seat, stealing a look at Mel again. Even *I'm* feeling uncomfortable on her behalf now. Her glare has turned icy but her head is still high.

When I turn back to Alex, she has tears streaming down her face and delicately pats at her cheek with her napkin. She's such a sap.

"I never thought I could be as happy as I am," Michael says, his own eyes moist. "Alex, I cannot wait to spend every day of my life with you. I'm the luckiest man in the world."

My throat cinches tight as we raise our glasses. Under the table I feel Luke's hand on my leg, brushing and gently squeezing, telling me something without words. When I let my gaze meet his, my heart expands at the tiny, almost shy smile on his face. And in that moment, I can't deny it anymore.

I've fallen in love with him.

I don't even know how I know that, but I do. It's this warm, insistent, exhilarating feeling behind my breastbone telling me that it doesn't matter that it's only been two and a half weeks; I'm in love with this man. And instead of feeling panicked, I just feel... calm. This feels right. Because I think he feels it too.

I slide my hand under the tablecloth and interlace my pinkie finger with his, deciding that I'm going to tell him. Today. I'm going to tell him how I feel, and I'm going to tell him the truth about Harriet 2.0. And while I'm not quite as fearless as I told him I was on the plane, I'm also not that far off, because telling him I'm in love with him is a totally different kind of leap—one that's more terrifying than going on the trapeze, or jumping from a plane. But I want this more than I've ever wanted anything, and I'm going to be brave enough to go after it.

Henry stands up next, his cheeks pink as he clutches a piece of paper to his chest. "Um, hello. I just wanted to say congratulations to Dad and Alex." He pauses to check his paper, then takes a faltering breath. "Last year, Alex saved my life when I had an allergic reaction. Dad said it was a sign she was meant for us, and I think he's right."

Alex is blubbering now and Michael squeezes her into his side, pressing a kiss to her temple with a little chuckle.

"I've loved spending time with Alex," Henry continues. "And it's been nice to see Dad so happy. It's made me really happy too."

My gaze swerves to Mel again, and there's a vein pulsing in her temple. But she's not glaring at Henry; she's shooting daggers at Alex. Instinctively I straighten up, as if preparing for battle.

"Congratulations, Dad and Alex. Alex, welcome to our family," Henry says finally. The whole room erupts into applause and Henry sinks down into his seat with scarlet cheeks. Alex stands and rushes over to him, pulling him into a tight hug. She whispers something in his ear and he grins, squeezing her. I smile as I watch them. Alex has nothing to worry about with Henry; he loves her dearly.

Dad is up next. He gives a gushing toast about how proud he is of Alex and all she's achieved moving over here and writing her books, which sets Alex off again, especially when Mum nods along in agreement. Then Dad talks about how wonderful Michael is and how pleased he is to welcome him to the family, and makes multiple hints about how he and Mum are expecting grandchildren in the very near future. This earns a grin from Michael in response.

Then William rises to his feet with a loud scrape of his

chair, and I tense in anticipation for some kind of rant about what a disappointment his sons are. Of course, he doesn't do that. His toast is sweet, about how Alex is lovely and he is happy to welcome her to the family—more glares from Mel, but honestly, what did she expect?—and how he looks forward to more grandchildren. In fact, it's all going swimmingly until he wraps it up with the comment, "Let's hope this one sticks, eh son?" Then he chuckles merrily to himself, raising his glass.

Crimson creeps onto Michael's cheeks and Alex, who has been smiling pleasantly throughout, looks down at her lap, her shoulders sagging.

For fuck's sake, William. Did he really have to get that last line in?

As we lift our glasses, I notice the smile is gone from Alex's eyes. There's a twist in my heart and I decide it's time for me to get over myself and put her needs first.

I pull in a deep breath, grasping my glass, ready to stand and say all the wonderful things I've been thinking. But to my absolute horror, Mel pushes her chair back and stands, bashing her knife against her glass to get attention. My eyes whip back to Alex and I see her rosy complexion pale.

Oh, no. This is not happening. Not on my watch.

I summon all my inner strength and stand, stalking over to Mel just as she draws a breath to speak. As respectfully as I can, I lean over and whisper, "I don't think you should make a toast. Maybe save what you want to say for later?"

But she waves me away, like I'm nothing more than a pesky mosquito. Then she turns to the expectant room, a savage smile spreading across her face. "As you may or may not know, Michael and I used to be married."

I glance at Alex again, wringing my hands. She looks

panicked as her fingers grip onto Michael's. Even Henry is looking slightly ill.

I have to stop this.

Clearing my throat, I turn to the room. "Thanks, Mel," I say jovially, forcing a laugh. "We don't need the prequel."

There's a smattering of nervous laughter around the room, and I catch Myles watching with concern. Mel stops, her severe gaze cutting to me. Then—I cannot believe this—she simply turns back and starts speaking again. The nerve!

Now I'm not so much worried for Alex as I am pissed off. Who the hell does she think she is? She shouldn't even *be* here right now, let alone standing up to speak. It's time to put her in her place.

Before I know what I'm doing, I grab her arm and pull—shit, she's strong—and somehow manage to yank her away from the table and out through a side door into an empty corridor. It's not until the door has slammed shut behind me and I've let go of Mel's arm that I realize what I've done.

Shit.

36

M el wheels around. "What the *fuck*?"

I inhale carefully, trying to calm my frenzied pulse. *You can do this, you can stand your
ground. You're not in the wrong here, she is.* But she takes a
menacing step forward, towering over me in her stilettos,
and her eyes are so dark with fury that I actually cower a
little.

"You can't give a toast," I say, trying to keep my voice
steady. "It's not appropriate."

"What?" she spits—literally—and I take a step back. "I
can do whatever I like."

I shake my head. "Not here. This is Alex's wedding,
and—"

"Oh for fuck's sake. She'll be alright. She's a *big* girl." Her
lips twist into a smirk and I realize she's trying to insult
Alex's body. It takes all my strength not to slap her.

The door opens beside us and I turn, surprised to find
Myles poking his head into the corridor. He slips through
the door and looks at me, ignoring Mel. I've only known the

guy five minutes but I've never been so relieved to see someone in my life.

"What the hell do you want?" Mel snaps, but Myles holds his hand up in her face and she jerks back.

He continues to ignore her, speaking to me. "You okay?"

I look at Mel. She folds her arms over her chest, glowering down her nose at me. And something inside me says that I need to do this on my own. I'm strong enough to fight my own battle.

I give Myles a firm nod. "Yes, thank you."

He reaches for the door handle, but it opens and Dena steps into the corridor. He glances between Dena, Mel and I, hovering. His eyebrows rise in silent question and I nod again. May as well face these two together. Two birds with one stone and all that.

"I'll be right in here." Myles gestures to the door and gratitude winds through me as he steps inside. How sweet of him to look out for me. Plus, I get the sense he's about ready to destroy Mel too.

The door clicks shut and Dena turns to Mel. "Are you alright?"

Mel huffs, shifting her attention back to me. "You know, you and Alex might be the new girls around here, but you're just nobodies from some hick town in the middle of nowhere. You're nothing compared to the real women here in New York."

Despite the sting of her words, I force myself to keep my gaze tethered to hers. This is misdirected anger, it's not about me. She's unhappy because of Michael and Henry's toasts, she's mad at Alex for marrying her ex, she's a narcissist who doesn't like to be challenged. I know that. But that doesn't make her any less intimidating.

"Just because Alex has snagged Michael doesn't mean you get Luke."

My heart jolts. "W-what?"

"Oh, come on. Don't think we don't know what's going on." She challenges me with her gaze and I glance at Dena, but she just shrugs.

"Let's go, Mel. It's not worth it."

"Oh, really?" Mel says, trying to stir the pot. "You're not bothered that she's moving in on your husband?"

"*Ex*-husband," I say shakily. "And I'm not—" The words lodge in my throat as Mel takes a step towards me, backing me closer to the wall. My pulse surges and my eyes fly to the door. *Myles, I was wrong. I can't fight this battle alone. Come back.*

Mel's hands go to her hips. "It must be so humiliating being here as Luke's dirty little secret."

"I'm not—"

"He obviously doesn't care about you. Why else would he be hiding it?"

Why would he want to hide what he has with you? Geoff's words from Bounce come back to me and my airway constricts.

"He must be having some kind of early mid-life crisis," Mel continues, sneering.

All the air has been sucked out of the room. My lungs feel tight. I dig my nails into my palms, trying to stay in control of my breathing. "Mel—"

"He's certainly not about to divorce Dena and settle down with *The Little Mermaid*." Mel laughs viciously, gesturing to me. It takes me a second to realize she's talking about my hair, and I shrink down, all the words I want to say dying on my tongue.

"Mel, just leave it," Dena says, but Mel ignores her as she closes the gap between us.

"You'll be gone soon and Luke will forget all about you."

She points a finger, jabbing me hard in the chest. I stumble backwards into the corner and lose my balance, grabbing the wall to steady myself. Suddenly, I'm back in high school being cornered in the bathroom as the walls close in. My vision blurs and the room swims around me. I trip over my feet, turning down the corridor blindly, all sense of direction gone.

Oh God. This can't be happening.

I'm vaguely aware of Mel and Dena leaving, but I can't move. My chest feels like it's being crushed and I can't breathe—I try to suck in air but I can't. I'm drowning.

Not again. No.

Sweat glazes my skin and I gasp—I gasp but I can't get any air, there's no air, and I lose my balance, I'm falling—

Strong arms wrap around me and pull me upright. I can hear a voice but I can't make out the words. I'm gasping for air and shaking—

"Breathe, Harriet, just breathe."

It's Luke, I realize through the fog. I try to take a breath but I'm still trembling, still gasping, my hands in fists gripping his shirt as I fight for breath. He strokes my hair, holding me, trying to soothe me.

"Breathe. Just breathe, baby. It's okay, I'm here, just breathe."

Somehow, I manage to rasp in the tiniest amount of air as Luke anchors me, keeping me safe in the middle of this raging storm.

"There you go. Just breathe. I'm here, baby."

I get another breath in, then another, and calm begins to ebb through me as the scattered pieces of myself come back together. I'm still shaking and when I raise a hand to my face, it's wet with tears.

Luke wipes my cheeks and strokes my hair, and I'm so spent I sag against him as my pulse slows in my veins. He holds me close, and I can hear his heart jackhammering through his shirt.

When I finally feel steady enough to pull back, his face is etched with concern. "Are you okay?"

I nod, loosening my grip in his shirt.

"Was that a panic attack?"

"Yes." My voice cracks as I stare down at my quivering hands, suddenly feeling more vulnerable than I ever have. I might have shared my awful past with him, but that was on my own terms. I never wanted him to actually *see* me like this, at my absolute worst. Shame washes through me and another tear slides down my cheek.

But Luke just gathers me into his arms, rubbing gentle circles on my back, holding me tight. "Hey, it's okay, baby. It's okay," he whispers again. And in that moment, I know without a doubt that he loves me, and that everything will be okay.

WHEN I GET BACK to the table, I'm still wobbly but I'm okay. Myles is shooting me worried looks, and I can't look at Mel, but I'm sure she knows she got to me. I missed Alex and Michael's first dance, and when Dena comes over to our table to ask Luke to dance, I know he has to go along with it. But he spends the entire song having a heated conversation with her, and while I don't catch any of it, I feel vindicated because I know he's standing up for me. And I'm more certain than ever that he and I will find a way to make things work. Mel knows nothing.

After their dance, Dena stalks off to the bathroom and Luke comes back over to the table, taking a seat beside me. He leans closer, keeping his voice quiet. "Dena told me what happened in the corridor. I'm sorry. Mel is..." He rubs the back of his neck. "She's really nasty. I never understood why Mike married her."

I fiddle with the napkin on the table in front of me, staying quiet.

"Don't let the muggles get you down," he says, trying to lighten the mood. But he knows it's not working, and sighs. "Look, I just have to get through today, okay? I just need this wedding to be over, then..." he trails off, his desperate eyes scanning my face.

Then what?

He turns to look out at the dance floor, so I do too, the question I can't ask hanging in the air between us. I watch Dena dance with William, laughing and smiling, and my stomach churns. When I glance back at Luke, his gaze is resting on me, his expression tender. He reaches out to tuck a loose tendril of hair behind my ear and I can't help myself; I soften against his hand, closing my eyes for the briefest second. In that moment, I feel the forcefield again and nothing else matters.

We share a smile then both sit back, turning to watch people dance again.

And that's when I see Alex. She's on the dance floor in Michael's arms, but she's looking at me. She has the strangest expression on her face and my heart stops in my chest.

She knows.

37

S hit, shit, shit.

Okay. No, it's okay. Maybe she doesn't know. I bet I'm overreacting.

But as Alex whispers something to Michael and threads her way through the tables towards me, my stomach begins to crumble.

"Can we have a word?" she asks. Her tone is pleasant but her gaze is steely.

Shit.

I swig back what's left of my champagne, then follow her across the room and back out the side door to the corridor. With every step I hear Admiral Ackbar in my head, saying *It's a trap!* But my unsteady legs won't let me run away.

Once the door clicks shut behind us, Alex turns to me and smooths the lace of her dress, not saying anything. I'm just wondering if I've misread this whole thing when she looks at me sharply.

"Is there something you want to tell me?"

I study the detailing on her dress. "What do you mean?"

"It's Luke, isn't it?"

I swallow hard, willing my pummeling heart to slow down. I'm not sure I'll survive two panic attacks today.

"The lake last night. All those late nights at his place..." I can hear the gears turning in her head as she thinks aloud. "And he was so enthusiastic about your cafe idea. I saw him, just now, with your hair. You said—" She stops, staring at me in disbelief. "Please tell me I'm wrong."

I open my mouth then close it again, unable to look at her. I don't know what I could possibly say to make this any better.

"But..." Her forehead scrunches in confusion. "I thought you were seeing the guy from the plane? Liam?"

I cringe, dragging my gaze to hers.

"Wait. Liam... is Luke? *Luke* was the guy on the plane?"

I give a tiny nod, chewing my cheek.

"So, this whole time..."

"I wanted to tell you." My voice comes out hoarse. "But I couldn't. It's not... We—"

"You do know he's *married*?" she says viciously. "His *wife* is here."

"Yes. Well, he's—" Fuck. I can't very well tell her he's getting divorced, can I? It's not my place to tell her, and he'd kill me. I won't break his trust.

"That didn't *bother* you?" Alex spits. "Here we are at my *wedding* and you're out there making a mockery of the whole thing by fucking a married man and destroying his marriage."

Her words are a knife in my gut, forcing a gasp from me. "It's not, I mean, he's—"

"Don't you realize how *messed up* this is?" She raises her hands to her head, massaging her temples. "You're my sister. This is Michael's brother. It's practically incestuous."

I grimace as she uses the one word I've been keeping

from my mind. She's wrong; it's not incestuous, not really. But—

"I cannot believe you've done this to me."

"What?" I say, surprised. "I haven't done anything to *you*—"

"What am I going to tell Michael?"

An icy feeling snakes its way up my spine. "Nothing! Please, you don't have to—"

"Of course I do! He's my husband. I can't keep this from him. You don't realize what an awful position this puts me in."

Shit. She can't tell Michael. It's one thing for *her* to be mad at me, but if she tells Michael I'm in trouble.

She shakes her head, gazing at me sadly. "I hardly recognize you, Harri. Ever since you got here you've been acting differently. At first I thought it was really cool that you were coming out of your shell, but now I find out you've been lying to me for weeks and sleeping with Michael's brother. His *married* brother."

Every word from her twists the knife. I suck in a trembling breath, my airway burning.

"Honestly, what is *wrong* with you?" Her eyes glisten with tears. "I don't even know who you are anymore." And without waiting for me to say anything, she turns and heads back into the reception hall, slamming the door behind her.

I stand there for a moment, focusing on counting my breaths. *In, out, in, out.* I cannot spiral again. *In, out, in, out.* Slowly, somehow, I blink back my tears enough to pull myself together.

Okay. It's okay. I know she's upset, of course she is. I would be too, if I were her. But she doesn't know the full story. She didn't mean what she said—of course she didn't—

she just needs to know all the facts and then she'll understand.

I open the door to the reception hall, my gaze seeking Luke. He's already looking at me in the doorway, his eyes flared with concern. I gesture surreptitiously for him to come over and he glances around, then wanders across the room, trying not to draw attention to himself. He slips into the corridor, closing the door behind him.

"Are you okay?"

"Alex has figured it out."

The color drains out of him. "What?"

"She thinks—" My words catch in my throat and I pause, trying to calm down. "She thinks I'm a home-wrecker, that I'm trying to break you and Dena up."

"How did she find out?"

I shrug helplessly. "I... I don't know. She saw us at the table and put it all together."

Luke wipes a hand down his face. "Oh. Shit."

"I'm sorry," I mumble.

"No—" He reaches for my hand and squeezes it. "*I'm* sorry. You shouldn't have had to deal with that."

"I think she's going to tell Michael. I know you didn't want to, but if we just tell them..."

He looks at me pleadingly. "I really don't want to do this right now."

"I know," I reassure him. "But we could ask them not to tell your dad, right?"

"It's not just that. I can't tell my brother, *on his wedding day*, that I'm getting divorced. Come on, Harri, you must be able to understand why I don't want to do that."

"Yeah, I do. But that was before... I mean, Alex already knows something is up now. I wanted to tell her the truth, but I didn't. I thought it should come from you."

His hand drops from mine and a frown stitches across his brow. He rubs the back of his neck, a muscle ticking in his jaw, and for the first time I feel a flicker of apprehension.

My hands shake and I try to hold them still. "I know the timing isn't ideal."

"No kidding." His frown deepens as he glares at the carpet. "Fuck."

My heart jerks but I speak calmly: "We need to tell them, Luke."

He breathes out hard, finally meeting my gaze. "I can't do this today. I can't be responsible for ruining my brother's wedding."

"But that wouldn't ruin his wedding, would it?"

"Well if that doesn't, telling him I've been fucking his new baby sister behind his back would."

My lips part in shock. There are so many things wrong with that statement I almost don't know where to begin. "I'm sorry, *fucking* me? Because that's all this was?"

Luke's features twist in agony. "I don't mean... No. But—" He lets out a low growl and shoves his hands through his hair. "I didn't want to make a scene at the wedding. You know that."

"I know, but..." My stomach is full of rocks now, because this isn't going at all how I thought it would. I wipe the sweat from my palms on my dress. "If you don't tell them, then that means I'm the only one taking the heat on this and that's not fair."

He stares at me, his jaw locked, saying nothing.

I can't believe this. Is he really refusing to tell them? I'm aware that I should be angry, that I probably *should* make a scene now, because that's what he deserves. But more than anything, I'm hurt. After everything he's seen me go through today, he's refusing to stand by me when I need him the most.

A lump lodges in my throat, but I manage to swallow it enough to speak. "I thought you and I had something here."

He blows out a frustrated breath. "Look, I didn't plan to meet you. I didn't plan to fall—" He stops himself abruptly and my heart drops. Was he about to say he's fallen in love with me? It was only a few moments ago that I felt certain he had, but now that he's standing here, letting me take the blame for everything, I realize how wrong I was.

"I can't, Harriet. I'm sorry." He shakes his head and looks away. As I gaze at him, I know the forcefield is totally gone. It's shattered into smithereens, dissolved into dust, scattered across the cosmos. The man I was with—the one who got me to go on the trapeze, who showed me the cafe I could have, who made love to me despite all my scars and held me only moments ago while I spiraled out of control—he's gone. Just like that. And, God, if that's all it took for him to disappear, then I never really had him to begin with, did I?

With blinding clarity, I can suddenly see what Mel and Geoff knew all along: he doesn't care. At least, not enough to fight for me.

"I need to get back in there," Luke mutters, his gaze glued to the carpet. I watch as he turns and enters the reception hall again without looking my way, without acknowledging the hurt he's just caused.

Tears press at my eyes and my breath comes in shallow, quick bursts. That's it. He's just walked away and left me. I'm too shocked to move, to do anything. I don't know how long I stand there, paralyzed. I don't know how I don't fall apart again, but I don't.

Then, as if in a trance, I walk into the reception hall. My gaze drifts over to where Alex and Michael are cutting the cake and posing for a photo. I catch Alex's eye and she gives a disappointed shake of her head, turning back to the camera. The photographer gestures for Luke and Dena to pose with the others, and I watch numbly as Luke slides his arm around Dena and smiles at the camera with ease. After everything he just said to me, he's smiling like nothing has happened. Like I don't even exist.

Something inside me breaks.

How could I have been so *stupid*?

I feel a sudden, hot rush of humiliation and spin on my heel. I fumble for my bag and stagger out the door, my vision blurry with tears. The cold night air hits me like a slap in the face, but I don't care. I need to leave. I need to not be here, with these people who don't care about me.

Before I know what I'm doing, I'm running. I'm running and I don't look back.

38

The seatbelt sign switches off and the plane levels out. This time I didn't bat an eyelash during take-off, which I'm putting down to two factors: one, I'm practically a seasoned traveler now, and two, I'm too bloody maudlin to care what happens to me at this point. Why should I? I'm in love with someone who doesn't love me back, and my heart feels like it has been slashed to bits with a machete.

Oh, and I ruined my sister's wedding, losing both her trust and respect.

The plane shudders as we hit a small patch of turbulence, but I just release a loud sigh and gaze out the window, thinking of Geoff. He was my savior in the end.

After fleeing the reception, I ran from the lodge down the road to the cabin, grabbed my things and was about to call a cab to take me back to the city when headlights swung up the driveway. For a moment I was overcome with joy because I thought Luke had followed me. He'd seen reason! He'd announced the truth to the whole reception! He'd come to declare his love! Oh, I *knew* he'd come through—

I was wrong, obviously.

Instead, Geoff leapt from the car and came running up the driveway, pulling me into a hug. When I told him I was getting a cab back to the city, he said it would cost me a fortune and offered to drive me.

I didn't know what to say. I think I burst into tears because of his kindness, and he ushered me into the passenger seat. I asked him why he was helping me and pointed out that after what had happened, Alex wouldn't be pleased. But he just shrugged and said that once Alex had calmed down, she'd be grateful I hadn't been alone when I was upset.

I wasn't so sure.

My phone wouldn't stop buzzing with calls from my parents, and in the end I sent them a text to say I wasn't feeling well and I'd check in with them later. I couldn't bear to explain over the phone what had happened.

Geoff and I drove in silence for at least an hour, until I couldn't stand it anymore. I had to get the words out. "It was Luke," I murmured in the dark.

I thought Geoff hadn't heard me, because he didn't say anything for the longest time. But then he sighed, and said, "I know."

"How?"

He shrugged again, glancing at me with a soft smile. "I don't know. I just had a feeling."

I waited for him to say more—that he'd told me so, that I was delusional because Luke wasn't divorced at all, and poor Alex, how selfish of me. But he said nothing like that. He did nothing that made me feel like he was judging me.

He took me straight to the airport, and even though I had three missed calls from Alex by then, I still just wanted to get on a plane and go home. After faffing about sorting out my ticket, I'm finally in the air. You'd think I'd be relieved, but instead I just feel... numb. The past two and a half weeks are a surreal blur in my mind, almost as if I dreamed them. And if it wasn't for the red hair tumbling over my shoulders, I might even think I did.

I give the flight attendant a thin smile as she hands me a glass of water. I was tempted to ask for whiskey but couldn't bring myself to say the words.

But the longer I sit here, processing the past couple of weeks, the more I do know one thing: I'm an idiot. Of course what Luke and I had couldn't last. I live on the other side of the planet, our siblings are married, he's barely divorced... not to mention the fact that I lied to him. There are so many reasons it could never work, no matter how much I wanted it to. He made that clear from the start, by refusing to tell anyone about us. *Talk about not taking the hint, Harriet.*

I laugh bitterly and the man to my right gives me a side-ways look.

Great. Now I'm turning into a nutter who laughs to herself in public. Ah, I'm too depressed to care.

This is all Harriet 2.0's fault. Who was I kidding with that whole thing? All I was doing was playing a foolish game —pretending to be someone I'm not, pretending to be adventurous, pretending I could have a little fling without consequences.

Pretending I was fearless.

I wish I'd never tapped into my alter ego. Well, I'm done with her, with her utter disregard for my feelings and how her outlandish actions might affect me. All she did was get me hurt.

Maybe Alex was right. She said she didn't know me anymore and I can't say I recognize myself right now, sitting here feeling sorry for myself because some guy rejected me.

I never thought I'd be that woman, falling apart over a man, but that's exactly what it feels like. It feels like I'm falling apart.

A lone tear escapes down my cheek but I don't bother to wipe it away. I hurt my sister and ruined her wedding. She'll probably never forgive me.

And I've lost the man who made me feel more alive than anyone ever has.

I just hope I haven't lost myself, too.

I'M GOING BACK to work today. I don't want to see Paula because she'll be all excited to hear about my trip, and even though it's been four days since I arrived home, I'm still in pieces. Tiny, fragmented little pieces that I can't put back together. Every time I try, there's a piece missing.

I haven't been sleeping well. At night I lie awake in bed staring at the ceiling, replaying the past few weeks. When I do drift off to sleep, it's fitful and full of messed-up dreams. I had one where I was drowning in the lake but Luke didn't notice, and when he finally tried to save me it was too late. I had another dream where I was down on a subway platform but it was empty and quiet, like at the museum. Then I noticed that Alex was on the tracks so I went down to talk to her, and a train came screaming around the corner. I woke before it hit us, but... clearly I have some issues.

It's been a weird few days. I've never missed someone like I miss Luke. It's an ache, a physical pain in my chest. My heart has been dropped off a cliff and now it's so bruised I'm not sure how it will recover. I know I shouldn't miss him, not after he left me to fend for myself at the wedding, but I can't help it. I keep thinking of things I want to share with him or say to him, then I realize I can't. It's like that phantom limb syndrome where people who've lost limbs keep thinking they're still there. How on earth can I feel like that after only knowing him for two and a half weeks? I must be losing my mind.

Alex has called a few more times and I've let it go to voicemail. I just can't face her yet. At least Steph hasn't been home, showering me with questions. She's been up in Auckland for work and I could not be more glad. It feels like a tiny mercy from this cruel and heartless universe.

Anyway. Enough moping. Enough feeling like shit over something so stupid. Time to get on with my life. Work today.

I do have a bit of a conundrum, though. It's going to sound silly, but I don't know what to wear to work. On autopilot I put on my slim-fitting jeans and a simple T-shirt, pulling my hair up into the tight bun on my head. But when I look at myself in the mirror, it doesn't feel right. I might be done with the outrageous version of myself, but I'm not the old me anymore, either. The trip to New York changed me, whether I like it or not.

In the end I stay in my jeans and T-shirt, but I put my red lipstick on and wear my hair half-up, half-down. It seems like a kind of compromise, and I smile at myself in the mirror when I'm done. The smile doesn't reach my eyes.

I drag my feet the whole walk to work, but when I finally push through the glass doors and inhale the familiar scent of coffee beans and Paula baking something delicious, a little part of me unfurls. It's nice to be back here, actually. Comforting. Maybe I can do this. Maybe today will be good.

Paula pops out from the kitchen, grinning when she sees me. "Hey, chick!" She wraps me in a tight hug, then releases me. "You look fantastic! How was your trip?"

I burst into tears.

Fuck. Not a brilliant start.

"Oh, love!" She takes my hand and guides me over to a table. "What's wrong?"

I sit there for a moment, studying the woodgrain in the table-top. Then, I draw a wobbly breath and tell her. Everything. The plane, the fling with Luke, his divorce, the wedding, how I let Alex down. How I convinced myself Luke was falling for me, then realized how deluded I was.

When I'm finally done, she puts an arm around my shoulder and squeezes. "Oh, chick. I'm sorry. That sounds..." She shakes her head. She doesn't give me advice, or make me feel bad, and I love her for it.

I dry my eyes and glance at the clock above the counter. Shit, I've been sitting here blubbering for twenty minutes. It's nearly time to open up.

"Thanks for listening and not judging. I haven't shared it all with anyone and it was good to get it out." And strangely, I do feel a little better. Not much, but a bit.

I stand and grab my apron from the counter, tying it around my waist, but Paula doesn't move from the table.

"I suppose we should get on with things," I say, trying to keep my tone bright. "It's good to be back here. I missed this place." I wait for Paula to stand, but she doesn't.

Instead, she sends me a worried look. "You should probably sit down again, love. I have some news."

Her tone makes a weight settle in my gut, and I lower myself back into the chair.

"I'm so sorry to drop this on you after everything you've just been through, but I need to tell you." She pauses, fiddling with the salt and pepper shakers on the table between us. "I'm selling—well, actually, I've *sold*—the cafe."

Oh shit. Of course, Mum and Dad said something about

that. With everything going on with Luke, I completely forgot.

"Right. What, er, what brought this on?" As far as I've always known, she loves running this place.

"Actually, it was you."

"*Me*?"

She nods. "When you left for New York, it got me thinking. I've always wanted to travel, to get out and see the world a bit more. I'm getting older and it sort of feels like now or never."

"Wow."

"It happened very quickly. I put the cafe on the market to see if there might be some interest, to see what response I'd get. But I got an offer after only three days and I couldn't turn it down."

"Right," I murmur. I'm so shocked I don't know what to think. "So... where will you go? What will you do?"

An excited smile plays on her lips. "I don't know! I thought I might go to New York, see what all the fuss is about. But you know, eventually, I'll want to do something like this again." She gestures around us. "I do love this place and I'm sad to leave, but I'm excited to explore somewhere new, build something new."

I give her a faint smile. She's brave, giving up something that she loves to see what else is out there.

"Anyway." Her smile fades. "Unfortunately—God, I hate to have to do this, chick—but the new owner doesn't want things to stay the same. He has ideas to redo the place and he'll be hiring new staff." She grimaces, reaching across the table for my hand. "So, that means—"

"Yeah. I get it." I push my mouth into a smile, but I can't stop my shoulders from sagging. The one good thing I had left in my life is now also being taken away.

Way to kick me when I'm down, universe.

"I'm sorry." Paula's face lines with remorse but I wave her apology away.

"Don't be silly. I'm really happy for you."

"What will you do?"

I chew my cheek, gazing around at the cafe. I've gotten so used to coming here all the time, to spending my days here, that I can't really imagine going anywhere else. Well, there was that one place in New York, that board game cafe that felt like my dream come to life...

"I could start my own cafe," I say, but it sounds like a joke to my ears.

Paula's face lights up. "Yes! You should! I've seen you scribbling ideas on that napkin."

"Oh..." I'm taken aback by her enthusiasm, and I did *not* know she'd seen my napkin. "Well, I don't know."

"Why not? You've worked for me for so long, wouldn't you love to be your own boss?"

I shrug, recalling Luke's enthusiasm and belief in me, the folder with all the numbers still in my bag, the empty store on the Lower East Side. I remember how I could see the ideas from my napkin come to life in that place, how I thought I'd call it something fun, like Game of Scones.

But thinking of that now sends a sharp sting through my chest and I quickly shake my head. The girl that stood in that empty shop space and pictured starting her own business was a different person. That was Harriet 2.0. When I think of that idea now it feels ridiculous. It feels impossible.

"I'd love to help you set something up," Paula says. "Maybe when I'm back from seeing the world, we could—"

"Thanks, but I don't think so." A shaky laugh drops from my lips. "I'll... I don't know. I'll find another job." As much as I hate the thought of having to redo my resume and find a new job, I guess that will give me something to focus on, to distract me from the pool of misery I've been wallowing in. And it's a lot less overwhelming than contemplating some wild fantasy of flitting off to start my own business in a new country.

Paula sighs, setting the salt and pepper shakers down, but she doesn't say anything more.

I force another smile and stand. "I'm so happy for you. Don't worry about me, I'll be fine." I wander to the counter and turn on the espresso machine, willing the tears brimming my eyes to go away, the hollowness inside to disappear.

It feels like I'm losing everything I know, and soon there won't be anything left.

39

P aula sends me home early. Apparently I'm not keeping it together as well as I think I am, and when she catches me having a little cry in the bathroom she decides I've done enough for the day.

But at home I just stand in the living room and stare blankly at nothing, unsure of what to do with myself. I should be preparing my resume to start job-hunting but, God, I can't face it. I'll start tomorrow.

In the end I curl up on the sofa and put on a movie (*The Empire Strikes Back*, if you must know. I wanted to, I don't know, "be" with Luke) but there's a knock at the door. I pause the opening credits and peel myself off the couch. When I swing the door open, my jaw sags at the figure on the doorstep. But before I can say anything, Alex throws her arms around me.

"Oh my God, Harriet. I'm so sorry!"

I let her hug me, dumbstruck. Over her shoulder, I spy Michael coming up the steps.

"Can you ever forgive me?" She pulls back, her eyes misty as she contemplates my face. Why on earth is she asking *me* for forgiveness? Shouldn't it be the other way around?

"Give her a minute," Michael says to Alex, chuckling.

I step aside and motion for them to come in. They enter the living room and Michael's gaze lands on the television, the corners of his eyes creasing in a smile.

"Luke and Henry are obsessed with this film."

I look away, blinking back the tears that spring to my eyes. Seeing Michael—with his uncanny similarities to Luke —is almost too much to bear.

"Honey," Alex admonishes, shaking her head at him. He looks chastened, and she turns her attention back to me. "Are you okay? You look..."

"Not really." I flop back onto the sofa.

"I'll make some tea, then we can talk."

I nod, my gaze involuntarily returning to Michael. He shifts his weight and I gesture to a chair. We sit in awkward silence, staring at the frozen film credits on the screen, while Alex clatters about in the kitchen. A few minutes later she appears with tea and settles onto the sofa beside me, folding her legs up underneath her and cradling her mug.

I take my tea with a weak smile. "What are you doing here?"

"Honeymoon," she says, as if it's the most obvious thing in the world. "Michael wanted to see where I grew up, and he promised we could stop over at Hawaii on the way home, so..." She shrugs, grinning, then her face turns serious. "First thing's first, I need to apologize."

"Why? If anyone should be apologizing, it's me. I'm sorry I lied to you, and I never meant to ruin your wedding. I thought you'd never speak to me again, and—"

"Oh, Harri. You don't have to apologize. I completely

attacked you for what happened with Luke and I had no right."

I blush, sliding an uncomfortable look to Michael. I can only assume she told him I was sleeping with Luke and I don't know what he must think of me. "Michael, honestly, it was an accident, me and Luke. I didn't know he was your brother and I didn't know he was married, at least not when we met, but..." I trail off, unsure of what else I can say. I can't tell him Luke and Dena are divorced because I'll sound delusional.

But it's more than that. Even after everything that happened, I still don't feel like I can tell them the truth. It's not my place. If Luke wants to tell them he can, but I'm not going to do it. I shouldn't have to.

Alex places a gentle hand on my arm. "Luke told us everything."

I nearly drop my tea. "You mean..."

"Yeah," Michael says. "He told us he separated from Dena five months ago, that they're divorced, and that he didn't want to ruin our wedding with the news. Then he told us about you." He shakes his head ruefully. "He's an idiot. He should have told me about his divorce. I knew things weren't great in his marriage, but I didn't realize how bad it was. I wish he hadn't gone through all that alone."

I gape at them, a strange combination of relief and frustration rippling through me. After everything that happened, he *told* them?

"Dad didn't take it very well," Michael mutters, running a hand over his beard.

"Wait." I set my tea down. "He told your parents too?"

Michael nods, reaching for his cup on the table. "Yep. Dad flipped out, but I played the wedding card—I told him it was my wedding and he needed to stop making a scene. It worked pretty well."

"*Wait*," I repeat, in utter disbelief. "Luke announced it *at* your wedding?"

"He did." Alex blows on her tea. "Once you'd gone, we tried to carry on. We danced for a bit, but Luke looked so miserable. I actually thought he was going to cry."

I glance wide-eyed at Michael and he nods. "Yeah, he was pretty cut-up once he realized you'd left."

"Really?"

"Dena asked him to dance and he lost it," Alex says. "We could hear him yelling, but we didn't know what was going on. Then he went out into the corridor and I followed him to see if he was okay. I think he felt really bad because he apologized for making a scene and tried to pull himself together. But I told him to sit down, and I went and got Michael, and we stayed with him until he'd told us everything."

I stare at her, my head spinning.

"I lost my shit at him," Michael says with a grimace. "You're Alex's younger sister. It just felt so... wrong."

I let my gaze fall to the floor, ashamed. "I know. I should never have—"

"No," Michael says, and I'm surprised by the sharp edge to his voice. "*He* shouldn't have gone after you."

"Michael was looking out for you," Alex explains. "You're basically his little sister now."

"Oh." I think back to the dinner before the wedding, when Michael said he was happy to have me as his sister-in-law and called me his "new little sister." And what Luke said, about how he didn't want to tell Michael we'd been sleeping together... Wow, I don't think I realized just how protective Michael actually feels of me. God, now I really *do* feel like his sister. I look at him and cringe. "I know it's weird, me sleeping with your brother. But it wasn't Luke's fault—he didn't *go after* me. We both, I mean, we—" I break off, my throat too clogged with emotion.

"I know," Michael murmurs, softening. "I didn't realize that at first. I just started yelling at him about how inappropriate it was for him to pursue you. And then... I don't know. The more I spoke to him, the more I realized it wasn't like that. I tried to tell him to go and talk to you, but he said he wasn't going to leave my wedding. So then I told him he needed to at least tell Mom and Dad, to stop worrying about my wedding and just get it over with. And then it was like once he had my permission, he just went for it. He told Dena he couldn't keep the act up anymore, then he told Mom and Dad everything." Michael gives a grim little laugh. "I've *never* seen him talk to Dad like that."

I wince, thinking of the horrible things William probably said to him. I wonder if he was as awful as Luke said he'd be. There's a tug in my heart at the thought of Luke hurting, and my eyes well with tears.

Alex puts an arm around me and squeezes me into her side. "I shouldn't have been so hard on you. I'm sorry for what I said. I didn't know the full story, and now I can see you were protecting him. You were just keeping your word."

I nod, wiping my eyes and trying to collect myself. "I'm so sorry this blew up at your wedding. We never—I never... I didn't want it to ruin everything and it did."

Alex smiles. "It didn't ruin everything. Please don't think that."

I let my breath out in a long exhale. Hearing Alex say the wedding wasn't ruined—knowing she isn't mad at me—makes the block of tension that has been sitting heavy in my middle since her wedding lighten ever so slightly.

"Besides," she adds, "that wasn't even the most dramatic thing that happened. After that, there was this huge blowup with Mel and Mark."

"What?"

"Apparently Mel has been having an affair with some married guy for the past few months. The wife must have found out, because she called Mark at the wedding and told him everything. He got super drunk and got up on the mic and told Mel he never loved her because he still loves Cat. It was crazy."

"Oh my God," I mutter. I think of how Mel called me Luke's "dirty little secret" and said that he was hiding me because he didn't care about me. That wasn't about me at all —it was about *her*.

"But you're not totally off the hook," Alex says, her lips quirking playfully. "Michael and I will figure out some kind of high-jinx to pull at your wedding to get you back."

I give her a funny look. "*My* wedding?"

"To Luke," she says, reaching for her mug again and taking a sip.

"What?"

She gazes at me for a second over her tea, then rolls her eyes. "He's in love with you, Harri."

My pulse leaps. "*What?*"

She laughs, and when I look at Michael, he just shrugs and smiles.

"But... he hasn't tried to get in touch with me."

"He knows he made a mess of everything." Michael sets his cup down with a sigh. "He shouldn't have brought Dena to the wedding in the first place, and he shouldn't have walked away from you. But... I can also understand why he felt like he had no choice. I mean, I did exactly what he thought I would do—I got mad at him. And it might sound like an excuse, but our father—" Michael's brow dips and he shakes his head. "Luke's spent his whole life trying to win Dad's approval."

"I know," I whisper.

Alex squeezes me again. "I think he was just really scared."

I suck in a shuddering breath as a tear slides down my cheek. Of course he was scared. How could I have let myself forget that? In the moment I'd been so focused on the idea that he didn't care enough, but what if it hadn't been about me at all? What if I'd underestimated just how terrified he was of confronting his dad and telling Michael the truth about us? I recall Luke's words in that corridor—*I can't, Harriet. I'm sorry*—and realization flashes through me. It wasn't that he was refusing to tell them, it was that he felt as though he *couldn't*.

More tears wash down my face as I think of him dealing with his brother's anger and facing his father alone. What if I hadn't run away, but had stuck by him? What if it hadn't been about me needing *him* in that moment, but about him needing *me*? At the cabin he confessed that he didn't feel brave—that he'd been living a lie. When I think about this now, a crack forms in my heart. He was there every step of the way for me when I needed help to be brave, but when it came time for me to help *him*, I didn't. I made it about me, and I ran.

Michael glances from me to Alex. "Maybe we should go settle in at your folks' place. Give Harriet some space."

Her gaze lingers on me for another moment, then she sighs, setting her empty cup down. "Alright. But I'm going to check in on you soon, okay?"

I nod numbly, then send them on their way. When I collapse back onto the sofa, I sit there in a daze for some time, playing Alex's words on repeat in my head: *He's in love with you.* He didn't turn his back on me at the wedding because he didn't care enough. It wasn't about me at all. Of course it wasn't, how could I have let myself believe that?

I'm so crazy about you, Harriet. Luke's words on the doorstep of the cabin echo through my head. My heart is sore as I think about what he was trying to say. Then the other words come back to me—*you make me feel alive, like no one ever has*—and despair rolls through me, breaking like a wave across my chest. Because if he *is* in love, it's not really with me, it's with a fantasy self I created, a "wild girl" who doesn't exist. I'd somehow convinced myself that it was just a tiny white lie—that it didn't matter because I was becoming that new, fearless version of myself—but that couldn't be further from the truth. Because I ran away when Luke needed me the most.

A sob escapes me and I curl into a ball on the sofa, hugging my knees, letting the tears stream down my face. I've fallen in love with a guy who can't really love me back, because I lied about who I am.

What a mess.

"Oh my God, hon!" I glance up and, through my tears, see Steph hurrying across the living room. She dumps a suitcase beside the sofa and crouches in front of me. "What's going on? Are you okay?"

"No," I manage through a fresh surge of tears.

She sits beside me, pulling me into a hug. She doesn't say any more; just holds me while I sob like a baby. It takes me some time, but gradually I feel the hysteria subside, and I straighten up, sniffling.

"Is this about the best man?"

I nod, reaching for a tissue to dry my eyes.

"You want to talk about it?"

I look at Steph, knowing I need to tell her the full story. Because while she knew I was sleeping with Luke—and that he was also Michael's brother—what I never told her about was Dena, and his divorce, and his dad. I take a deep breath, and with a heavy heart, I finally tell her everything.

"Wow," Steph says when I finish. "That's... a lot."

"Yeah."

Her eyebrows tug into a frown. "Are you angry with him for not sticking up for you at the wedding?"

I look down at my hands, thinking about this. It was humiliating and I was hurt. I should be mad as hell—I should want him to suffer, like I did. But I don't feel that way. I know he's a good guy—I know he *has* suffered. He acted from a place of pain and fear, and that's a place I know all too well.

"No," I whisper. "I understand why he didn't. And... he did, in the end. I just ran away before he could."

Steph reads something on my face I didn't know was there. "You're in love with him."

I nod.

"Oh, Harri," she says, hugging me again. "You need to go and fight for him. Harriet 2.0 would."

I sigh, pressing my fingers to my eyelids in frustration. "That's the problem, Steph. I'm not Harriet 2.0, am I? But that's who I told him I was. He kept going on and on about how I made him feel alive, how he loved my wild side. I don't have a bloody wild side!"

Steph gives a disgruntled huff. "Bullshit."

"What?"

"*Bullshit*. You *do* have a wild side."

I laugh humorlessly. "Oh that's right, what did you say? Returning library books after the due date. Somehow I don't think that's the kind of outrageous things Luke had in mind."

"For fuck's sake, Harriet. Did you even *listen* to the story you just told me? You dyed your hair bright red, went on a freaking trapeze and went skinny-dipping. You had your first orgasm with a stranger on a plane, then had a secret affair with him! I'm sorry, but if that's not outrageous then I don't know what is." She folds her arms across her chest, leveling her gaze at me.

And for a moment, I'm speechless. Hearing everything listed out like that certainly does sound, well, wild.

"Okay," I say at last. "I can see what you're saying. But..." I shake my head, thinking of my panic attack at the wedding. I didn't tell Steph that part before, but I think it's time she knows the full truth. Not just about the wedding— about all of my past. "There's something you don't know about me." My voice shakes, but I continue, regardless. I tell her what I told Luke—about the girls who tormented me at high school, about how I couldn't hold it together, about what I did to cope with it all. And then I tell her about the wedding. By the time I'm finished I'm in tears again, and Steph hands me a tissue, her face etched with concern.

"Why have you never told me this?"

"I guess..." I blow my nose loudly. "I was worried you might think less of me."

"Why would I think less of you? Harriet, if anything, that makes me think you're a badass. You lived through all that shit and came out the other side, stronger. Sounds exactly like Harriet 2.0 to me."

"No." I curl into a ball again, feeling exhausted. "She's fearless and I'm not."

"No one is fearless. Everyone is afraid of something. And

Luke saw that side of you, Harri. He knows you're not fearless."

"Maybe," I mumble. Tears fill my eyes again and I turn my head away so Steph doesn't see. "I'm going to have a lie-down." I drag myself to my feet and shuffle out of the living room before Steph can say anything else.

"MERRY CHRISTMAS." I'm woken by Steph sitting on the edge of my bed, thrusting a sheet of paper towards me.

"What?" I wriggle up in bed, rubbing my eyes and taking the paper from her.

"I said, Merry Christmas."

"It's not even November yet."

She grins, her eyes shimmering with mischief. "I know. This is your early Christmas present."

I glance down at the paper and blink the sleep out of my eyes. When I figure out what I'm holding, I look up at Steph again in shock.

She chuckles. "This might also have to be your Christmas present for next year, and the year after. And maybe your birthday present too."

"You've bought me a ticket to New York," I say in disbelief.

"Yep. You're going to tell Luke how you feel."

"Oh God." I press my eyes shut in exasperation. "Steph, this is *very* generous, but I really don't think—"

"This cost me a fortune, Harri. You're going."

"Well, what about work?" I huff. "I have a job, you know, and—"

"I know Paula sold, and I know you know. So that excuse isn't flying either."

I shove the air from my lungs as I look at the date and time printed on the ticket. It's tomorrow night. She's bought me a bloody flight to New York for *tomorrow night*. This must have cost her a couple thousand at least, and in big, bold text it says it's non-refundable. She's a maniac.

"So what am I supposed to do? Just show up on his doorstep and say 'Hi, Luke! I'm in love with you!'"

"You can word it however you like, but yeah, that's the gist of it." She shrugs. "Come on, Harriet. You did all these amazing things in New York and totally faced your fears, but now you're letting your fear win."

I chew on a nail. She's right about that, and not just now. I let my fear win at the wedding, when I ran away from Luke. And I never once actually told him how *I* felt, how he made *me* feel so alive, too. But...

"What about the fact that I lied to him?"

Her face softens. "I know you think you have to be some outlandish version of yourself for him to like you, but you don't. You're better than that, because you don't have to pretend to be fearless. You can be your *own* kind of brave, even when things are scary."

I glance down at the ticket again and my stomach seesaws with nerves. Can I be that brave?

"Go to New York and tell Luke how you feel," Steph says again, more gently. "Tell him the truth about Harriet 2.0. He's seen the real you anyway. He won't care."

I look up at Steph again, swallowing. She's right about that, too. He *did* see the real me, the one that no one else has ever seen. I just have to tell him the truth and hope that he'll still want me.

I just have to be that brave.

40

It's nearly midnight when my plane touches down in New York. I had a layover in Houston like last time, but I was so amped up I couldn't sit still. I paced around the airport terminal for four straight hours, walking from gate to gate, just to keep moving. Every time I sat still my gut would rage with anxiety and I'd feel nauseous.

It took the edge off quite nicely, though, because I dozed off on the flight from Houston to JFK. I guess the fact that I haven't slept since Steph gave me the ticket also helped.

Now, sitting in the back of a cab as we bump along through Queens, I'm strangely excited. The familiar breathtaking skyline of Manhattan comes into view, twinkling like a glittery postcard in the distance, and my heart does a little dance. I'm back in New York, just like that, and it feels okay. More than okay—it feels like where I'm supposed to be. It feels good.

The cab pulls up at the hotel and I tip the driver like a local. By the time I'm in my hotel room, I'm tired. I know I could have stayed at Alex and Michael's, but I didn't tell them I was flying over here. Truthfully, I'm not sure how this will work out, and I don't need the extra pressure from Alex texting me every five minutes to ask.

Anyway. I'm here now. I fire off a quick text to Steph to tell her I landed safely, then I crawl into bed and stare at the ceiling. And, after running through a thousand different scenarios for how things could go with Luke tomorrow, somehow, I fall asleep.

I WAKE EARLY the next morning. I kill some time by making coffee and trying to read, but I don't take anything in. I'm too anxious to go and see Luke.

By 7 a.m. I decide I've waited long enough. I dress in one of my prettiest dresses, do my hair and makeup, and pull on my jacket as I head outside into the fading darkness of early morning to find a cab. Even though it's only a short drive, I can feel myself getting more and more wound up the closer we get to Luke's. Maybe I should have had a shower session with John Stamos before I left.

I chuckle quietly at the thought, but I'm not fooling myself. I'm freaking out right now. What have I gotten myself into? Why on earth did I agree to this?

I wipe my sweaty palms, keeping my breathing steady. No, I know why I'm here. I know what I came to do. I'm here to be brave. I'm here to fight for the man I love.

I nod to myself, hardening my resolve. Adrenaline courses through me, and as I pull out my compact to check my makeup, my stomach is full of thrashing butterflies.

Then, just like that, we're in front of Luke's apartment building. I sit in the cab for a moment, gazing at the entrance.

Shit. I don't know if I can do this.

Come on Harriet! You've come all this way, Steph mentally cheers me on.

I pay the driver and step out, pulling my bag onto my shoulder. I key in Luke's code and climb the stairs with shaking legs, barely registering what I'm doing. My heartbeat is like hailstones on a tin roof as I step onto Luke's floor, but I don't let that deter me. I knock on his door, then suck in a breath and wait.

Nothing happens.

What if he's not home? I'd never considered that. Uncertainty tugs at me, but I push it away. I'm just looking for excuses.

Besides, it's still early. He's probably asleep.

I raise my hand and knock again, louder this time. A corkscrew twists through my gut while I wait, until finally, I hear footsteps approaching. My heart vaults into my throat as the door opens, and my eyes fasten on a redhead in an oversized T-shirt.

She rubs her eyes. "Um, hi?"

I lose track of time and space at this point. I think my jaw unhinges. I think I stop breathing.

"Can I help you?"

I blink, frozen. My stomach is plunging and I can't find any words. I just gape at her, willing this not to be true.

But it is. There's a woman answering his door. There's a half-naked woman answering his door, early in the morning.

Oh my God.

I manage to get some air into my lungs and it burns. I can't believe he would—

"Are you looking for Luke?" she asks. "I'm Andrea, his house-sitter. He's out of town."

Andrea. House-sitter.

It takes a second for this information to slot into my brain, then relief floods through me in such great torrents that I have to lean against the wall.

Her brows flick together. "Are you okay?"

I nod, breathing out a small laugh. "Yes. I'm... yes. You're the turtle lady."

"I guess you could call me that."

Okay, alright. Luke isn't sleeping with someone else. He's just out of town.

Oh. Fuck.

"Um—" I rub my nose, trying to catch up with this unexpected turn of events. "Did Luke say when he'd be back?"

"No. He called me in the middle of the night and left in quite a rush, so I didn't get much out of him. But you could call him?"

"Right," I say, absorbing this. Maybe he got contacted by that company in Houston he was looking to partner with and had to fly back there. "Okay... thanks."

"No problem." She smiles, one hand on the door. "I'm going to head back to bed."

"Yes," I mumble, straightening my bag on my shoulder and stepping away. "Sorry. And thanks again."

The door closes and I stare at it for a minute, as if Luke will somehow materialize in front of me.

He doesn't, of course.

With a sigh, I turn for the stairs and head down. When I step out onto the street, I feel a little lost. This is very inconvenient, to say the least. I don't often fly halfway across the world to tell men I love them, but when I do I kind of expect them to be home. Talk about an anticlimax.

I survey the streets around me, shivering as the cold air bites through my thin jacket. I'm not really sure what to do now. Luke could be back at any time, so... I should stay, right? I did fly all the way over here and it's not like I have a job to rush back to. I guess I could call him, but the thought of telling him over the phone that I flew to New York to see him somehow makes me more nervous than doing this face to face. Maybe I should go back to the hotel, have a cup of tea, and decide on a plan of action.

I find a taxi down the street and climb inside. We head towards the hotel and I gaze out the window, watching the city slowly wake and sparkle in the morning light. A smile sneaks onto my lips at how beautiful it looks, and at how it actually feels good to be back here on my own terms. While this isn't exactly how I wanted this to go, I'm glad I took the leap, even if I haven't quite landed safely yet. There's a powerful sensation buzzing through me, one that's familiar from my last visit. It's like muscle memory; I've slipped back into the way I was when I was in New York before. Not fear-less, but definitely more bold than I gave myself credit for.

After everything that happened with the wedding, I somehow let myself forget all the ways I had grown during my time here. But I did grow—I grew a lot. I think back over Steph's list: the hair, the trapeze, the skinny-dipping, the orgasm, and Luke—Luke who helped me see the inner strength I didn't even know was there, who helped me connect with my sexuality, who made me feel so full of life and possibility.

Yes, coming back here was the right thing to do. As soon as Luke is back in town, I'm going to tell him the truth about Harriet 2.0, and I'm going to show him that we belong together. I'm done living in fear, and I'm not going to let it rule anymore of my decisions. In fact, the next opportunity I have to challenge my fears, I'm going to dive in head-first. It doesn't matter if—

The cab turns a sharp corner and my bag slides off the

seat, the contents scattering along the floor, my thoughts halted.

Bloody hell.

I unbuckle my seatbelt and scramble to gather my things from the floor of the cab, stopping as something catches my eye. My heart does a tiny hiccup as I reach to pick up Isaac's card, the one he gave me when Luke showed me the empty shop. It almost feels like a sign. Wasn't I just thinking about how I want to face my fears?

Before I can talk myself out of it, I call to the driver, "Can we go to the Lower East Side instead, please?"

He mutters a string of curse words under his breath, then does what I can only assume is an illegal U-turn across four lanes of traffic. My bag goes flying again. This time the clasp on the back pocket pops open and Luke's folder of numbers half slides out. I forgot that was still in there.

I reach for it with a trembling hand. If that's not a sign, I don't know what is. Maybe Luke isn't the only reason I came back to New York.

Okay. I take a deep breath and make a little deal with myself. If we get to the store and it's still for lease, I'm going to call Isaac. If it's still available, I'll take that as the ultimate sign. A current of nervous excitement runs through me at the thought.

"Where on the Lower East Side?" the cabbie demands from the front.

Crap. Where was it? I know it was somewhere off Grand Street, at least I think it was...

"Er, maybe left here..." I do my best to give him directions, and we make several wrong turns—followed by much colorful language on his part—but eventually we're on the right street, and we're pulling up outside the store.

And there, across the front window, is a sign for a pet store. It's been leased, and it's been turned into a pet store.

I wait for relief to take hold of me, but it doesn't. In fact, the longer I sit in the back of the cab, peering out the window at the pet store, the more I feel like I might cry.

God, I didn't realize just how badly I wanted this dream, but the sense of sheer disappointment is so crushing it steals my breath. When the driver turns back to ask me what's going on, I struggle to respond.

"Sorry. Never mind," I mutter, swallowing against the lump blocking my throat. "Back to the hotel."

He peels away from the curb and I lean back, absently watching the shops pass by, feeling hollow with remorse. If only I'd taken the opportunity when it was there. Now I've lost the chance to—

"Wait!" I hear myself cry, before I can even comprehend what's happening. But my eyes have spied it: the empty store. It *is* there, I got the wrong place! Of course I did, I had no idea where I was going!

The driver gives an almighty harrumph, pulling the cab over hard, and I press my hands to the window, looking at the store. My heart is pounding again, but this time in a good way. Because it's not over, my dream. The store is still here. And I said—I *promised* myself—if it was here, that was a sign...

"Lady, what are we doing?" the driver barks, interrupting my thoughts. "Are you getting out here or not?"

A smile stretches wide across my face. "Yes," I say resolutely. "Yes, I am."

Isaac exits a cab, scanning the sidewalk. His face lights up when he sees me, leaning back against the empty storefront, gnawing my fingernails down to stumps.

"Harriet!" He steps forward and takes my hand in a hearty handshake.

"Hi," I say, with more confidence than I feel. It took him an hour to get here—unsurprising, considering I called him at 8 a.m. on what I now realize is a Sunday—and in that time my certainty about this whole thing has been whittled down to a tiny nub. Honestly, what am I doing?

"I didn't expect to hear from you," he admits as he opens the door.

I shuffle in behind him, watching him turn on the lights. "Well, I wasn't planning to call. But thanks for coming out so early on a Sunday. I, er, I thought I'd take another look." Probably best to leave out the part where I felt like the universe was giving me signs to open a cafe here.

"No problem. I'm glad." He turns to me with a grin. "So... do you have any questions?"

I nibble my lip, glancing around the space. Now that I'm here, actually contemplating this whole thing, it suddenly looks... well, not as good as I remember. I mean, look at that peeling paint. And that hole in the drywall. And was that water stain always there, running down the wall?

I clear my throat, glancing back at Isaac's expectant face. "Why is this place still available? It must be costing the owner, sitting here empty."

"Fair question. In all honesty, most of the people I show it to only see the surface. It's not much to look at." He gestures around and I wince. It really isn't. "People don't want to deal with the work. They want a place that's ready for them to move into right away. The owner wants the tenant to fix it up." He lifts his shoulders in a light shrug.

"And I guess most people don't want to be this far down on the Lower East Side. It's not as trendy as the East Village."

I nod, taking all this in, my mind whirring with possibilities.

"But, you know," he continues with a sincere smile, "that's why it's a good price. The owner is nice enough and he'll leave you to it. If you don't mind setting it up, you could have a cool place here. Look at some of these features." He gestures to a wall behind me. "If you strip away this drywall, there's brick under there. That could look really good cleaned up. And the bar top here is solid oak. Give that a little TLC and it would come up real nice."

I glance around again, seeing the place through Isaac's eyes. A little bud of hope unfurls in my chest, blossoming quietly as I picture it anew.

But... as optimistic as I want to be about things with Luke, what if it doesn't work out and I don't have him beside me on this journey? He was the one who gave me all the information in this folder, the one I'm clutching to my chest like a life-preserver in a stormy sea. Without his numbers and his guidance—without his belief in me—I wouldn't be standing here.

I turn to run my hand along the wooden bar top, thinking. Alex moved all the way to New York when she didn't know a soul, just for the adventure. Even if I don't have Luke, I'll have her, and Michael. And—of course, why didn't I think of this before?—Cat runs her own business and Geoff manages a bookstore, surely they'll be able to help me with some of the business stuff.

Besides, I'm not going to throw my dream away just because things with Luke are up in the air. I'm sick of living my life in a safe bubble, watching everyone around me have adventures. It's my turn to roll the dice and make my move.

"The owner really wants it leased," Isaac says thoughtfully. "I could talk to him, see if he'd lower the rent. And if you want, I could possibly talk him down to a six month term, just to start. I'm sure he'd go for it."

Six months is about what Luke said it would take to turn a decent profit. And, really, what's the worst that could happen? I waste six months, I lose a bit of money—but I would have tried, at least. I wouldn't have to live wondering *what if*. A thrill runs up my spine as I realize I've already made up my mind.

Isaac can read my face. "Should I call him?"

I nod, my pulse picking up its pace as Isaac steps out with his phone.

While he talks, I pull out my napkin and wander around the store, picturing how I can bring my ideas to life in this space. With that brick wall exposed, I could hang some artwork, and a chalkboard menu behind the counter. I could have rows of tables down the center here, and sofas against that back wall. Then the shelves with the games could go over there, and an espresso machine could sit here on the counter, the cases with the baked goods could go...

Hmm. I'm going to have to hire people to work here, of course. I don't know anything about hiring or managing staff.

And then I see Paula's face, as if she's right there behind the counter, serving up a plate of her delicious brownies. I wonder—

"Okay." Isaac enters again, his face broad with a grin. "He's on board. We'll just need to draw up a new lease agreement for you to review."

"Review?"

"Yeah." He gives me a kind smile, clearly sensing that I'm out of my depth. "You'll want to have a lawyer look over the agreement before you sign, but that's pretty standard. I can put you in touch with a few if that helps. Once they're satisfied, you can sign the lease and get to work."

I stare at Isaac for a second, unable to move as I process what he's saying. It can happen. It's happening.

He tilts his head to one side with a chuckle. "Don't back out on me now."

"I just have to call someone," I say in a rush, fumbling in my bag for my phone. "One sec." I step out onto the street and, with trembling fingers, I press the call button.

"Hello?" Paula's voice is groggy on the other end and I curse myself. It must be the middle of the night.

"Er, hi."

"Harriet?" Her voice rises with alarm. "Is everything okay?"

"Yes," I say quickly. "Sorry, I forgot the time difference."

She exhales, then her laugh comes down the line. "No problem. What's up?"

"Well..." I glance down at the folder in my arms, suddenly feeling stupid. But if I don't ask, I'll never know. "You know that cafe idea I had?"

"Sure."

I reach deep inside for my courage. "I'm doing it. I'm doing it here in New York. And, I know this is a bit out there, but I was wondering... do you still want to help?"

There's a pause on the other end and I hold my breath. Then Paula speaks, and I can hear the grin in her voice.

"When can I start?"

41

I step from the shower, wrapping the towel around myself. My feet sink into the plush hotel carpet as I pad across the room and slip into my pajamas, my tired body protesting.

After my meeting with Isaac two days ago, I found a lawyer to help me negotiate the terms of the rental agreement. There was a lot of back and forth before I finally signed the lease, then I began looking for contractors so they can come and strip out all the old fixtures and the damaged drywall. I started to clear out some of the mess myself today, which was both thrilling and terrifying.

It's good, though, to have a distraction from things with Luke. I may as well use this time while he's out of town productively. It's either that or I stay holed up in my hotel room, binge-watching *Star Wars* and torturing myself with what may or may not happen between us. Because even though I want to stay positive, whenever I let myself think about it, my mind conjures worst-case scenarios. I can't help it; I'm hard-wired that way, especially when there's so much uncertainty in my life right now. At least Paula is on a flight tomorrow. Having her here will be good.

I'm just crawling into bed, ready to devour a pizza in front of a movie, when my phone buzzes beside me. I see it's Alex calling from New Zealand, and there's a nervous spasm in my stomach. I haven't spoken to her since arriving in the city, but we've texted, so she knows I'm here. I was hoping to have an update on the Luke situation when we finally spoke, not to mention I have to explain my cafe to her. Part of me worries she might think it's absurd. I can't deny I would love to speak to someone about this, though. And when I think of her moving here to pursue her own dreams, it occurs to me that out of everyone, she might understand the most.

With a deep inhale, I press the talk button. "Hey."

"Harriet!" she shrieks. Her excited tone makes me giggle. "Switch to video."

I glance down at my PJs—red shirt with the Hogwarts emblem—then press the video button. It's just my sister; she's seen me in worse.

But when the video connects, it's not Alex on the screen.

It's Luke.

My heart launches into the stratosphere. My brain short-circuits, attempting to explain what's happening. What the... How is this possible? How is he—

"Hey, Harri." Luke's voice is low and gentle, clearing away my scattered thoughts.

Alex leans over his shoulder, grinning. "He came all the way here to see you!" she squeals and Luke flinches, shooting a look back at her.

"Honey, let her talk to him!" I hear Michael say somewhere off camera.

"Sorry." She raises her hands, following Michael out of what I can now see is her old bedroom at our parents' place.

"We'll give you guys a moment." The door clicks shut behind her and Luke turns back to the screen.

I shake my head, trying to make sense of this. "You're in New Zealand."

He chuffs an ironic laugh. "You're in New York."

"I... Yeah."

There's a beat of silence while we just stare at each other, neither of us knowing where to begin. He's wearing his glasses again and it's making my pulse do crazy things.

"Nice PJs," Luke says at last.

Oh God. I glance down at my *Harry Potter* top, feeling my face turn a matching crimson. Not to mention my hair is probably a mess. "Shut up," I mutter.

"I mean it. I love them."

I look back at the screen. Something bright and hot fills my chest as I gaze at the man on the other side. Of course he loves my pajamas—he's the biggest nerd. He's my favorite nerd. "Why are you there, Luke?"

He sighs, setting the phone down and leaning back on a chair. He's sitting at Alex's old desk. "Mike called me after he saw you and told me to get my ass down here. I jumped on the first plane I could. I had to see you." He pauses, then adds with a rueful chuckle, "Of course, I thought you would actually *be* here."

I utter a small laugh, not sure what to say.

He studies me for a long moment, then his face crumples and his head drops into his hands. "Argh, Harriet... I am so sorry. I fucked everything up." His voice breaks and it makes my heart clench. "At the wedding... God, I was such a coward. I can't believe what I asked you to do. I was just... I was afraid."

I nod, my throat thickening. "I know."

"No." He shakes his head forcefully. "It wasn't just my

dad or pissing Mike off or ruining the wedding. It was having to finally step up and live my life on my own terms. I hadn't realized how much I'd let my fear of what others think dictate how I live. But you helped me see that so clearly, even down to decorating my own damn apartment. You've made me so much better, Harri. But..." He pauses, gazing at me. "I was also afraid of how quickly I was falling for you. It scared the shit out of me. I never expected... I didn't think... You just came out of nowhere and changed everything."

My throat feels like it has closed up now, watching his agonized face.

"I should never have asked you to go along with everything at the wedding," he continues, staring down at his hands. "And when Alex figured it out, I should have stood by you. I should never have walked away from you. I know I was spineless and I'll always regret it." He glances up at me again and his eyes are shining. "When you left, I was devastated, but I guess I felt like I deserved it. Then Mike called me and told me that he almost lost the woman he loved once too, and that I needed to fight for you. That's why I got on the plane, Harri, to fight for you, to tell you..." He drags a hand through his hair, tugging on a tuft of it, his miserable eyes searching the screen. "Do you think... could you ever forgive me?"

A tear spills over my cheek and I wipe it with the back of my hand. "Yeah," I say, leaning closer to the screen. He's thousands of miles away and I wish, so desperately, that he was right beside me. And when I see a tear slide down his face, my heart feels like it's being torn in two, knowing I can't hold him. "I've already forgiven you."

"I'll do everything I can to make it up to you," he says, lifting his glasses and wiping his cheek. "I swear."

"Luke, I'm sorry too. I shouldn't have run away. I know it put you in a really difficult position, and I wish I had stuck by you. I wish I could have helped you stand up to your dad."

He shakes his head. "You leaving was the wake-up call that I needed. And in a way, it was good to stand up to Dad alone." He lets out a long, shuddering sigh, as if he's finally releasing the weight of the world after carrying it for so long. "God, I want to see you. When are you coming home?"

"Um..." A breath of realization rushes out of me. "Not anytime soon, actually."

"Then I'll get on the first flight I can out of here. Can you wait a few days?"

Happiness is blossoming inside me and I can't help a watery laugh. "Yeah. I'm going to be here for a while, so... I can wait a few days."

"Okay." His eyes soften with relief. "Don't go anywhere."

"I won't." I smile to myself. He's going to be so shocked when he sees the cafe. Shit, I need to get moving. I want to show it to him when it's finished and perfect, not as the mess it is now.

He leans closer, smiling that gorgeous lop-sided grin of his. "I can't wait to kiss you again. I've missed my wild girl so much."

My wild girl.

His words steamroll over my happiness, crushing it into dust. Somehow, talking to him again, I let myself forget the most important thing of all: that I lied to him.

It's okay, I reassure myself. *He'll understand. Just tell him the truth.*

"Luke, there's something I have to tell you. I—"

His head whips around and in the back of the frame I

see Alex creep into the room. "How are you two getting on? Did you make up yet?"

Luke chuckles, which Alex takes as an invitation to come closer and peer at the screen.

"Yes," I mumble. "We made up. But—"

"Yay!" She hugs Luke around the shoulders and he grins.

"Yep, I'm going straight back to New York. I need to see my girl."

I coax my mouth into a smile, trying to ignore the way my stomach is tilting uneasily. Maybe it's best to tell him this in person, anyway. And I can only hope, once I tell him the truth, he'll still want me as his girl.

42

It's been a rough week. Luke was supposed to be back by now, but he couldn't get on a flight out of New Zealand for three days, and then out of the blue he got a call to say that the Houston company *does* want to partner with him, so he's had to stop there before he can come back to New York.

Since our video chat I've been keeping busy with the cafe, and I haven't been doing it alone; I reached out to Geoff and Cat, who have been very enthusiastic, and Myles is working on branding and a website for me. I haven't told Alex yet, but I did tell her I'll be sticking around in New York for a while. I could hear her squeal from the other side of the planet.

I've been staying at the hotel but it's getting pricey. As soon as my visa comes through, I'll have to find a place of my own. Mum will have a hernia that she's losing another daughter over here, but right now that's the last thing on my mind.

It's a crisp morning as I wander along the street towards work, my breath coming out in a cloud in front of me. I

arrive at the front door and unwind my scarf, pulling my
keys out of my bag, but the door is already unlocked. When
I push my way inside, I hear the hum of the espresso
machine—one of the first things I bought, because I figured
we'd all work much more efficiently with a regular supply of
coffee.

"Hey, chick!" Paula's head pops out. "Coffee?"

"Morning! Yes. *Please.*" I smile, shrugging off my coat as
the high-pitched screech of the milk-frother fills the space.
Seeing Paula behind the counter over the past few days has
brought a sense of comfort and familiarity to what has been
a daunting endeavor. I asked her if she wanted to run the
place with me, but she insisted that it should be all mine.
I'm kind of glad she did.

We sip our coffees in silence, gazing around at the blank
slate before us. All the broken drywall and old fixtures have
been removed and the wooden floor and counter have been
sanded back to the grain. It's good progress, but it's a far cry
from where it needs to be.

Coffee consumed, Paula disappears to clean and organize the kitchen, and I set out some little pots of yellow
paint to test on the bare walls. As I work, my mind wanders
to Luke. I'm trying to be positive, I really am, but he told me
he couldn't wait to see me and it's been a whole week now. I
know he's busy—and, you know, he did fly to the other side
of the world for me and everything—but I can't shake the
feeling that something is off. We've been texting since our
video chat but over the past couple of days I've hardly heard
a peep. What if he's changed his mind, or somehow figured
out that I lied to him?

I try to push the thought from my mind for the rest of
the day but it's a struggle. I'm tired after working my ass off

all week and my nerves are frayed to bits from worrying about things with Luke.

We're just finishing up for the day when my phone buzzes. I hear it, sitting on the counter, and my heart lunges against my ribs when I see a message from Luke.

Luke: Hey, Harri. Can you come by tonight?

I stare at the words, trying to decipher the tone. There's no "I've missed you, baby!" or "I'm back and I can't wait to see you!" Just cool, casual, detached. He didn't even text to tell me he was leaving Houston.

Shit. I don't want to think about what this means.

My belly fills with butterflies as I lock up the store and take a cab to Chelsea. I can't sit still; I'm a jittery ball of nervous energy. Now that I'm seeing him, I have to tell him the truth. I don't know what I'm more worried about—that he'll be shocked to realize I'm not who he thought I was, or hurt because I lied. It doesn't matter, really. All that matters is that if he decides he can't be with me after everything, I don't think I'll be able to come back from that.

The door is ajar when I get to his floor, so I give it a tentative push. "Hello?" I call, and the butterflies in my middle turn into a furious swarm of hornets.

But as I step inside, I realize I've made a mistake. The walls are dark, the floors exposed wood, the lighting dim and warm.

"Sorry, wrong apartment," I say, hastily backtracking through the door.

"Wait!" Luke wanders out of the kitchen, grinning. "Harriet, come in here."

I blink, taking in his familiar, tall figure and the huge smile lighting his handsome face. My feet have a mind of their own as they lead me back inside, and I peel my eyes away from him to take in the space around us, my jaw hanging open.

It's not the wrong apartment, but everything is different. Gone are the gleaming, sterile, white surfaces, the chrome and LED lights. He's stripped back the carpet to reveal wooden floorboards which are stained a dark chocolate brown. The walls, once blindingly white, are Prussian blue, and the bright lighting has been replaced with yellow bulbs which give the place a warm, golden glow. The kitchen has been redone with a dark granite countertop, the white sofa has been replaced with a chunky, tan leather three-seater, and his fancy gaming wall panel is gone. In its place is an exposed brick wall, and a low wooden cabinet with the TV sitting right on top—not hiding.

"What do you think?" Luke's voice is close behind me and I spin around, breathless.

"It's... It's... Wow." I'm shaking my head, trying to process how different the place feels from before. It's like night and day. And this is *fresh*—I can smell the paint. I notice he's kept the huge metal bookshelves along the wall, and I'm glad.

Luke cocks his head, keeping his eyes on mine. "You like it?"

"I *love* it," I breathe.

He nods, not saying anything more.

Now's your chance, the rational voice in my head says. *Tell him the truth.* But my lips won't move. Instead, I drink in the man before me like an oasis in the desert. He's had a haircut recently, and his beard is thicker. His eyes look tired, but they're sparkling as they silently roam my face, making my pulse rush. He's wearing jeans and a black long-sleeved tee with the *Star Wars* logo on it, and when I spot a clock on the kitchen wall in the shape of the Millennium Falcon, I think my heart is going to burst.

This man... look at him. I love him so much it hurts. He's everything.

"I got back from Houston two days ago," he says at last. "But I couldn't call you. Not until I was ready. I wanted to make sure this place was perfect when I asked you to move in with me."

My breath stills in my lungs. "What?"

"I told you I would do everything I could to make up for what I did at the wedding. I let you down in the worst way, at the worst time, and I didn't want to face you until I could prove that I wouldn't let you down again. Alex told me you're sticking around for a while, and"— he shrugs, his mouth lifting into a shy smile—"I was hoping you might... move in here."

Holy fuck. Is he for real?

"I love you." The words jump from my mouth before I can register what I'm saying. Seeing him again—in this dream apartment that he's *asking me to share with him*—I can't think straight.

His eyes light with surprise, the smile on his face growing wider, but I can't enjoy it. I need to come clean.

"But there's something I have to tell you." I swallow, knowing it's now or never. "I lied to you, Luke. I told you I was someone who loves to be adventurous, who goes skydiving and lives life on the edge. I told you those things because you were a stranger on a plane and I thought I'd never see you again. Then, the more time we spent together, the more it seemed like you liked that wild side of me and the more I became afraid that if you knew the truth you wouldn't like the real me."

His face softens and he opens his mouth to speak, but I

can't stop now. My heart is knotted into a tight ball in my chest, my breathing shallow as I keep going.

"The real me doesn't seek out thrills, because most of the time I'm too scared. I didn't even want to come to New York for Alex's wedding, I was so afraid of the city. I let you believe I was someone who loves to do crazy, outrageous things, and I shouldn't have. Because that's not who I am." I stop here, thinking I'm done, but more words come spilling out, desperate to be heard. "Since the wedding, I've learned something, though. I thought I had to be fearless, but I don't. What really matters is being brave—choosing to act, even if I'm scared." Tears well in my eyes and I swipe at them quickly before they fall. "So I might not be the woman I told you I was on the plane, but I'm learning how to look at things that scare me and not let them win. And that includes telling you the truth, telling you I'm in love with you, and hoping you still want me." My voice is so shredded with emotion it's barely audible, but it doesn't matter. I have no words left.

Luke gazes at me for what feels like an eternity. "You're wrong," he says at last, and my pulse crashes.

"What?"

"You said you're not wild, but I've seen that side to you. On the trapeze, skinny-dipping in the lake, in the reception hall that night, and fuck"—he gives a little grunt, his eyes glinting—"that time I bent you over the kitchen island... You are wild. You make *me* wild. I think we bring out that side in each other."

In spite of everything, a smile touches my lips. He's right. I might not be naturally adventurous, but with him I've done more outrageous things than I ever have. He *does* make me want to be wild.

"Harriet..." Luke takes a step towards me, shaking his

head with a funny little smile. "You are the bravest, most amazing woman I've ever met. I don't care about some stupid lie you told me when we were strangers, because I know who you are now. I know you were bullied in high school and you had panic attacks and it scared you. I know you love books and games, that you're anxious when you're on the subway, that you dream of running your own cafe. I know how you like to be touched, what makes you feel good, what makes you feel safe. I know that you're sweet and caring and you'll do anything for your sister—or anyone who asks for your help." He pauses, his eyes gleaming, and my heart takes off at a gallop. "I *do* know you, Harri. And if there's anything else I don't know, then I want to get to know it. Because I'm in love with you, too."

I press my eyes shut, letting tears spill down my cheeks. His words pour over me, a balm to my raw heart, my frazzled nervous system, my anxious mind. All that worrying, but he wants me just as I am. He always has.

When I open my eyes, I find him watching me hopefully, his cheeks moist. I step forward and reach a hand up to him, dragging my thumb over his cheek.

"Are you sure?" I whisper. "Are you sure you don't care that I'm not fearless?"

His eyes crinkle into a smile, his hands settling on my waist. "The only thing I care about is you—is having you in my life. And since you're sticking around, will you stick around here, with me?"

I nod eagerly. Because now that I know he's in love with me—the *real* me—fuck. That's all I want.

The corner of his mouth twitches. "Even though I'm not John Stamos?"

"Actually," I say, smothering a smile, "if you must know, I am more of a Bob Saget girl."

He throws back his head in laughter and the sound makes my whole body tingle. God, I missed him.

"Luke..." I look around the apartment in disbelief. "I can't believe you finally redecorated. How did you get it done so fast?"

"When I came back from the cabin to this empty, miserable apartment, I kind of lost it. I couldn't stand the sight of this place, the way it made me feel. I started ripping things out and called contractors in the next day. When I had to fly out to New Zealand, Andrea offered to oversee the work."

"It looks amazing. Like a totally different place."

Luke nods. "Good. That's what I wanted. I should have done this a long time ago, but I needed you to help me see. Not just with the apartment, Harri, with everything. I thought working on this place would take my mind off you, but the more I tore out, the more I realized what a mistake I'd made by walking away from you at the wedding. And then when Mike called..." He lowers his gaze in shame, then brings it back to mine, resolute. "I will never let you down like that again. I want you to know, I'm all in."

Those words send happiness rolling through me like a wave. "I am too," I murmur. His hands are still resting on my waist and I reach down, pushing his sleeves back. Then I slide my fingers over the warm skin of his forearms, squeezing the muscle. "I missed these arms."

He chuckles. "I missed your everything."

That might be the sweetest thing anyone has ever said to me. "Me too," I say, stepping forward to kiss him. But before I can, he cocks his head.

"Why did you come back to the city? Was it for me?"

I nod.

"But I wasn't here. So why did you stick around?"

"Um..." I chew my lip, trying to play it cool. I don't want

to tell him, not yet. I want to show it to him when it's finished and looking amazing. But that will be weeks away and I can't wait that long. "I rented that space Isaac showed us."

Luke's eyebrows spring up. "Seriously?"

"Yeah." My mouth pulls into a ridiculous grin. I am so *not* playing this cool.

"Oh my God, Harri!" He beams, practically vibrating with excitement. "That's amazing! You're doing the cafe?"

"I am. It's because of your help, Luke, and your encouragemen—"

My words die away as Luke hauls me into his arms and covers my mouth with his in a hot, ravenous kiss. "Fuck, I love you," he says against my lips, and I let out a blissful sigh. As he kisses me, I forget everything but the feel of his hands on my back, the sweep of his tongue over mine, the way he makes my heart feel full and happy.

Then he picks me up and carries me into the bedroom, and we make love under the stars as if the world is ending and we're the only two people alive.

43

Luke slips his hand into mine, squeezing gently. "There's nothing to be nervous about."

"I know. I just hope everyone loves it as much as I do."

It's been three weeks since Luke arrived back—three weeks of living at his place and finishing off my cafe. I've worked my butt off and I'm so pleased with how it's turned out. The exposed brick wall behind the counter looks really good, and the solid oak countertop has been polished to a fine finish. The hardwood floors are gleaming with a stain and polish, and the wall opposite the counter is painted golden yellow, lined with heavy wooden shelves that are packed with games. A row of warm, low-hanging bulbs run the length of the space, and with the leather sofas at the back, it feels like someone's living room. It's exactly the vibe I imagined when I scribbled on that napkin, believing this could never be more than a fantasy.

Tonight we're having a soft opening, inviting friends and family to celebrate before I open the doors to the public. After all my hard work, all my dreaming... Gah, I'm about to crawl out of my skin with nerves. But Luke, bless him, has been doing everything he can to keep me calm.

He drops my hand and cups my jaw, tilting my face up to his. "They'll love it," he murmurs, smiling, and the certainty in his tone relaxes me. His gaze tracks over my face, dipping down to my dress. "You look gorgeous. I wish I'd gotten here earlier so we could have celebrated privately." There's a raw edge to his voice and his eyes flash with heat, sending a shiver of desire through me.

"Ugh, no thank you." Alex sashays past, setting down a tray of nibbles. "I know I was *instrumental* in getting you two together"—she gives a self-satisfied smile—"but that doesn't mean I'm used to seeing *this* yet; my sister and my—"

"If you say 'my brother,' I'm going to kill you," I mutter. It's nice that Luke and I don't have to hide now, but Alex thinks it's hilarious to joke about our unusual situation.

She smirks. "You said it, not me. But it is nice to see you both so happy." She squeezes Luke's shoulder, then pulls me into a hug. "I still can't believe you're staying in New York and that you've made this place! It's awesome, Harri. I'm so proud of you."

I smile, hugging her tight. I've never felt closer to my sister.

"Is everything ready?" Michael asks, appearing beside us. "Should we open the doors?"

I glance between him, Alex, and Luke. Henry is munching a brownie, with chocolate crumbs on his chin and a grin on his mouth.

Paula wanders over and sets down another tray of food, looking at me. "We're ready. Let's do this!"

I nod, taking a deep breath to settle the tornado in my stomach. Luke catches my hand again, pressing his lips to the back of it as Michael opens the doors.

Here we go.

"THIS PLACE IS AMAZING!" Cat says when I join her, Myles, Geoff, and a few others I don't know at a table.

"Thanks." I smile modestly, looking around. The turnout has been great; Cat invited some friends, Geoff and Alex brought people they know through the bookstore, and Luke and Michael invited others too. Even Isaac is here with his wife, Julia. Having all these people here to celebrate, playing games and enjoying themselves, means the world to me.

"I love the brownies," the girl beside me says. "It's hard to find good vegan brownies."

"Thanks! They're Paula's specialty."

"I'm Josie." She sticks her hand out and I shake it, noting her short, dark hair and green eyes. She has a sprinkle of freckles across her nose and I hesitate, sure I've seen her before. "I work at Bounce," she adds at my bemused expression.

"Right!" I chuckle. "I knew I recognized you."

"You'll be seeing a lot more of me now that I know there's delicious vegan baking here."

I grin. I knew getting Paula on board was a good idea.

A loud cheer goes up a few tables away and I turn to see Henry looking triumphant. I don't know what game he's playing, but apparently Luke and Michael aren't doing so well. I giggle at the expression of dismay on Luke's face.

Steph waves to me across the room and I excuse myself, heading over. I decided to repay her generosity with a ticket to New York for my opening night. I wouldn't be here if it weren't for her helping me find my courage. And, you know, forcing me onto a plane.

"Okay, who is *that?*" she asks with a flick of her hand. "He's hot."

I follow her gaze to take in Cory's tall, fit frame, short beard, and disheveled dirty-blond hair. I'm not going to disagree with that assessment. He gives a friendly wave in our direction and Steph swoons. I've never seen her swoon in my life.

"That's Cat's brother," I say with a laugh. "He owns a bar in the East Village."

"Fuck," she says softly, and I laugh again, elbowing her in the side.

"You have a boyfriend."

"I know." A resigned sigh trickles out of her. "But the men here are something else." Her gaze darts to Luke and she tilts her mouth into a sly grin. "You've done well for yourself, Harri. Luke is gorgeous and he seems really sweet."

"Yeah, he is."

"And," she says, dropping her voice, "he must be pretty good in bed. Have you had any more—"

"Steph," I hiss, cutting her off before she can say "orgasms." My face warms at her knowing smile, and she snickers.

"That's a yes."

This time, I can't stop the grin that creeps onto my lips. "Yes. He's very... Yes." That's an understatement. Luke went to all that trouble to redo his apartment—*our* apartment— and we've hardly left the bedroom. But he doesn't seem to mind.

Actually, living with Luke is better than I could have imagined, and not just because of the sex. When I've come home exhausted from setting up the cafe all day, we've ordered take-out and spent the night on his sofa—him playing his games and me working my way through the books from his shelves I haven't read. I missed reading, and while I now have an exciting life of my own in the real world, I know it's okay to get lost in make-believe worlds from time to time, too. Especially when Luke is eagerly waiting for me to finish a series so we can chat about it.

I meet his gaze across the room. His mouth curves into a sexy smile, his eyes filled with affection as he gazes back. I still can't believe this gorgeous, nerdy man is in love with me. Without his love—his belief in me—I would never have created this place. It was my vision, and I chose to do it for myself, but having him push me along the way meant everything.

And as I look around at everyone having fun in this dream I made a reality, my heart feels like it will overflow.

THE DOOR CLICKS SHUT and I turn to Luke, grinning. "I think that went well."

"It was fantastic! Everyone had a great time."

I glance at the tables behind him. I sent everyone home, insisting they didn't need to help me clean up this late, but now I'm having some serious regrets. There are glasses and empty bottles and food trays scattered everywhere.

As if reading my mind, Luke grabs a few plates from a nearby table. "Let's get this cleaned up then we can head home, okay?"

Home. Home, with Luke. It's like I've traveled through space and time into some parallel universe where I have everything I want. I'm worried I'm going to wake up and find myself back in my old flat, back in a life that—in hindsight—was only making me miserable.

But I won't. I'm here, and this is real. *Luke* is real.

He sets about collecting discarded glasses and bottles, but I'm rooted to the spot, watching him. I don't want to clean, or even go home. I want him right here, right now.

He pops out from the back, gathering more glasses together, pausing to look at me when I don't join him. Whatever he sees in my eyes makes him abandon tidying, and he takes my face, sliding his fingers into my hair and stroking the pad of his thumb across my cheek. "I'm so proud of you, baby."

My body hums at his touch, his words. "I couldn't have done this without your help. Thank you."

"I might have given you a nudge, but *you* did this. It's all you." He shakes his head, glancing around us before returning his gaze to mine. "I can't believe you think you don't take risks or do big things. You're everything you think you're not, you know that?"

I look up at him, at the warmth and love in his eyes, and I see myself reflected back. I see myself the way he sees me, and it's pretty freaking awesome. "Thank you," I whisper, tightening my grip on his back. My heart is glowing like an ember in my chest as he lowers his mouth to mine.

He skates his hands down my back, over my butt and under my thighs, lifting me up so I wrap my legs around him. Then he carries me to the counter and sets me down, leaning his body forward into mine. His hand caresses my jaw tenderly, then trails down across my collarbone.

"I'm never going to stop kissing you," he murmurs against my lips, and I smile.

"Good. But..." I pull back. "Could you stop and go turn the lights off? And maybe lock the door?"

He frowns, puzzled, then I see the understanding dawn on his face. And he's off—flicking the lights and pushing the bolt through the door—and back faster than I would have thought humanly possible. When he takes my mouth again, his tongue laps hungrily at mine and he grinds the hard bulge below his waist against me.

I moan into his mouth, sliding my hands down his front and unbuckling his belt to take hold of him, remembering the first time I touched him on the plane and how that changed the course of our lives forever. I thought it was Harriet 2.0, but it wasn't. It was me. It was always me.

"I love you," I breathe, stroking him, kissing his ear.

I can't see his face in the darkness, but I don't need to. "I love you more," he says gruffly, before claiming my mouth again.

And for the next hour, we don't leave the darkness of the cafe. We don't leave that counter. And it is very outrageous, indeed.

EPILOGUE

Head to:
https://www.jenmorrisauthor.com/oil-epilogue
to read an exclusive *Outrageously in Love* epilogue!

Did you enjoy *Outrageously in Love*? Reviews help indie authors get our books noticed!

If you liked this book, please leave a review on Amazon. Or you can leave a review on Goodreads. It doesn't have to be much—even a single sentence helps! Thank you.

ACKNOWLEDGMENTS

It was almost a year ago that I published my first novel, followed by another a few months later. Since then, I've been welcomed into an online community who support me and lift me up in every way. It's because of this community that people are finding and taking a chance on my work. Thank you to everyone who has bought, read, reviewed, or shared my books. The fact that people even read—let alone enjoy—my writing still blows my mind.

I have to thank my partner, Carl. Not just because he supports us financially so I can write, but also because he inspired a lot of this story. Luke's love of space, *Star Wars*, and gaming are all traits I borrowed from Carl.

I got the idea for this story while on a flight from Houston to New York. No, I didn't join the mile high club (ha ha), but I wouldn't have been on that flight if it wasn't for Carl pushing me to take a solo trip across the globe while he stayed home with our son. I'm forever grateful that he gave me the gift of New York, where I finally decided I was going to commit to writing, and where the idea for this series really came to life. Thank you for always supporting and believing in me, Carl.

My son Baxter already loves space and will no doubt grow up to be a space geek like his dad (and, probably, a book nerd like his mum). Regardless of who he becomes, I hope I can show him the acceptance and support every child deserves from their parents. Baxter, your curiosity about the universe inspires me every day and I'm so proud to be your mum.

Behind the scenes of my launches (and, really, every other day of the year) I have two friends who look out for me, make me laugh, and indulge my love of books (and hot men). Kira Slaughter and Tammy Eyre, your belief in me and my work—your unfailing support and enthusiasm—means the world to me. I wouldn't enjoy this half as much without you. Thank you for everything.

Sarah Side is the kind of friend who is always there when I need someone to read my writing, brainstorm ideas, and basically just listen while I rant/spiral/implode. Her support of my work from day one has made me believe in myself. Thanks, Sarah, for being there whenever I need you.

My friend Louise Ryan originally asked me the question at the beginning of this story: "What's the most outrageous thing you've ever done?" While I didn't have an interesting answer, the question stuck with me. I already knew I wanted to write about someone meeting a stranger on a plane, but it was this question that helped me develop Harriet's character and her journey. So thank you, Louise, for the inspiration.

I have to say a huge thanks to my critique partners, Lauren H. Mae, Mia Heintzelman, Jennifer Evelyn Hayes, and Andrea Gonzalez, who each spent many hours reading this story and giving thorough, detailed feedback to help me shape it into something I'm proud of. Thank you to Alicia Crofton, whose keen eye always picks up things I miss, and special thanks to Julie Olivia, who helped me with all the Harry Potter and Star Wars references, as well as a lot of the board game stuff.

My beta readers are a wonderful team of people who always help me improve my work. I'd be lost without their honest feedback. Emma Grocott, Emilie Ahern, Michele Voss, Laura Harris, Ayla Russell, Caroline Chalmers, Kristen Fairgrieve, Kelly Pensinger, and Elliot Andrews—thank you for the time and energy you put into reading and answering questions about this book. I'm so grateful for you.

Thanks to all my advanced readers who shared their excitement over this story and helped to promote it. There are far too many to name, but just know that I appreciate every single review, share, post, comment, and mention.

My cover designer Elle Maxwell always manages to take my vision and make it better than I could imagine. I'm super grateful for her talent, her attention to detail, and her patience when I insist on tweaking something that doesn't really need to be tweaked. Thanks for everything, Elle.

A big thanks to you, my lovely reader, for spending time with Harriet and Luke. I love this couple and their connection, and I hope you do too.

And finally, to anyone who has ever been bullied for who they are and/or what they love, to anyone who suffers anxiety... you are not alone. You are not broken. And you will not be defeated.

ABOUT THE AUTHOR

Jen Morris writes sexy romantic comedies with heat, humor and heart. She believes that almost anything can be fixed with a good laugh, a good book, or a plane ticket to New York.

Her books follow women with big dreams as they navigate life and love in the city. Her characters don't just find love—they find themselves, too.

Jen lives with her partner and son, in a tiny house on wheels in New Zealand. She spends her days writing, dreaming about New York, and finding space for her ever-growing book collection.

Outrageously in Love is her third novel, and the third book in the *Love in the City* series.

ALSO BY JEN MORRIS

Have you read book one in the series, *Love in the City*? Follow Harriet's sister Alex as she ventures to New York in search of her dreams, and finds a sexy bearded man along the way.

You might also enjoy book two, *You Know it's Love*. Join Cat as she tries to save her vintage clothing business—and fight her feelings for the cocky new bartender at her brother's bar.

Next up in the series is book four—Cory and Josie's story! Sign up to my mailing list and/or follow me on Instagram so you don't miss anything.

Find me on Instagram and Facebook: @jenmorrisauthor

Subscribe to my newsletter for updates, release info, and cover reveals: www.jenmorrisauthor.com

See all the book inspiration on Pinterest: www.pinterest.com/jenmorrisauthor/

Made in the USA
Las Vegas, NV
06 June 2022

49878775R00225